V. Fausboll

Jataka Together with Its Commentary

Vol.7

V. Fausboll

Jataka Together with Its Commentary
Vol.7

ISBN/EAN: 9783337384920

Printed in Europe, USA, Canada, Australia, Japan

Cover: Foto ©Andreas Hilbeck / pixelio.de

More available books at **www.hansebooks.com**

INDEX TO THE JĀTAKA

AND ITS COMMENTARY,

CONTAINING

A COMPLETE INDEX OF PRO... TOGETHER WITH

A LIST OF THE ...

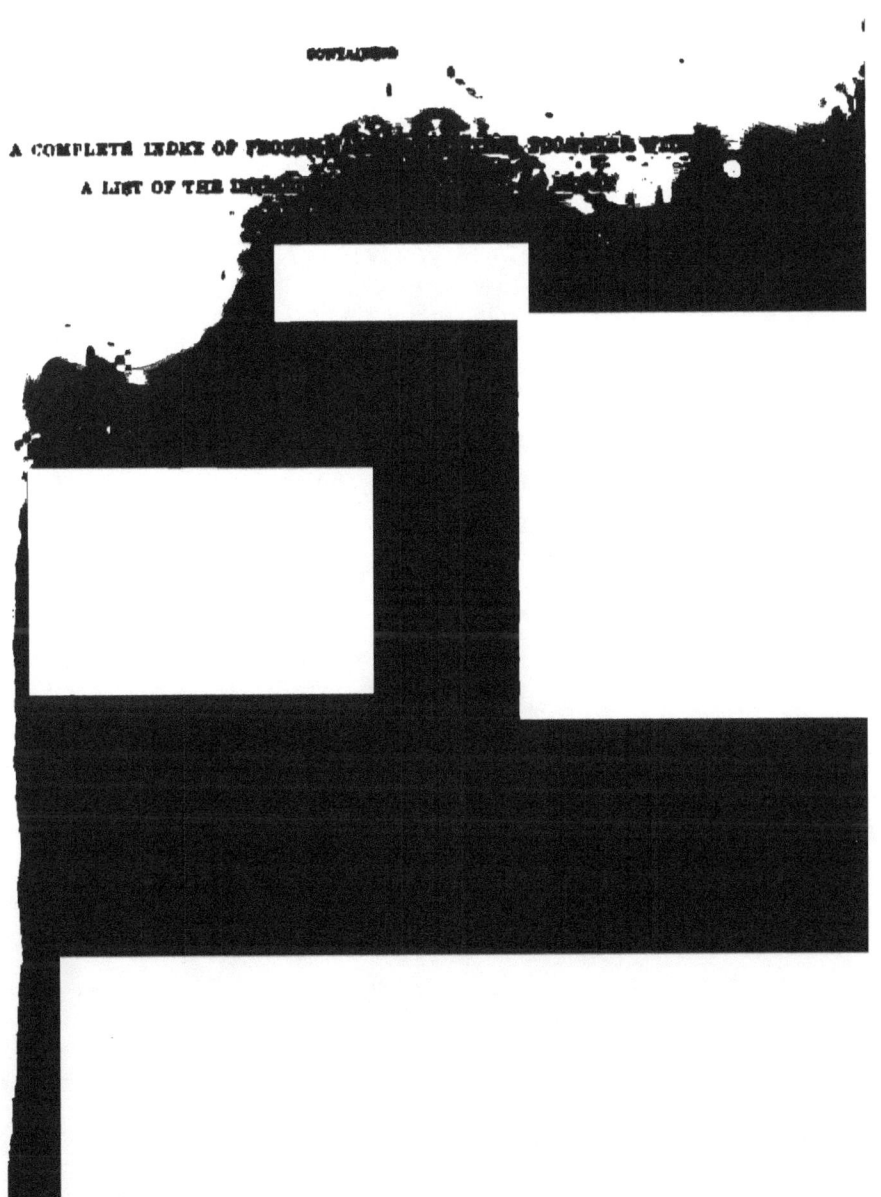

TO

ALBRECHT WEBER

WHO FOR MORE THAN A GENERATION HAS BEEN

AN ILLUSTRIOUS LEADER

OF

THE STUDY OF INDIAN LANGUAGES AND LITERATURE

THIS VOLUME IS MOST RESPECTFULLY DEDICATED

BY

V. FAUSBØLL AND D. ANDERSEN.

CONTENTS.

		Page
Postscriptum by V. Fausbøll		I—XII.
Preface to the Index		XIII—XVII.
I.	Index of Proper Names and Titles	1—186.
II.	Alphabetical List of all the introductory Gáthas to the Játakas	189—199.
III.	Index of Gáthás or parts of Gáthás which more than once occur in the Játakas and the Commentary	201—235.
IV.	List of Quotations from other works by the Editor	237—242.
V.	Additions and Corrections	243—247.

POSTSCRIPTUM

—

Born in a country parsonage I, until my twelfth year, associated much with peasants, and listened with attentive interest to their legends and stories. Amongst these there were two especially which made a strong impression upon my childish mind:

One was the legend of the sunken church lying at the bottom of the lake where it might be seen deep down in the water when it was clear and calm, and whose bells might still be heard ringing in the stillness of the evening; the other was the story of the treasure-seeker who at sunset, in perfect silence, without uttering a word, sought to bring the long burried treasure up to the surface.

I also laboured and strove for years digging silently, until I could bring the treasure forth to the light of day. Here we have it! But it has long lain hidden and may require a little furbishing in coming times, before it can shine in all its glory.

—

What induced me with eagerness to begin to work at the Jātaka Book was particularly three utterances I met with: The first I found in Spence Hardy's Manual of Budhism. p. 1, viz. „The Singhalese will listen the night through to recitations from this work without any apparent weariness, and a great number of the Jātakas are familiar even to the women". The second I read in Clough's Singhalese Dictionary under the word Jātakapota where it says: „this book is so sacred amongst the Buddhists that they will offer to it and worship it". And the third I noticed in the Ceylon Friend 1837 where it says: „The more I think of Buddha, the more I love him". When we have read the Jātaka through no one will wonder at these sentiments.

In 1849 I had already commenced transcribing parts of the Jātaka, but I did not seriously take it up until I had finished my edition of the Dhammapada in 1855. The further I got into the book, the clearer I saw its importance, not only in a linguistic sense but also from a culture-historical point of view, and in order to awaken interest for it in the literary world I began publishing specimens of it in 1861. Professor Westergaard was not at first in favour of a complete edition, he would have preferred an analysis only. Perhaps he thought the undertaking beyond my abilities. Later on he altered his opinion and supported the work. It was however principally the encouragement I, from the very beginning, received from Professor A. Weber that kept up my courage. And when material failed me, it was especially the Rev. Subhūti's untiring perseverance in sending me a paper transcript in parts, and Colonel Duncan's splendid present of a complete Burmese copy of the Jātaka (at the instigation of Missionary C. H. Chard) that made it possible for me to finish my undertaking.

I now trust that the fact will not be overlooked, that I have had but little material to work from, also that when I began the study of Pāli, the language was nearly uncultivated. I therefore venture to hope for a mild criticism of this my work.

I. As is well known, a „Jātaka" in the Jātaka Atthavaṇṇanā consists of four parts, viz. (see Jāt. I $\frac{126}{19}$) a) a Paccuppanna-vatthu, an incident from the time of the Gotama Buddha, that frames, as it were, and gives rise to Gotama Buddha telling an event of olden times, b) an Atītavatthu which latter has originally been in verse, but afterwards been retold by G. B. partly in prose and partly in verse, with moral teaching in view. c) (J. I $\frac{411}{1}$) a Veyyākaraṇa or Commentary which elucidates both the tale and certain words in the metrical pieces, and ultimately d) a Samodhāna, a winding up of the story. The two last belong properly to the Paccuppannavatthu.

In the Paccuppannavatthu a number of books are quoted appertaining to the Tipiṭaka, it consequently belongs to the period following the Buddhistic canon's genesis, and is therefore doubtless an utterance of clerical tradition. The P. V. ends in J. 1—13 with „pākaṭam akāsi", but in all the others with „atītam āhari" (cfr. I. $\frac{104}{1}$). That the Nidānakathā is a part of the P. V., we must conclude, as it appears, from I $\frac{187}{16}$, and that the P. V. belongs to the Aṭṭhakathā (i. e. the Jātakaṭṭhakatthā I $\frac{82}{94}$) may be seen from the postscript of J. 77 which runs as follows:

„Parinibbute pana Bhagavati usabhā-rukkhādīni tīṇi padāni Aṭṭhakathaṁ āropetvā lābūniti ādīni pañca (for pañca read ca) padāni ekaṁ gāthaṁ katvā Ekanipātapāliṁ āropesun ti", i. e.

„When Bhagavat was dead the Council-holders put the three padas usabhā-rukkhā etc. into the Aṭṭhakathā (see p. 336), and made lāpūni and the other padas into one gāthā and put it into the verses (Pāli) of the Ekanipāta.

So the Aṭṭhakathā and its translation into Pāli (Jātakassa Atthavaṇṇanā) begin with: Sā panāyaṁ Jātakassa Atthavaṇṇanā, see vol. I p. 2.

As a contrast to Aṭṭhakathā, Pāli is often mentioned by which is understood the verses both in the present Jātaka and in the Singhalese Aṭṭhakathā on which it is founded. Thus when it is said in J. I $\frac{258}{30}$: pāliyaṁ pana phalaṁ pāpetīti likhanti taṁ vyañjanaṁ Aṭṭhakathāya n' atthi, we must by this understand „in the verses (pāli) of the Aṭṭhakathā", likewise in II $\frac{261}{17}$ $\frac{292}{4}$. VI $\frac{29}{24}$ $\frac{276}{20}$; sometimes Potthakā (IV $\frac{393}{18}$ V $\frac{25}{6}$) and Pālipotthakā (VI $\frac{242}{27}$) are used, as it seems, with the same meaning as Pāli.

In the Atītavatthu we have the oldest element of the Jātaka. The tale of the A. V. is founded on an ancient story, originally composed in verse, from which Gotama Buddha quotes sometimes single verses sometimes more. We have here an entire parallel to many of the Icelandic Saga-works which are also built up on the old lays of the Bards. That G. B. himself is not the author of these verses, is most clearly seen from the later Jātakas, the verses of which in many places say the same as has just been told in prose. It would indeed be ridiculous to suppose that G. B. should have exerted himself to express in poetry and even in old language what he had just said in prose. No, he only affirms what he has said in prose by quotations from the poem on which his tale is founded. In many instances he does not even convert the old song into prose, but lets the tale go on in the very words of the song, only now and then putting in some explanatory remarks, see f. ex. II [illegible], III,809, IV,504, V,514; VI [illegible]; 220,28-221,19; 485,10-12; 513,17-26; 548,1-10, 557,2-6 etc. Compare this with what I have said in my edition of the Sutta-Nipāta p. VII—VIII. It is also worth noticing certain recurring phrases which seem to point to our having here before us fragments of old popular epic poetry, f. ex. kacci vo kusalaṁ VI [illegible] [illegible] cfr. Mahābhārata (Calcutta edition) XII,13727; see further VI [illegible] foll. [illegible] [illegible] [illegible] [illegible] [illegible] [illegible], V [illegible] [illegible] VI [illegible].

That the Atītavatthu is the oldest part of the Jātaka may be clearly seen from the language of the Pāli Verses, as in these we find many peculiarities, especially old forms which do not occur in the prosaic Pāli, and some of which point to the north-west of India, they being found in the Vedas. A few of them are due to the metre. I shall make a note of he following:

1. A vowel may be made long, f. ex. āraho VI [illegible] [illegible], anūdake VI [illegible], khaṇāsi IV [illegible], seti III [illegible] [illegible], satām iva III [illegible], ivā III [illegible], or short: attanaṁ III [illegible], pāsamha IV [illegible], akataññuna dubbhinā IV [illegible], vijanahi VI [illegible], disva III [illegible] [illegible], pasavetva VI [illegible], and a half-vowel may be

dissolved: tvaṁ becomes tuvaṁ IV $\frac{45}{1}$, daṭṭhu — S. dṛṣṭvā V $\frac{249}{7}$ cfr. IV $\frac{109}{4}$; e becomes y: ky-āhaṁ — ko ahaṁ III $\frac{204}{21}$ and o v or uv: sv-āyaṁ — so ayaṁ V $\frac{140}{7}$, kuvidha — ko idha V $\frac{237}{23}$.

2. A consonant may be omitted: jaggato for jagganto III $\frac{420}{10}$, dakkhisāma for -issāma III $\frac{62}{7}$, dukhaṁ for dukkhaṁ II $\frac{235}{12}$, or inserted: Añjanaṁvanaṁ III $\frac{272}{4}$, varaṁdhanena VI $\frac{278}{4}$, also in the sandhi-combination, f. ex. ya-d-esamāna IV $\frac{247}{10}$, sattiyā-m-api IV $\frac{216}{30}$, .. kiṇṇa-m-antare for .. kiṇṇā III $\frac{239}{11}$, VI $\frac{246}{16}$, na-y-ime IV $\frac{259}{16}$, VI $\frac{60}{12}$, pāṇa-r-iv' ettha rakkhitā for pāṇā III $\frac{180}{9}$, jīva-r-eva for jīvo III $\frac{489}{17}$, jalanta-r-iva for jalantaṁ V $\frac{129}{3}$ yay-ime VI $\frac{104}{24,\ 53}$.

3. Anusvāra may be dropped: mayha for mayhaṁ V $\frac{27}{4,\ 21}$, corāna for corānaṁ I $\frac{120}{9}$, together with the preceding a: kākān' asmāka ñātinaṁ I $\frac{104}{11}$, yes' āyaṁ IV $\frac{115}{17}$, mayh' etaṁ V $\frac{240}{7}$.

4. In the declension of words I mention: kuṭṭhuṁ va III $\frac{119}{6}$, sūciṁ III $\frac{204}{1}$ cfr. Dhammapada p. 287. māyā — māyāya VI $\frac{210}{24}$, pitus sataṁ III $\frac{183}{24}$, mātuc ca IV $\frac{341}{21}$, bhattur atthe II $\frac{225}{15}$, Bārāṇassaṁ for Bārāṇasiyaṁ II $\frac{486}{14}$ V $\frac{19}{21}$, rukkhāse III $\frac{209}{1}$, dhanuggahāse V $\frac{124}{30}$; padasā, balasā, kāmasā etc. III $\frac{407}{19}$, II $\frac{60}{6}$, VI $\frac{162}{14}$, are I suppose adverbial forms originating in the Sanskritic -ças. Tvaṁmātarā — te mātarā IV $\frac{40}{7}$.

5. In the conjugation: ñāmi — jānāmi VI $\frac{43}{20}$, pūrenti — pūriyanti V $\frac{580}{10}$, saṁsaraṁ for saṁsarantā I $\frac{44}{3213}$, gantā for gantāro V $\frac{279}{12}$, bhātha for bhāyatha I $\frac{24}{241}$, hañchati IV $\frac{109}{6}$, gañchisi, V $\frac{124}{27}$, VI $\frac{47}{11}$, āgañchuṁ IV $\frac{451}{18}$, jānitaye IV $\frac{483}{6}$, jagghitāye III $\frac{396}{18}$, pucchitāye V $\frac{207}{6}$, khāditāye V $\frac{33}{7}$, kātave V $\frac{210}{17}$, padātave I $\frac{142}{3}$, nidhetave III $\frac{17}{6}$, gantave IV $\frac{220}{1}$, pamottave IV $\frac{181}{21}$, padahitvāna I $\frac{10}{4}$, hātūna IV $\frac{220}{37}$, paribhuñjiyāna V $\frac{203}{24}$, anumodiyānaṁ — anumoditvā V $\frac{143}{13}$, adhiyānaṁ V $\frac{451}{6}$.

6. Na-kāro upamāne, na — as, like V $\frac{241}{19}$. A as affirmative particle: ahāpita — hāpita V $\frac{139}{15}$, adūsema — dusit' amha

VI $\frac{143}{2}$, cfr. S. B. E. X, S. N. XI: apucchasi; accasara — atisara IV $\frac{4}{19}$, vyavajanti V $\frac{27}{4}$.

That the Atītavatthu contains the oldest part of the book, is also clear when we look at the scenes of the tales.

In the A t ī t a v a t t h u-tales the scene is laid:

428 times in Kāsiraṭṭha (Bārāṇasī)
25 — in Gandhāraraṭṭha (Takkasilā)
9 — in Kururaṭṭha (Kampilla, Indapattanagara, Uttarapañcālanagara)
7 — in Magadharaṭṭha (Rājagaha)
3 — in Siviraṭṭha (Ariṭṭhapuranagara, Jetuttaranagara)
3 — in Kosalaraṭṭha (Sāvatthī, Sākala)
twice in Bharuraṭṭha
twice in Kāliṅgaraṭṭha (Dantapuranagara)
twice in Vaṁsaraṭṭha (Kosambī)
once in Sovīraraṭṭha (Roruvanagara)
once in Mahiṁsakaraṭṭha (Sakulanagara)
once in Mallaraṭṭha (Kusāvatī)
once in Serivaraṭṭha
once in Tambapaṇṇidīpa
once in Avantiraṭṭha (Ujjenī)
once in Videharaṭṭha (Mithilā)
once in Uttarāpatha
once in Himavanta (Chaddantadaha)
once in Kampillaraṭṭha (Uttarapañcālanagara) cfr. Kururaṭṭha supra.

In the P a c c u p p a n n a v a t t h u-tales the scene is laid:

428 times in the Kosala-
58 — in the Magadha-
4 — in the Sākiya-
3 — in the Vaṁsa-
twice in the Licchavī
twice in the Malla-
once in the Sumbha-
once in the Bhagga-

once in the Kâsi-
once in the Koliya-
once in the Videha-

In these two lists the following names are in common:

Kâsiraṭṭha occurs as the scene of the tale			in the P. V. once
			in the A. V. 428 times
Magadha-	—	—	in the P. V. 58
			in the A. V. 7
Videha-	—	—	in the P. V once
			in the A. V. once
Malla-	—	—	in the P. V. twice
			in the A. V. once
Kosala-	—	—	in the P. V. 428 times
			in the A. V. 3 times
Vaṁsa-	—	—	in the P. V. 3 times
			in the A. V. twice

But the following are only to be found in the P. V.:

Licchavî	twice
Sâkiya-	4 times
Sumbha-	once
Bhagga-	once
Koliya-	once

and the following only in the A. V.:

Gandhâra-	25 times
Kuru-	9 times
Sivi-	3 times
Sovîra-	once
Mahiṁsaka-	once
Seriva-	once
Bharu-	twice
Tambapaṇṇidîpa	once
Kâliṅga-	twice
Avanti-	once
Uttarâpatha	once
Himavanta	once

That is to say: The tales of the Atītavatthu play mostly in the northern and western part of India, and the tales of the Paccuppannavatthu principally in the eastern India. In other words: the Atītavatthu is the oldest element of the Jātaka. This seems especially to be evident from the tales in which the Takkasilā is mentioned as a University-town to which young men resorted from Bārāṇasī and other easterly cities to study the three Vedas and acquire every sort of accomplishment under the guidance of a renowned master. (See the Index under Takkasilā).

The Paccuppannavatthu and the Atītavatthu together with the Veyyākaraṇa and the Samodhāna then make up the Jātaka-Aṭṭhakathā (I $\frac{47}{94}$) that was translated into Singhalese with the exception of the verses which were left in the original Pāli; and this Singhalese Jātaka-Aṭṭhakathā has later been re-translated into Pāli under the name of Jātakassa Atthavaṇṇanā or Jātakass' Atthavaṇṇanā (see I $\frac{1}{94}$?, VI $\frac{594}{9}$, V $\frac{419}{4}$) which is the Jātaka that now lies before us and begins at page 2 of the first volume.

That the prosaic part of the Atītavatthu belongs to the old Jātaka is quite clear from the fact that the verses would be thoroughly unintelligible without it.

It may be doubted whether the Introductory Verses at p. 1, although they are to be found both in C and B, originally belong to the Jātakassa Atthavaṇṇanā, as they do not appear in S which has quite a different Introduction (see vol. IV) and only agrees with C and B from the beginning of p. 2: Sā panāyaṁ Jātakassa Atthavaṇṇanā. If we suppose that they are part of the J. A. then the author of it has been called upon by three persons viz. Atthadassin, Buddhamitta and Buddhadeva to write it.

II. But who is the Author? To be sure, we are told by the writer of the Gantha-Vaṁsa (see Journal of the P. T. Soc. 1886 p. 59) that Buddhaghosa is the author, but on this you can scarcely rely. It is certain that Buddhaghosa has written Visuddhimagga, Sumaṅgalavilāsinī, Papañcasūdanī, Sāratthappakāsinī, Manorathapūraṇī and Samantapāsādikā, for this clearly appears from the Introductory Verses to these commentaries, but that he, besides these voluminous works, should have written six others equally large whose author he is supposed to be, is very incredible, especially if he only stayed three years in Ceylon, and was not barely a translator, but an independent writer.

Further, it is not granted either, that the **Buddhamitta** who is spoken of in the Introductory Verses of the Jātaka-Atthavaṇṇanā, is the same with the one that is mentioned in the Samantapāsādikā and the Papañcasūdanī, this one being more likely to be identical with the Buddhamitta that, according to Vasilief's Bouddhisme p. 218 lived „vers la neuf-centième année après la mort de Bouddha“ and consequently was a contemporary of Buddhaghosa. This last mentioned Buddhamitta, further, may be the same with the one who is mentioned as having, in the time of Kumāragupta. Samvat 126 erected a Statue of Buddha. (Cfr. Westergaard's Indiske Kejserhuse p. 108, and A. Cunningham's Archæol. Survey of India X p. 7).

III. That the **original Pāli Aṭṭhakathā** (see Index) — **Jātaka-Aṭṭhakathā** (I $\frac{1}{2}\frac{2}{6}$) which was translated into Singhalese, already has existed as a **Book** at the time when the Saṅgītikārakas made the above-mentioned transposition (see supra p. III) seems evident.

IV. The now existing **Jātakassa Atthavaṇṇanā** presents itself partly as a recast of the Jātaka-Aṭṭhakathā, an earlier arrangement of the stuff being kept formally but having in reality been altered, while several, formerly independent, Jātakas have been incorporated in others. We find namely that 12 (110. 111. 112. 170. 192. 350. 364. 452. 471. 500. 508. 517.) from their original place have been transferred to 546 Mahā-Ummagga-, 2 (341. 464) to 536 Kuṇāla-, 1 (441) to 546 Vidhura-, and 1 (470) to 535 Sudhābhojana-; consequently, when we subtract these 16 from the current statement of 550, we only get 534, but formally there are 547 according to the older redaction. In this both C and B agree. It would be of interest to learn what position the Siamese Jātaka holds in regard to

C and B, if, on the whole, a complete copy nowadays exists in Siam.

V. The Buddhist Canon is mentioned in the Jātaka under three names: Tīṇi Piṭakāni, Piṭakattaya and Tepiṭaka Buddhavacana (see for these names the Index).

And if we can depend upon the statement in J. II $\frac{327}{18}$ of the following import:

„Tadā kira pañcasatā brāhmaṇā tiṇṇaṁ vedānaṁ pāragū sāsane pabbajitvā Tīṇi Piṭakāni uggaṇhitvā mānamadamattā hutvā 'Sammāsambuddho pi Tīṇ' eva Piṭakāni jānāti, mayam pi tāni jānāma, evaṁ sante kiṁ tassa amhehi nānākaraṇan' ti Buddhupaṭṭhānaṁ na gacchanti i. e.

„At that time five hundred Brāhmaṇas who where perfect in the three Vedas, and had embraced the doctrine (of the Buddha) and acquired the three Piṭakas, were seized with the madness of pride and said: „Sammāsambuddha, to be sure, knows the three Piṭakas, but we too know them, in what then consists the difference between him and us", so thinking they do not go and serve Buddha,

then the Tipiṭaka must have existed at the time of Gotama Buddha, and G. B. wòuld consequently, like his antagonist Devadatta (II $\frac{412}{18}$), have been Tipiṭaka-dhara, one who knows the three Piṭakas. Compare with this J. I $\frac{116}{17}$, II $\frac{441}{7}$: „āvuso Devadatta, Sammāsambuddho tuyhaṁ ācariyo, tvaṁ S-sambuddhaṁ nissāya Tīṇi Piṭakāni uggaṇhi"; and the beginning of the Commentary to Dhammapada vv. 19—20: Bahum pi ce ti. Imaṁ dhammadesanaṁ Satthā Jetavane viharanto dve sahāyake ārabbha kathesi. Sāvatthivāsino hi dve kulaputtā naṁ sahāya (pahāya?) vihāraṁ gantvā Satthu dhammadesanaṁ sutvā kāme pahāya sāsane uraṁ datvā pabbajitā pañcavassāni ācariyupajjhāyānaṁ santike vasitvā Satthāraṁ upasaṁkamitvā sāsane dhuraṁ pucchitvā vipassanādhurañ ca ganthadhurañ ca vitthārato sutvā eko tāva „ahaṁ bhante mahallakakāle pabbajito na sakkhissāmi ganthadhuraṁ pūretuṁ vipassanādhuraṁ pana pūressāmīti" yāva arahattā vipassanaṁ kathāpetvā ghaṭento vāyamanto saha paṭisambhidāhi arahattaṁ pāpuṇi, itaro „ahaṁ ganthadhuraṁ pūressāmīti" anukkamena Tepiṭakaṁ Buddhavacanaṁ uggaṇhitvā gatagatatthāne dhammaṁ kathesi ... „kiṁ pana tumhehi tassa santike gahitaṁ, kiṁ Dīghanikāyādīsu aññataro nikāyo, Tīsu Piṭakesu ekaṁ piṭakan" ti vatvā catuppadikam pi gāthaṁ na jānāti etc. Mark further Alwis' quotation from Vibhanga ātuvā in his Introd. to Kachchāyana's Grammar p. V: Sammāsambuddho pi tepiṭakan Buddhavachanan Tantin āropento Māgadhībhāsāyeva āropesi 'Buddha who rendered his (?) tepiṭaka words into Tanti (or tantra or doctrines) did so by means of the Māgadhi language'.

That the Tipiṭaka has existed before Gotama Buddha, even long before at the time of Koṇḍañña-Buddha, would also result from the Nidānakathā I $\frac{29}{10}$, where we are told that the king Vijitāvin mastered the three Piṭakas; likewise from I $\frac{41}{1}$ $\frac{42}{16}$ and IV $\frac{31}{7}$. So it will be understood how we already in the Atītavatthu (II $\frac{147}{5}$) occasionally meet with the formula: appamāṇo Buddho, appamāṇo Dhammo, appamāṇo Saṁgho, this Buddha being of course the Buddha of the time and not Gotama Buddha.

And perhaps in time we may find out that several of the anterior, so-called mythical, Buddhas have been real historical persons; one of them at least has proved to be so, since a stūpa was erected to him, and Asoka worshipped before it and restored it. (See Bühler in the Academy 1895. 27. April p. 360). On the whole, I think we must admit that such a complicated system as that of Gotama Buddha's is scarcely one man's work, but must indeed have had its forerunners. And that a large old poetic literature in Pāli has existed before Gotama Buddha is proved by the many identical fragments of verses that recur in different Jātakas, in fact in all Pāli books, and seem to have been common property at the time: compare below Dr. Andersen's List of Parallel Verses.

VI. In the Jātaka to write is called likh. Lekha means a streak, a line, writing, and the Indians wrote on a paṇṇa or a paṭṭa. An epistle is called paṇṇa, and a letter akkhara. Examples: imaṁ gāthaṁ paṇṇe likhitvā II $\frac{173}{24}$, IV $\frac{55}{17}$; tena hi likhathā 'ti suvaṇṇapaṭṭe likhāpesi II $\frac{377}{23}$, IV $\frac{7}{24}$ $\frac{487}{14}$; jātibiñgulakena bhittiyā akkharāni likhitvā V $\frac{114}{9}$ $\frac{487}{24}$, IV $\frac{335}{28}$: paṇṇākārena saddhiṁ paṇṇāni pahiṇiṁsu V $\frac{489}{14}$: pāsāne lekhaṁ khananto V $\frac{149}{15}$ $\frac{114}{9}$ $\frac{487}{24}$.

Lipi that appears in the Inscriptions of Asoka, is not to be found in the Jātaka and is no doubt a loan from the Persians.

I cannot conclude this Postscriptum without especially thanking the Berlin Academy of Sciences for its repeated liberality in granting a sum towards the printing of this last volume of the Jātaka.

Finally I have to thank Mr. P. C. Madsen, the compositor, for the care and attention with which he for the space of twenty years has worked at this not very easy task.

Kopenhagen 20. February 1897.

V. Fausbøll.

PREFACE.

On beginning this Index to the Jātaka, four years ago, it was first my intention to give an index of both names and matter. But I have altered this plan since the appearance of the English translation published by Prof. Cowell. In this translation we have not only a short account of the contents of the tales, but a complete index has been held in prospect, when the work is finished. I have therefore particularly confined my work to proper names and Gāthās. In reality I think that indexes to proper names and verses in Pāli literature are at present of much greater consequence than a new Pāli Dictionary. Prof. E. Müller's Index of proper names published in J. P. T. S. is, it is true, of great importance, and I have myself derived much benefit from it, but it is clear that after a space of nine years it cannot longer be satisfactory. I therefore hope that the present index will be a considerable step forward. My plan has been to collect all places where the names occur. How far I have been fortunate in this respect, the use of the book will show. The names are arranged alphabetically according to the Pāli Alphabet, and the words of the text itself are everywhere, as far as possible, employed in the explanations; my own additions are marked (—). The index refers to the six volumes marked I—VI, and each place is indicated page and line. Only quotations from Nidānakathā are separately designated by the letter N. In accordance with the now published edition I have tried to introduce a further denotion as to whether the quotations are from the Jātaka-text itself, from the frame story, or the commentary, whereas the quotations from the commentary are marked with (—) enclosing the number of line, whilst quotations from the principal text are marked with *. I admit that it would have been of interest to have had a special mark for all quotations from the verses, but the fear of making the whole too complicated has prevented me doing so. Beside the proper names are added all names of tales[1]) or portions of the work and titles of other Pāli works quoted. Amongst the number of references to passages in the Jātaka itself, many of course are incorrect, in such cases I have exerted myself to point out the one really meant. I will here merely give an example: Vol. IV 360.$_{24}$ we have the following quotation „Aṭṭhanipāte Sucirajātake". There is however no tale with this title in the whole Jātaka. The only way of finding out what is referred to is the word „amdisadānaṁ", which shortly mentions the subject of the introductory tale. Thereby is found in Aṭṭhanipāta Ādittajātaka, and attention is directed besides to Jāt. (499), where it is clear the same quotation appears again in the form of „Aṭṭhanipāte Sovīrajātake". Neither is there any Sovīrajātaka, but when one gets accustomed to the different ways in which the tales have come by their names in the last redaction of the text, it is easy to be seen that the name Sovīrajātaka must be the right reading, as Ādittajātaka begins just with the words „alte Sovīraraṭṭhe". Sucira must therefore be a misscript for Sovīra. Vidūra-jāt. (Cod. B) is doubtless Vidhūra-jāt. or another name for Dhūmakārijāt. (413). Here is consequently a confounding of the Atītavatthu and the Paccuppanna-vatthu. On the other hand the Birman variation of Sovīra IV 401 is Sivira (cfr. III 470 Siviraṭhe B), which also implies that Sucira is a perversion.

The importance of having the words of the Paccuppannavatthu, pointing out the subject of the tale, included in the index, may thus be seen; I have therefore unhesitatingly introduced them in alphabetical order with the proper names, for it is practical to

[1]) The numbers of the tales are always marked with (—).

have as much as possible in one list, and several of them are proper names.

The titles of the stories are in most cases formed in either of the following ways: 1) the Jātaka is called after the hero, generally Bodhisatta, but also sometimes after some other person taking part in the tale, 2) the title can be formed according to the first Gāthā, but in certain cases after the prose beginning. The same methods may be seen in the titles of the Jātakas that are preserved in the Bharhut-Inscriptions. For instance that Mahāummagga-jātaka is called Yavamajhakiyaṁ, agrees very well with our text, that VI 331,1 is as follows: „Mithilāyaṁ.... pācīnayavamajjhake Sirivaḍḍhako nāma seṭṭhi ahosi". Ruru-jāt. is named after Bo. in the text, but on the Stūpa we find Miga-jāt. after the first Gāthā. Jāt. (62) is, as we know, likewise named on the Stūpa after the opening words in the first Gāthā: yaṁ brāhmaṇo etc. Nacca-jāt. is named after an important occurrence in the tale (the peacock's dance), but the Stūpa has Haṁsa-jāt. after Bo. At the beginning of Bhallāṭiya-jāt. (504) prose and verse are much the same: Bhallāṭiyo nāma ahosi rājā; the Stūpa here has Kinnara-jāt. This seems to infer that we cannot from the titles draw any direct conclusion as to the original form of the tales. I do not think it right to assert, that the Jātakas have originally only existed in metre. As these tales have been represented at an early period under the form of reliefs, they must have been widely circulated and well known, and have doubtless also been early narrated in prose. That great parts of the present redaction are selected from longer poems in narrative style, there is little reason to doubt, but at the time they were first related as Jatākas (i. e. stories of Buddha's earlier existences), they may very well have been somewhat in their present shape. For closer examination of such problems it is therefore of importance to have a list of all the verses that occur in more than one place. This I have striven to do in Index III, which not only contains an alphabetical list of the beginnings of those Gāthās that are to be found repeated in their entire length, but also several recurring parts of Gāthās, as far as I can make out [1]). Prof. Franke's opinion [2]) of the verses in the Jāt. seems to be confirmed here in several points. A good example of this is given in the verses in Jāt. (262) and (263) which we refind in succession vol. IV 471 (cfr. V 451). Still I do not think that we can safely admit a poetical „Ur-Jātaka", even if we allow that the prose in the Atītavatthu on the whole shews evidence of editorship. I shall not however enter closer into the question here; what has been most important to me was that this index should follow as quickly as possible on the completion of the text, and I hope it may deserve some appreciation and a lenient criticism of its deficiencies that it is now, in less than a year's time, presented to the public. One result of the hasty preparation, for which I beg indulgence, is the rather long list of additions and corrections.

In reference to Index I I would further remark that, as it first of all is an index to the present edition, I have, from principle, not voluntarily corrected the text which is given by the editor; the corrections I have ventured to make are therefore few. I here mention a couple of examples of incorrect names. Vol. IV 343 speaks of two Theras Mantidatta and Dhanuggahatissa. These names can be shortened to Datta and Tissa, which may be seen from II 403, where the same tale occurs; but instead of Datta the Singhalese text has Utta. This last mentioned name is undoubtedly false, as B has the form Datta, and the signs for „u" and „da", in Singhalese might easily be mistaken. In accordance with this I have also understood „mitto" and „datto" IV 478,27 as proper names of undefined persons. I avail myself of the opportunity here offered, of correcting a mistake which unfortunately has crept into Chalmer's translation of Vol. I p. 230. The Pāli Text (Jāt. I 391,21) has the following: »Sāriputtatthero Nālagāmake jāto varake pari-

[1] I have prepared a complete index of all the verses, but have refrained from printing the whole of it, as it would be too voluminous; still I hope to be able, on another occasion, to prepare an index of the parallel verses in the Jātaka & the rest of Pāli literature.

[2] Anzeige von Gurupūjākaumudī, Bezz. Beitr. 1897 p. 291 ff.

nibbāyi", which is rendered: „The Elder S., who was born in Nāla village, died at Varaka". Here, a town of the name of Varaka figures, but it is a delusion. The mistake is brought about through an insignificant misprint: it ought to be „jātovarake", as in V 125,21 where the same passage occurs. The word is formed of jāta + ovaraka (birth-room, cfr. jātabhūmi), and the passage is to be translated thus: „S. died in Nālagāmaka in the same room, he was born in".

Of deviating readings I have taken several, as far as they appeared to me to be of importance, particularly the more uncommon names. On the other hand I have left out the number of epithets Bodhisatta, Mahāsatta, Tathāgatha etc., as they seem to me unnecessary; still I have in the article Bodhisatta given an alphabetical list of all his names and existences. I have adopted a simpler method with the names Bārāṇasī and Brahmadatta, merely mentioning vol. & page. In solitary cases (f. ex. Vedā) I have only selected a few places and notified this by adding „etc.".

The editor has in many instances in the text and notes added parallels from other works (especially Dhammapada). These quotations are, although not exhaustive, still of great importance, and I have considered it useful to give a list of them in Index IV.

In conclusion I wish to thank Prof. Fausbøll, my teacher and guide of many years standing, in grateful acknowledgement of the aid he has rendered me throughout the whole of my work. Our deceased countryman V. Trenckner also deserves to be mentioned here: his copy of the printed text and his transcript have, in not a few places, been of much use to me.

I must address a special acknowledgement to the Directors of the Carlsberg Fund, who munificently, have granted me pecuniary support, which has enabled me to devote so much of my beforehand fully occupied time to this work.

Kopenhagen, May 1897.

D. Andersen.

I

INDEX

OF

PROPER NAMES AND TITLES

A.

Akataññu-jātaka (90) I 377—79. — III 196,4.

Akaniṭṭhabhavana III 487,1.

akālarāvī bhikkhu I 435,20.

Akālarāvi-jātaka (119) I 435—36.

Akitti, isi VI 99,29*.

Akitti, brāhmaṇo (= Bodhisatto) V 45,18. IV 237,6*. 242,24.

Akitti-jātaka (480) IV 236—42. — V 241 (30).

Akittitittha IV 237,26*.

Akittidvāra, Bārāṇasiyaṁ IV 237,26*.

Akkha-khaṇḍa, Vidhurapaṇḍita-jātake VI 286,8.

aggasāvakā, dve III 191,4.

Aggāḷava (Aggālava), cetiyaṁ Āḷavinagaraṁ nissāya I 160,21. — II 282,15. 25. — III 78,23. 351,23.

Aggi Bhagavā I 285,16*. 494*,11. 13. 14. 20. 22. 24. Aggideva VI 202,21* (25. 29).

Aggika-jātaka (129) I 461—62.

Aggika Bhāradvāja, sigālo I 462*,8. 17. 21.

aggijuhanaṁ II 43,10.

Aggidatta, brāhmaṇo pitā Kakusandha-Buddhassa V 42,25.

Aggideva, Devagabbhāya putto pañcamo IV 81,8*.

Aggimāla, samuddo IV 139,25*. Aggimāli IV 140,2*.

Aṁkura, Devagabbhāya putto dasamo IV 81,7*. 84*,4. 8.

Aṅga, rājā Aṅgaraṭṭhe IV 454*,10. 14. 15. 19. 28. — V 316,13*. — VI 271,29. 272 (9).

Aṅga, Bārāṇasi-rājā VI 203,14* (21).

Aṅga-raṭṭha N 87,18. — II 211*,1. 15. — IV 454*,10. 11. 13. — V 316,12*. — VI 256,8*. 317 (1). — Aṅgā V 317,28*. — VI 274,1* (5).

Aṅgati (Aṁgati), rājā Mithilāyaṁ Videharaṭṭhe VI 220,26*. 221,11. 222,16. 223 (5). 229,8. 230,10. 232,31. 233 (1). 239 (25). 241,11. 242,26 (30).

Aṅgīrasa, tāpaso, isi V 135,24*. VI 99,29* (32). — Aṅgīrasa Gotama.

Aṅgīrasa Gotama (isi) V 144,1*. 145 (7).

Aṅguttaraṭṭhakathā I 131 (23).

Aṅgulimāla, thero I 275,30. — III 330,8. — IV 180,23. — V 36,5. 456,19. 25. 511,19. 20. — VI 329,24 (coro).

Aṅgulimālasutta-vaṇṇanā V 456,30.

Aciravatī, nadī I 418,8. — II 96,5. 366,2. — III 137,8. 228,8. — IV 167,8. 21. 168,4.

Accimukhī (Accīmukkhī), Bhūridattassa (Bodhisattassa) vemātikabhaginī VI 190,20*. 195*,1. 4. 6. 196,15*. 219,25.

Accuta, tāpaso, isi VI 532,2 (7). 9 (10). 12. 540,16*. 593,28.

Accuta, seṭṭhi N 94,16.

Accutavarupadanta, hatthi Bārāṇasirañño VI 185,26*.

Ajapāla, purohitaputto IV 476,8*. 482,9*. 491,4.

Ajapālanigrodha N 16,8. 78,11. 81,5. — I 469,15.

Ajātasattu, putto Bimbisārassa Magadharañño I 185,27. 28. 186,20. 508,10. 510,5. 11. 511,17. — II 237,17. 19. 23. 27. 239,18. 242,21. 403,10. 17. 19. 21. 404,11. 19. 23. — III 121,17. 122,7. 215,15. 406,1. 536,24. — IV 343,1—3. 15. 18. 23. 27. — V 261,32. 262,30. 277,5. — VI 129,22. — Ajātasattussa asantapaggaho I 508,10. — °pitughātakammaṁ V 261,33. — Ajātasattu-mātā II 237,20 (cfr. Kosaladevī).

Ajita, brāhmaṇo (Bodhisatto) N 85,16.

Ajita-Kesakambali, diṭṭhigatiko V 246,11. Ajitakesakambala I 509,13.

Ajīvaka (purisanāma) I 402,27*. 403,14*.

Ajjuna, Devagabbhāya putto sattamo IV 81,7*.

Ajjuna, Paṇḍurājaputto V 135,24*. 143*,12. 27. — V 424,20. 426 (10. 31. 36). 427 (15). — Kekakādhipa V 267,5*. — Ajjunavatthu V 119 (15).

Ajjuna-rukkha, bodhi Anomadassi-Buddhassa N 36,6.

Ajjhobāra, mahāmaccho V 462,17*.

Añjanadevī, dhītā Devagabbhāya IV 80,21*. 84,3*. 88,13*. 89,11*.

Añjana-pabbata V 133,22*. 415,23.

Añjanavana, Sāketaṁ nissāya I 308,26. 309,10. — III 270,21*.

Añjanavasabha, maṅgalahatthi Dhanañjayassa Koravyarañño II 368,12*.

aññatitthiyā (cfr. titthiya-) III 74,10.

Aññākoṇḍañña-thera N 82,11. (cfr. Koṇḍañña brāhmaṇa).

aṭṭha varā Visākhāya IV 314,29.

Aṭṭhaka, rājā V 135,21*, 137,3*. 149,30*. 150 (2). — VI 99,10*. 251,14. (27).

Aṭṭhakathā N 44,1. 66,32. — I 345 (15). 488, (29). — II 241 (17). 294 (9). 299 (5). 334 (15). 395 (10). — V 95 (7). — VI 36 (20). 279 (29). sevaṭṭhakathā N 62,22.

Aṭṭha-nipāta III 422—482. — I 153,24. — II 113,14. — IV 360,24. 401,12.

Aṭṭhasadda-jātaka (418) III 428—434.

Aṭṭhāna-jātaka (425) III 474—478.

Aṭṭhisena, Bārāṇasi-brāhmaṇo (— Bodhisatto) III 352*,5. 22. 26. 353 (2. 27). 354 (6). 355,19.

Aṭṭhisena-jātaka (403) III 351—355.

Aḍḍhamāsakarāja III 449*,6. 8. 11. 454,3. — IV 174 (9).

Aḍḍha-vagga III 211—227.

Aṇimaṇḍavya, tāpaso (— Maṇḍavya) IV 30*.18. 24. 37,1.

Aṇḍabhūta-jātaka (62) I 289—295.

Atideva, brāhmaṇo (— Bodhisatto) N 35,3.

Atipaṇḍita, kūṭavāṇijo I 404*,21. 24—26. 28. 29. 405*,1. 7. 9. 11. 15. 16. (18. 19).
Atimuttaka-susāna, Bārāṇasiyaṁ IV 28,22*.
Atula, nāgarājā (= Bodhisatto) N 34,20. 41,12.
Atula, ambarukkho IV 324*,13. 14.
Attadaṇḍa-sutta V 413,23. 414,23.
Atthakāma-vagga I 234—261.
atthakusalo putto I 366,8.
Atthadassi-thera N 1,14.
Atthadassi-Buddha N 38,27. 39,9. 19. 44,8.
Atthassadvāra-jātaka (84) I 366—367.
Adīnasattu V 26 (8) = Alīnasattu.
Adhanapālī (purisanāma) I 403*,5. 16.
Adhamma, devaputto kāmāvacaraloke (= Devadatto) IV 100,23*. 101*,3. 7—9. 16. 24. 102*,6. 9. 11. (16. 20). 103*,2 (11. 18. 26. 27). 104,6. Adhammayāna, ratho Adhammassa IV 101,19*. 102 (17).
Adhogaṅgā II 283,13*. 329,19*. — V 3,4*.
Anattalakkhaṇa-sutta IV 180,14. — Anattalakkhaṇa-suttanta N 82,18.
Ananusociya-jātaka (328) III 92—97.
Anantarapeyyāla, Vidhurapaṇḍita-jātake VI 304,10.
Anabhirati-jātaka a) (65) I 301—2. — b) (185) II 99—101.
Anāthapiṇḍika, seṭṭhi Sāvatthiyaṁ, N 77,5. 92,14. 93,10. 94,5. 7. 28. — I 95,9. 17. 96,6. 11. 97,27. 105 (16). 217,3. 226,23. 229,20. 230,27. 231,13. 24. 248,18. 251,21. 252,3. 268,22. 25. 364,3. 4. 14. 377,15. 19. 25. 28. 378,8. 412,25. 441,4. 7. 11. — II 286,27. 347,6. 8. 12. 410,28. 411,3. 416,1. 431,4. 11. — III 119,1. 4. 128,20. 22. 141,22. 196,2. 257,3. 7. 435,2. 24. 26. — IV 144,7. 11. 188,20. 228,10. 25. 229,4. 9. 10. — VI 15 (9). — Culla-Anāthapiṇḍika (I 148,4. — II 267,1. — III 520,6. — Anāthapiṇḍikassa dāsī Rohiṇī nāma I 248,13.

— °dāsī III 435,2. — °micchayamitto I 441,4. — °bhāgineyyo II 437,4. — °mitto Kāḷakaṇṇī nāma I 364,3.

Anitthigandha-kumāra, putto Bārāṇasirañño (= Bodhisatto) II 329,2*. 331,9. — IV 469,3*. 472 (8). 473,9.

Animisa-cetiya N 77,31.

Anukevaṭṭa, brāhmaṇo, VI 406,8*. 407,29*. 408*,8. 9. 29. 409,1. 23.

Anujjā, bhariyā Vidhurapaṇḍitassa, VI 290,11* (15).

Anutīracārin, uddo, III 333*,19. 25. 334,21*. 335, (1).

Anurādha-pura V 254 (21).

Anuruddha-thera N 30,14. — I 140,7. — II 93,23. 125,8. 257,10. — III 147,15. 469,21. 494,19. 496,21. — IV 14,21. 242,24. 288,21. 314,20. 332,22. 360,30. 412,23. 491,4. — V 67,24. 151,29. 412,10. 511,22. — VI 95,9. 129,15. 329,17. 593,27.

Anuḷā, aggasāvikā Kassapa-Buddhassa N 43,28.

Anusāsika-jātaka (115) I 428—430.

anusāsika-bhikkhunī I 428,18.

Anusāsikā, caṇḍā sakuṇikā I 429*,17. 22. 430,6.

Anusissa, tāpaso, jeṭṭhantevāsiko Sārabhaṅgassa (Bodhisattassa), III 463,19*. 469,22. — V 133,11*. 134,3*. 136,10*. 138*,4. 23. 139,12*. 140*,1. 12. 151,(9).

Anūnanāma (= Puṇṇako yakkho) VI 273,30*.

Anūpiya, ambavanaṁ N 65,29. — I 140,3.

Anūpiya, nagaraṁ I 140,2. 9.

anesanā II 82,3.

Anotatta-daha, mahāsaro Himavante N 50,14. 80,15. — I 232,6*. — II 92,26. — III 257*,22—23. 264,19*. 379,18*. — IV 213,5*. 368,14*. 379,20*. 497 (81). — V 314,20*. 320,10*. 321 (20). 27*. 324 (13). 392,22*. 415,25. — VI 432,21*.

Anopama, nagaraṁ, Vesabhu-Buddhassa N 42,11.

Anoma, upaṭṭhāko Sobhita-Buddhassa N 35,21. — aggasāvako Anomadassi-Buddhassa N 36,5.

Anoma, nagaraṁ Piyadassi-Buddhassa N 39,3.
Anomadassi-Buddha N 35,27. 36,8. 10. 44,6.
Anomā, mātā Nārada-Buddhassa N 37,6.
Anomā, nadī N 64,12. 20. — IV 119,10.
Anta-jātaka (295) II 440—441.
Andhakaveṇhu, dāso Devagabbhāya, sāmiko Nandagopāya IV 79,20*. 81,18*.
Andhakaveṇhu-dāsaputtā, dasa bhātikā puttā Devagabbhāya IV 81*,8. 12. — V 18,7*. 19 (28). — Andhakaveṇhuyo V 267,12*.
Andhapura, nagaraṁ I 111,8*.
Apacara = Upacara-rājā (paṭhamakappe) Cetiyaraṭṭhe Sotthivatinagare III 454,18*.
apaccavekkhitaparibhogo I 379,7.
Apaṇṇaka-jātaka (1) I 95—106. — N 1,8. — IV 282,20.
apaṇṇaka-dhammadesanā I 95,6. 104,5. 106,3.
Apaṇṇaka-vagga I 95—142.
Apanthaka (purisanāma) I 403*,11. 16.
Aparagoyāna-dīpa VI 279 (8). (cfr. Goyāniyā).
Aparaṇṇa, gijjho (= Bodhisatto) III 255,9*. 256,12. 26.
aparissāvanako bhikkhu I 198,10—22.
Apāyimha-vagga I 360—379.
Appacintin, maccho I 427*,9. 16. 428,1. 9.
Appamādovāda V 66 (28).
Abbhantara-jātaka (281) II 392—400. — II 433,5.
Abbhantara-vagga II 392—430.
Abhaya, upaṭṭhāko Atthadassi-Buddhassa N 39,15.
Abhaya-mahārāja II 414 (10).
Abhayaṁkara, hatthi VI 135,28*.
Abhiṇha-jātaka (27) I 188—190.
Abhidhamma-kathā IV 265,10.
Abhidhamma-piṭaka N 78,4.
Abhibhū, aggasāvako Sikhi-Buddhassa N 41,30.

Abhimārapayojanā I 142,18.
amacco Kosalarañño I 354,16. — II 400,7. — III 168,11.
Amata-mahānibbāna N 3,24. — II 130,8. — Amata-mahānibbāna-talāka, Amata-nibbāna-mahātalāka N 4,20.
Amatantala-nibbāna N 4,27—28.
Amara-nagara N 2,33. 3,2. 6,10.
Amaravatī, nagaraṁ N 2,14. 32. 3,15.
Amarā-devī, purāṇaseṭṭhikulassa dhītā, VI 364*,10. 24. 365,7*. 366*,3. 9. 21. 27. 368*,6. 9. 27. 369*,25. 30. 372,24*. 392,22*. 478,12*.
Amarādevī-pañha (112) I 424,19—21.
Amitā, aggasāvikā Padumottara-Buddhassa N 37,22.
Amittatāpanā, brāhmaṇa-dhītā, bhariyā Jūjakassa VI 521,13—14*. 16*. 22. 524,30*. 593,20.
Amba-jātaka a) (124) I 449—451. — b) (474) IV 200—207.
ambagopaka-thero III 187,3.
Ambacora-jātaka (344) III 137—139.
Ambaṭṭha (māṇavo?) VI 478,17*. — Ambaṭṭha-kula III 413,19*. 414 (1).
Ambhaṭṭhavessā (plur.) IV 363,21*. 366 (18).
ambarasadānaṁ Bimbādevītheriyā II 392,11.
Ayakūṭa-jātaka (347) III 145—147.
Ayoghara-jātaka (510) IV 491—499.
Ayoghara-paṇḍita, putto Brahmadattassa Bārāṇasi-rañño (= Bodhisatto) N 45,28. — IV 490,27. 492,12*. 499,24. — Ayoghara-samāgama VI 30,8.
Ayojjhana-nagara IV 82,22*.
Ayyakākāḷaka, go (= Bodhisatto) I 194,10*. 196,14.
Araka, satthā, isi (= Bodhisatto) N 46,5. — II 61,10*. 62,30.
Araka-jātaka (169) II 60—62.
Arañjaragiri, pabbato Majjhimadese III 463*,21. 22. — V 134,2*. — VI 514,3*. (Ārañjara VI 493,20*. (22).)
araññakuṭikā Rājagahaṁ nissāya, Mahāmoggallānassa III 33,10. — °Mahākassapassa III 71,6.

Arañña-jātaka (348) III 147—149.
Arañña-vagga II 354—392.
Aratī, dhītā Mārassa N 78.20. — I 469.17.
Arahaṁ Sugato (— Buddho) N 79.32.
Ariṭṭha, putto Dhataraṭṭhassa nāgarañño, VI 168*.2. 4. 5. 10. 189.22*. 27. 190*.21. 22. 204.28*. 205*.18. 23. 26. 206.2*. 208.25*. 210 (9. 25). 212.10*. 215 (8. 25). 216 (34). — (cfr. Kāṇariṭṭha.)
Ariṭṭhajanaka, putto Mahājanaka-rañño, rājā Mithilāyaṁ, VI 30*.21. 23. 32.26*. 33.26*. 42.21*.
Ariṭṭhapura, nagaraṁ Siviraṭṭhe IV 401.27*. — V 210.18*. 212.26*. — VI 419 (11). 27*.*
Arindama, Bārāṇasirājā putto Magadharañño (— Bodhisatto) N 41.25. — III 489 (24) (Arindamaka). — V 247*.8. 20. 248.9*. 249.15*. 251 (28). 252.12*. 255.7*. 261.29.
Arindama, Kāsirājā V 380.14*. (19).
ariyasāvako Kassapabuddhakāle II 111.18*.
Aruṇa, khattiyo pitā Sikhi-Buddhassa N 41.29.
Aruṇarāja (— Assaka-rāja) III 3.24*. 26. 4 (1).
Aruṇavatī, nagaraṁ Sikhi-Buddhassa N 41.29.
Arūpabhava N 55.4.
Alakkhī V 114 (24).
Alambusa-jataka (523) V 152—161. — V 193.11*.
Alambusā accharā V 152.22*. 153.8. (8). 10. 17*. 26*. 154.17*. 30. 157.14*. 22*. 28. 159 (8). 20*. 160.16*. 20. 161.17.
alasabhikkhu III 139.21.
Alāta, amacco Aṁgatissa rañño (— Devadatto) VI 221.8*. 32. 222.4. 22. 26. (30). 223 (4). 227.5. (18). 25. 228.17. 19. 233.23. (30—31). 234.30. 32. 235 (7). 237 (15). 255.6. — Alātaka VI 221.16. 230.14.
Aḷāra, see: Āḷāra.
Alīnacitta, putto Bārāṇasirañño. rājā (— Bodhisatto) II 21.17*. 22.18*. 22. 23 (1). 28.

Alīnacitta-jātaka (156) II 17—23.

Alīnasattu-kumāra, putto Jayaddisarañño Uttarapañcālanagare (— Bodhisatto) N 45,22. — V 22,5*. 26,2. (7). 29,7. (29) (Ālīnasatta). 30 (1). 35,5 (Alīnasatta). 36,8.

Avanti-mahārāja, Ujjeniyaṁ IV 390,14*.

Avanti-raṭṭha, Dakkhiṇāpathe III 463,16*. — IV 390,14*. 397 (27). — V 133,24*. 318 (6). — Avantīsu IV 397,5*.

Avavādakā, Licchavi-dārikā paribbājikā III 1,14.

Avāriya-jātaka (376) III 228—232.

Avāriya-pitā, nāviko III 230,1*. 8. (11). — Avāriyā, tassa dhītā 230 (11).

Avāriya-vagga III 228—274.

Avidūrenidāna N 47—77. — N 2,1. 9.

Avīci, mahā-nirayo N 70,2. 6. 18. — I 96,21. 232,17*. 322,4*. 366,8. — III 42,20*. 243 (30) 454,9. 459,30*. 460 (9). 12*. 15*. — IV 100,21. 103,3*. 142,4*. 158,20. 23. 29. 169,6. 7. 200,7. — V 87,18*. 144,5*. 145 (28). 271 (12). 502,13*. — VI 354,16*. 398 (82). — Avīci-nirayasantāpa VI 8,20*.

Asaṁkiya-jataka (76) I 332—334.

Asadisa-kumāra, putto Bārāṇasirañño (— Bodhisatto) II 87*,3. 11. 17. 90*,6. 16. 91,1. 4. (5). 92,2.

Asadisa-jātaka (181) II 86—92.

asadisa-dānaṁ III 469,25. — IV 360,23. 401,11.

Asadisa-vagga II 86—113.

asaddahanaṁ IV 50,7.

Asanarukkha, bodhi Tissa-Buddhassa N 40,25.

asantapaggaho Ajātasattussa rañño I 508,10.

Asama, aggasāvako Sobhita-Buddhassa N 35,21.

Asamā, mātā Paduma-Buddhassa N 36,24. — aggasāvikā Padumuttara-Buddhassa N 37,22.

Asampadāna-jātaka (131) I 465—469.

Asampadāna-vagga I 465—486.

Asātamanta-jātaka (61) I 285—289.

Asātarūpa-jātaka (100) I 407—410.

Asita Devala (cfr. Devala, Kāḷadevala) III 466,27.

Asitañjana, nagaraṁ Uttarāpathe Kaṁsabhoge IV 79,9*. 82,20*.

Asitābhū-jātaka (234) II 229—231.

Asitābhū, devī Brahmadattakumārassa II 230*,1. 4. 12. 231,2*. (7).

Asilakkhaṇa-jātaka (126) I 455—58.

asilakkhaṇapāṭhaka-brāhmaṇo I 455,6. 23*.

Asītinipāta (XXI) V 333—511. — IV 413,4.

Asubhakammikatissa-thera-vatthu III 534 (28).

Asura[gaṇa]ppamaddana (= Sakko) V 139,18*.

Asura-nagara I 204 (6. 9). — °bhavana I 202*,12. 13. 203,24*.

Asura-yoni VI 595,27. — Asurādhipa (-rājā) IV 135,31*. 136, (6)

Asurā (pl.) I 202*,9. 11. 21. 203*,6. 10. 16 17). 20. 204 (6. 8).

Asurādhipa (Indo?) V 243,20*. 245 (23) (cfr. Inda).

Asurinda N 66,9. — Asurinda, Vepacittiya I 205,28*.

Asoka, upaṭṭhāko Vipassi-Buddhassa N 41,16.

Asokā, aggasāvikā Maṅgala-Buddhassa N 34,9.

Assaka, rājā VI 99,10*.

Assaka, rājā Kāsiraṭṭhe Potalinagare II 155,18*. 157*,12. 13. 18. 21. 24. 158,7*. 14. — Assakaraṭṭhe Potalinagare III 3*,4. 16. (27). 4*,3. 7. 14. 20. 5*,2. 7. 6,7*. 8 (2). 6*.

Assaka-jātaka (207) II 155—158.

Assaka-raṭṭha III 3*,4. 15. — V 318 (6). — Assakā (pl.) III 6,26*. 7,24*. 8 (5). — Assakāvanti V 317,24*. 318, (6).

Assakaṇṇa, giri VI 125,14. (24).

Assaji-thera (Chabbaggiya-bhikkhu) N 82,16. 85,16.

Assaji-Punabbasukā, Chabbaggiyānaṁ dve janā Kiṭāgiriṁ upanissāya II 387,12.

Assattha, bodhi Gotama-Buddhassa N 16,16.

Assapāla, putto purohitassa Esukārirañño IV 476,5*. 479,21*. 481,7*. 491,4.

Assapura, nagaraṁ Upacarassa rañño dutiyena puttena māpitaṁ, III 460,23*.

Ahiguṇḍika-jātaka (365) III 197—199.
Ahidīpa (— Kāradīpa) IV 238,10*.
Ahipāraka, putto senāpatissa Sivirañño Ariṭṭhapuranagare. senāpati. V 210*,20. 23. 211,21*. 212,28*. 213*,10. 16. 214,10*. 215,1*. 216*,2 (10). 24. 218*,1. 11. (19). 220,28*. 222*,8. 11. 223,2*. 224 (6. 10. 16. 20. 26). 225 (1). 226 (2. 27). 227 (9). 14*. 17.
ahivātakaroga-muttaka II 79,9.
ahetukavādi amacco Bārāṇasi-rañño V 228,20—22. 237,7*.

Ā.

Ākāsagaṅgā I 95,19. — II 63,27. — III 344,5*. — IV 422,33* (Cod. B.). — V 124,29*.
āgantukasaṁgaho Kosalarañño III 400,6.
āgantukaseṭṭhi III 299,3.
āghātabandhanaṁ paṭhamaṁ Devadattassa Bodhisatte I 113,11*.
Ājañña-jātaka (24) I 182—82.
ājīviko aññataro I 257,3. — ājīvikānaṁ micchātapo I 493,17.
Ādāsamukha-kumāra, rājā Bārāṇasiyaṁ (— Bodhisatto) II 297,14*. 300,1*. 305,14*. 310,11*. 18.
Ādiccupaṭṭhāna-jātaka (175) II 72—73.
Āditta-jātaka (424) III 469—474.
Ādittapariyāya-desanā N 82,32. — IV 180,16.
Ānaka, mutiṅgo II 344,18*.
Ānanda, khattiyo Padumuttara-Buddhassa pitā N 37,20.
Ānanda-kumāra, vemātikabhātā Maṅgala-Buddhassa N 30,21.
Ānanda-kumāra VI 427*,22. 23. 463,27*.
Ānanda-thera I 15,24. 16,18. 124,4. 6. 133,19. 139,20. 140,7. 153,10. 161,12. 178,0. 181,1. 182,7. 185,23. 188,27. 198,4. 206,14. 213,5. 289,16. 299,10. 306,23. 315,24. 327,21.

330,5. 7. 332,22. 345,12. 354,12. 365,27. 375,14. 381,3. 382,6. 8. 16. 383,16. 19. 387,19. 391,19. 29. 420,13. 440,26. 443,31. 446,22. 486,27. 496,30. 501,18—20. 508,6. — II 5,8. 17,21. 23,27 (-assa sātakasahassapaṭilābho). 24,3. 7. 9. 25,26. 30,6. 32,26. 38,18. 40,28. 50,8. 62,17. 65,22. 76,11. 81,27. 92,2. 93,28. 95,21. 96,9. 97,27. 99,16. 121,11. 127,8. 134,16. 170,15. 16. 175,15. 178,3. 202,30. 209,24. 231,15. 20. 23. 26. 257,10. 277,4. 286,6. 291,22. 310,17. 314,19. 318,20. 321,15. 393,8. 400,2. 403,9. 415,8. 420,28. 426,27 (-assa aṭṭhavaralābho). 429,13. 436,14. — III 8,17. 13,6. 15,20. 18,11. 23,3. 8. 9. 25,21. 30,14. 33,4. 56,5. 81,23. 100,2. 112,14. 121,13. 145,18. 155,5. 170,15. 190,22. 206,10. 232,16. 248,14. 274,25. 293,3. 298,7. 11. 15 (-assa jīvitapariccāgo). 298,23. 307,21. 321,14. 330,8. 351,18. 355,19. 368,16—18* (Vedehatāpaso). 369,24. 375,13. 28. 388,14. 397,3. 402,20. 405,26. 27. 434,25. 444,9. 454,3. 469,22. 478,29. 532,5. — IV 7,2—6. 14,20. 22,3. 27,23. 36,28. 43,18. 59,12. 69,24. 89,16. 95,7. 95,12. 22 (-ena laddhavarā). 96,12. 15. 100,10—11. 113,25. 123,22. 130,18. 157,26. 168,12—13. 186,18. 196,19. 199,5. 207,19. 218,27. 228,2. 228,5. 10. 16. 18. 24 (-ena kataṁ mahābodhipūjā). 229,2. 23. 28. 30. 230,2. 236,16—17. 263,4. 264,31. 275,6. 282,14. 304,24. 314,20. 326,18. 368,28. 369,12. 13. 374,4. 401,8. 412,23. 413,3. 6. 423,19. 22. 24. 430,9. 437,1. — V 20,29. 67,24. 125,16. 161,30. 177,7. 192,7. 227,17. 246,12. 312,12. 332,23. 333,3 (-assa jīvitapariccāgo). 335,4. 27. 30. 337,14. 16. 18. 354,1. 3. 382,7. 412,10. 456,11. 511,21. — VI 68,21. 95,9. 17. 18. 129,16. 219,25. 255,9. 329,17. 478,13*.

Ānandabodhi II 321,9. 11. 13. — IV 229,20.

Ānanda, gijjharājā V 424,3*. 447,29*. 32. 450,4*. 8. 456,3*.

Ānanda, maccharājā I 207,2*. — II 352,11*. — V 462*,16. 19. 23. 25. 463*,10. 11. 12. 14. 464,5*. (21).

Ābhassara-brahmaloka I 406,17*. — Ābhassarato I 473,9*. —

Ābhassaresu I 474,6*. — III 358,25. — Ābhassarūpago I 474,10*. (17—18). — Ābhassarā devā VI 55,24*. (25).

Āmalaka-rukkha, bodhi Phussa-Buddhassa N 41,5.

Āyācitabhatta-jātaka (19) I 169.

āyu Buddhassa N 49,29.

Āyura, amacco Maddavaraññño Bārāṇasiyaṁ III 337,24*. 338*,4. 19. 339*,9 16. 341,8*. 17.

Ārañjara, giri VI 493,20*. (22). (cfr. Arañjara).

Ārāmadūsa(ka)-jātaka a) (46) I 249—251. — b) (268) II 345—347.

Āruppa-(bhava) I 406,18*.

Ālamba, see: Ālambāyana.

Āḷambara, bheri II 344,19*. — Āḷambara-megha II 344,21*.

Ālambāyana (Ālambāna), brāhmaṇo VI 179,25*. 180*,1. 20. 181*,4. 13. (16). 182*,2. 9. 183,29*. 184,1. 17. 23. 24. 29. 185*,21—22. 186,19*. 191*,7. 10. 12. 16. 20. 30. 192* (3). 10. 23. 193*,19. 28. 194*,8. 21. 196*,11. 15. 197*,17. 20. 26. — Ālamba VI 194,7*.

Āḷavaka, yakkho IV 180,23. — VI 329,34.

Ālavakā bhikkhū, Ālaviyaṁ nagare II 282,17. 27.

Āḷavī, nagaraṁ I 160,21. — II 282,15. 21. 24. 25 (Ālavī). — III 78,22. 351,22.

Āḷāra, kuṭumbiko Mithilanagare V 164*,12. 19. 22. 168 (8). — Aḷāra: V 166,15*. 167*,7. 10. (28). 170*,27. 29. 172,25*. 173,10. 21. 174,9*. 175 (25). 176,21*. *177,7.

Ālāra Kālāma N 66,34. 81,15.

Ālīnasatta, see: Alīnasatta.

Āsaṁka-jātaka (380) III 248—254.

Āsaṁkā, dhītā Bodhisattassa III 250*,5. 17. 253,5*. 254*,9. 15. (25).

Āsā, Sakkassa dhītā V 392,21*. 393,12. 398,18*. 28. 400*,9. 29. 401*,4. 8. 20. 21. (30). 402 (4. 5). 408,16. (19). 409,18. 410,4*. (9).

Āsāḷhi-puṇṇamā N 81,28

Āsāvatī, latā Cittalatāvane Tāvatiṁsadevaloke III 250,22*. 251,7. (14).

Āsiṁsa-vagga I 261—284.

I.

Itivuttaka III 409 (21). (plur.).

Itthī aññatarā II 341,3. — itthiyo pañcasatā surāpāyikā, Visākhāya sahāyikā V 11,5.

Itthi-vagga I 285—315.

Inda III 146,26*. 515,28*. 517,20*. — IV 347*,10. 18. — V 33,17*. (21). 115 (1). 158,9. (31). 322,22. 410,24*. 411 (11. 22). 506,3*. — VI 125,34. 126,9. 127 (10). 212,11*. 215 (26. 27). 219 (6). 240,26. 568,8. 571,12. — Indassa gotta VI 500,24. 501 (29). — Indo Vatrabhū V 152,2. — Indo asurādhipo (? cfr. IV 135,31*. 136 (6)). V 243,20*. 245 (22—23). — Sakko devānaṁ indo N 80,11—12. — I 204*,22. 26. — III 146,30*. — Inda-paṭimā VI 125,31*. 126 (24). — Indapurohitā VI 127,4. (9). — Indavajira I 354,3*. — III 146,0*. — V 92 (11). — Inda-sagotta V 411,19*. 21. — Inda-sahavyatā V 411,20*. 412,2 (7). — sa-Indakā devā V 568,10. — Indagopaka-vaṇṇābhā gandhārā VI 500,1*.

Indapatta, nagaraṁ Kururaṭṭhe II 213,3*. 214 (18). 366,23*. 368,11*. — III 400*,18. 21. 27. — IV 361,4*. — V 57,7*. (23). 59,4*. 67,20*. 457,8*. 474,7*. 484,15*. 510,26*. 511,6*. — VI 255,27*. 272,32*. 311,23*. 323* (14). 19. (22). 30. 324,2*. (9).

Indasamānagotta, tāpaso II 41*,12. 15. 42,11*. 43,2*. 6.

Indasamānagotta-jātaka (161) II 41—43.

Indriya-jātaka (423) III 461—469. — I 153,24. 495,19. — II 113,15. 443,4. — III 58,27. 248,18. — V 152,3.

Irandatī, nāgakaññā (dhītā Varuṇassa nāgarañño) VI 263,25*. 264,7*. 265,28*. 266*,14. 17. 21. 267*,5. 11. (16). 20. 268* (2).

8. 30. 270,4*. 304,22*. 307,10*. 308,6*. 323,1*. 5. 324,31*. 325,33*. 326*,17. 18. 20. 327*,3. 4.

Illisa, seṭṭhi Bārāṇasiyaṁ I 349,21*. 350,24*. 351*,4. 5. 17. 23. 25. 352,5*. 353*,6. 11. 14. 22. 23. 25. 354,4*. 7*. 12.

Illisa-jātaka (78) I 345—354.

isigili, pabbato V 125,28 (Isigilipassa).

Isipatana, (udapāno) Bārāṇasiṁ nissāya N 68,5. 81,26. 86,24. — II 354,6. 17*. 19*.

Isisiṅga, Bodhisattassa putto, V 152*,17. 22. 153,10. (14). 16*. 154,30. 155,1. 4. (7). 157,28. 160,30. 161,18. — V 193,12*. 194,9*. 195*,20. 22. (25). 196,5*. 10. (15). 201,14*. 209,18.

issarakāraṇavādi amacco V 228,21—23*. 238,7*. 241,10*.

Ī.

Īsadhara, pabbato VI 125,18. (19—21).

U.

Ukkaṭṭhā, (nagaraṁ Kosalaraṭṭhe) II 259,18. 26. 28.

ukkaṇṭhita-bhikkhu I 265,4. 289,10. 295,20. 367,24. 499,9. — II 33,8. 127,12. 132,16. 134,19. 184,8. 227,8. 271,5. 310,22. 323,14. 328,8. — III 30,18. *90,16. 187,11. 200,3. 265,8. 474,22. 496,26. 514,20. 527,3. — IV 27,25. 104,10. 382,27. — V 209,21. 278,3.

Ukkala, janapado N 80,17.

Ugga, seṭṭhi Koṇāgamana-Buddhassa kāle N 94,19.

Uggata, rājā pitā Sujāta-Buddhassa N 38,18.

Uggasena, rājā Bārāṇasiyaṁ IV 458,18*. 464,11. 467,28*. 468,23.

Ucchaṅga-jātaka (67) I 306—308.

Ucchiṭṭhabhatta-jātaka (212) II 167—169.
ucchedavādi amacco V 228*,31—26. 239,12*. 241,11*.
Ujjenī, nagaram Avantiraṭṭhe II 248*,28. 28. 250,4*. — IV 390*,14. 15. 19. 397 (27)
Uṇṇanābhi, see: Unnanābhi.
Utta-thera II 403,28. 404,3. 6.
Uttara, aggasāvako Koṇāgamana-Buddhassa N 43,9.
Uttara, aggasāvako Vessabhu-Buddhassa N 42,12.
Uttara, khattiyo pitā Maṅgala-Buddhassa N 34,7.
Uttara, māṇavo (Bodhisatto) N 37,31.
Uttara, seṭṭhi Sāvatthiyaṁ I 432,28. — Uttara-seṭṭhiputto I 432,26. 433,3. 5. 22. 26. 434,12. 18.
Uttara, nagaraṁ Maṅgala-Buddhassa N 34,7.
Uttarakuru (janapado) V 316,20*. — VI 100 (28). — Uttarakurū VI 279 (4).
Uttarapañcāla, nagaraṁ, catutthena puttena Upacarassa rañño māpitaṁ, III 461,1*. — Kampilla-raṭṭhe II 213,3*. — III 79*,1. 6. — IV 396 (17). 430,23*. — V 21,6*. 98,24*. — VI 391,6*. 392,28*. 409,25*. 412 (18). 415,7*. 417 (2. 5). 419 (12). 426,20*. 461,6*. 466*,12. 28. 475 (11). — Kururaṭṭhe IV 444*,10. 13.
Uttarapañcāla-rāja IV 392,23*.
Uttarapañcāla-raṭṭha III 379,3*. — Uttarapañcālā: II 214 (17). — III 381 (27). — VI 405,9*.
Uttaramadhurā, nagaraṁ Uttarāpathe, IV 79,21*.
Uttarasāḷha-nakkhattayoga N 82,9.
Uttarahimavanta II 195 (9). — III 377,23*. 471,3*. — IV 114,16*. 119,4*. 328*,7.*24. 367,19*. 368,2*. — V 42,19*. — VI 56,9*. 100 (13). 101 (18).
Uttarā, aggasāvikā Koṇāgamana-Buddhassa N 43,10.
Uttarā, aggasāvikā Nārada-Buddhassa N 37,7.
Uttarā, brāhmaṇī mātā Koṇāgamana-Buddhassa N 43,8.
Uttarā, mātā Maṅgala-Buddhassa N 34,8.

Uttarāpatha, janapado II 287,15*. — IV 79,9*.
uttastabhikkhu I 414,23.
udakakalaho ñātakānaṁ Buddhassa I 327,20.
udakadhārā, dve N 53,6.
Udakapabbata, Himavante V 38,8*.
Udañcani-jātaka (106) I 416—417.
Udapānadūsaka-jātaka (271) II 354—355.
Udaya, aggasāvako Tissa-Buddhassa N 40,34.
Udaya, rājā Bārāṇasiyaṁ (= Bodhisatto) III 446,9* (Udayakumāro). 447,7*. 449,8*. 450*,16. 19. 22 (23). 454,4.
Udaya-jātaka (458) IV 104—113. — IV 119,27*.
Udayabhadda, Kāsirājā (= Bodhisatto) IV 104*,22. 25. 111,16*. — Udaya: IV 107,8*. (11). 111,8* (10). 19*.
Udayabhaddā, rājadhītā vemātikabhaginī Udayabhaddassa IV 104,25*. 105*,9. 12. 19. 23. 112 (17). — Udayā: IV 110 (22). 111*,25. 29. 112*,4. 8.
Udāyin V 456,10. — Udāyitthera (= Kāḷudāyī) N 86,25. 87,8. 11. — VI 479,5. (= Lāḷudāyī) I 123,14. 27. 124,6.
Udumbara-jātaka (298) II 444—446.
Udumbara-rukkha, bodhi Koṇāgamana-Buddhassa N 43,10.
Udumbara-devī, bhariyā Piṅguttarassa VI 348*,10. 14. 15. 352,18*. 355,23*. 363,23*. 368,6*. 384*,6. 17. 465 (27). 478,19*.
Udena, rājā Kosambiyaṁ, III 157,24. 384,8. 5. 9. 385,17*. — IV 375,8 (Udenavaṁsarājā). 375,10. 22. 390,1. 2.
Udena, upaṭṭhāko Tissa-Buddhassa, N 34,27.
Uddaka Rāmaputta N 66,34. 81,17.
Uddāla, vātaghātarukkho IV 298,8*. 301 (20).
Uddālaka, putto Bodhisattassa (Bārāṇasirañño purohitassa) IV 298*,9. 12. 299*,4. 10. 22. 300,16*. 301*,10. 16. (20). 22. 302*,8. 22. 303*,11. 23. 304*,16. 18. (24).
Uddālaka-jātaka (487) IV 297—304. — Uddāla-jātaka: I 375,18. II 68,3. — III 232,21.
Uddha-gaṅgā II 283,18*. VI 427,23*.

Unnanâbhi (Uṇṇanâbhi?), makkaṭako IV 484 (20).
Upaka, âjîviko N 81,24.
Upakaṁsa, putto Mahâkaṁsassa rañño Asitañjane IV 79*,10. 16. 24. 26. 27. 80,4*.
Upakañcana, brâhmaṇaputto bhâtâ Bodhisattassa IV 305,10*. 306,18*. 308,11*.
Upakârî, Pañcâlanagaraṁ VI 448,10. (15. 16). 450,21*. 458,13. 459,15.
Upakâḷa, nirayapâlo VI 248,3*. (6). — Upakâḷa-niraya VI 248 (7).
Upacara (Apacara), putto Carassa râjâ Cetiyaraṭṭhe Sotthivatinagare (paṭhamakappe) III 454,18*.
Upacâlâ, aggasâvikâ Phussa-Buddhassa N 41,5.
Upajotiya, dovâriko IV 382,13*. (17).
Upajjhâya, dovâriko IV 382,14*. (18).
Upatissa, thero, aggasâvako Gotama-Buddhassa (— Sâriputto) N 15,23. 16,12.
Upatissâ, aggasâvikâ Koṇḍañña-Buddhassa N 30,14.
Upananda, Sakyaputto thero II 441,5. 15. 18. 23. 24. 442,25. III 332,5. 27. 31. 333,2. 8. 336,18.
Upanâmâ, aggasâvikâ Paduma-Buddhassa N 36,25.
Upari-gaṅgâ IV 230,23*. 231,10*.
Uparidevaloka VI 2,8*.
Uparibrahmaloka III 358,27.
Uparimaṇḍaka-mâla (Sihala-dîpe) VI 30,5. —
Uprimaṇḍalaka-malaya (Tambapaṇṇadîpe) IV 490,21.
Upavâṇa, Bhagavato anibaddhaupaṭṭhâko IV 95,14.
Upasanta, aggasâvako Atthadassi-Buddhassa N 39,15.
Upasanta, upaṭṭhâko Vessabhu-Buddhassa N 42,13.
Upasâgara, putto Mahâsâgarassa rañño Uttaramadhurâyaṁ IV 79*,22. 24. 80*,6. 7. 12. 19. 81,17.
Upasâla, aggasâvako Paduma-Buddhassa N 35,25.
Upasâḷha-jâtaka (166) II 54—56.

Upasāḷhaka, brāhmaṇo II 54,10. 55*,6. 22. 56,1*.
Upasena (Vaṅgantaputta) II 449,16.
Upasenī, dhītā Candakumārassa (Bodhisattassa) VI 134,25*.
Upasoṇā, aggasāvikā Sumana-Buddhassa N 34,27.
Upāli, thero I 140,5. 6 148,6. — IV 266,7.
upāsako I 188,30. 301,15. — III 403,8. — n. Sāvatthivāsī I 299,14. 332,26.
upāsakā uposathikā, see: uposathikā.
Upāhana-jātaka (231) II 221—24.
Upāhana-vagga II 221—42.
Uposatha, putto Varakalyāṇassa rājā paṭhamakappe II 311,11*. — III 454,16*.
Uposatha-kumāra, Bārāṇasiraññо putto, Saṁvarassa bhātā IV 133*,11. 25. 135*,2 (24). 27. 136,18.
Uposathakula (nāgakulaṁ) IV 232,13*. 234 (11. 13).
uposathakammaṁ III 444,11. — IV 454,8. — V 1,3. 161,21.
Uposathakhaṇḍa, Bhūridattajātake VI 170,1.
uposathikā upāsakā IV 325,17. 355,2. — VI 157,25.
Uppalavaṇṇā, dutiyasāvikā Gotama-Buddhassa N 15,25. 16,14. — I 160,10. 164,24. 196,14. 306,24. 375,14. — II 381,21. — III 168,6. 264,24. 310,10. 324,22. 383,23. 405,14. — IV 22,2. 314,21. 423,19. — V 11,2. 36,5. 125,16. 227,18. 412,6. — VI 29,30. 68,19. 95,9. 157,21. 219,25. 478,11*. 481,15*. 593,29.
Ubbarī, aggamahesī Assakassa Kāsiraññо Potalinagare II 155,19*. 156,24*. 157*,5. 7. 10. 12. 158,14.
Ubbarī, aggamahesī Brahmadattakumārassa III 161,14* (17).
Ubhatobhaṭṭha-jātaka (139) I 482—484.
Ummagga-jātaka (= Mahā-ummagga-jātaka 546) I 424,13. 18 (21). — II 76,16. — III 152,8. 341,21. — IV 72,15. 186,24. — V 81,23. 147 (7). — VI 485,16*.
Ummadantī, dhītā Tiriṭavacchassa seṭṭhino Ariṭṭhapure V 210,27*. 211*,8. 15. 213*,1. 18. 214*,11 (16) 21. 215,28*.

216,3*. 217*2. 8. 9. 23. 24. 218*,6 (9). 11. 18. 27. 219,8. 9. 220*,2. 5. 221*,15. 18. 23. 26. 222,2*. 224 (11). 225 (22). 226 (2). 227,15*. 18.
Ummadantī-jātaka (527) V 209—227. — I 285,5. — II 115,18.
uyyānadūsako I 249,21.
uyyānapālaputto aññataro II 345,5.
Uraga-jātaka a) (154) II 12—14. — II 52,21. — b) (354) III 162—168.
Uracchadā, Kikissa rañño dhītā VI 481,6*.
Uruvelakassapa (cfr. Kassapa), Uruvelavāsi jaṭilo Tathāgatena damito N 82,30. 83,7. 8. 10—12. 27. — IV 282,20. VI 220,1. 5—10. 22. 255,4. 10. — Uruvelakassapa-damana VI 219,30.
Uruvelā, nagaraṁ N 56,25. 67,2. 68,6. 82,28. 30. 86,25. — Uruveḷā IV 180,15.
Uruveḷā, aggasāvikā Kassapa-Buddhassa N 43,28.
Uḷuṁkasaddaka, Mahākassapa-therassa paṇṇasālājhāpako daharo III 71,24. 28. 72,5.
Uḷumpa, nigamo Sakyānaṁ IV 151,25.
Ulūka-jātaka (270) II 351—354.
Usinnara, rājā (— Usīnara) VI 251,16* (28).
Usīnara, rājā Bārāṇasiyaṁ Kassapa-Buddha-kāle IV 181,7*. 182,15*. 183,20*. — VI 99,10*.
Usīraddhaja, pabbato Majjhimadese N 49,14.
Ussada-niraya III*206,17*. — IV 3,12*. 405 (17). 493,24*. VI 2,6*. 4,5*. 112, (20). — Ussadanirayā sojassa I 168 (17).

E.

Ekanipāta I 95—511. — II 179,17 (— Jāt. 102). 234,28 (— Jāt. 68). 429,18 (— Jāt. 86). — III 196,4 (— Jāt. 90). — V 446 10 (— Jāt. 63 [Takkāriya-jāt. ɔ: Takka-jāt.])

VI 126 (15) (– Jāt. 31). 336 (16) (– I 424,12). 343 (32) (– I 424,17). 365,19* (– I 424,20). — Ekanipātapāli I 345 (15).
Ekapaṇṇa-jātaka (149) I 504—508.
Ekapada-jātaka (238) II 236—237.
Ekabala-raṭṭha VI 390*,24. 29.
Ekarāja-jātaka (303) III 13—15. — N 47,2 (cfr. Cariyāpiṭaka 351).
Ekādasanipāta (XI) IV 90—143. — I 136,12 (– Jāt. 462). — II 27,24 (Jāt. 462). II 426,28 (– Jāt. 456). — III 18,8 (– Jāt. 459).
Ekūnavīsatipañha (Mahāummagga-jātake) VI 345,28.
Eṇī, nadī III 361 (20). — Eṇikūla III 361,1 (20).
Erāpathā — Erāpatha-nāgarājakulaṁ II 145,19* (22).
Erāvaṇa, hatthī Sakkassa III 392,5*. — V 137,17*. — VI 147,9* (26). 278,26* (nāgarājā).
Eḷakamāra, Kosalarañño putto V 424,28. 430 (1).
Esukārin, Bārāṇasirājā IV 473,18*. 475,9*. 477,11*. 481,14* (16). 486,26. 491,2.

O.

okāsa-vilokanaṁ Buddhassa N 49,7.
Okkāka, rājā Kusāvatiyaṁ Mallaraṭṭhe V 278,22*. 280,5*. 283,12*. 284,19*. 285*,22. 24. — Okkāka-paveṇi V 300 (6) Okkāka-putta V 306*,22 (23). 27. 307,9*. — Okkāka-rājavaṁsa II 438,17.
Oparakkhī (bhariyā Candakumārassa (Bodhisattassa)) VI 148,10*.
omasavāda-sikkhāpadaṁ I 374,30. — c. chabbaggiyānaṁ bhikkhūnaṁ I 191,3.
ovādo Kosalarañño IV 176,2. — V 109,3.
Osadha-dāraka, nāmaṁ Bodhisattassa Mahosadhattabhāve N 53,28. — Osadhakumāra VI 332,2*. See: Mahosadha.

ossaṭṭhaviriyo bhikkhu I 106,14. 110,30. 136,11. 178,14. 181,5. 261,26. 268,8. 272,18. — II 17,25. 335,7. — IV 130,22.

K.

Kaṁsa, rājā — Kāsirājā VI 198,30* (25).
Kaṁsa, rājā Bārāṇasiggaho (— Kosālarājā, Jāt. 51) II 403,2 (4). — V 112,13* (15).
Kaṁsa, putto Mahākaṁsassa Asitañjana-nagare IV 79*,10. 16. 27.
Kaṁsa-bhoga, Uttarāpathe IV 79*,9. 12. 26.
Kaṁsa-vaṁsa IV 79,18*.
Kakaṇṭaka-jātaka (170) II 63,1—3.
Kakaṇṭaka-vagga I 487—511.
Kakudha-Kaccāyana [— Pakudha-Kaccāyana], diṭṭhigatiko I 509,13. — V 246,11 (var. lect.).
Kakusandha-Buddha X 42,18—19. 24. 30. 43,12. 44,10. 94,16.
Kakkaṭa-jātaka (267) II 341—345.
Kakkara-jātaka (var. lect. Kukkura-j.) (209) II 160—162.
Kakkāru (var. lect. Kakkaru-, Takkaru-) (326) III 86—90.
Kaccāna (Kasāna), thero (— Kaccāyana, Mahā-Kaccāyana) II 381,22. — III 469,31.
Kaccāna (— Puṇṇaka), see: Kaccāyana.
Kaccānī, sassū kālakaṇṇī III 425,18* (21). 426,5*. 427,16*. — Kaccānagottā III 428 (1) (cfr. Kātiyānī).
Kaccāni-jātaka (417) III 422—428.
Kaccāni-vagga III 422—82.
Kaccāyana (Mahā-Kaccāyana), thero V 151,29 (cfr. Kaccāna).
Kaccāyana (— Puṇṇaka) VI 273,29*. — Kaccāna VI 283,11*. 286,3*. 301,28. 327,17*. — Kātiyāna VI 299,22*. 306,4* (19). 308,29*.
Kacchapa-jātaka a) (178) II 79—81. — b) (215) II 175—178. — c) (273) II 359—361.

Kajaṅgala, nigamo Majjhimadese puratthimadisāya N 49,8.

Kajaṁgalā, nagaraṁ III 226*,17 (20). 28 (— Bārāṇasī). — IV 310,14*. 311 (14. 27).

Kañcana-guhā, Himavantapadese I 491*,17. 18. 24. 492*,5. 20. 29. 31. — II 6*,9. 13. 17. 9,3*. 176,6* (Cittakūṭapabbatatale). 396,16*. — IV 484 (19). — V 37,11*. 38*,25—26. 316,21*. 357,4*. 368 (30). 381,13*. 392,28*.

Kañcanadevī, dhītā Bārāṇasirañño, bhaginī Bodhisattassa IV 305*,12. 25. 311 (14).

Kañcanapaṭṭī, paṇṇasālā Jotirasa-tāpasassa II 399,10*.

Kañcana-pabbata N 34,19. — Himavante II 396,27*. 397,15*. 399,9*. — V 415,22. — Uttarahimavantapasse VI 101 (18). — Kañcana-pabbatā VI 100,4* (17).

Kañcanakkhandha-jātaka (56) I 276—278.

Kañcanamāla-setacchattaṁ Sakkassa V 386,3*.

Kaṭakandhakāra, vihāro (?) Tambapaṇṇadīpe (Sīhaladīpe) IV 490,21. — VI 30,4.

Kaṭāhaka, dāso (vikatthiko) I 451,22*. 452*,18. 24. 453*,11. 15. 22. 26. 27. 454*,7. 17 (26). 29. 455,2.

Kaṭāhaka-jātaka (125) I 451—455. — I 458,16.

Kaṭṭhavāhanarāja, Bārāṇasiyaṁ (— Bodhisatto) I 136,3*. 7. — IV 148,7.

Kaṭṭhahāri-jātaka (7) I 133—136. — IV 148,7.

Kaṇavera-jātaka (318) III 58—63. — III 436,11*. — V 446 (13).

Kaṇikārarukkha, bodhi Siddhattha-Buddhassa, N 40,10.

Kaṇḍari, rājā Bārāṇasiyaṁ V 437,25. 440,12 (16—17).

Kaṇḍari-jātaka (341) III 132,18—29. — V 437,25—440,20.

Kaṇḍina-jātaka (13) I 153—156.

Kaṇṇapeṇṇā, nadī Mahiṁsakaraṭṭhe Saṁkhapāladahato nikkhantā V 162*,8. 14. 163,5*. 168 (11). — Kaṇṇapeṇṇa-daha V 168 (5).

Kaṇṇamuṇḍaka, dabo Himavante V 415,24. — Kaṇṇamuṇḍa II 104,9*.

Kaṇha (cfr. Kaṇhāyanagotta). — Vāsudevarājā IV 84,22* (25). 86*,10. 22. — VI 421,20*.

Kaṇha, sunakho, see: Mahākaṇha.

Kaṇha, brāhmaṇakumāro, isi (— Bodhisatto) IV 7,6. 12*. 9*4. 16. 11,3*. 13*,12. 22. 14,21.

Kaṇha, see: Kaṇhadīpāyana.

Kaṇha-jātaka a) (29) I 193—196. — b) (440) IV 6—14.

Kaṇhadīpāyana, tāpaso (— Bodhisatto) IV 29,27*. 31,24*. 37,1. — IV 83,8*. 87,17*. — V 114 (12). 267,12*. 273 (5—6). — Kaṇha IV 33,9* (18—26). — Dīpāyana IV 28*,17. 22. 29*,17. 24. 30*,1. 10. 23. 33*,1. 10 (16).

Kaṇhadīpāyana-jātaka (444) IV 27—37.

Kaṇhā, see: Kaṇhājinā.

Kaṇhā, dvepitikā (dhītā Kosalarañño ca Kāsirañño ca), pañcapatikā (pañcasu Paṇḍurājaputtesu paṭibaddhacittā ahosi) V 424,16. 426 (8. 9. 16).

Kaṇhāgotamakā, Kaṇhāgotamaka-nāgarājakulaṁ II 145 (20 24).

Kaṇhājinā, dhītā Vessantarassa N 77,18. — VI 487,3*. 509,24 (26). 29. 513,3. 583,8. 544,21. 545,21. 547,14. 16. 550 (1. 4). 12. 14. 16. 18. 553,34. 554,9*. 12. 556,19 (28). 557,32. 559,9. 12. 16. 19. 23. 26. 27. 561,18. 563,11. 14. 17. 565,7. 570,18. 574,16. 576 (7). 11. 577,9 (11). 583,10*. 585,10. 589,2 (7). 593,28. — Kaṇhā VI 546,15*. 548,7. 553,13. 17. 19. 21. 23. 25. 27.

Kaṇhāyanagotta (— Vāsudeva) IV 84 (25). — VI 421 (21)

Kanthaka, asso Buddhassa N 54,7. 62,5. 6. 24. 26. 63,7. 8. 10. 12. 33. 64,25. 28. 65,22. 27. — IV 119,18. — Kanthako nāma devaputto hutvā Tāvatiṁsabhavane nibbatti N 65,26. — Kanthaka-nivattana-cetiyaṭṭhānaṁ N 63,32.

Kandagala(ka), sakuṇo (— Devadatto) II 162*,20. 23. 25. 163,7*. 164,8*. 12.

Kandagalaka-jātaka (210) II 162—164.

Kandhaka, see: Khandhaka.

Kaṇṇamuṇḍa-daha, see: Kaṇṇamuṇḍaka.

Kapallapūva, ṭhānaṁ pabbhārante Jetavanaṁ nissāya, I 348,31.

Kapi-jātaka a) (250) II 268—270. — b) (404) III 355—358.

Kapila, brāhmaṇo purohito Upacarassa Cetiyarañño (= Bodhisatto) III 454*,23—24. 455,2*. 457,16*. 461,12. — Kapilatāpasa V 273 (7) (= isi V 267,14*).

Kapilavatthu, nagaraṁ Gotama-Buddhassa, Sākiyaraṭṭhe N 15,22. 49,20 (Kapilavatthuka). 50,8. 52,11. 54,10—11. 87,14—16. 89,6. — I 208,9. — IV 6,26. 145,2. 147,5. 152,15. V 412,16. 22. 26. 413,32. 415,15. — VI 479,2. 8. — Kapila N 16,1. — Kapilapura N 91,17. — II 97,7—8. — IV 50,8. 282,17. — V 415,4. — Kapilavatthu-gamanaṁ Buddhassa N 89,6. — IV 282,21.

Kapota-jātaka a) (42) I 241—244. — b) (375) III 224—227.

Kappa, brāhmaṇa-kumāro (māṇavo), isi (= Bodhisatto) III 142,30*. 143*,16. 17. 27. 28. 144*,6. 9 (12). 16 (16). 20). 145,18. — III 361,10. 362 (21. 25. 28). 363,17.

kappahalāhalaṁ N 47,22. 48,5.

Kappāsiya-vanasaṇḍa, Uruvelaṁ nissāya N 82,27.

Kampilla — Kampillarājakumāra (Alīnasatta) V 34,5* (7).

Kampilla-nagara II 214 (17) (Uttarapañcāla-raṭṭhe). — III 379,3*. 381 (26). — V 35,6. — Kampilliya-pura VI 433,15 (16).

Kampilla-raṭṭha (cfr. Uttarapañcāla) III 79,1* (Kampillaka-). — IV 396 (17). — V 21,6*. 34 (10). 98,24*. — VI 391,6*. 433 (16). — Kampilliya-r. VI 464,8* (12).

Kambalassatarā, nāgā Sinerupāde VI 165,4* (6).

Kambojaka-raṭṭha IV 465 (7). V 446 (28). — Kambojakā assatarā IV 464,4*. — Kambojakā — Kambojaraṭṭhavāsino VI 208,30*. 210 (26).

Kammāsadamma (var. lect. Kammāsadhamma), nigamo Kururaṭṭhe V 511,15*.
Kayanibbinda-jātaka, see: Kāyavicchinda-.
Karaṇḍaka, assamapadaṁ IV 95,1*.
Karaṇḍaka-jātaka (= Samugga-jāt. 436) V 455, (2).
Karaṇḍu (var. lect. Karaṇḍaka, Karakaṇḍa, Karakaṇḍaṁka), rājā Dantapuranagare Kāliṅgaraṭṭhe III 376,12*. 381,16* (24).
Karambiya-paṭṭana V 75,13*. — Karambiya-acelo (vāṇijo) V 75,20*. — Kārambiyo acelo V 86,1.
Karavīka, pabbato VI 125,15 (16. 16).
Kalaṇḍuka, dāso Bārāṇasiseṭṭhino I 458,17. 20. 22. 459*,1. 5. 6. 11 (20). 21. 459,20.
Kalaṇḍuka-jātaka (127) I 458—459.
kalaha, udakakalaho ñātakānaṁ Buddhassa I 327,26. — kākoluka-kalaho II 351,17.
Kalābu, Kāsirājā (= Devadatto) III 39,13*. 40,2*. 43,12. — V 135,22*. 143,12* (17). 144,5*. 145 (28—29).
Kalāyamuṭṭhi-jātaka (176) II 74—76.
Kaḷārajanaka, putto Nimirañño VI 129,12*.
Kaliṅga, see: Kāliṅga.
Kalyāṇa, putto Vararojassa, rājā paṭhamakappe II 311,10*. — III 454,15*.
Kalyāṇadhamma-jātaka (171) II 63—65.
Kalyāṇadhamma-vagga II 63—86.
Kalyāṇī, nadī Tambapaṇṇidīpe II 128,16*.
Kalyāṇī (= Janapada-K.?) IV 422bis 11.
Kaviṭṭha-vana, Godhāvarītīre V 132*,4. 7. — Kaviṭṭha(ka)-assamapadaṁ V 132,22*. 133*,12. 26. — Kaviṭṭhaka-assamaṁ Sakkadattiyaṁ III 463*,7. 11. — Kaviṭṭha-ārāmo V 115 (5).
Kasmīra-raṭṭha III 365,2*. 378,3*.
Kassapa, isi VI 99,29*.
Kassapa (Lomasa-Kassapa), purohitaputto (= Bodhisatto)

III 514,20*. 515,2*. 517*,21. 25. 518*,10. 23. 519,11* (cfr. Lomasa-Kassapa).
Kassapa, brāhmaṇo tāpaso, pitā Nāradassa (— Bodhisatto) IV 221,25*. 222 (1).
Kassapa, — Akittipaṇḍito (Bodhisatto) IV 240*.10. 28. 241*,1. 2. 10. 11. 22.
Kassapa, māṇavo (— Bodhisatto), Piyadassi-Buddhassa kāle N 38,30.
Kassapa, pitā Isisiṅgassa, mahāisi (— Bodhisatto) V 157,16*. 159,28*. — Kassapagotta 157 (19).
Kassapa, brāhmaṇo tāpaso, pitā Bodhisattassa III 38,4* (12).
Kassapa-Buddha N 42,19. 43,14. 27. 44,10. 16. 65,11. 90,5. 94,20. — I 116,17. 413,27. 236,28*. 240,1*. 363,8 — II 111,18*. 255,6*. 256,4*. — III 474 (9). — IV 1,9*. 181*,7—8. 311 (20). — V 212,9*. 476,13*. 477,8*. 479 (22). 483,6*. 484,8*. 488*,6. 19. — VI 117 (26). 118 (28). 119 (26). 120 (27). 121 (24). 122 (26). 123,24. 124,22. 227 (13). 228 (25). 481,4*.
Kassapa, thero (— Mahākassapo) II 17,21. 381,24. - III 71,4. 72,29. 73,1. 90,11. 469,21. 514,16. 543,6. — IV 69,24. 314,10. 332,23. 491,3. — V 67,25. 151,28. 177,6. 192,6. 412,10. 511,21. — VI 95,9. 157,22. — Mahākassapa II 93,22. 262,21. — IV 180,17. 390,6.
Kassapa — Uruvelakassapa N 83,12. — VI 220,6. 10.
Kassapa — Kumārakassapa I 148,25.
Kassapa — Nārada-tāpasa VI 58,9*. (15).
Kassapa, see: Nārada Kassapa.
Kassapa, see: Purāṇa-Kassapa.
Kassapa, Kassapagotta, — Guṇo ājīviko VI 222,24. 223 (10). 224,19. 225,19. 227,5. 25. 228,21. 229 (7). 22*. 233,6. 235,25 (20).
Kassapamandiya-jātaka (312) III 36—39.
Kāka-jātaka a) (140) I 484—486. — b) (146) I 497—499.

— c) (395) III 314—316 (— Jāt. (42) I 242—244). — Kākajat.-Navanipāte I 241,28. — II 318,24 (— Kākātaj. (395) Ohanipāte & Cakkavākajāt. (434) Navanipāte).

Kākātī, devī, aggamahesī Bārāṇasiraññо (Bodhisattassa), Naṭakuverena pāpaṁ akāsi III 90,25*. 91*,3. 15. (19). — bhariyā Venateyyassa (cfr. Sussondijāt. Nr. 360) V 424,28.

Kākāti-jātaka (327) III 90—92. — V 428 (30). cfr. Jāt. 360.

Kākaneru (pabbato) VI 204,14*. 212,20*.

Kākola-niraya VI 247,1*.

kākolūka-kalaho II 351,17.

Kāṇamātā, upāsikā Sāvatthiyaṁ I 477,7. 12. 24. 26. 31. 478,2. 480,9. — Kāṇā, tassā dhītā I 477,9. 11. 18. 21. 22. — Kāṇamātā-sikkhāpadaṁ I 477,8.

Kāṇāriṭṭha (—Ariṭṭha) VI 168,16*. 190,18*. 197,12*. 200*,15. 21. 201,6*. 219,26.

Kātiyāna, see: Kaccāna.

Kātiyānī (— Kaccānī) III 427,8*. 25.

Kāpilānī, therī 289,15.

Kāma-jātaka (467) IV 167—175 — II 212,14.

Kāmanīta-jātaka (228) II 212—216.

kāmanīta-brāhmaṇo II 212,12.

Kāmavilāpa-jātaka (297) II 443—444.

Kāmasutta IV 168,18.

Kāyavicchinda-jātaka (v. l. Kayanibbinda) (293) II 436—438.

Kāraṇḍiya (Kāraṇḍika), māṇavo (— Bodhisatto) III 171,20*. 172*,9. 28. 173,21*. 174,2. — Kāraṇḍiko 173,17*.

Kāraṇḍiya-jātaka (356) III 170—174.

Kāradīpa (— Ahidīpa), Nāgadīpa-samīpe IV 238,9-10*.

Kārāyana — Dīgha-Kārāyana IV 151,28—30.

Kāḷa, thero Kosalajanapade I 165,1. 2. 4. 166,2.

Kāla, nāgarājā N 70,18. 21. 72,18. — Mahā-Kāla N 72,10.

Kāḷa (nirayapālo) VI 248,3* (6). — Kāḷa-niraya VI 248 (7).

Kāḷa-pabbata (Himavante) VI 255,24. 264 (27). 265,15*. 303 (7. 9) (cfr. Kālāgiri).

Kāla, migo, putto Bodhisattassa (— Devadatto) I 143,13*. 144*,1. 14. 21. 145 (8). 11.

Kāla (Kāḷa), senāpati, see: Kālahatthi.

Kāḷaka, senāpati Yasapāṇi-rañño Bārāṇasiyaṁ (— Devadatto) II 186,20*. 187,18*. 188,13*. 189*,2. 16. 21. 196,3*. 9.

Kālakañjakā asurā: I 389,19 (Kālakañjaka-asura-yoni). — Kalakañjakā, pl. N 44,33.

Kālakaṇṇī (Kāḷakaṇṇī), mitto Anāthapiṇḍikassa I 364,5. 9. 12. 365,2. — mitto Bodhisattassa I 365,6—16*. 27. — Dhītā Virūpakkha-mahārājassa Cātummahārājika-devaloke III 257,20*. 258*,5. 21. 259*,10. 12. 261,8*. — Kālī III 259*,12. 20. 261,2*. Kāḷakaṇṇī — alakkhī IV 378,12*.

Kālakaṇṇi-jātaka (83) I 364—365. — Kālakaṇṇi-vatthu I 441,10.

Kālacampā-nagara (Kāḷa-), Aṅgaraṭṭhe VI 31*,28. 30. 42,19*. 256,8*. 274 (5). 317 (1) (cfr. Campā).

Kāḷadevala, tāpaso, kulūpako Suddhodana-mahārājassa N 54,15. 67,28. 88,22. — VI 479,23.

Kāḷadevala, isi Avantiraṭṭhe Dakkhiṇāpathe, jeṭṭhantevāsiko Sārabhaṅgassa (Bodhisattassa) III 463*,10. 21. 464*,2. 8. 466,11*. 469,20. — V 133*,11. 24. — Asita Devala III 466,27. — Devala III 466,25. 467 (1). — V 151,29.

Kāḷabāhu, makkaṭo (— Devadatto) III 98*,8. 9. 99*,15. 20. 100,2.

Kālabāhu-jātaka (329) III 97—100.

Kāḷamattiya-aṭavī IV 82,15*. — Kāḷamattika- IV 88,15*.

Kāḷavalli-maṇḍapa, Tambapaṇṇidīpe IV 490,23.

kāla-vilokanaṁ Buddhassa N 48,21.

Kāḷavela, vihāro (?) Sīhaladīpe VI 30,6.

Kālasilā, Isigili-passe V 125,23. 126,7.

Kāḷasutta, nirayo V 266,18*. 267,23*. 268,6*. 270 (28). 272 (8).

Kāḷasena, rājā Ayojjha-nagare IV 82,22*.

Kālahatthi (Kāḷahatthi), senāpati manussamaṁsakhādaka-rañño Bārāṇasiyaṁ V 460,1*. 461*,4. 21. 462 (8). 11*. 464,4*. 465,1*. 466,4*. 468*,9. 14. 469 (11). 18*. 470,27*. 508*,23. 31 509*,3. 12. 510 (8). 511,20. — Kāla (Kāḷa) V 461,26. 462,1 (8). 465,6*. 468,20*.

Kālāgiri (Himavante) VI 302,28. 304,30* (29). 309,27*. 326,23* (cfr. Kāḷa-pabbata).

Kāḷāgiri-khaṇḍa, (Vidhurapaṇḍita-jātake) VI 314,28.

Kālāma, see: Āḷāra Kālāma N 66,34.

Kālikarakkhiya, isi VI 99,28*.

Kālikā, see: Kālī.

Kāliṅga-raṭṭha (Kaliṅga) II 367,16*. — 381,15*. — III 3,8* (26). 376,12*. 540,12*. 542 (6). — IV 230,6*. — V 144 (24). — VI 487,5*. 490 (17). 521*,8. 14. 522 (18). — Kaliṅga 574,8*. 581 (31). — Kāliṅgā III 6,25*. 381,16* (24). 541,18*. 542,5. — VI 521,21. 522 (18) (Kaliṅgā).

Kāliṅga-rāja, Dantapura-nagare Kāliṅgaraṭṭhe II 367,17*. 369,17* (22). 370,2. 6. 381,12*. — III 3*,3. 5. 20 (27). 4*,9. 17. 20. 5*,2. 3. 7. 12 24. 6*,4 9. 12. 15. 17. 18. 21. 22. 23. 8 (8). 6–7*. 18. — IV 230,6*. — V 135,20*. 137,4*. 149,31*. — Kāliṅga, rājā Kāliṅgaraṭṭhe putto Cullakāliṅgassa IV 231,23*. 232,23. 233,9*. 12. 24. 234,29. 235,8. 14*. 236,6. 17. — Kāliṅgakumāra — Cullakāliṅga IV 230,28*. 231*,7. 10.

Kāliṅgabodhi-jātaka (479) IV 228–236. — II 321,10.

Kāliṅgabhāradvāja, purohito Kāliṅga-rañño (— Bodhisatto) IV 232,10*. 233,12. 234 (17). 25* (28). 235,14*. 236,18. — Kāliṅga-brāhmaṇo IV 235,19.

Kālī — Kāḷakaṇṇī.

Kālī, gaṇikā Bārāṇasiyaṁ IV 248*,20. 21. 249*,3. 17. — Kālikā 249,25*.

Kāḷudāyin, amacco Suddhodanassa N 54,9. 86,13. 15. 88,4. — IV 314,24.

Kāvinda, dhammānusāsako Vedeha-rañño VI 330,6*. 343 (15). 354,2*. 368,20*. 369,11*. 380,17*. 383,12*. 387*,21. 24. 388,1*. 441,19*. 478,17*.

Kāvīrapaṭṭana, Damiḷaraṭṭhe IV 238,6*.

Kāsayo (Kāsiyā, cfr. Kāsiyo) — Kāsiraṭṭha-vāsino II 402,9*.

Kāsāva-jātaka (221) II 196—199.

Kāsāva-vagga II 196—221.

Kāsi, nagaraṁ Phussa-Buddhassa N 41,8.

Kāsi — Kāsi-raṭṭha IV 113,9*. — V 51,15*.

Kāsi-kuttama- VI 49,7*. 50,28*.

Kāsi-gāma(ka) (Kāsika-, Kāsaka-) II 57,15*. 68,8*. 70,8*. 173,28*. 203,24*. 387,28*. 394,8*. — III 45,10*. 59,2. 248,26*. 310,21*. 510,21. — IV 44,30*. 114,24*. 115*,1. 8. 224,18*. — V 68,4*. — Kāsigāma, nahānamūlaṁ dhītu Bimbisārarañño II 237,18. 404,20. nahānacuṇṇamūlaṁ II 403,15. 19. nahānīyamūlaṁ IV 342,17.

Kāsi-gāmaka (Kāsigāmakavāsika), adj., K. māṇavako II 221,18*.

Kāsi-nigama (Kāsi-gāma) III 36,29*. 308,10*. 388,28*. 467,6. — IV 22,14*.

Kāsi-pura, — Bārāṇasī V 54,23. 56,1. — VI 165 (30).

Kāsi-raṭṭha (Kāsika-) I 96,8*. 107,20*. 120,11*. 124,10*. 127,10*. 169,11*. 238,27*. 245,4*. 247,10*. 262,19*. 303,28*. 357,14*. 361,19*. 478,6*. 495,25*. — II 15,21*. 70,10*. 72,9*. 85,18*. 101,21*. 103,3*. 131,13*. 134,28*. 145,8*. 149,4*. 155,18*. 165,5*. 167,28*. 246,26*. 257,25. 269,8*. 314,24*. 359,7* 402 (23). 411,10*. — III 42 (9). 93,22*. 142,30*. 213,30*. 267,21*. 281,18*. 293,16*. 304*,8. 10. 21. 391,16. 406,24. 527,16*. — IV 28,16*. 50,20*. 100 (8). 113 (9). 114,1*. 115,28*. 137 (7). 220,12*. 370,7*. 377,22*. 476,11*. 488,30*. — V 12,1*. 41*,6. 8. 159,9*. 193,18*. 227,25*. — VI 3,18*. 118 (28). 138 (5). 177,22*. 462 (21). — Kāsi IV

113,9*. — Kāsi-rajja III 153,8*. — VI 198 (36). — Kāsi-Kosala III 32,2*.

Kāsi-rāja N 46,19. — III 39,13*. 43,2. 4. 12. — IV 94,18*. 96,27*. 99 (23). 104,18*. 462,8. 464,29. 30. 465,2. 22. 469,2*. 492,26*. — V 90,5*. 135,22*. 252,12*. 260,8*. 371,15. 377, (18). 14*. 19. 379,30*. 380,24. 381,8. 426(27). 427 (17). 457,8*. — VI 1,10*. 2,10*. 3,18*. 7,10*. 11,2*. 12,15*. 13,18*. 21,18*. 29,14*. 82*,3. 5. 87,10*. 88,25*. 89,28. 196*,19. 31. 198 (25). — Kāsissa rājā V 51,15*. — Kāsi-pati IV 99,9*. 100 (8). — V 113,6*. 114 (30). 131,6*. 373,16*. 375,23*. 376,3*. — Kāsi-vaddhano (-vaḍḍhano) IV 462,3. 464,24. VI 82,8*. 88,25*. — Kāsīnaṁ raṭṭha-vaddhano (-vaḍḍhano) IV 94,14*. 226,23*. 227,21. — V 68,28. 264,23. 265,27. — Kāsīnaṁ rājā VI 77,28*. 85,19*. — Kāsirājadhītā VI 198 (26). Kāsiputto (Kāsirājadhītāya putto — Bhūridatto) VI 175,7* (10).

Kāsika, adj. Kāsika-vatthaṁ I 355,20. — Kāsikaṁ (— Kāsika-vatthaṁ) VI 151,10* (20). 450,25*. — Kāsikāni vatthāni IV 352,15*. — Kāsika-sucivattha- (— Kāsiyāni sucīni vatthāni) VI 144*,23–27. 145 (9). 154*,1–5. — Kāsika-vilepanaṁ I 355,30.

Kāsiyani (vatthāni) VI 500,11*. 506,20. 510,6.

Kāsiyo — Kāsiraṭṭhavāsino V 377,6 (11). — VI 165,21* (31) (Kāsīnaṁ). — VI 462,17* (21). 464,25* (Kāsisu).

Kiṁsukopama-jātaka (248) II 265–266.

Kiṁsukopama-suttanta II 265,8.

Kiki, rājā Kassapadasabalassa kāle VI 481*,4. 10.

Kiṁchanda-jātaka (511) V 1—11.

Kitavāsa, rājā Bārāṇasiyaṁ II 194,22* (24). 195 (17).

Kinnarā devī, bhariyā Kaṇḍari-rañño Bārāṇasiyaṁ V 437,29. 33. 438,29. 33. 439,7. 440,7. 12 (16. 17).

Kimpakka-jātaka (85) I 367—369.

Kimbila, thero I 140,6.

Kimbilā, nagaraṁ (Kassapabuddhakāle) VI 121,18 (34).

kilesaniggaho I 501,3. — III 18,8. 208,6. 375,17. 397,6. — IV 113,20.

Kilesamāra (cfr. Namuci) V 455 (11). — VI 46 (12).

Kisavaccha, isi, jeṭṭhantevāsiko Sārabhaṅgassa (Bodhisattassa), uyyāne Daṇḍakiraññо Kumbhavatīnagaraṁ nissāya III 463,18*. 469,22. — V 133*,11. 27. 134*,5. 9. 135*,6. 25. 136*,13. 14. 143,19*. 151,30. — VI 99,28*. Vaccha Kisa: V 150,24. 267,7*.

Kisāgotamī, therī N 60,27. 61,10. — III 543,5.

Kīṭāgiri II 387,12.

Kīḷanakhaṇḍa, Bhūridattajātake VI 186,17.

Kukku-jātaka (396) III 317—321.

Kukku-vagga III 317—363.

Kukkuṭa-jātaka a) (383) III 265—67. — b) (448) IV 55—59 (var. lect. Kukkuha-jātaka).

Kukkura-jātaka (22) I 175—178 (cfr. Kakkara-jāt.)

Kukkula-niraya V 114 (9). 143,21*. 144 (18).

Kukkuha-jātaka, see: Kukkuṭa-jātaka (448).

Kuṭikāra-sikkhāpadaṁ II 282,16. — III 78,21. 351,23.

Kuṭidūsaka-jātaka (321) III 71—74.

Kuṭidūsaka-vagga III 71—102.

kuṭumbiko (kuṭumbiyo) II 236,3. 337,11. — III 56,9. 66,20. 106,21. — IV 369,2.

Kuṭumbiyaputtatissa-thera I 316,4. 28. 317,9. 18. 20.

Kuṇāla, sakuṇarājā (= Bodhisatto) V 416,29*. 417*,2. 4. 6. 8. 10. 12. 15. 19. 21. 22. 27. 419 (5). 421*,13. 14. 17. 19—22. 24. 25. 422*,6. 7. 9. 11. 16. 423 (4. 5. 7. 12). 24*. 33*. 424,8*. 15. 427 (15). 428 (31). 430 (7). 440,10. 443,32. 444,28. 447,29*. 33. 451 (7). 456,10.

Kuṇāla-kathā V 415,12.

Kuṇāla-jātaka (536) V 412—456. — I 208,11. 327,30 (cfr. V 412—16). — III 91,4* (cfr. Jāt. 360). 132,30 (cfr. V 437—440). — IV 144,3 (cfr. V 444—45). 207,23 (cfr. V 412—16).

Kuṇāla-daha, Himavantapadese V 412,14. 415,25. 419 (22. 24).
Kuṇāla-dhammadesanā V 415,11.
Kuṇḍakakucchisindhava-jātaka (254) II 286—291.
Kuṇḍakakumāra, brāhmaṇo (— Bodhisatto) III 39,15*.
Kuṇḍakapūva-jātaka (109) I 422—424.
Kuṇḍadhāna-vana, Kuṇḍiyanagaraṁ nissāya I 407,20.
Kuṇḍalinī, sālikā-sakuna-dhītā V 111,1*. 116*,1. 3. 5 (8. 9). 120*,1. 8. 6. 15 (18). 125,18. — Kuṇḍalini-pañho V 120,7*.
Kuṇḍalī (?) VI 478,19*.
Kuṇḍiya-nagara I 407,19.
Kuddāla-jātaka (70) I 311—315.
Kuddāla(ka)-paṇḍita, paṇṇika-putto (— Bodhisatto) N 46,5. — I 312,28*. 314*,22. 27. 30. 315,0*. 14*. 25. — Kuddāla-samāgama IV 490,24. — VI 30,7.
Kuntani-jātaka (343) III 134—136.
kuntanisakuṇikā, Kosalarañño gehe III 134,14.
Kundālī, gadrabhī II 338,24*. 340,17.
Kumārakassapa, thero I 148,26. 30. 32. 149,6. 153,14. 19. — Kassapa 148,25. — -assa mātā I 145,16.
Kumārapabba, Vessantara-jātake VI 555,32.
kumārikā aññatarā Jetavane II 224,20. 229,7.
Kumbha-jātaka (512) V 11—20.
Kumbha-vagga II 431—451.
Kumbhakāra-jātaka (408) III 375—383.
Kumbhavatī, nagaraṁ Daṇḍakirañño vijite III 463,18*. — V 29 (19). 134,1*.
Kumbhīra, yakkho VI 272 (27).
Kumbhīla-jātaka (224). II 206. — II 206 (14) — Vānarinda-jātaka (57).
Kummāsapiṇḍa-jātaka (415) III 405—414. — III 451,25* (cfr. III 410). — V 88,7.
Kuraṅgavī, dhītā Bārāṇasirañño V 424,28. 429 (19). 430 (2. 5. 7).

Kurayo, see: Kuruyo.

Kuraraghariya-Soṇatthera VI 15 (12).

Kurukhetta-vāsī rājā (Janasandho) VI 291,11.

Kuruṅgamiga-jātaka a) (21) I 173—174. — b) (206) II 152—155.

Kuruṅgamiga-vagga I 173—198.

Kurudhamma (pañcasīlāni) II 367*,2. 10. 371*,18. 23. 372*,1. 3. 4. 5. 18. 22. 373*,5. 6. 18. 374*,1. 5. 12. 17. 21. 375*,10. 12. 376*,4. 6. 26. 377*,1. 21. 23. 378,11*. 379*,4. 22. 24. 380,2*. 381,14*.

Kurudhamma-jātaka (276) II 365—381.

Kuruyo (var. lect. Kurayo) — Kururaṭṭhaṁ II 214,9* (16. 18). — VI 278,16*. 279 (3). 322,27*. 323,11. 325,16*. — Kurūnaṁ amacco VI 284,16*. — Kurunaṁ (Kurūnaṁ) kattu-seṭṭho (Dhanañjayo) VI 306,22* (32). 309,8. 313,22*. 319,21*. 323,7. 23*. 29*. 325,2. — Kurūnaṁ raṭṭhaṁ VI 284 (20). — Kurunaṁ (Kurūnaṁ) rājā (Dhanañjayo) IV 450,4*. — VI 260*,16. 22. 282,16*. — Kurūnaṁ sabhā VI 272,28*. 273 (8).

Kururaṭṭha II 214 (18). 366,23*. — III 400,18*. — IV 361,4*. 444,10*. — V 57,7* (24). 457,8*. 474,7*. 484,15*. — VI 255,17*. 273 (23). 322 (30). 329,11*.

Kururāja II 381,26 (= Bodhisatto). — VI 260 (25). 283,16*.

kula-vilokanaṁ Buddhassa N 49,21.

kuladhītā ekā, Sāvatthiyaṁ III 182,8.

Kulavaddhana, seṭṭhi V 185*,1. 9. 12. * 192,6.

Kulāvaka-jātaka (31) I 198—206. — VI 126 (15).

Kulāvaka-vagga I 198—234.

Kuvera VI 201,25*. 307,6*. 325,29*. — Vessavaṇa Kuvera 269,2*. — VI 269,2*. 270 (3). 271,9.

Kusa-kumāra, putto Okkākassa rañño (= Bodhisatto) V 282,1*. 284,24* — Kusarājā V 285*,27—28. 287,11*. 288*,3. 6. 290,23*. 291*,20. 22. 294*,24. 27. 30. 295,1*. 296 (17). 21*. 300 (6). 11*. 21*. 307,11*. 308,1—2*. 12 (13). 310,7* (25)

312,18. 455 (4). — VI 340 (8). 383,22*. 388 (9). — Kusa V 293,24*. 296*,4. 25. 298,18*. 304,18*. 305*,15. 17. 21. 35. 310,7*. 11. 18. 16. 17. — Kusanarinda V 298 (15). 299 (26). 305 (2). 12*. 311 (18). 18. 20. 28.

Kusa-jātaka (531) V 278—312. — IV 27,26. 104,11. 304,28. — VI 1,18*.

Kusa-rāja, see: Kusakumāra.

Kusarāja-kula V 305 (9).

Kusanāḷi-jātaka (121) I 441—443. — IV 77 (17).

Kusanāḷi-vagga I 441—465.

Kusamāli, samuddo IV 140,28*. — Nīlavaṇṇa-kusamāla IV 140,16*.

Kusāvatī, nagaraṁ Mallaraṭṭhe (— Kusinārā), rājadhānī Mahāsudassanassa I 392,6*. — rājadhānī Okkākassa V 278,22*. 285*,6. 14. 293,24*. 294 (2). 8*. 296 (11). 297*,16. 21. 311,23. 24. — Kusāvatīrājakula V 305 (6).

Kusinārā, nagaraṁ I 391,23. — IV 148,11. 151,20.

Kuhaka-jātaka (89) I 375—377.

kuhaka-bhikkhu I 375,18. 460,8. 461,26. 480,13. — II 68,8. 72,7. 233,24. 268,23. — III 84,9. 115,11. 232,20. 267,15. — IV 297,22.

Kūṭadanta, brāhmaṇo VI 329,23.

kūṭavāṇijo, Sāvatthiyaṁ I 404,8. — II 181,3. 423,18.

Kūṭavāṇija-jātaka a) (98) I 404—405. — b) (218) II 181—184.

Kūṭāgārasālā, Vesāliṁ upanissāya II 5,11. 262,8.

Keka-rājadhānī, Mahiṁsakaraṭṭhe V 145 (9) (cfr. Kekaya-).

Keka-rāja VI 280 (20).

Kekaka, nagaraṁ II 213,8* (— Kekaya-rājadhānī).

Kekakā (pl.) — Kekaya-raṭṭhaṁ II 214,9* (16. 19). — VI 280,24* (29). 281 (8). — Kekakādhipo (Ajjuno) V 267,5* — Kekaraṭṭhādhipati 273 (2—8).

Kekaya-raṭṭha II 214 (19).

Kekaya-rājadhānī, Kekayaraṭṭhe II 214 (20) cfr. Keka-.

Ketakavana, Naḷakapânagâmaṁ upanissâya Kosalesu I 170,4.
Ketumatī, nadī (Himavante) VI 518,12. 519,21*.
Ketumatī-pura VI 594,11.
Kebukā, nadī III 91,22* (24). 92,2*.
Keḷavāhā, see: Telavāhā.
Kelâsa, pabbato V 53 (26). — Kelāsakūṭa I 321,26*. — V 39,11. 52,17*. — Kelāsa-sadiso VI 490,12*. 515,22.
Keḷisīla-jātaka (202) II 142—144.
keḷisīlakā bhikkhū II 447,3. — III 310,14.
Kevaṭṭa, brāhmaṇo Uttarapañcala-nagare VI 391,7*. 392*,14. 16. 28. 393*,3. 8. 10. 12. 19. 28. 394,2*. 395*,13. 26. 400,23*. 401,27*. 402*,11. 12. 403*,8. 18. 20. 22. 29. 404*,2. 12. 13. 405*,4. 6. 15. 18. 406,1*. 407,13*. 408,16*. 409*,20. 27. 411*,19. 25. 29. 412*.2. 6. 413*,1. 13. 414*,4. 5. 11. 415,16*. (30). 416 (32). 417 (22). 419 (1. 2. 8). 424,26*. 430,15*. 438 (16). 452,1* (7—11). 461*,8. 14. 478,15*. — Kosiyagotta (Kosiya) VI 418,17. 419 (8).
Kesava, tāpaso Himavante III 143*, 3. 6. 7. 12. 16. 28. 144,3*. (11. 13). 14*. 145,6*. 15*. 18. 362 (20). 363,17. — Kesī III 144,9* (11). 362 (25).
Kesava, — Vāsudevarājā IV 84,24* (29). 85,3. 20*.
Kesava-jātaka (346) III 141—145.
Kesi, assataro VI 135,28*.
Kesinī, bhariyā Candakumārassa (— Bo.) VI 134,31*.
Kesī, see: Kesava, tāpaso.
Kokanada, pāsādo Bodhirājakumārassa III 157,28.
Kokanadā (-a?), vīṇā V 281,14*. 290,4*.
Kokālika, bhikkhu I 431,16. 17. 432,20. 22. 491,6. — II 65,28. 66,1. 8. 22. 28. 67,23. 25. 108,10. 13. 109,14. 18. 110,27. 175,19. 20. 178,2. 356,3 4. 10. 14. 358,22. 438,15. 16. 20. 21. 24. 440,2. 441,2. — III 102,11. 104,14. 112,21. — IV 166,26. 242,28—30. 243,14. 20. 21. 24. 27. 244,2. 3. 22. 23. 30. 245,2. 8. 11. 14. 255,10. 11.

Kokālika-jātaka (331) III 102—104.
Kokālika-raṭṭha II 356,5. 6. — IV 242,29. 243,30.
Kokālika-vatthu II 356,8 (cfr. Jāt. 481).
Kokila-vagga III 102—132.
Kokilā, dhītā Candakumārassa (— Bo.) VI 134,26*.
Koñca, pāsādo Vidhurapaṇḍitassa VI 289*,10. 12.
Koṭigāma, Gaṅgātīre Bhaddiyanagaraṁ nissāya II 332,20. 27.
Koṭisimbali-jātaka (412) III 397—400.
Koṭisimbali-niraya V 275 (7).
Koṭumbara-raṭṭha VI 51 (26). — khoma-koṭumbarāni — K.-raṭṭhe uṭṭhita-vatthāni VI 47,18*. 51 (29), cfr. Kodumbara-raṭṭha.
Koṇāgamana-Buddha N 42,19. 43,1. 13. 27. 44,10. 94,18.
Koṇḍañña — Candakumāra (Bo.) VI 137*,1 (4). 20. 138,2*.
Koṇḍañña-Buddha N 30,1. 12. 34,14. 44,4. 90,5.
Koṇḍañña, brāhmaṇo N 56,4. 12. 24. 57,1. 67,4. — Aññā-Koṇḍañña-thera N 82,11.
Koṇḍañña, — Sarabhaṅgasatthā (Bodhisatto) V 140*,17. 19 (21). 141,13. 30*. 142 (5).
Kodumbara-raṭṭha (— Koṭumbara-r.) VI 501 (25). — khoma-kodumbarāni (vatthāni) VI 500,11*.
kodhana-bhikkhu II 277,8. — III 15,24. 39,8. — IV 22,5.
Kontimārā, nadī VI 493,20* (23). 514,2*.
Komāyaputta, brāhmaṇo (— Bodhisatto) II 447,18*. 449,11.
Komārabhacca, see: Jīvaka K.
Komāyaputta-jātaka (299) II 447—449.
Korakkhattiya, (titthiyo) I 389,18. 19. 390,9.
Korakalamba(ka), kaniṭṭho Kapilabrāhmaṇassa (Bodhisattassa) III 454,25*. 455*,11. 13. 457*,14. 18. 458*,18. 27. 459,9*.
Korabya, see: Koravya.
Koravya, rājā Kururaṭṭhe Indapattanagare, pitā Sutasomassa V 457,3*. 474,8* (Korabya).
Koravya-rāja — Dhanañjaya, Indapattanagare II 368,11*. — III 400,19*. 402,29. — IV 361,4*. 362*,1. 10. 15. 363*,1. 13.

23. 364*,6. 16. 26. 365,8*. — V 59,21* (26) (Korabya-). 61,1* (25). 65,16*. — VI 256*,15. 20. — Koravya-kumāro — Dhanañjaya-rājā (putto Dhanañjayassa) VI 256,26*. 268,5*. 273*.16. 20.

Koravya-seṭṭha — Sutasoma V 479*,2. 31.

Kolita, dutiyasāvako Gotama-Buddhassa (Moggallāno) N 15,24. 16,12. — II 381,22.

Koliya-nagara, Rohiṇiṁ nadiṁ nissāya V 412,16. 415,4. — Koliyanagara-vāsino V 412,19. 413,24. 414,1. — Koliya-kammakarā V 412,29. — Koliyā V 412,15. 413,9. 11.

Koliyarājadhītā, Soppavāsā upāsikā I 407,20.

Kosamba-kkhandaka (Vinayapiṭake) III 486,10.

Kosambaka, rājā Kosambiyaṁ IV 28,8*. — Kosambika IV 56,4*.

Kosambakā, bhaṇḍanakārakā bhikkhū III 211,4. 490,2.

Kosambika, see: Kosambaka.

Kosambī, nagaraṁ I 160,19. 161,8. 360,8. 19. 20. — III 64,2. 384,2. 486,9. 10. 490,1. 2. — IV 28,8* (Vaṁsaraṭṭhe). 56,4*. 375,5. 392,21*. 398 (1). — VI 237,1 (31). 238,20. 239 (18). — Kosambiyanagara VI 239 (27).

Kosambī-jātaka (428) III 486—490.

Kosala-gāmako, aññataro I 249,21.

Kosala-janapada I 164,28. 198,20. — III 490,15.

Kosala-devī, Bimbisārarañño bhariyā, dhītā Mahākosalassa II 403,14. 16. — Kosalarājadhītā III 121,18. — Ajātasattu-mātā II 237,20.

Kosala-nagara IV 158,11.

Kosala-raṭṭha I 234,15. 16. 306,27. 329,25. 330,14. 20. 88. 331,7*. 332,16*. — III 270,15*. 307,26. — IV 130,27. — V 315,24*. — Kosala-rajja III 116,6*. — V 425 (27).

Kosala-rāja I 133,25. 136,5. 262*,19. 21. 263*,6. 11. 16. 17. 22. 24. 28. 264,1*. 307,3. 334,28. 369,8. 381,4. 455,6. — II 1,6. — 3,8* (Malliko). 3,12* (Kosalarajjasāmiko). 3,17*. 4 (8.

5,6. 12,8. 21*,9. 10. 16. 23. 22*,3. 7. 12. 23,21 (Kosalo). 23 (8). 28. 74,3. 4. 76,7. 125,12. 127,5. 139,6. 169,22. 206,19. 208,3. 237,17. 21. 314,19. 359,3. 393,15. 404,6 (mahodara-Kosalo). 404,23. 433,7. — III 13,16* (Dabbaseno). 22,27. 48,16—17. 115*,16. 17. 116,21*. 134,14. 153,6*. 155,5. 212,30*. 270*,15. 18 (Sāketo). 274,9* (16) (Kosalo). 400,6. 405,28. 406,1. 21. 410,24* (27) (Kosalādhipo). 414 (14). 428,10. 444,7. 469,28. 487,18. 520,7. — IV 144,9. 145,4. 148,28. 152,7 (Kosalanarindo). 176,3. 177,18. 188,19. 229,2. 27. 342,2. 13. 17. 361,1. 368,23. 401,18. 444,3. 4. — V 98,20. 108,5. 109,3. 315,31*. 316*,6. 10. 425 (28). 427 (17). 428 (32). 429 (8. 28). 430 (16. 19).
Kosalarāja-dhītā III 407,27*. 412,26* (30—32). 413,12* (18 (sukosalā). — Kosalaraññо amacco I 354,16. — II 400,7 (— Kosalarājasevako III 13,11). — III 168,11. — °atthacaro amacco IV 196,23. °paduṭṭhāmacco III 153,5 (cfr. II 125 & 206). — °purohito III 104,18. — (cfr. Pasenadi).
Kosalā (pl.) I 170,2. 215,16. 249,31. 316,32.
Kosikī V 5,23*. — Kosikigaṅgā V 2,10*. 6 (14. 19).
Kosiya, Kosiyagotta — Sakka II 252,8* (11).
Kosiya, see: Kosiyagotta, Maccharikosiya.
Kosiya-jataka, a) (130) I 463—465. — b) (226) II 208—209. c) (470) IV 186.
Kosiya-vagga II 321—354.
Kosiyagotta (Kosiya), isi VI 181,24*. 182 (3).
Kosiyagotta (Kosiya), — Kevaṭṭo brāhmaṇo VI 418,17. 419 (8).
Kosiyagotta, brāhmaṇo, Sāliudiyagāme Magadharaṭṭhe IV 276,14*. — Kosiya IV 278,7*. 280*,3. 14. 21. 281,12*. 282,2*. 6.
Kosiyagotta (Kosiya), brāhmaṇo, pitā Sonakumārassa (Bodhisattassa). V 319,18* (17. 18). 20. 321,1*. 7*. 10. 322,3. 324*,27. 29. 326*,28. 31. 327 (4).
Kosiyā, brāhmaṇī dussīlā Bārāṇasiyaṁ I 464*,1—23. 465,7*.
Kosiyāyana, brāhmaṇo Kāsiraṭṭhe I 496,12*. — Kosiyāyanī brāhmaṇī I 496 (16).

Kh.

Khajjopanaka-jātaka (364) III 197.

Khajjopanaka-pañha III 197,19. — VI 371,9*. 372,10*.

Khaṇḍa, aggasāvako Vipassi-Buddhassa, N 41,16.

Khaṇḍahāla-jātaka (542) VI 129—157. — I 140,9. 142,12. — III 293,9. — IV 77,28. 119,29*.

Khaṇḍahāla, brāhmaṇo purohito Bārāṇasiyaṁ, atthadhammānusāsako Candakumārassa (Devadatto) VI 131*,13. 19. 24. 28. 132,4*. 6*. 11. 21*. 134,15*. 137 (11). 138*,11. 13. 15 (20). 31. 139,2*. 140*,1. 7. 9. 11 (16. 31). 141*,4. 14. 15 (19). 142*,19. 21. 30. 143*,1 (3—4). 28. 144,4*. 146 (11). 148*,26. 28. 149*,2. 5. 8. 10. 12. 14. 16. 22. 24. 26. 28. 154,22*. 29. 155,20—23 (28—32) 157,30.

khattavijjavādi amacco V 228*,22—28. 240,7*.

Khadiraṅgāra-jātaka (40) I 226—234. — II 410,1. — III 128,21.

Khadiravaniya, rukkhakoṭṭha-sakuṇo khadiravane Himavantapadese (— Bodhisatto) II 162*,19. 22. 163*,3. 21. 164,8*. 12.

Khantivaṇṇana-jātaka (225) II 206—207.

Khantivādi-jātaka (313) III 39—43. — N 46,17. — III 178,4. — IV 11 (24). — V 101 (5). 113 (31). 119 (15). 145 (30).

khantivādi-tāpasa, (Kuṇḍaka-kumāro — Bodhisatto) III 40,26*. 41*,9. 17. 43,13. — V 135,22*.

Khandhaka, (Vinaya-Piṭake?) II 415,13. (var. lect. Maṇikhandha-jātaka.) (cfr. Sundari-māraṇaṁ.)

Khandhavatta-jātaka (203) II 144—148.

Kharadāṭhika, yakkho, N 31,9.

Kharaputta-jātaka (386) III 275—281.

Kharassara-jātaka (79) I 354—355.

Kharādiyā, migī, bhaginī Bodhisattassa I 160,3* (4).

Kharādiya-jātaka (15) I 159—160.

khipitakaṁ Buddhassa II 15,3.

khīṇāsavathero I 236,30*.

Khujjuttarā, upāsikā (dāsī). III 168,6. — IV 314,21. — V 192,6. 312,12.

Khuddakatissa, thero Maṁgaṇa-vāsī Sīhaladīpe VI 30,3.

Khuradhāra, nirayo V 269,11*. 274 (30). 275 (8).

Khurappa-jātaka (265) II 335—337.

Khuramāla, samuddo IV 139,4*. Khuramālī IV 139,18* (17).

Khema, nagaraṁ Kakusandha-Buddhassa N 42,14. nagaraṁ Tissa-Buddhassa, N 40,22. nagaraṁ Sumana-Buddhassa N 34,25.

Khema, migadāyo Bandhumatīnagaraṁ upanissāya VI 480,12*.

Khema, saro IV 424,4*. 427,13*. — V 356,5* ff.

Khema, rājā Kakusandha-Buddhassa kāle (— Bodhisatto) N 42,21.

Khema, Khemaka, see: Khemanesāda.

Khemaṁkara, upaṭṭhāko Sikhi-Buddhassa N 41,30.

Khemanesāda V 356,20*. — Khemaka V 356,26*. 358,8. 8. 28. 362,1*. 364,26*. 370, (15) 19*. 371,16 (20). — Khema 362,9*.

Khemā, devī, aggamahesī Bārāṇasiraññο II 36*,4. 16. — IV 256,28*. 334,14*. 413*,10. 22. 418,28*. 423,26*. — V 354*,9. 11. 355*,2. 12. 373,8*. 381,3*. 382,5.

Khemā, bhikkhunī, aggasāvikā Gotama-Buddhassa N 15,25. 16,14. — III 168,7. — IV 423,18. 430,8. — V 362,6. — VI 68,20. 481,15*.

Khemā, aggasāvikā Dhammadassi-Buddhassa N 39,27.

Khemā, nadī Himavantā pavattā V 199,22*. 200 (7).

Khemī, pokkharaṇī V 374,19* (27).

G.

Gagga, brāhmaṇo, pitā Bodhisattassa II 16,14*.
Gagga-jātaka (155) II 15—17.
Gaggali-gāma, Pāragaṅgāya VI 431,15*.
Gaṅgamāla, nahāpito III 451*,3. 17. 26. 452*,11. 24 (28) 453,14*. — IV 174(9).
Gaṅgamāla-jātaka (421) III 444—454.
Gaṅgā, nadī I 295*,25. 29. 296*,7. 16. 298,3*. 502,16*. — II 117*,4. 6. 11. 13. 120,4*. 145*,10. 12. 151*,20. 23. 152,19. 158,28*. 159*,7. 8. 13. 258*,2. 8-10. 12 (23-27). 259,(2). 283,12. 15. 284,7*. 329,19*. 331,12. 332,23. 333,17. 338,23*. 339,12*. 344*,1 (8). 13-16. 359*,9. 16. 412,15*. 423,24*. 424,6*. 450,5-6*. — III 52*,13-16. 133,7*. 134,(5). 159,19*. 160,7*. 230,1-3*. 8. 231,14*. 345,18*. 361,6. (23). 362,(8. 9-11). 370*,8. 18. 371,27*. 372*,4. 24. 476,11*. 477,(9). 491*,4. 7. 14. 494,2*. 496 (18). 507,24. 520,14. 17*. — IV 70*,13. 15. 22. 224,25*. 225*,1. 5. 17. 227 (14). 231*,4. 7. 256*,5. 7. 8. 10. 260 (12—15.) 318*,16. 22. 437*,20. 479*,13. 14. 21. 480,1*. 482,14*. 483,15*. 489,6*. — V 3*,7. 20. 22 (29). 7, (30). 60*,2. 5. 61,29*. 93 (21). 191,2*. 255*,9. 16. 256 (9—10). 392,18*. 448,24. 449 (23). 496 (2). — VI 72*,24—26. 203,11* (19. 26). 359*,7. 9 (14—17). 392,7*. 412 (30). 415 (31). 427,22*. 431*,18—25. 432,10*. 433,18*. 445,10*. 452,5*. 455,18*. — Gaṅgaṭṭhakavimāna V 6 (16) — Gaṅgādevatā II 425,23*. (cfr. Adhogaṅgā, Ākāsagaṅgā, Uddhagaṅgā, Uparigaṅgā, Kosikigaṅgā, Bhāgīrathī, Mahāgaṅgā, Pāragaṅgā).
Gaṅgeyya-jātaka (205) II 151—152.
Gajakumbha-jātaka (345) III 139—141.
gaṇadānaṁ II 85,7.
Gaṇḍa, uyyānapālo Bimbisāra-rañño IV 264,23.
Gaṇḍatindu-jātaka (520) V 98—108.

Gaṇḍambamūla N 88,20.

Gadrabha-pañha (111) I 424,16—18. — Mahāummagga-jātaka VI 344,9.

Gandhakuṭi, Dasabalassa N 92,23. — I 119,8. 10. 22. — 316,9. 330,27. 501,21. — II 216,23. — III 67,2. — V 337,17. 382,20. 413,27. 456,27.

Gandhabbarāja, (— Sakko) VI 260*,15 (17). 21.

Gandhamādana, pabbato Himavante, III 452,8*. 453,27*. 478,8*. — IV 16*,4. 23. 287*,12. 14. 438,2*. 14. — V 63,13* 64 (5). 196,27*. 197 (1). 393,2. 395,13*. — VI 79*,7 (14) 83,22*. 84,9. 92,17. 19. 22. 518,5. 519,19. 528,22. 529 (6). 533,28. 579,28.

Gandhara, pabbato (Himavante) VI 579,23.

Gandhāra-jātaka (406) III 363—369.

Gandhāra-raṭṭha I 191,11*. 273,5*. 285,9*. 317,27*. 375,1 395,28*. II 47,11. 217,1*. — III 364,9*. 365,2*. 377,23*. — VI 501,22.

Gandhāra-rāja I 191,11*. — II 219,14*. 220,25*. 221,4. — IV 98,13*. — pitā Bodhisattassa III 364,9*. — Bodhisatto III 364,16*. 365,27*. 369,24. Gandhāratāpaso: III 365,14*. Gandhāro: III 366,21*.

Gandhāra-vagga III 363—421.

Gandhāra-visaya III 367,12*.

Gandhārā, (Gandhāra-raṭṭha-vāsino) III 378,8*. 381,16* (25). — VI 500,1*. 501,22 (Gandhārā paṇḍukambalā).

Gambhīra, paṭṭanagāmo I 239,24*.

Gambhīracārin, uddo III 333*,19. 20. 334*,2. 21. 335,(2).

Gayā, nadī V 388,24*. 389,(1).

Gayāsīsa, pabbato I 142,22. 185,29. 186,8. 10. 18. 14. 18. 425,2. 490,24. 28. 508,13. — II 38,23. 196,18. — IV 180,16.

Garahita-jātaka (219) II 184—186.

Garahita-piṭṭhipāsāṇa II 186,9*.

Garuḷa, (— Kuṇālo, Bodhisatto) V 428 (31). — Garuḷa Venateyya VI 260*,14. 20 (34.) 261,25*. 440,(7). (cfr. Venateyya).

Gahapati-jātaka (199) II 134—137.

Gāmaṇi-Caṇḍa, pādamūliko Janasandhassa Bārāṇasirañño II 300*,10. 21. 302*,5. 14. 304*,19. 21. 22. 305,21*. 306,9*. 307*,5. 6. 309,25*. 310,1*. 17. Gāmaṇi 300,25*. 301*,17. 20. 302*,9. 12. Caṇḍa-Gāmaṇi II 301,30*. Caṇḍa II 302*,13. 28. 303,9*. 304*,1. 14. 305*,1. 9. 11. 16. 22. 306*,1. 2. 7. 11. 12. 16. 17. 21. 22. 307*,1. 8.

Gāmaṇicaṇḍa-jātaka (257) II 297—310.

Gāmaṇi, rājakumāro I 136,14. 20 (28). 137, (2). 6.

Gāmaṇi-jātaka (8, cfr. 462) I 136—137.

Gāyikā, bhariyā Caṇḍakumārassa (Bo.) VI 148,10*.

Gijjha-jātaka a) (164) II 50—52. — b) (399) III 330—332. — c) (427) III 483—486 I 430,11. II 41,5.

Gijjhakūṭa, pabbato II 54,19. 55,11*. — III 536,21. — V 333,6. Gijjhapabbata II 50,20*. — III 255,10*. 484,4*. 485 (8). — V 424,4*. — VI 129,19. 130,2. — Gijjha VI 204*,10. 18. (18). 212,19*.

Giridanta (Giridatta, Giridattha), assabandho Sāmaraññо (— Devadatto) II 98*,10. 20. 99,15.

Giridanta-jātaka (184) II 98—99.

Giribbaja, pabbato (— Vaṁkagiri) VI 589,9 (16)

Girimekhala, hatthi Mārassa N 72,2. 73,28. 74,30.

Giriya, sigālo (— Devadatto) III 322,18. 323,21*. 324 (3—4).

Guṇa, ājīviko (Kassapagotto) VI 222,24. 223 (8). 21. (34). 224,12. 227,24 (28). 230,1. 2. 231,8. 233, (12. 32). 234,4 (16). 240 (21). 242 (29). 255,8.

Guṇa-jātaka (var. lect. Sīha-jāt.) (157) II 23—30. (— Sigāla-jātaka II 314,21.)

Guttā, dhītā Kiki-rañño VI 481,12*.

Guttila-gandhabba, (— Bodhisatto) II 248*,20. 22. 249*,3. 16. 22. 251*,15. 27. 254,20*. 256,18*. 257,10.

Guttila-jātaka (243) II 248—257.

Gumbika (— Gumbiya) III 200,8.

Gumbiya, yakkho III 200,16*. 201,5 (16).

Gumbiya-jātaka (366) III 200—202.

Gūthaniraya IV 493*,7. 22. — VI 8,15*.

Gūthapāṇa-jātaka (227) II 209—212.

Gotama Buddha N 15,16. 21. 16,10. 26,10. 33,34. 84,1. 67,18. 81,27. — I 147,32. 156,23. 227,10. 26. 28. 228,32. 229,1. 2. 5. 6. 34. 372,20. 23. 25. 28. 31. 32. 34. 373,1. 389,20. 22. 390,6. 425,2. 434,2. — II 169,29. 170,1. 8. 248,10. 415,18. 20. 25. 28. 416,5. 9. 12. 19. 417,12. 18. — III 359,18 (22. 25). — IV 37,9. 167,7. 11. 15. 17. 168,3. 9. 187,7. 15. 21. 24. 188,7. 10. 200,5. 263,13. 20—22. 264,11. 371*,11. — V 144*,1. 267*,6. 333,7. 8. 11. 18. 335,13. — VI 130,2. — Mahā-Gotama II 216,18. — III 44,25.

Gotamakacetiya, Vesāliṁ nissāya, II 259,26.

Gotamaka-suttanta II 259,27.

Gotamā, devī, aggamahesī Bārāṇasirañño, mātā Candakumārassa (Bo.) VI 134 (9). 157,20. — Gotamī VI 148,5*. 151 (29). — Gotami-putto VI 151,6* (16). 152,18*. 153,2*.

Gotamī, see: Mahāpajāpatī Gotamī. — Gotamā (read: Gotamī?) VI 481,15*.

Godha-jātaka a) (138) I 480—482. — b) (141) I 487—489. — c) (325) III 84—86. — d) (333) III 106—109. — V 241 (20).

Godhāvarī, nadī V, 132*,3. 6. 25. 136*,4. 6. 10.

Gopāla, putto purohitassa Esukāri-rañño IV 476,6*. 481*,5. 20. (30). 482,4*. 491,4.

Goyāniyā (— Aparagoyānadīpa) VI 278,15*. 279 (3).

Gorimanda, seṭṭhī VI 357,21* (24. 30).

Goḷakāla, puriso VI 337 (17. 32. 39). 338 (30) (Goḷa).

Govaḍḍhamāna, gāmo Uttarāpathe Kaṁsabhoge IV 80*,22. 23.

Gh.

Ghaṭa-jātaka, see: Ghaṭa-jāt.
Ghaṭīkāra, kumbhakāro, mitto Bodhisattassa Kassapa-Buddhassa kāle N 43,17. — Mahābrahmā N 65,12. 69,29.
Ghaṭṭiyā, bhariyā Candakumārassa (Bo.) VI 148,19* (21).
Ghata-kumāra, putto Brahmadattassa Bārāṇasi-rañño, rājā (— Bodhisatto) III 168,22*. 169,6*. 170,15.
Ghata-paṇḍita, putto Devagabbhāya navamo (— Bodhisatto) IV 81,7*. 84*,14. 18. 24. 85,5*. 86*,6. 31. 87*,2 (13). 15. 89,17.
Ghata-jātaka a) (355) III 168—170. b) (454) IV 79—89. — V 114 (11). 273 (6) (Ghaṭa-jāt.)
Ghatāsana-jātaka (133) I 471—472.
Ghanasela, pabbato Dakkhiṇāpathe Avantiraṭṭhe V 133,24*.
Gharāvāsa-pañha, Vidhurapaṇḍita-jātake VI 287,30.
Ghositārāma, Kosambiyaṁ upanissāya I 360,4. — III 384,3. 486,8.

C.

Cakkadaha IV 232,12*.
cakkavatti-rājā (Bodhisatto) N 38,12.
cakkavatti-sampatti N 48,19.
cakkavatti-halāhalo N 47,23. 48,11.
Cakkavāka-jātaka a) (434) III 520—524 (cfr. Kākajāt.). — b) (451) IV 70—72.
Cakkavāḷa-pabbata VI 282,7*.
Caṇḍa, nāgarājā I 472,2*.
Caṇḍa, Caṇḍagāmaṇi, see: Gāmaṇicaṇḍa.
Caṇḍapajjota, rājā (Avantiraṭṭhe) V 133,15*. (cfr. Pajakarājā III 463,18*.).
caṇḍabhikkhū dve II 30,10.
Caṇḍoraṇa, pabbato Himavantapadese, IV 90,14*. 93*,6 (9. 18. 16.

Catukuṇḍika-niraya III 243 (29—31). 244 (3).

Catukkanipāta III 1—152. — V 109,7 (— III 110,8). — VI 370,17* (— III 152,7).

Catudvāra-jātaka (439, — Mahā-Mittavindaka-jāt. I 363,8) IV 1—6. (cfr. Jāt. 41, 82, 104, 369).

Catuposathika-khaṇḍa, Vidhurapaṇḍita-jātake VI 262,2.

Catuposathika-jātaka (441) IV 14. — VI 257,25*.

Catumaṭṭa-jātaka (187) II 106—108.

Caturakkha, sunakho III 535,28*.

Cattālīsa-nipāta (XVII) V 109—192.

Canda, kinnaro Candapabbate Himavantapadese (— Bodhisatto) IV 283,20*. 284*,1. 7. 287,25*.

Canda, devaputto IV 63*,6. 19. 23. 64,17*. 68*,20. 28. 69,28. — V 383,12*. 386*,8. 15. 388*,3. 21. 390,20*. 412,10. — VI 1,15*. 89,9*. 90,8. 223,17 (32). 242,21*. 247,4*. 263,11*. 278,17*. 279. (5). 426,9*. 459,12*. 596,17. — Candimā VI 201,25*. 243,13. 20*. 443,5.

Canda, pabbato Himavantapadese IV 283*,14. 19. 288*,13. 10. Candaka-pabbato V 162,8*. Candapassa-pabbato V 38,7*.

Canda, brāhmaṇaputto — Vidhurapaṇḍito (Bodhisatto) VI 262,5*.

Canda, Candaka, see: Candakumāra.

Candaka, pāsādo (Sivirañño) IV 411,17*. — (Videharañño) VI 229,22. 230,12 (19). 231, (3). 35. Candapāsādo 242,22*.

Candakinnara-jātaka (485) IV 282—288. — N 91,9. — IV 282,24.

Candakumāra, putto Bārāṇasirañño, rājā (— Bodhisatto) N 45,14. — VI 131*,17. 18. 21. 24. 132,23*. 133,15*. 134 (9). 136 (28). 138,7*. 139,17*. 143 (4—5). 13*. 145 (10). 147, (4). 148 (22). 151 (2. 6). 156,14*. 157 (8—9). — Canda VI 133,6* 136,24*. 137,21*. 144*,24. 26. 28. 146,2. 4. 6. 8 (9). 147,25*. 148*,9. 20. 29. 149,6*. 150,24*. 151 (1). 152 (10). 154,2. 4. 6

9. 12. 15. 156,17. 19. 21. 23. 157,23. — Candaka VI 144,16. — Candiya VI 137,21*. 152,7*. (18). 154,27. (cfr. Koṇḍañña).

Candakumāra, putto Brahmadattassa Bārāṇasi-rañño, bhātā Bodhisattassa I 127,20*. 128*,21. 23. 133,10*. 19.

Candadeva, Devagabbhāya putto tatiyo IV 81,5*.

Candapassa, see: Canda-pabbata.

Candamittā, aggasāvikā Vipassi-Buddhassa N 41,17.

Candavatī, dhītā Bārāṇasi-rañño III 517*,3. 23. 518,6* (16). 519* (4). 9. 16.

Candavatī, nagaraṁ Anomadassi-Buddhassa N 36,4.

Candasena (— Bhaddasena, cod. B[d]) VI 157,22.

Candā, aggasāvikā Vipassi-Buddhassa N 41,17.

Candā, kinnarī, bhariyā Bodhisattassa IV 283,14*. 284*,2. 9. 10 (18). 285*,6. 24. 286, (1). 4*. 288*,6. 15. 288,22. Candī 284*,12. 14. 16 (19—20).

Candā devī, aggamahesī Mahāpatāpassa Bārāṇasi-rañño, mātā Bodhisattassa III 178,20*. 179*,9. 12. 180*,3. 6. 11. 17. 26. 181,11*. 182,1*. 4.

Candā devī, aggamahesī Kāsirañño, Maddarājadhītā, mātā Bodhisattassa VI 1,16*. 2*,3. 11. 3,11*. 5,1*. 10,7*. 11,12*. 19,16*. 20,18*. 24,17*. 28,30*.

Candā devī, aggamahesī Sutasomassa Bārāṇasi-rañño (Bodhisattassa) V, 177,19*. 182,10* (14). 192,5.

Candā, aggamahesī Candakumārassa (Bodhisattassa) VI 151,22*. 152*,4. 17. 152,22. 153*,15. 22. 154,23*. 157,21.

Candā, mātā Piyadassi-Buddhassa N 39,4.

Candābha-jātaka (135) I 474.

Candiya, see: Candakumāra.

Campaka, nagaraṁ Paduma-Buddhassa N 36,23.

Campaka-rukkha, bodhi Atthadassi-Buddhassa N 39,15.

Campakā, aggasāvikā Kakusandha-Buddhassa N 42,27.

Campā, nagaraṁ (— Kāḷacampā) VI 32*,13—15. 20.

Campā, nadī Aṅga-Magadha-raṭṭhānaṁ antare IV 454*,11. 16. 455,1*.

Campeyya, Campeyyaka, nāgarājā (— Bodhisatto) N 45,21. — IV 454*,12. 18. 455,7*. 462,2 (9). 464,26. 29. 30. 465, (6). 22. 468,22.

Campeyya-jātaka (506) IV 454—468.

Cammasāṭaka-jātaka (324) III 82—84.

cammasāṭako paribbājako III 82,8.

Cara, putto Varamandhātussa, rājā paṭhamakappe III 454,13*.

Cariyāpiṭaka N 47,12. — IV 406,14.

Cātummahārājā, N 48,16. Cātummahārājika-devaloka II 311,4. 24*. 312,3*. — III 257,10*. 262 (7). 264,18*. — °bhavana II 89*,4. 14. 91 (10).

Cāṇura, mallo IV 81*,21. 26. 82*,3. 6. 8.

Cālā, aggasāvikā Phussa-Buddhassa N 41,5.

Ciñcamāṇavikā, paribbājikā Sāvatthiyaṁ I 280,20. 487,3. 6. 440,25. — II 121,10. 160,21. — III 298,26. — IV 187,2. 12. 15. 188,28. 189,9. 196,18. — VI 593,26.

Citta, gahapati IV 314,22. Cittassa gahapatino vatthuṁ VI 15 (8).

Citta, caṇḍālaputto (— Bodhisatto) IV 390*,17. 391*,18. 17. 28. 392*,3. 21. 26. 393*,7. 15. 394*,11 (19. 21). 26. 27. 395* (1—8). 7. 13. 24. 396*,4. 19. 401,8.

Citta, Cittaka, migo, kaniṭṭho Bodhisattassa IV 413,12*. 415*,7. 12 (15. 27). 417*,1. 22. 418,20*. 419,27*. 421,16*. 423,19.

Cittarāja, yakkho II 372*,10. 13.

Citta-Sambhūta-jātaka (498) IV 390—401.

Cittakūṭa, pabbato Himavante II 107*,10. 12. 24. 176,5*. — III 208,18*. 209,22*. 247*,1. 2. 248,10*. — IV 212,22*. 213*,3. 28. 214,4*. 216,4*. 218,24*. 423,28*. 424,3*. 427,10*. 430,4*. — V 337,27*. 338,2*. 343 (4). 347 (29). 352,31*. 354,11*. 355,27*. 356,1*. 357,4*. 358*,5. 27. 361, (5). 365,1*.

368 (29). 369 (14). 381*,12. 15. 469 (26). — Citrakūṭa IV 212,26*. 216 (19). — V 338,18*. 344 (2). 347 (28).
Cittakūṭa-dvārakoṭṭhaka, Tāvatiṁsabhavane VI 125,30*. 127,14*. devarājapavesanaṁ VI 126,8.
Cittakūṭa-latāvana, see: Cittalatāvana.
Cittacūḷa, kacchapo VI 162*,13. 24. 163,30*.
Cittapāṭalī, kappaṭṭhiyarukkho Asurabhavane I 202,15*.
Cittalatāvana, uyyānaṁ Tāvatiṁsabhavane I 204,29*. 205,5*. — II 188,21*. — III 250,22*. 251,7* (15. 17). — VI 590,17. — Cittalatā VI 278,28*. — Cittakūṭalatāvana V 392,25*.
Cittahatthasāriputta, thero Sāvatthiyaṁ I 311,23. 312,9.
Cittā, itthī gehe Bodhisattassa I 201*,2. 24. — pādaparicārikā Sakkassa I 204,27*.
Citrakūṭa, see: Cittakūṭa.
cīvaravaḍḍhako bhikkhu I 220,16.
Cunda, Bhagavato anibaddhaupaṭṭhāko IV 95,14.
cumbaṭakalaho I 208,10. (cfr. V 412 ff.)
Culla- cfr. Cūla, Cūḷa.
Culla-anāthapiṇḍika II 287,1. — III 520,8. Cūḷanāthapiṇḍika I 148,4.
Cullakammāsadamma-nigama V 35,28*.
Cullakaseṭṭhi, (= Bodhisatto) I 120,18*. 122*,11. 14. 123,8.
Cullakaseṭṭhi-jātaka (4) I 114—123.
Cullakāla-pabbata, Himavante V 38,7*.
Cullakāliṅga, putto Kāliṅgaraññe Dantapūranagare IV 230,7*. 232,7*. — Cūlakāliṅga IV 230,14*. — Kāliṅgakumāra IV 230,28*. 231*,7. 19.
Cullakāliṅga-jātaka (301) III 1—8?
Cullakuṇāla-jātaka (464) IV 144 (cfr. V 444—445).
Cullakuṇālavagga III 132—152.
Cullatāpasa, putto Bodhisattassa I 416,30*. 417,27. [= Nārado, putto Kassapassa, Cullanārada-jātake (477)].

Cullatuṇḍila, sūkaro, bhātā Bodhisattassa III 287*,5. 19. 25. 288*,1. 24. 289,20*. 290,1* (27). 291 (1). 292,25*. 293,3. (cfr. Tuṇḍila).

Culladaddara, putto Sūradaddara-rañño Daddaranāgabhavane Himavantapadese, bhātā Bodhisattassa III 16*,8. 19. 17,25.

Culladhanuggaha-paṇḍita, udiccabrāhmaṇaputto (— Bodhisatto) I 356,15*. 359,20*. 27. — Culladhanupaṭṭhāka I 357,4*. — Cullupaṭṭhāka I 357,11*.

Culladhanuggaha-paṇḍita, Bārāṇasibrāhmaṇo III 219*,25. 30. (— Dhanuggaho)

Culladhanuggaha-jātaka (374) III 219—224. — V 446, (15).

Culladhammapāla-jātaka (358) III 177—182. — III 178,1. IV 11 (24). V 113 (31—32).

Cullanandaka-jātaka, see: Cullanandiya-jāt.

Cullanandika, see: Cullanandiya.

Cullanandikā (?) VI 478,15*.

Cullanandiya, vānaro kaniṭṭhabhātiko Bodhisattassa II 199,19*. 201,2*. Cullanandika II 200,2*. 201,9*. 202,(3).

Cullanandiya-jātaka (222) II 199—202. Cullanandaka-jāt. III 178,7.

Cullanārada-jātaka (477) IV 219—224. — Cullanāradakassapa-jāt. I 196,19. 416,10. 18*. II 419,8. III 147,20.

Cullantevāsika, duggatakulaputto (seṭṭhi) I 121*,3. 8. 122,1*. 123,7.

Cullapaduma-jātaka (193) II 115—121. — VI 15 (9).

Cullapanthaka, thero I 114,9. 10. 115,3. 24. 116,7—10. 25. 32. 117,1. 7. 8. 10. 14. 15. 18. 24. 25. 118,6. 18. 27—31. 119,4. 18. 120,4. 6. 123,3. 8. — IV 224,11.

Cullapalobhana-jātaka (263) II 328—331. — Cūlapalobhana IV 469,1*.

Cullapiṇḍapātika-tissa, thero (— Tissakumāro) I 156,9. 17. 157,18. — Cullapiṇḍapātiyo: I 159,11.

Cullabodhi-jātaka (443) IV 22—27. — cfr. III 93,8*.

Cullabodhi-tāpasa, see: Cūḷabodhi-tāpasa.

Cullalohita, go, kaniṭṭhabhātā Bodhisattassa I 196,28*. 197*,2. 7. 24. 198,4. — II 419*,12. 16. 420,28.

Cullavanavaṇṇanā, Vessantara-jātake VI 532,10.

Cullasuka-jātaka (430) III 494—496.

Cullasutasoma-jātaka (525) V 177—192. — IV 119,28*. — Cūlasutasoma-jāt. N 45,30. Cūlasutasoma-samāgama IV 490,24.

Cullasubhaddā, aggamahesī Bodhisattassa V 37,10*. 39*,2. 6. 24. 46,10*. 51,24*.

Cullahaṁsa-jātaka (533) V 333—354. — I 142,19. — III 293,10. — IV 413,4. — V 147 (26). 382,4.

Cullupaṭṭhāka, see: Culladhanuggaha.

Cūla-, Cūḷa-, cfr. Culla-

Cūḷajanaka-jātaka (52). I 268.

Cūḷanāthapiṇḍika, see: Culla-anāthapiṇḍika.

Cūḷani-Brahmadatta, rājā Uttarapañcālanagare Kampillaraṭṭhe VI 391*,7. 11. 392,28. 393*,8. 12. 394*,13. 16. 395,30*. 399,23*. 400,20*. 402,26*. 405,10*. 409*,2. 15. 410,21*. — Cūḷanī VI 411*,17. 23. 24. 27. 415,7*. 416 (2). 14* (27. 32). 420,23*. 424 (1). 426*,3. 6. 428,2*. 433,21* (27). 434,1* (19). 435,4*. 436 (18). 445,9* (30). 448,6*. 450*,21. 29. 30. 454 (32). 461,13*. 463*,14. 16. 22. 464*,1. 23. 466* (2). 4. 22. 467,27*. 470 (29). 471 (11. 26. 35. 36). 472. (7. 11). 474 (30). 478,18*. — Cūḷanīya VI 437,3*. 448,8. 11. 477,29*. — Cūḷaneyya VI 437,24*. — Brahmadatta VI 393*,14. 17. 31. 394*,2. 22. 395*,3. 4. 14. 25. 398 (21). 399,9* (11). *400,16*. 401*,9. 10. 402*,1. 16. 403,9*. 405,14*. 406*,11. 17. 23. 408,4*. 409*,12. 25. 411,18*. 415,10*. 416,9*. 424 (2). 433,23. 434 (9). 15 437,4*. 441*,7. 17. 21. 446*,17. 25.

Cūḷabodhi-tāpasa, (Bodhisatto) VI 257 (29). (cfr. Cullabodhi-).

Cūlasubhaddā, seṭṭhidhītā N 93,2.

Cūḷāmaṇicetiya N 65,5.

Cūḷāmaṇiveṭhana N 65,3.

Cecca, — Cetiya-rājā V 267,15*. 273 (7).

Cetapāmokkhā, — Cetarājāno VI 515,5. (11).

Cetaputta VI 519,17*. 526 (4). 527,6*. 528*.2. 6. 10. 18. 531*.25. 31. 593,28. Ceta VI 527,12. 532,8.

Cetaputtā (Cetaraṭṭhavāsino) VI 517,10.

Cetaraṭṭha VI 514,9. 11*. 18. 516,16. 517. (20). (cfr. Cetiya-raṭṭha).

Cetā, suṇisā Vidhurapaṇḍitassa Anujjāya ca VI 290,18*. (20).

Cetā, Cetiyaraṭṭhavāsino I 256,7*. (11). — VI 516,17. 19. 517,3. 13 (20).

Cetiya-giri, Tambapaṇṇi-dīpe N 7 (28).

Cetiya-jātaka (422) III 454—461. — V 101 (6). 113 (24). 273 (9). — VI 362 (1).

Cetiya-raṭṭha I 253,11*. 256 (11). — III 454,19* (cfr. Ceta-raṭṭha).

Cetiya, Cetiya-rājā (— Devadatto) III 457,28*. 458*,17. 24. 459*,6. 16. 26. 460 (6. 8). 11*. 461,12. — V 273 (7). — Cecca V 267,15*. 273 (7).

Cetiyo (Cetaraṭṭha-itthiyo) VI 514,22.

Ch.

Chakkhattiya-khaṇḍa, Vessantara-jātake VI 587,16.

Chatta, māṇavo brāhmaṇa-putto II 428*,10. 20. 429,2*.

Chatta, putto Kosalarañño III 115,17*. 116*,13. 16. 117,23*. (26). 118 (6). 21.

Chattapāṇi, anāgāmiupāsako I 381,20.

Chattapāṇi, kappako Yasapāṇi-rañño Bārāṇasiyaṁ II 186,22*. 191,26*. 192*,1. 3. 8. 18. 193 (1). 18*. 195,30*. 196,9.

Chaddanta, (— Bodhisatto), nāgarājā: N 45,22. — V 38,26*. mahāgajissaro: V 36,22. vāraṇo: V 36,16. 50 (5). 54, (28).

Chaddanta-jātaka (514) V 36—57.

Chaddanta-daha, Himavante V 37*,1. 12. 38*,11. 13. 23. 39,10*. 45 (11. 14). 56 (20). 415,25.

Chanipāta, III 228—316.

chandakadānaṁ II 45,12.

Channa, amacco Gotama-Buddhassa N 54,6. 62,1. 12. 32. 63,7. 9. 18. 64,20. 24. 65,20—22. 27. — III 187,7. 332,1. — IV 119,18. 282,14. 423,17. 430,7. — V 354,2. 382,5. — VI 593,26.

Channapatha-pañha, Mahāummagga-jātake VI 366,6.

chabbaggiyā bhikkhavo I 191,8. 217,11. 24. 360,24. — II 287,10. — III 27,12. 14. 149,12.

Chabbyāputtā, chabbyāputtanāgarājakulaṁ II 145,20*. (24).

Chambhī, brāhmaṇo VI 470,21* (26. 27). 471, (18).

Chaḷaṅgakumāra, senāpati (— Kuṇāla-sakuṇo (Bodhisatto)) V 425,1. 430 (4. 9—10. 13).

Chavaka-jātaka (309) III 27—30.

J.

Jaṭila, Mahāraṭṭhiyo (— Bodhisatto) N 37,16.

Janaka, rājā (— Bodhisatto) I 268,15. — VI 59*,2. 4. (cfr. Mahājanaka).

Janaka, rājā Bārāṇasiyaṁ III 341,28*. 348,26* (30).

Janapadakalyāṇī, (vadhū Nandassa) N 91,18. — I 393,20. 22. 26. 394 (6. 24. 28). 395,5. — II 92,12. 17. 93,8—10. — III 281,28*. (— Kalyāṇī IV 422bis 11 (?)).

Janapadakalyāṇi-suttaṁ I 393,19. 394,4.

Janasandha, khattiyo, pitā Tissa-Buddhassa N 40,28.

Janasandha, (adj.?) rājā Kurukhetta-vāsī VI 291,11.

Janasandha, rājā Bārāṇasiyaṁ, pitā Ādāsamukhassa (Bodhisattassa) II 297,10*. 298,23*. 299 (1. 20). 300,10*.

Janasandha-kumāra, putto Brahmadattassa, rājā Bārāṇasiyaṁ (— Bodhisatto) IV 176,19*. 177,20. 178 (21). 180,6.

Janasandha-jātaka (468) IV 176—180.

Jambāvatī, caṇḍālī, mātā Sivi-rañño, bhariyā Vāsudeva-Kaṇhassa VI 421,19*. (21).

Jambuka, suka-sakuṇa-putto (— Bodhisatto) V 111,6*. 120*,8. 11. 16 (17). 125*,1. 8. 9. 125,16.

Jambuka, suṇakho III 535,23*.

Jambuka-jātaka (335) III 112—115.

Jambukhāda(ka)-jātaka (var. lect. Jambu-vādaka-, -sākhāda-) (294) II 438—440.

Jambudīpa N 49,5—6. 85,9. — I 166,14. 179,5*. 191,18*. 228,20. 263,15*. 272,20*. 356,25*. 357,8*. 359,21*. 446*,17. 18. — II 21,2*. 22,16*. 49,26*. 81,22*. 112,4*. 119,7*. 156,6*. 170,3. 212,18*. 216,9. 14. 248,22*. 250,20*. 257,15. 258,3*. 291,16*. 296,6*. 321,12. 367*,14. 16. — III 3*,15. 18—19. 32,3*. 129*,5. 10. 158,14*. 159*,11. 16. 21. 414,21*. 485 (17). 515,21*. 516,4*. (28). 526 (14). 538,9*. — IV 40,8*. 82,21*. 83,28*. 95,4*. 101*,3—4. 105,8*. 136,28. 153,9*. 160*,4. 5. 12. (13). 176,25*. 212,23*. 214,14*. 230,28*. 245,22*. 304,18*. 341,19*. 342,4*. 355,8*. 361,6*. 378,9*. 379,5*. 391,12*. 468,19*. — V 14,13*. 20,27*. 59,6*. 65,8*. 127*,17. 24. 130,10*. 133,4*. 135,19*. 162,26*. 226 (14). 231,26*. 282,8*. 283,11*. 285,27*. 295,7*. 301,13*. 304,9*. 312,17. 314*,24. 26. 315*,9. 12. 316,14*. 317,1*. 319 (1). 440,4. 443,18. 457,24*. 464,3*. 471,15*. 472,21*. 473,28*. 474,10*. 475 (19—20). 476,6*. 489 (21). 493,16*. 509,5*. 510,25*. — VI 8,27*. 39,4*. 56,15*. 100 (24). 148 (23). 162,27*. 242,20. (29). 255,30*. 262*,9. 10. 278,16*. 279 (4). 391*,1. 5. 12. 25. 392*,4. 8. 27. 393*,18. 19. 25. 400*,1. 4. 404,10*. 411,4*. 415*,10. 13. 426,5*. 435,24*. 460*,18. 24. 461,5*. 464,18*. (21). 483 (7). 485,2*. 505,1*.

Jambudīpa-samudda III 91 (24).

Jayaddisa, rājā Kampillaraṭṭhe, pitā Alīnasattukumārassa (Bodhisattassa) N 45,22. — V 22*,2. 27. 23,22*. 30*,21. 26.

Jayaddisa-jātaka (513) V 21—36.

Jayampati, putto Okkākassa rañño V 282*,8. 286,26*. 287*,2. 17.

Jayasena, rājā, pitā Siddhattha-Buddhassa N 40,8. — pitā Phussa-Buddhassa N 41,8.

Jarā, luddo IV 88.26*. 89.3*.

Jarāsuttaṁ I 309.8.

Jarudapāna-jātaka (256) II 294—296.

Java, Javana, devaputto VI 239.4. (33). 240 (10).

Javanahaṁsa-jātaka (476) IV 211—218.

Javasakuṇa-jātaka (308) III 25—27.

Jāgara-jātaka (414) III 403—405.

Jātaka, N 1,12. — Jātakass' Atthavaṇṇanā N 1.30. 2.1. — VI 594.2. — Jātakaṭṭhakathā N 62.30.

Jātaveda, = Aggi I 214*.17. 29.(22—24). 494.28*. 495 (4). — II 326.16*. 330.13*. — III 17*.9. — V 452.22. 454 (25). VI 201.31*. 202 (7). 204.12*. 206.20*. 371.12* (22). 528.25. 529.5. 530.28. 578.30.

Jātimanta, brāhmaṇo Vettavatīnadītīre IV 388*.8. 12. 24.

Jātiyāvana, Bhaddiyanagaram nissāya II 331.16.

jānapadittthi aññatarā I 306.27.

Jālaroruva, nirayo V 271 (6. 7).

Jālikumāra (Jāli), putto Vessantara-rañño (Bodhisattassa) N 77,12. — VI 487,1*. 509.24 (26). 29. 513.4. 533.8. 541.22*. 24. 542.5*. 544.21. 545.21. 546*.2. 8. 25. 28. 547.14. 16. 553.24. 556.19 (28). 557.32. 559.9. 12. 15. 17. 23. 25. 27. 561.3. 18. 563.9. 14. 17. 565.7. 570.18. 574.16. 578.5 (12). 579 (7). 581*.14. 17—23. 582.6*. 583.19*. 585.10. 589.2 (7). 593.28.

Jitamitta, aggasāvako Nārada-Buddhassa N 37.7.

Jina-cakkaṁ, IV 100.19.

Jina-sāsanaṁ, I 229.32.

Jinā pubbakā I 214.11*.

Jīvaka (purisanāma) I 402*.25—27. 403*.14. 20.

Jīvaka Komārabhacca, (vejjo) I 116.27. 117.18. 118.12—13. 15—16. 24. 119.3—5. 508.27—28. 30. 509.8. 15—17. 25. — IV 430.17. — V 262.17. 21. 333.14.

Jīvakambavana, Rājagahaṁ nissāya I 114.9. 509.26. — V 261.32. 262.23.

jīvitapariccāgo Ānandassa IV 413,8. 423,28. — V 333,8. 354,6.

Juṇha, thero Kosalajanapade I 165,2. 4. 166,8.

Juṇha(kumāra), putto Bārāṇasi-rañño, Bārāṇasi-rājā (= Bodhisatto) IV 96*,18. 28. 97*,1. 9 (12). 99 (23).

Juṇha-jātaka (456) IV 95—100. — II 426,28.

Jūjaka, brāhmaṇo Kāliṅgaraṭṭhe Dunniviṭṭhabrāhmaṇagāmavāsī (= Devadatto) VI 521,8*. 21. 523*,5. 16. 20. 531,25*. 532 (18). 33*. 533,14*. 540,16*. 541,15*. 543*,4. 30. 544,26*. 545*,7. 14. 22. 548,3*. 551,10*. 553,10*. 554,8*. 568,21*. 573*,23. 27. 574*,2. 25. 575,7*. 581,9*. 593,26.

Jūjaka-khaṇḍa, Vessantara-jātake VI 528,17.

Jeṭṭhamūla-māsa V 412,18.

Jeta-rājakumāra II 216,19. (cfr. Jetavana-dvārakoṭṭhaka).

Jetavana N 77,4. 92,21. 31. — I 95,11. 96,10. 106,16. 123,11. 126,16. 133,22. 136,10. 145,15. 147,29—30. 153,22. 156,8. 15. 159,14. 164,27. 169,2. 175,2. 178,13. 181,5. 182,9. 188,29. 191,2. 193,21. 25. 196,17. 198,9. 13. 18. 206,16. 210,14. 215,14. 220,15. 32. 221,1. 4. 12. 14. 19. 224,14. 22. 226,21. 25. 234,18. 241,27. 244,26. 248,12. 251,20. 252,4. 20. 257,2. 259,4. 261,25. 268,7. 18. 269,11. 270,14. 272,17. 283,7. 284,12. 285,8. 289,19. 295,19. 299,13. 301,14. 302,28. 306,26. 310,5. 311,22. 316,3. 7. 317,5. 327,25. 329,28. 332,25. 334,27. 345,18. 347,4. 348,15. 19. 349,8. 354,16. 25. 355,24. 363,6. 364,2. 366,8. 10. 367,28. *369,6. 370,2. 3. 375,17. 377,14. 379,6. 381,2. 32. 387,22. 391,20. 401,27. 404,2. 405,27. 411,8. 25. 412,24. 413,24. 414,22. 416,8. 418,2. 426,21. 27. 428,12. 430,9. 431,16. 432,25. 435,19. 437,2. 441,3. 446,24. 449,19. 451,18. 455,5. 458,14. 460,2. 461,24. 463,2. 13. 469,14. 471,10. 18. 473,2. 474,2. 28. 477,5. 480,12. 484,11. 493,10. 495,17. 497,2. 499,8. 501,2. 5. 9. — II 1,4. 9,11. 12,7. 15,8. 17,24. 23,26. 30,9. 11. 15. 33,2. 41,3. 43,10. 45,11. 50,11. 52,20. 54,9. 58,22. 60,28. 63,7. 11. 65,25. 68,2. 72,6. 74,2. 6. 12.

76,14. 79,8. 17. 82,2. 85,6. 86,26. 92,5. 93,18. 95,24. 99,18. 26.
106,23. 108,9. 109,17. 111,2. 4. 113,18. 115,17. 125,11. 14.
127,11. 132,16. 134,18. 137,6. 139,4. 142,2. 9. 144,20. 148,21.
151,2. 155,11. 158,17. 160,24. 164,16. 167,14. 169,21. 173,12.
175,18. 178,5. 179,16. 181,2. 184,7. 196,14. 202,24. 203,10.
206,28. 208,2. 209,26. 28. 212,12. 216,8. 13. 19. 25. 219,2. 4.
224,19. 227,8. 229,6. 231,14. 233,22. 236,2. 6. 239,21. 246,8.
257,13. 17. 263,17. 265,2. 266,23. 268,28. 271,4. 277,7.
286,9. 291,25. 294,10. 297,2. 310,21. 314,18. 318,22. 321,8.
14. 323,18. 328,2. 335,6. 337,10. 338,18. 341,2. 345,6.
347,5. 349,10. 351,16. 20. 356,2. 5. 359,2. 361,15. 365,2. 24.
385,2. 387,9. 18. 390,26. 392,10. 400,6. 403,12. 409,28.
415,11. 416,15. 17. 419,2. 420,26. 423,15. 426,26. 429,16.
431,3. 433,2. 436,17. 22. 441,9. 13. 443,2. 444,18. 449,14. —
III 1,4. 8,16. 13,9. 15,28. 18,2. 9. 20,16. 27,11. 30,17. 36,2.
7. 9. 10. 12. 39,7. 43,16. 44,28. 48,18. 20. 51,10. 56,8. 58,25.
66,19. 27. 71,3. 74,18. 19. 22. 82,2. 84,8. 86,17. 90,16. 92,19.
102,10. 104,17. 106,20. 26. 110,2. 115,10. 118,25. 26. 126,5.
128,30. 134,13. 137,2. 4. 139,20. 141,21. 145,21. 147,18.
149,10. 153,4. 155,8. 162,2. 168,10. 170,18. 182,7. 187,10.
191,3. 193,21. 194,7. 196,2. 197,22. 200,2. 204,2. 206,13.
208,5. 211,3. 5. 213,8. 219,17. 224,22. 226,4. 232,20. 238,2.
246,10. 248,17. 255,2. 257,2. 265,2. 267,14. 270,7. 275,3.
281,13. 286,9. 299,2. 18. 303,10. 307,24. 25. 308,4. 312,12.
314,16. 317,4. 324,16. 330,11. 332,4. 25. 336,22. 341,20.
355,21. 358,20. 359,2. 363,15. 21. 369,27. 375,17. 25. 388,17.
391,9. 397,5. 400,5. 15. 403,2. 19. 405,10. 423,4. 428,9.
435,2. 439,6. 444,11. 454,6. 461,15. 469,25. 474,21. 479,2.
483,8. 490,18. 494,21. 496,24. 501,21. 502,5. 9. 514,19. 520,2.
524,12. 527,2. 532,2. — IV 1,3. 15,2. 22,5. 27,25. 43,21.
59,5. 62,14. 70,2. 72,18. 79,4. 90,3. 95,11. 100,14. 104,10.
113,20. 123,25. 130,22. 131,5. 7. 136,22. 144,6. 148,12.
152,23. 158,2. 167,2. 176,2. 180,9. 187,2. 27. 28. 188,2. 4. 6

189,5. 196,28. 200,3. 7. 211,24. 219,2. 224,8. 228,5. 8. 10. 24. 236,20. 242,27. 244,20. 263,7. 276,3. 288,25. 297,21. 304,27. 314,20. 316,1. 4. 325,16. 332,26. 342,25. 350,19. 351,7. 355,2. 360,23. 369,2. 8. 375,3. 5. 21. 390,5. 401,11. 437,4. 444,7. 454,6. 468,25. 473,15. 491,8. — V 1,3. 11,5. 14. 21,2. 36,9. 57,5. 75,6. 88,6. 98,22. 109,3. 125,21. 152,2. 161,21. 177,10. 193,8. 209,21. 227,21. 247,3. 278,3. 312,15. 382,9. 456,19. — VI 1,3. 30,15. 68,25. 29. 69,22. 24. 70,5. 9. 157,26. 255,14. 329,20. — Jetavana-koṭṭhaka II 142,8. — Jetavana-dvārakoṭṭhaka I 329,26. 348,14. 17. 30. — II 216,20 (Jeta-rājakumārena kārito). 239,23. 286,30. 321,11. — III 2,9. — Jetavana-dvāra IV 158,15. 228,23. 26. 27. — V 262,3. — Jetavana-piṭṭhi I 493,18. — II 170,10. 16. — piṭṭha II 170,5. — Jetavana-pokkharaṇī, I 329,25. 330,4—6. 10. 13. 21. 331,8*. — IV 158,16. — Jetavana-magga II 416,7. — Jetavana-vihāra I 93,10. 14. 230,24. 348,10. — II 46,1. 403,24. — -mahāvihāra I 95,7. — IV 228,21. 23. — -piṭṭhivihāra II 203,9. 341,12. — VI 70,4.

Jetuttara, nagaraṁ Siviraṭṭhe VI 480,7*. 484,14*. 486,14*. 487*,15. 21. 489 (17). 504 (8). 514*,1. 6. 10. (27). 541 (26). 545,23*. 561,7. 566,16*. 572 (11). 573 (15). 574,4*. 580,23*. 592*,5. 9. 25.

Jotipāla-(kumāra), māṇavo purohitaputto (— Sarabhaṅgasatthā — Bodhisatto) N 43,16. — III 463,4*. — V 127,29*. 128*,7. 19. 27. 129*,1. 5. 8. 16. 26. 130,8*. 131,11*. 132,5*. (cfr. Sarabhaṅga). Jotipāla-vatthu VI 14 (29).

Jotirasa, tāpaso Kañcanapabbate, kulūpako Vessavaṇassa II 399,10*.

Jh.

Jhānasodhana-jātaka (134) I 473.

Ñ.

ñātatthacariyā I 175,2. 484,12. — III 369,28. — IV 144,6.
ñātakānaṁ kalaho IV 207,22. (cfr. V 412,15).

T.

Takka-jātaka (63) I 295—299. Takkāriya-jātaka — Takka-jātaka V 446 (16).
Takka-paṇḍita, isi (= Bodhisatto) I 296,26*. 297*,8. 12. 298*,1. 11. 15. 16. 17. 299,10.
Takkaru-jātaka, see: Kakkāru-jāt.
Takkaḷa-jātaka (446) IV 43—50.
Takkasilā, nagaraṁ Gandhāra-raṭṭhe I 191,11*. 259,11*. 273*,5. 9. 285*,9. 18. 22. 286*,3. 11. 317,27*. 356*,13. 16. 375,1. 395,24*. 396*,15. 397*,24. 27. 402,14*. 406,9*. 431,21*. 447,10*. 463,24*. 470*,2. 8. 471,7. 505,27*. 510,14*. — II 2,6*. 39,7*. 47*,11. 12. 16. 58,1*. 68,9*. 72,10*. 85,19*. 87,8*. 100,10*. 137,27*. 165,6*. 173,21*. 200,9*. 217*,1. 2. 11. 218 (3. 4). 219,13*. 272,6*. 277,25*. 278,2*. 282,6*. 314,26*. 319,4*. 323,22*. 349,25*. 359,8*. 366,25*. 400,27*. 411,11*. 427,3*. — III 31,8*. 39,16*. 64,11*. 79,3*. 93,11*. 115*,18. 19. 119,20*. 122,19*. 126,2. 143,1*. 147,23*. 149,22*. 158,13*. 159*,17. 22. 24. 168,23*. 171,11*. 194,16*. 215,23*. 219,20*. 221,4*. 228,22*. 235*,7. 8. 238,11*. 249,1*. 308,11*. 337,9*. 341,25*. 352,6*. 377,24*. 381 (24). 392,1*. 400,21*. 403,25*. 407,24*. 415,10*. 428,22*. 463,5*. 497,10*. — IV 7,14*. 22,18*. 38,28*. 50,27*. 52,2*. 55,18*. 74,3*. 96,18*. 98,14*. 171,6*. 176,20*. 200,14*. 203,8*. 224,19*. 237,8*. 298,15*. 305,18*. 315,30*. 316,12*. 391,9*. 401,26*. 456,29*. — V 23,1*. 26,23*. 127,31*. 161,27*. 177,17*. 210,22*. 227,27*. 247,12*. 263,7*. 426 (12). 457,7*. 476,20*. 479 (22). — VI 347,7*.

Takkasilâcariya, (— Bodhisatto) II 279,23*.

Takkasila-jâtaka (— Telapatta-jât. 96) I 470,1*.

Takkasila-râja, (— Bodhisatto) I 399,25*. II 218,9).

Takkârika-jâtaka (— Takkâriya-jât.) III 102,11.

Takkâriya-mâṇava, T-paṇḍita, (— Bodhisatto) IV 245,29*. 247*,11. 255,11. Takkâriyâ (!) IV 247,24*. 248 (4).

Takkâriya-jâtaka (481) IV 242—255. — I 431,16. II 356,4. — (Takkâriyajâtaka — Takka-jâtaka V 446 (19).)

Tagarasikhin, paccekabuddho III 299,28. 300,10.

Tacasâra-jâtaka (368) III 204—206.

Tacchasûkara-jâtaka (492) IV 342—350.

Taṇḍulanâli-jâtaka (5) I 123—126.

Taṇhaṁkara-Buddha N 44,8.

Taṇhâ, dhîtâ Mârassa N 78,29. — I 469,17.

Tapana-niraya (var. lect. Tâpana), V 266,14*. 267,25*. 270,2*. 271 (25—28). 275, (34—35).

Tapassu, vâṇijo N 80,16.

Tapodârâma, Râjagahaṁ nissâya II 56,23.

Tamba, râjâ Bârâṇasiyaṁ III 187*,17. 21. 189,15* (19. 20). 190,7* (15).

Tambapaṇṇi-dîpa, (— Sîhaladîpa), N 85,11. — II 127,23*. 129,10*. — IV 490,20.

Tambapaṇṇi-sara II 129,11*.

Tayodhamma-jâtaka (58) I 280—283.

Talatâ-devî, (mâtâ Cûḷani-Brahmadattassa Pañcâla-rañño) VI 398 (9). 434,27*. 435,19*. 471 (8). 472 (9—11). 474 (10). 478,15*.

Tâpana-niraya, see: Tapana.

Tâlavana (Ck Nâḷapana?), I 392,4*.

Tâvatiṁsa-bhavana N 54,13. 16. 65,5. 26. — I 202*,7. 9. — II 37,20*. 89,16*. 91 (10). 92,29. 93,1. 312,16*. — III 87*,2. 5. 249,3*. 252,11*. — IV 63,4*. 69,19*. 105,21*. 111 (11). 113,14*. 170,16*. 180,24. 236,14*. 265,10. 318,24*. 360,16*. 445,26. 475*,5. 7. — V 15 (14). 158 (32). 168 (16). 280,2*.

281,8*. 392,24*. 400 (81). — VI 2,7*. 97,7*. 125,30*. 132,3. 238,24. 239 (14. 34. 37). 256,18*. 278,25* (Tāvatiṁsa). 331*3. 4. Tāvatiṁsa-devaloka I 202,14*. — II 93,20. 26. 311,4. 312,9*. — III 87,13*. 250,21*. — V 19 (24). — VI 484,18*. — Tāvatiṁsa-nagara VI 279 (18). — Tāvatiṁsā devā I 202,8*. — V 153,9. — VI 105,5. 568,10. — Tāvatiṁsā VI 279,9*. — Tāvatiṁsā accharā VI 590,16.

Timsanipāta (XVI) V 1—108.

Tikanipāta II 271—451. — IV 473 (8). (— II 330).

Tikūṭa, nadī (pabbato?) IV 438,28*. 439 (4).

Tikhiṇamanti-kumāra, bhātā Cūḷanī-Brahmadattassa VI 469 (26). 473,28*. 474,8* (6. 22).

Tinduka-jātaka (177) II 76—79.

Tittira-jātaka a) (37) I 217—220. — b) (117) I 431—432. — c) (319) III 64—66. — d) (438) III 536—543.

Tittiriya-brahmacariyaṁ I 219,18.

Tittha-jātaka (25) I 182—185.

titthanāviko III 228,5.

titthiyasāvakā pañcasatā, Anāthapiṇḍika-seṭṭhissa sahāyakā I 95,8.

titthiyā hatalābhasakkārā III 126,6. (cfr. II 415,15. IV 187,5.)

Titthiyārāma II 415,22. 416,7. — IV 187,17. 188,3.

Tidasapura, (Tāvatiṁsabhavane) III 413 (14). — VI 168,25*.

Tidasā, (devā Tāvatiṁsabhavane) III 357,16*.

Tidiva, (— Tāvatiṁsabhavana) IV 322,23*.

Tipallatthamiga-jātaka (16) I 160—164. — III 64,4.

Timanda, maccho V 462,16*.

Timirapiṅgala, maccho V 462,18*.

Timbaru-tittha V 388,25*. 389 (1).

Tiyaggala, daho Himavante V 415,26.

Tiracchāna, (Tiracchāna-yoni) VI 395,27.

Tirīṭavaccha, brāhmaṇaputto tāpaso (— Bodhisatto) II 314,23*. 315,5*. 316,24*. 317 (8). 19*.

Tiriṭavaccha, seṭṭhi Ariṭṭhapuranagare, pitā Ummadantiyā V 210,25*. 211,3*. Tiriṭi V 215,19*.

Tiriṭavaccha-jātaka (259) II 314—318.

Tiriṭi, see: Tiriṭavaccha, seṭṭhi.

Tilamuṭṭhi-jātaka (252) II 277—282.

Tissa, aggasāvako Dīpaṁkara-Buddhassa N 29,21. — aggasāvako Vipassi-Buddhassa N 41,16.

Tissa, amacco IV 11 (24).

Tissa-kumāra, seṭṭhi-putto Rājagahe, — Cullapiṇḍapātika-tissa-thero, I 156,10.

Tissa-Buddha N 40,14. 15. 28. 44,9.

Tissa, thero, — Dhanuggaha-tissa-thero, II 404,3.

Tissa, thero, — Losaka-tissa-thero, I 236,9. 11.

Tissā, aggasāvikā Koṇḍañña-Buddhassa N 30,14.

Tītimīti, mahāmaccho V 462,17*.

Tīlavāhā, see: Telavāhā.

Tuṇḍila, bhātā Kāliyā gaṇikāya IV 248*,21. 26. 249*,4. 16. 24.

Tuṇḍila, sūkaro (— Cullatuṇḍila) III 289,6*. 291 (21. 34). 292 (7).

Tuṇḍila-jātaka (388) III 286—293.

Tudu Brahmā IV 244,31. 245,3.

Tusita-devatā (pl.) N 49,32.

Tusita-pura N 2,6. 47,18. 21. 49,32. 52,4. 77,1. — VI 573 (9) 593 (23). 594,8.

Tusita-bhavana N 2,7. 47,17. 48,18. — VI 573 (9). Tusitā (devā) VI 279,9*.

Tepiṭakaṁ Buddhavacanaṁ IV 37,7. — Tepiṭaka-abhidhammika-vinayadharā IV 219,12. (cfr. Piṭaka-).

Tebhātika-jaṭilā (Uruvelāyaṁ) N 82,31. 86,28.

Temiya-kumāra (— Mūgapakkhapaṇḍita), putto Kāsirañño (— Bodhisatto) VI 3,19*. 4,14*. 5,25*. 6,8*. 8*.11.24. 10*,17. 21. 11,4*. 12,12*. 19 (8. 32). 20,28*. 21,2*. 22,31. 23,2.

Temiya-jātaka — Mūgapakkha-jātaka (538).

Terasa-nipāta (XIII) IV 200—275. — I 193,23. 196,18. 416,10. 431,16. — II 356,3. — III 524,13.

Telapatta-jātaka (96) I 393—401. — Takkasila-jāt. I 470,1*.

Telavāhā, nadī Serivaraṭṭhe (var. lect. Kelavāhā, Tīlavāhā) I 111,7*.

Telovāda-jātaka (246) II 262—263.

Tesakuṇa-jātaka (521) V 109—125. — I 177,29*. — II 1,5. — III 110,8. 317,5. — VI 94 (30).

Th.

Thuṇa, nagaraṁ, see: Thūṇa.

thullakumārika-palobhanaṁ I 196,18. 416,9. — II 419,3. — III 147,19. 524,18. — IV 219,2.

Thullanandā, bhikkhunī I 474,27. 475,2. 9. 10. 476,20. 23. 477,1.

Thusa-jātaka (338) III 121—126. — III 215,16.

Thūṇa, nagaraṁ (var. lect. Thuṇa) VI 62,23*. 65,30. — brāhmaṇagāmo Majjhimadese N 49,18.

therassa pañhavyākaraṇaṁ I 474,3.

D.

Dakarakkhasa-jātaka (517) V 75,1-4.

Dakarakkhasa-pañha, Ummaggajātake VI 469*,11. 21. 477,26*. 478,8*.

Dakkhiṇāgiri-janapada I 224,18. — II 345,4. 6.

Dakkhiṇāpatha V 133,24*.

Daṇḍakahiraññā-pabbata, Himavantapadese II 33,18*. 36*,2. 11. 18. 38,13*.

Daṇḍakāraññā V 29,1 (Daṇḍakāraññagato Rāmo).

Daṇḍakin, rājā Kumbhavati-nagare III 463,18*. — V 29 (18). 133,27*. 134,4*. 135,25*. 143*,11. 19. 267,7*.

Datta, thero (= Mantidatta) IV 343,12. 16. — (purisanama?) IV 478 (27).

Datta, putto Dhataraṭṭha-nāgarañño = Bhūridatto (Bodhisatto) VI 167,30*. 168,28*.

Daddabha-jātaka (322) III 74—78. — V 414,18.

Daddara, = Mahādaddaro putto Sūradaddara-nāgarañño (Bodhisatto) III 16,24*.

Daddara, pabbato Himavantapadese II 8,19. 20. (23—25) = Rajata-pabbata. 67,12* (14). — III 16,5*.

Daddara-jātaka a) (172) II 65—67. — b) (304) III 15—17. — III 178,2.

Daddara-nāgabhavana, Daddarapabbatapāde Himavantapadese III 16,5*.

Daddara-pura, nagaraṁ Upacarassa rañño pañcamena puttena māpitaṁ III 461,7*.

Dadhimāla, samuddo IV 140,6*. — Dadhimāli IV 140,12*.

Dadhivāhana, rājā Bārāṇasiyaṁ II 104*,17. 29. 105*,5. 21. 106,5*.

Dadhivāhana-jātaka (186) II 101—106.

Dantapura, nagaraṁ Kāliṅgaraṭṭhe II 367*,17. 22. 371,15*. 381,12*. — III 3,3*. 376,12*. 381 (23). — IV 230,6*. 231,28*. 232,2*. 236,14*. — V 144 (24).

Dabba Mallaputta, saṁghassa bhattuddesako I 123,13. 16.

Dabbasena, Kosalarājā III 13*,16. 17. 14*,1. 13 (25). 15,14*. 20.

Dabbhapuppha-jātaka (400) III 332—336.

Damana, V 126,28 (read: Nandopananda-damana).

Damiḷa-raṭṭha IV 238*,6. 13.

Darīmukha, purohitaputto Rājagahanagare, paccekabuddho III 238*,9. 19. 24. 239*,2. 17. 20. 240*,4. 5. 7. 10. 17. 243,10*. 244,15*. 245,17 (18. 19).

Darīmukha-jātaka (378) III 238—246.

Daḷha-vagga II 1—40.
Daḷhadhamma, rājā Bārāṇasiyaṁ III 385,10*. 386,8* (19).
Daḷhadhamma-jātaka (409) III 384—388.
Daḷhadhammasuttanta-desanā IV 211,24.
Dava, see: Deva, devaputto.
Dasaṇṇa-raṭṭha VI 239 (9). — Dasaṇṇaka-raṭṭha III 338 (25). Dasaṇṇā VI 238,17. 239 (9. 20). — Dasaṇṇako (adj.) III 338,21*.
Dasaṇṇaka-jātaka (401) III 336—341.
Dasanipāta IV 1—89. — I 363,8 (— Jāt. 439.) — III 93,8* (— Jāt. 443.) — VI 257,25* (— Jāt. 441.) — VI 379,31* (— Jāt. 452).
Dasabrāhmaṇa-jātaka (495) IV 360—368.
Dasaratha, — Janasandho Bārāṇasi-rājā, II 299,14*. (18. 21).
Dasaratha, mahārājā Bārāṇasiyaṁ IV 124,6*. 125,18*. 126,11*. 130,17. — Dasaratha-rājaputto (Rāmo) VI 558 (22).
Dasaratha-jātaka (461) IV 123—130.
Dasavara-gāthā (Vessantara-jātake) VI 484,4.
daharabhikkhu Sāriputtattherassa saddhivihāriko II 160,26.
daharabhikkhunī V 36,9.
daharabhikkhū dve II 151,8.
Dānakhaṇḍa, (Vessantara-jātake) VI 513,10.
dānajjhāsayo bhikkhu V 382,9.
dānapati Sāvatthivāsī IV 236,21.
dānavato bhikkhu IV 62,14.
Dāmā, aggasāvikā Vessabhu-Buddhassa X 42,18.
Dāyapassa, uyyānaṁ Brahmadatta-kumārassa V 264,8*. 27. 32. 265 (17). 28.
dārako kuṭumbiyaputto Sāvatthiyaṁ III 501,22.
dāvagginibbānaṁ I 212,8.
dāsī Anāthapiṇḍikassa III 435,2.
Diṭṭhamaṅgalikā (?) VI 478,19*.
Diṭṭhamaṅgalikā, Bārāṇasi-seṭṭhino dhītā IV 376*,4. 6. 7. 15.

19. 21. 377*,8. 8. 18. 20. 27. 378*,5. 18. 20. 379,16*. 383,22*. 385,2*. 386,4. — dve Diṭṭhamaṅgalikāyo (?), Ujjeniyaṁ, ekā seṭṭhidhītā ekā purohitadhītā, IV 390,21*.

diṭṭhigatikā, pañca V 246,10. (cfr. I 509,10).

Dibbacakkhu (Dibbacakkhuka), kubakatāpaso IV 445,25*. 446*,1. 16. 448 (16).

Dīghakārāyana, bhāgineyyo Bandhulassa senāpatino Kosalarañño IV 151,21. Kārāyana IV 151,28. 30.

Dīghatālā, bhariyā Goḷakāḷassa VI 337 (18). 338 (6. 15. 16).

Dīghati, Kosalarājā (— Dīghīti. cfr. Vin. I 342) III 487,18.

Dīghapiṭṭhi, duggatamanusso VI 337 (28). 338 (10. 19).

Dīghabhāṇakā (pl.) N 59,31.

Dīghāvu-kumāra, putto Arindama-rañño (Bodhisattassa) V 249,14*. 258*,14. 18. 20. 260*,4. 8. 10.

Dīghāvu-kumāra (var. lect. Dīghayu-kumāra), putto Dīghatissa Kosalarañño (— Bodhisatto) III 211,18*. 212,30*. 213,5. 487,19. 489,14. 490,10.

Dīghāvu-kumāra, putto Mahājanaka-rañño (Bodhisattassa) VI 44,11*. 61 (28). 62,1* (4). 68,21.

Dīghitikosala-jātaka (var. lect. Dīghītikosala) (371) III 211—213.

Dīghīti, see: Dīghati.

Dīpaṁkara-Buddha N 2,5. 10,33. 11,5. 8. 10. 12,3. 18. 13,4. 14. 31. 14,2. 15,11. 30. 16,18. 21. 24. 17,14. 19,11. 26,20. 23. 27,4. 7. 28,16. 25.* 29,1. 12. 14. 20. 22. 25. 30,1. 8. 43,28. 44,4. 14. 17. 23. 47,17. — III 242 (19).

dīpa-vilokanaṁ Buddhassa N 49,11.

Dīpāyana, see: Kaṇha-Dīpāyana.

Dīpi-jātaka (426) III 479—482.

Duka-nipāta II 1—270. — II 314,21 (— Jāt. 157) — II 359,4 (— Jāt. 154).

Dukūla(ka), paṇḍito nesādaputto VI 72*,2. 6. 12. 18. 73*,6. 18. 74,19*. 85,2*. 87*,1. 3. 18. 88 (18).

Dukkhakkhanda, °sutta-pariyāyo II 314 (5). — °ādīni suttāni IV 313 (7). °-pariyāyo IV 480 (17).

Dujīpa (Dujipa), rājā VI 203,2* (4. 5). (cfr. Dudīpa).

Duṭṭhakumāra, putto Brahmadattassa Bārāṇasiraññо (= Devadatto) I 325,5*. — Duṭṭha-rājā I 327,20.

Duṭṭhakumāra, putto Kitavāsa-rañño Bārāṇasiyaṁ II 194 (26). 195 (7).

Duṭṭhakumārī, Bārāṇasi-seṭṭhino dhītā I 295,28*.

Dutiyapalāyi-jātaka (230) II 219—221.

Dutiyamakkaṭa-jātaka, see: Dūbhiyamakkaṭa.

Dudīpa, rājā Bārāṇasiyaṁ VI 99,9* (13). (cfr. Dujīpa).

Duddada-jātaka (var. lect. Dudda-, Dudada-) (180) II 85—86.

Dunniviṭṭha, brāhmaṇagāmo Kāliṅga-raṭṭhe VI 514,3*. 521*,8. 14. 522 (18).

Dubbaca-jātaka (116) I 430—431.

dubbaca-bhikkhu I 159,16. 244,27. 252,27. 283,8. 363,7. 413,25. 430,10. — III 206,14. 255,3. 483,4. — IV 1,8. — dubbacajātiko bhikkhu II 41,4.

Dubbalakaṭṭha-jātaka (105) I 414—416.

Dummedha-jātaka a) (50) I 259—261. — b) (122) I 444—446.

Dummukha, rājā Kampillanagare Uttarapañcālaraṭṭhe III 379,3*. 381,17* (26).

Duyyodhana, putto Magadha-rañño, rājā Magadhānaṁ V 161,26*. 171,31*. — Saṁkhapāla-nāgarājā (Bodhisatto) V 162,28*.

Durājāna-jātaka (64) I 299—301.

Dussalakkhaṇa, brāhmaṇo Rājagahanagare I 373,18*.

dussasahassapaṭilābha-vatthu II 314,20. (cfr. saṭakasahassapaṭilābho Ānandattherassa II 23,27.

Dūta-jātaka a) (260) II 318—321. — b) (478) IV 224—228.

Dūbhiyamakkaṭa-jātaka (var. lect. Dutiyamakkaṭa-) (174) II 70—72.

Dūrenidāna N 2,11—47,18. — N 2,1. 7. — IV 282,18.

Deva, aggasāvako Sujāta-Buddhassa N 38,19.

Deva, devaputto, bhātā Kālakaṇṇiyā III 261,12* (18) (v. l. Davo).

Devagabbhā, dhītā Mahākaṁsa-rañño Asitañjana-nagare IV 79,11*. 80*,2—4. 8. 10. 13. 14. 19. 23. 26. 81*,2—4.

Devatāpañha, Catukkanipāte VI 370,17*.

Devatāpañha-jātaka (350) III 152.

Devatāpucchitapañha, (Ummaggajātake) VI 378,21.

Devadatta I 106,8. 114,5. 140,7. 142,17. 18. 26. 143,5. 7. 147,8. 14. 15. 18. 19. 25. 148,1. 149,5. 153,17. 172,26. 173,4. 5. 7. 10. 11. 174,23. 26. 185,27. 29. 186,2. 5. 6. 8. 15. 17. 19. 20. 22. 26. 28. 29. 31. 32. 210,11. 268,8. 278,13. 14. 280,17. 20. 26*. 283,4. 319,16. 17. 20. 322,20. 22. 27. 28. 323,2. 327,18. 21. 424,24. 425,1. 5. 7. 426,13. 444,3. 4. 11. 13. 446,21. 465,20. 21. 24. 469,11. 482,18. 21. 25. 484,8. 489,2. 9. 490,21. 25. 491,1. 7. 12. 13. 14. 493,14. 506,11. 16. 510,3. 6. 7. — II 38,22. 26. 39,2. 40,27. 70,3—5. 72,1. 8. 99,15. 121,11. 15—17. 125,8. 148,22. 23. 25. 150,23. 152,23. 24. 155,8. 158,19. 20. 160,21. 162,8. 13. 14. 164,12. 186,17. 196,9. 198,15. 17. 25. 197,1. 3. 4. 5. 10. 199,5. 9. 10. 15. 202,17. 19. 206,7. 221,8. 10. 13. 224,16. 239,21. 22. 24. 240,4. 242,16. 21. 243,2. 5. 246,5. 248,6. 7. 10. 16. 257,10. 384,22. 438,16. 19. 20. 440,2. 441,2. — III 25,28. 27,9. 43,12. 86,18. 21. 90,11. 97,13. 18. 100,2. 112,19. 28. 115,8. 134,11. 161,27. 174,6. 7. 177,22. 177,27. 178,10. 182,4. 202,18. 203,27. 298,21. 324,21. 355,24. 356,1*. 358,17. 372,12*. 414,30. 421,13. 454,9. 461,11. 12. 536,23. 537,1. 543,3. 5. — IV 37,4. 5. 12. 43,17. 18. 55,28. 59,1. 2. 100,16. 104,5. 6. 158,12. 18. 30. 159,4. 166,23. 25. 196,18. 200,3. 4. 6. 11. 207,17. 19. 255,16. 21. 23. 263,3. 4. 350,16. 430,12. 18. 21. 436,29. 30. 454,2. 468,21. — V 56,2 (20. 21). 68,1. 2. 74,29. 30. 75,8. 88,1. 2. 261,33. 262,1. 4. 12. 333,4. 7. 17. 334,5. 10. 19. — VI 129,19. 22. 130,1. 23. 26. 29. 131,1. 6. 9. 157,19. 20. 219,25. 236 (23). 255,6. 478,15*. 593,26.

Devadatta-parisā I 153,18. — III 358,17. — IV 104,6. 437,1.

Devadatta-Kokālikā II 438,15. 24.

Devadattassa akataññutā III 25,25. — °assa āghātabandhanaṁ paṭhamaṁ Bodhisatte I 113,10°. — °assa niraye paviṭṭhabhāvo IV 158,2. — °assa paṭhavipavesanaṁ III 355,22. 457,7. — IV 100,14. — V 75,7. — °assa vatthu V 117 (28). — °assa vadhāya parisakkanaṁ I 278,12. 382,26. 489,7. — II 158,10. 186,16. 382,3. — III 133,3. 177,28. 414,29. 536,22. — IV 55,27. — °assa silāpavijjhanaṁ V 67,29. — °assa Gayāsīse Sugatālayadassitabhāvo I 490,34. — °assa Sugatālayo II 38,22. 148,22. 162,8. — °assa Sugatālayakaraṇaṁ III 112,17.

Devadaha-nagara N 52,10—12.

Devadhamma-jātaka (6) I 126—133. — I 206,18.

Devala, aggasāvako Padumuttara-Buddhassa N 37,21.

Devala, (— Kāḷadevalo) III 466,25. 467 (1). — V 151,29. — — Asito Devalo III 466,27.

Devinda, dhammānusāsako Vedeharañño VI 330,5°. 343 (15). 354,7°. 366,21°. 369,12°. 370,7°. 380,26°. 383,20°. 388,2°. 6 (10). 441°,23. 27. 478,18°.

Desaka, nigamo Sumbharaṭṭhe I 393,18 (cfr. Sedaka, Saṁy. Nik. V (Mahāvagga) 45,30. 46,19).

devorahanaṁ IV 263,10.

Doṇa, pokkharaṇī V 388,25°. 389 (1).

Dohaḷakhaṇḍa, Vidhurapaṇḍita-jātake VI 274,30.

Dvādasa-nipāta IV 144—199. — I 133,24; 175,8; 484,13 (— Jāt. 465). — I 259,5 (— Jāt. 469). — I 437,4 (— Jāt. 472). — II 212,14 (— Jāt. 467). — VI 355,21 (— Jāt. 471).

Dvāraka IV 85,8° (10). — Dvāravatī-nagaraṁ.

Dvāravatī, nagaraṁ IV 82,25°. 83,7°. 84,8°. 85,11. — VI 421, (23. 29).

Dvāravatī-rajja IV 83,8°.

Dh.

Dhaja, brāhmaṇo N 56,3.

Dhajaviheṭha-jātaka (391) III 303—307.

Dhaññavatī, nagaraṁ Nārada-Buddhassa N 37,5.

Dhataraṭṭha, mahārājā Cātummahārājika-devaloke III 257,21*. 258,12*. 262,3*.

Dhataraṭṭha, rājā VI 251,14* (27).

Dhataraṭṭha, nāgarājā VI 162*,7. 12. 14. 15. 25. 28. 163*,14. 15. 20. 29. 164*,15. 15. 166 (12. 15. 23. 28). 32*. 167*,15. 23. 28. 171,20*. 186,24*. 195,3*. 196,19*. 200,4*. 219,11*. — Dhataraṭṭhā nāgā VI 219,18*.

Dhataraṭṭha, haṁsarājā (= Bodhisatto) IV 425,2. 6. 16. 426,28*. 428,13*. — V 337,26*. 338,2*. 343,27*. 345,27*. 353,2. 360*,9. 11. 362,4*. 365*,2. 30. 366,2. 5*. 9. 368,1*. 371,11*. 372*,6. 26. 28. 373,2*. 377,5. 379,12*. 382,7. — Dh.-mahissaro V 357*,7. 22. — Dh.-kulaṁ V 345 (19). 355*,20. 26. 357,5*. — Dhataraṭṭhā (pl.) V 340,14*. 342 (13). 343,17*. 345,11* (18). 346,7. 20. 347 (16). 353,23 (25). 382,3.

Dhanañjaya, rājā Bārāṇasiyaṁ III 97,28*. 98*,9. 16 (18).

Dhanañjaya, rājā Kururaṭṭhe Indapattanagare (pitā Bodhisattassa) II 366,28*.

Dhanañjaya, Koravya-rājā (Korabya-rājā) Indapattanagare putto Dhanañjayassa (= Bodhisatto) II 368,11*. 371,18*. — N 45,13.

Dhanañjaya, Yudhiṭṭhilagotto, Koravya-rājā Indapattanagare III 400*,19. 24. — V 57,7* (Dh-korabya). 59 (26). 67,24. — VI 255,27* (Dh-korabba). 256*,21. 25. 258,29*. 259,15*. 261,28*. 262,8*. 268,5*. 318,3*. 329,17* (cfr. Yudhiṭṭhila).

Dhanañjaya, seṭṭhi, pitā Visākhāya ca Sujātāya ca II 347,6

Dhanapāla(ka), hatthi (Rājagahe) = Nālāgiri, N 66,3. — III 293,12. — V 337,1—2. — Dhanapāla-gajjito (?) III 293,9. — Dhanapāla-damanaṁ I 142,19. — IV 413,4.

Dhanapālī (purisanāma) I 402,31*. 403*,3. 4. 14. 20.

Dhanavatī, brāhmaṇī, mātā Kassapa-Buddhassa N 43,22.

Dhanuggaha, Bārāṇasi-brāhmaṇo III 220*,4. 12. 17. 20. 221,2*. 224,18. — Culladhanuggaha-paṇḍito III 219*,25. 30.

Dhanuggaha-tissa, thero II 403,13. 28. 404,1. 9. 23. 26. 409,25. — IV 343,9. 11. 27. 31. 350,14. 16. — Tisso II 404,3.

dhanuggaha-payojanaṁ III 293,9. 536,26 (cfr. Jāt. 542).

Dhanusekha, bhattakāraka-putto, sahāyo Cūlanissa VI 469 (26). 471 (11). 475,3* (10). Dhanusekhavā 475,5* (10).

dhamma N 1,3. 80,31. — II 147,3*. — dhammānussati-kammaṭṭhānaṁ I 97,13

Dhamma, devaputto kāmāvacaraloke (— Bodhisatto) IV 100*,22. 24. 101*,7. 9. 15. 22. 23. 102*,6. 9 (17). 103,23 (29). 104 (2). 7.

Dhamma-jātaka (457) IV 100—104.

Dhammaka, pabbato Himavantassa avidūre N 6,11. 24. 7 (5. 9).

Dhammagutta, thero Tambapaṇṇidīpe IV 490,20.

Dhammacakkappavattana-sutta N 82,10.

Dhammacetiya-sutta IV 151,29.

Dhammadassi-Buddha N 38,27. 39,21. 30. 40,12. 44,8.

Dhammadinnā, aggasāvikā Piyadassi-Buddhassa N 39,5.

Dhammadinnā, (bhikkhunī) VI 481,16*.

Dhammaddhaja, purohito Yasapāṇirañño Bārāṇasiyaṁ II 186,21*. 187*,10. 19. 190,2*. 196,9.

Dhammaddhaja-jātaka a) (220) II 186—196. — b) (384) III 267—270.

Dhammantari, vejjo IV 496,7*. 498 (32).

Dhammapada N 79,31. — I 349,16. — II 441,28. — III 73,3. 333,8.

Dhammapāla, brāhmaṇo (pitā Bodhisattassa) IV 50,22. — Mahā-Dhammapāla IV 50,15. 52,3*.

Dhammapāla, Dhammapāla-kumāro, putto Dhammapāla-brāhmaṇassa (— Bodhisatto) IV 50,25*. 51*,3. 15. 19. 24. 52*,7. 12. 55,3*. 28.

Dhammapâla, Dhammapâla-kumâra, putto Mahâpatâpassa rañño Bârâṇasiyaṁ (= Bodhisatto) III 178,16-21. 179*,3. 11. 17 (22). 180*,8. 10. 181,13*. 182,4.

Dhammapâla, — Vidhurapaṇḍito (Bodhisatto) VI 289,30*. 291,2 (20).

Dhammapâla-kumâra, putto Vidhurapaṇḍitassa VI 290,25*. 300,18*.

Dhammapâla-kula IV 50,21*.

Dhammapâla-gâma, Kâsiraṭṭhe IV 50,20*.

Dhammapâla-jâtaka N 90,17. (cfr. Culla-dhammapâla-jâtaka (358), Mahâdhammapâlajât. (447).)

Dhammasena, aggasâvako Maṅgala-Buddhassa N 34,8.

Dhammasena, aggasâvako Phussa-Buddhassa N 41,4.

dhammasenâpati, see: Sâriputta.

Dhammâ, dhitâ Kikissa rañño (Kassapa-buddha-kâle) VI 481,18*.

Dhammika, sigâlo I 460,14*.

Dhâtar, devarâjâ VI 201,24*. 202 (1).

Dhâtaraṭṭhâ, nâgâ VI 219,18* (cfr. Dhataraṭṭha-).

Dhûmakâri, brâhmaṇo III 401*,18. 26. 402,6*. 29.

Dhûmakâri-jâtaka (413) III 400—402.

Dhûma-roruva, nirayo V 271 (6. 7. 9).

Dhonasâkha-jâtaka (v. l. Venasâra-, Venasâ-) (353) III 157—161.

N.

Nakula, Paṇḍurâjaputto V 424,20. 426 (11).

Nakula-jâtaka (165) II 52—54.

Nakulâ, aggasâvikâ Sobhita-Buddhassa N 35,21.

Nakkhatta-jâtaka (49) I 257—259.

Nagara, puraṁ V 310,19 (29-30).

Nagara-khaṇḍa, Bhûridatta-jâtake VI 167,27.

Nagarapavesana-khaṇḍa, Bhūridatta-jātake VI 197,8.
Naggaji, rājā Takkasilanagare Gandhāraraṭṭhe III 377,24*. 381,16* (25).
Naṅgalīsa jātaka (123) I 446—449.
Naṅguṭṭha-jātaka (144) I 493—495. — II 43,11.
Nacca-jātaka (32) I 206—208.
Naṭakuvera, gandhabbo III 91,5*. 92,1* (16). — V 424,27.
Naṭaṁdaḷha-vagga II 139—164.
Nanda, kaniṭṭhabhātiko Buddhassa N 91,10. 17. — II 92,7. 9. 15. 16. 18. 20. 24. 29. 93,1 6. 7. 11. 15. 20. 28. 94,6. 12. 95,21. — IV 224,10 (Nando kulaputto). — Nandakumāro II 92,10. Nandatthero II 92,6. 93,25. 94,9. — V 449 (26). — Nandapaṇḍito II 381,24.
Nanda, dāso I 225*,5. 7. 12. 16. 20. 27. 28 226,12*. 18. — Nandako I 226,1*.
Nanda, brāhmaṇo Takkasila-vāsī V 23,1*. 24,11*. 25,21*. — 476,20*. 486 (4). 493,29*. 511,21.
Nanda, Nandakumāra, brāhmaṇaputto tāpaso, bhātā Bodhisattassa V 312,20*. 313*,3. 21. 314*,3. 5. 9. 11. 315,18*. 316*,1. 5. 19. 24. 25. 318,10*. 319,3* (28. 26). 320,11*. 321*,27. 30. 322,23. 324*,6-9 (15—17). 19. 326*,1 (22). 24. 327*,6. 9. 19. 24. 328*,2 (10). 18. 21. 23. 26—29. 329*,1—4 (7—11). 13. 26. 332,19*. 22.
Nanda-jātaka (39) I 224—26.
Nandakovada II 392,16.
Nandagopā, paricārikā Devagabbhāya IV 79,19*. 80*,5. 7. 12. 16. 24. 26. 27. 81,3*.
Nandana-pokkharaṇī, Tāvatiṁsabhavane II 189,13*. — Nandanavana-pokkharaṇī VI 333,18* (cfr. Nandā-p.).
Nandana-vana, Tāvatiṁsabhavane N 49,32 (Tusitapure). 49,33 (sabbadevalokesu). — II 188,21*. — III 494,13. 495,26. — V 153,29*. 154,9*. 158,9 (31 32). 190 (12). 392,25*. 453,31. — VI 132,1*. 144,18 (20). 147,14*. 238,23. 239,3. 240 (9).

278*,23. 28. 333,20*. 395,2*. 449,9*. 481,28*. 529,31. 530,8. 531 (8). 534,13. 590,14 (31).

Nandamûla(ka)pabbhâra, Uttara-Himavante II 195 (9). — III 240*,1. 16. 245,26*. 304,19*. 377*,15. 23. 379,18*. 407,13*. 433,19*. 439,12*. 471,4*. 472,6*. — IV 114*,17. 23. 115*,1. 17. 27. 116,7*. 342,9*. 367,20*. 368,2*. 370,16*. — V 248,28*.

Nandâ, aggasâvikâ Dîpaṁkara-Buddhassa N 29,23.

Nandâ, itthî gehe Bodhisattassa I 201*,2. 26. — pâdaparicârikâ Sakkassa I 204,29*.

Nandâ, tisso dhîtaro Bodhisattassa I 475,20*.

Nandâ, dhîtâ Candakumârassa (Bodhisattassa) VI 134,27*.

Nandâ-devî, aggamahesî Cûḷani-Brahmadattassa Pañcâla-rañño VI 434,27*. 435,19*. 445*,11. 12 (28. 32). 453,27*. 454*,6. 14. 455,18*. 456,12*. 457*,24. 25 (27—29). 458,*1. 6. 462,24*. 466*,10. 14. 467*,6. 26. 469 (25). 473 (12. 20). 475 (26).

Nandâ-pokkharaṇî, Tâvatiṁsabhavane I 204,31*. 205,5*. — VI 132,2*. 232 (14). 531 (8) (cfr. Nandana-p.).

Nandiya, vânaro (— Bodhisatto) II 199,18*. — Mahânandiko II 202,21.

Nandiya, migo (— Bodhisatto) III 270,16*. 271*,1. 5. 17. 25. 272*,6 (9). 12.

Nandiyamiga-jâtaka (385) III 270—274

Nandivisâla, go (— Bodhisatto) I 191,14*. 192*,3. 10. 21. 23. 28. 193 (13). 18.

Nandivisâla-jâtaka (28) I 191—193. — I 374,31.

Nandisena, amacco Assaka-rañño III 3*,17. 24. 4 (2). 10*. 5*,7. 17. 6*,7. 19. 8,7. 13*.

Nandopananda, (nâgarâjâ) V 126,22 (Nandopananda-damanaṁ).

Namuci, Kilesamâro V 453,17. 455 (11) (cfr. Kilesamâra).

Nammadâ, nadî II 344,1* (3). — IV 392,18*. 397,6* (30).

Naradeva, yakkho VI 383,13*. 387,24* (28).

Naḷakapāna, gāmo Kosalesu I 170,3. — Naḷapāna-pokkharaṇī I 170,3.

Naḷakāra, devaputto IV 318,12*. 323,2*.

Naḷapāna-jātaka (20) I 170—172.

Nalamāla, samuddo IV 140,27*. — Nalamālī IV 141*,6. 13.

Naḷini-jātaka, see: Naḷinikā-jāt.

Naḷinikā, Kāsirājadhītā V 194*,14. 20. 195 (3). 18*. 198,25*. 199,20*. 209,18. — Naḷiniyā V 194,30*.

Naḷinikā-jātaka (526) V 193—209. — Naḷini-jāt. V 209,19. 449 (25).

Naḷinī, rājadhānī Vessavaṇassa VI 313,9* (19) (Naḷiññaṁ — Naḷiniyaṁ).

Navanipāta III 483—543. — I 241,28: II 318,24 (— Jāt. 395 & 434). — I 430,11: II 41,5; IV 1,4 (— Jāt. 427).

nahāpitaputto Vesāli-vāsiko II 5,12.

Nāgadīpa II 128,16*. — III 187,20* (— Serumadīpa). 118*,5. 26. — IV 238,9*.

Nāgabhavana VI 256*,14. 17. 24. 257,5*.

Nāgamuṇḍā, dāsī, mātā Vāsabhakhattiyāya I 133,25. — IV 145,8.

Nāgarukkha, bodhi Maṅgala-Buddhassa N 34,9. — b. Sumanassa N 34,28. — b. Revatassa N 35,10. — b. Sobhitassa N 35,22.

Nāgasamāla, thero IV 95,13.

Nāgasamālā, aggasāvikā Sujāta-Buddhassa N 38,20.

Nāgā, aggasāvikā Sujāta-Buddhassa N 38,20.

Nāgita, Bhagavato anibaddhaupaṭṭhāko IV 95,14.

nāṭakitthiyo N 61,14—28.

Nāthaputta-nigaṇṭha, diṭṭhigatiko I 509,14. — Nigaṇṭha-Nāthaputto II 262,13. 15. 263,14. — III 128,17. — V 246,12.

Nānacchanda-jātaka (289) II 426—29.

Nāmasiddhi-jātaka (97) I 401—403.

nāmasiddhiko bhikkhu I 401,22.

Nārada, amacco Bārāṇasirañño III 143*,24. 28. 144*,3. 16. 23. 145,15*. 18. 362 (21. 23. 28).

Nārada, isi Majjhimapadese Arañjaragirimhi, kaniṭṭho Kāḷadevalassa III 463*,20. 26. 464*,8. 11. 16 (18). 23. 465* (3. 7). 11. 12 (18). 466 (5. 15. 22). 25. 467,3*. 469,10. — jeṭṭhantevāsiko Sarabhaṅgassa V 133,11*. 134,2*.

Nārada, upaṭṭhāko Sujāta-Buddhassa N 38,19.

Nārada, tāpasakumāro, putto Kassapassa (Bodhisattassa) IV 222*,21. 23. 25. 27. 29. 223,2*. (cfr. Cullatāpasa).

Nārada, brāhmaṇatāpaso (devabrāhmaṇo) V 392,24*. 393,13. 18. 394*,8. 10. 13. 394,25. 395,12*. 412,11. — pañcabhiññātāpaso V 424,6*. — devabrāhmaṇo V 450,5*. 7. 451,24*. 452,1. 456,4* (11). — tāpaso gottena Kassapo VI 56,12*. 58,8*. 68,11*. 20.

Nārada, rājā Mithilāyaṁ IV 358*,18. 24. 27. 359*,7 (12). 17. 21. 360* (4). 11. 18. 360,20.

Nārada, Buddha N 35,27. 36,10. 37,11. 12. 25. 44,6.

Nārada, Mahābrahmā (= Bodhisatto) VI 220,25. 242,3*. 26. 243 (4). 11. 22* (23. 24) (Nārada Kassapa). 243,29*. 244*,1. 17. 21. 245*,2. 3. 8. 17. 251,3*. 254,31*. 255,11 (Mahābrahmā).

Nāradakūṭa N 29,3.

Nārada-Pabbatā, dve devanikāyā VI 568,7 (18). 571,11.

Nārivana, Himavante V 152,18*.

Nāla-gāmaka I 391,21. — V 125,21.

Nālaka, bhāgineyyo Kāḷadevalassa N 55,13. 14. 26.

Nālapana, see: Tālavana.

Nālāgiri (Nāḷāgiri), hatthi (Rājagahe) II 199,12. — III 178,12. 415,2. — V 333,19. 334,4. 9. 18. 20. 23. 335,12. 19. 22. 336,5. 8. 9. 15. 337,1. 15. — Nāḷāgiri-damanaṁ V 335,2. 11. — Nāḷāgiri-vissajjanaṁ III 97,14. 536,25. (cfr. Dhanapāla).

Nālika, pabbato (Himavante) VI 518,17. 519,26*.

Naḷikīra, rājā Dantapuranagare Kāliṅgaraṭṭhe V 132,23* (v. l.

Nāḷikera). 143*,11. 25. 144 (22. 24). — Nāḷikera-rājassa vatthu V 119 (15).

Nigaṇṭha-Nāthaputta, see: Nāthaputta-Nigaṇṭha. — Nigaṇṭhā (pl.) II 262,10.

Nigrodhārāma, Kapilavatthuṁ nissāya N 88,11. — IV 6,27. 7,1. 50,7. 282,18. — VI 479,8. 13. — Nigrodhasakkassa ārāmo N 88,6. — VI 479,8.

Nigrodha(kumāra), putto seṭṭhino Rājagahe, rājā Bārāṇasiyaṁ (= Bodhisatto) IV 38*,20. 28. 39*,1. 7. 23. 26. 40*,1. 10. 22. 28. 41*,3. 8. 25. 42*,5. 21. 43,13*. 15*. 19.

Nigrodha-jātaka (445) IV 37—43.

Nigrodhamiga-jātaka (12) I 145—153. — Nigrodha-jāt. III 273,23*.

Nigrodhamigarājā, (= Bodhisatto) I 149,23*. 150,7*. 153*,1 3. 153,19. — Nigrodha I 152*,15. 17. 18 (20. 22).

Nigrodharukkha, bodhi Kassapa-Buddhassa N 43,24.

Nidānakathā I 1—94. — I 137,16. — IV 262,19. — tīṇi nidānāni I 2,2.

Nibbāna-nagara N 5,11. 18. 23.

Nibbānapurapavesanadīpanaṁ udānaṁ III 433,25*.

Nimi, rājā Mithilanagare Videharaṭṭhe (= Bodhisatto) N 45,14. — I 139,21*. — III 378,14*. 381,17* (26). — VI 96,28*. 97,9*. 15 (19. 23). 98,7. 10. 16 (22). 102*,22. 28 (34). 103*,2. 7. 11. 105,38. 125,12*. 128,19*. 129,7. 16. — Nemikumāro VI 96,24*.

Nimi-jātaka (541) VI 95—129. — V 275 (8). 276 (2. 5. 13).

Nimmānarati-devaloka II 349,3.

Niraya-khaṇḍa, Nimi-jātake VI 116,28. — Mahānāradakassapa-jātake VI 250,20. — Nirayakathā VI 250,21*.

Nilīya, nesādaputto III 330,25* (26) (v. l. Nīlīya).

Nisabha, aggasāvako Anomadassi-Buddhassa N 36,5.

Nisabha, pabbato VI 204,14*. 212,20*.

Nīlavaṇṇa-kusamāla, see: Kusamāli.

nekkhammaṁ IV 473,15. — nekkhamma-pāramī V 177,10. 247,3.

Nemikumāra, see: Nimi.

Nemindhara, pabbato VI 125,14 (22. 23).

Nerañjarā, nadī N 15,27. 16,4. 5. 70,4. — IV 392,12*. 397,6* (28).

Neru, pabbato Himavante III 247*,3. 17 (10). 248*,1. 2. — V 425,17. 23. 432 (15) (cfr. Kākaneru, Mahāneru, Sineru, Meru).

Neru-jātaka (379) III 246—248.

P.

Pakiṇṇaka-nipāta (XIV) IV 276—374. — II 68,8 (— Jāt. 487) — II 333,27 (— Jāt. 489).

Pakudha-Kaccāyana, diṭṭhigatiko (v. l. Kakudha-) V 246,11. (cfr. Kakudha-Kaccāyana).

Paccaya, maṅgalahatthi Vessantarassa VI 485,25*.

paccekabuddho I 232,3*. — II 194 (31). — III 240,11* (Dummukho). 299,27 (Tagarasikhī). 307,11*. 429,7*. 439,11*. 453,1*. — IV 15,15. 318,15*. 328,8*. 340,27*. 373,28*. — V 245,15* (Sonako). 288,25*. 440,24. — VI 53,2*. — paccekabuddhā (pl.) I 395,14*. 470,16*. — III 257,25*. 304,19*. 377,11*. 407,31* (cattāro). 470,18*. — IV 114,14*. 368,3*. V 54,6*. — VI 41,6*. etc. — paccekabodhisatto IV 340,22* — paccekabuddhaveso II 197,19*.

Pajaka, rājā (Avantiraṭṭhe) III 463,13* (Pajaka-rañño vijitaṁ — Caṇḍapajjotarañño vijitaṁ V 133,15*.

Pajāpatī V 28,26. — VI 568,8. 571,12.

Pajjunna, devarājā I 331*,21. 22. 28. 332*,1. (3). 15.

Pajjota, see, Caṇḍapajjota.

Pañcagaru-jātaka (v. l. Bhiruka-jāt.) (132) I 469—471.

Pañcanipāta III 153—227. — VI 371,9* (— Jāt. 364).

Pañcapaṇḍita-jātaka (508) IV 473. — Pañcapaṇḍita-pañha, Ummagga-jātake VI 389,30. — V 81,30*. 122 (6). — Paṇḍitapañha VI 379,14*.

Pañcapāpā, dhītā ekassa daliddassa Bārāṇasiyaṁ, bhariyā Baka-rañño ca Pāvāriya-rañño ca V 440,22. 441,2. 17. 443,18.

pañcamahāvilokanaṁ Buddhassa N 48,24.

pañcavaggiyatherā N 57,8. 81,26. 82,10. — pañcavaggiyā bhikkhū N 67,31. 81,18.

Pañcasikha, gandhabbaputto III 222*,10. 12. 17. 19. — IV 63*,7. 15. 18. 66*,2. 20. 67*,4. 13. 68,27*. 69,1*. 24. — V 383,18*. 386,9*. 389*,10. 17. 27. 390,29*. 412,10.

Pañcāla, rājā Uttarapañcālanagare Kampillaraṭṭhe III 79,1*. — IV 398*,8. 12. 16. 20 (— Sambhūta-paṇḍito). — 430,28*. 433*,20. 22. — V 21,6*. 23,21*. 98,25*. 102,7*. 104,15*. 105*,15. 21. 106,7*. 107,1*. — VI 280,23* (27). 281 (2). — Pañcālo, Pañcāla-rājā — Cūḷani-Brahmadatto VI 329,20. 396,25*. 397,4* (10). 398 (23). 411,2*. 418,15. 419 (3). 423,27* (30). 424,13*. 426,28*. 427,16. 443 (23). 446,12. — Pañcālarājadhītā VI 154,28. — VI 411,18 (— Pañcālacaṇḍī).

Pañcāla, — Uttarapañcāla-nagaraṁ VI 416,16*. 417 (3). 437,26*.

Pañcāla-raṭṭha III 81 (3). — Pañcālā II 214,9* (16. 17). — III 80*,24. 26. 81 (3. 6). 381,17*. — IV 432,2. — VI 412,15. 424,17*. — Pañcālā — Pañcālanāgarā VI 477,29*. — Pañcālino VI 397,2*. 398 (23).

Pañcāla, adj. Pañcālā kākasenā VI 443,17* (22). — Pañcālā (pl.) VI 475,6* (11).

Pañcālacaṇḍa, brāhmaṇakumāro Bārāṇasiyaṁ (— Kuṇālo — Bodhisatto) V 425,3. 430 (21. 32). — purohito 437,30. 440,10.

Pañcālacaṇḍa, putto Cūḷani-Brahmadattassa Pañcāla-rañño VI 435,27*. 445,24. 453,23*. 454*,2. 10. 462,25*. 466,15*.

Pañcālacaṇḍī, dhītā Cūḷani-Brahmadattassa VI 409,31*.

410,13*. 426,20*. 427,19. 434,28*. 438 (12). 445,18*. 26 (31). 453,25*. 454*,4. 12. 466*,19. 24. 478,16*.

Pañcāliya, adj. Pañcāliyā senā VI 396*,28. 32. 397 (29). 399,9*.

Pañcālī, Pañcālarājadhītā, devī Esukāri-rañño IV 486,12* (16).

Pañcāvudha-kumāra, putto Brahmadattassa Bārāṇasi-rañño (— Bodhisatto) I 273,2*. 274,1*. 275,30.

Pañcāvudha-jātaka (55) I 272—275.

Pañcūposatha-jātaka (490) IV 325—332.

Pañña-jātaka, see: Pānīya-jāt.

paññāpasaṁsanaṁ II 297,8. — IV 224,8.

paññāpāramī II 76,15. 173,12. — III 204,8. 281,18. 341,21. — IV 136,22. — V 57,5. 227,21. — VI 255,14. 329,20.

pañhavyākaraṇaṁ therassa I 474,3.

Paṭācārā, Licchavi-dārikā III 1,14. — VI 481,16* (therī?).

paṭhamakappikā (manussā) II 352,6*. (cfr. Jāt. 32).

Paṭhama-paṇṇāsa — Jāt. (1) — (150), I 261,22.

Paṇḍara, nāgarājā V 76,22*. 77,5*. — Paṇḍaraka V 77*,7. 13. 17. 78 (18). 79*,18. 20 (25). 28. 82 (14). 19*. 83,16*. 84,25*. 86,11. 19* (22).

Paṇḍara-jātaka (518) V 75—88. — VI 177,19*.

Paṇḍarakā, nadī IV 438,28*. 439 (4).

Paṇḍava, asso Sāmarañño Bārāṇasiyaṁ II 98*,9. 20.

Paṇḍava-pabbata, (Rājagahaṁ nissāya) N 66,14.

Paṇḍita, vāṇijo (— Bodhisatto) I 404*,19. 25. 405*,7. 8. 16 (17).

Paṇḍitapañha, see: Pañcapaṇḍitapañha.

Paṇḍukaṇṇa, nāṭako IV 324,11*. — Paṇḍukaṇṇa-nāṭo 324,19*.

Paṇḍukambalasilāsana, Sakkassa N 32,12. — II 92,2. — IV 8,28*. 238,18*. — V 92,1*. 136,6*. 386,2*. — Paṇḍukambalāsilā IV 265,19. — Paṇḍukambalāsana IV 357 (4).

Paṇḍuka-Lohitakā, Chabbaggiyā bhikkhū II 387,10. 12. 20.

Paṇḍurāja-puttā V 426 (11. 18). — Paṇḍurāja-gotta V 426 (10).

Paṇṇāsa-nipāta (XVIII) V 193—246.

Paṇṇika-jātaka (102) I 411—412.

paṇṇiko upāsako I 411,8. — II 179,16.
Patāpana, nirayo V 266,14*. 271 (26). 453,27.
Patikolamba, bhattarandhako IV 431,26*. 432 (16. 24). 31*.
Padakusalamāṇava-jātaka (432) III 501—514.
paduṭṭhāmacco Kosalarañño III 153,5 (cfr. II 125 & 206).
Paduma, aggasāvako Dhammadassi-Buddhassa N 39,26.
Paduma, Buddho N 35,27. 36,11. 23. 29. 37,10. 44,6.
Paduma, pitā Paduma-Buddhassa N 36,24.
Paduma-kumāra (Paduma-rāja), putto Brahmadattassa Bārāṇasi-rañño (= Bodhisatto) II 116,3*. 118,22*. 119,6. 24. 121,11. — IV 189*,16. 24. 191*,2. 8. (cfr. Mahāpaduma).
Paduma-jātaka (261) II 321—323.
Paduma-niraya IV 245,8. 12.
Padumā, aggasāvikā Sikhi Buddhassa N 41,31.
Padumā, mātā Tissa-Buddhassa N 40,23.
Padumuttara, Buddho N 37,13. 18. 26. 44,16. — I 148,18. 409,26.
Panāda, rājā = Mahāpanādo II 334,3. — IV 325,7*.
Panthaka, thero = Cullapanthako I 116,22. 118,25. — Mahāpanthako I 114,23.
Panthaka (purisanāma) I 403*,9. 10. 15. 21.
Pabbajjā-sutta N 66,32.
Pabbata, isi, jeṭṭhantevāsiko Sarabhaṅgassa (Bodhisattassa) III 463,15*. 464,7* (Pabbatissaro). 469,21. — V 133*,10. 12. 151,29.
Pabbata, see: Nārada-Pabbatā.
Pabbata, rājā Koṇāgamana-Buddhassa kāle (= Bodhisatto) N 43,3.
Pabbatūpatthara-jātaka (195) II 125—147.
Pabhāvatī, dhītā Maddarañño, aggamahesī Kusarañño (Bodhisattassa) V 283,23*. 284*,3. 6. 17. 25. 285*,11. 26. 286*,3. 5. 7. 14. 12. 23. 287*,3. 5. 21. 27. 289*,13. 15. 17. 22. 290*,10. 21. 26. 291*,4. 6. 17. 23. 30. 292*,1. 6. 7. 13. 20. 293*,10. 13.

294*,6. 9. 12. 27. 295,2*. 297*,5. 12. 17—20 (25). 298*,3. 7. 27. 299*,9. 11—23 (26). 300*,19. 21. 22. 29. 301*,1. 4. 6 (9—10). 11. 16. 20. 302*,22. 27. 303 (21). 26*. 305,17*. 306*,10. 19. 307*,10. 28. 308,5*. 11. 30*. 309,4*. 310,5*. 10. 311,6*. 22. 312,12.

Pabbāvatī, mātā Sikhi-Buddhassa N 41,20.

Pabhāvatī, mātā Sujāta-Buddhassa N 38,18.

Payāga, titthaṁ (v. l. Payāta-, Payāka-) VI 198,3* (6).

Paranimmita-Vasavattin N 48,17. (cfr. Vasavattin).

Parantapa, dāso Bārāṇasirañño III 417*,2. 8. 10. 11. 20. 22. 23. 25. 418*,3. 6. 9. 12. 26. 419*,2 (7). 14. 20 (24). 420,11*.

Parantapa-jātaka (416) III 414—421.

paribbājikānaṁ catunnaṁ pabbajjā III 1,5.

Paribhindana-kathā, Mahāummagga-jātake VI 389,31.

Pariyesana-khaṇḍa, see: Māhāsattassa pariyesanakhaṇḍa (VI 200,14).

Parosata-jātaka (101) I 410—411.

Parosata-vagga I 410—424.

Parosahassa-jātaka (99) I 405—407. — I 411 (1).

Palāyi-jātaka (229) II 216—218.

palāyi-paribbājako II 216,8. 219,3. — palāyiko paribbājako II 257,14.

Palāsa-jātaka a) (307) III 23—25. — b) (370) III 208—210.

Pasenadi, Kosalarājā, putto Mahākosalassa I 344,21. — II 15,3. 403,13. 17. 21. — IV 342,27. — Pasenadi-Kosala I 148,3. — II 286,24. — III 402,29. (cfr. Kosalarājā).

Pāṭala, naṭo III 507,10. 19. 24. 508,1.

Pāṭali-rukkha, bodhi Vipassi-Buddhassa N 41,17.

Pāṭika, (acelako) N 77,24 (Pāṭikaputta-samāgamo).

Pāṭikārāma, Vesāliyaṁ upanissāya I 389,16.

Pādañjali-jātaka (247) II 263—64. — V 122 (12).

Pādañjalin, putto Bārāṇasi-rañño II 264*,3. 14 (16) 24. 27. — V 122 (12). — Pādañjaliko II 264,6*.

Pāṇīya-jātaka (459) IV 113—119. — III 18,4. 375,18 — Paññajāt. III 208,8. 397,8. (cfr. Jāt. (148)).

Pāpaka, kulaputto nāmasiddhiko I 401,29. 402,1. — Pāpaka, māṇavo I 402,16*. 403,21*.

Pāragaṅgā II 333,17. — VI 427,27*. 431,14*.

Pārāpata-jātaka, see: Romaka-jāt.

Pārāsariya, brāhmaṇo, disāpamokkho ācariyo Takkasilāyaṁ II 202*,1. 3 8). — (= Bodhisatto:) III 160,21*. 161 (2).

Pārikā, nesāda-kumārikā, mātā Suvaṇṇasāmassa (Bodhisattassa) VI 72*,3. 10. 86,30*. 87,10*. 88,17* (19). — Pārī: VI 73*,9. 13. 28. 74*,2. 8. 10. 87,14*. — Pāri-tāpasī VI 73,25*.

Pāricchatta(ka), rukkho Tāvatiṁsabhavane I 202,14*. — VI 265,18. — VI 278,25*.

Pārileyya, (hatthi?) IV 314,23. — Pārileyyaka III 489 (28).

Pārileyyaka-vanasaṇḍa III 489,22.

Pāli (Pāḷi) I 488 (28). — II 294 (8). 299 (16). — IV 236 (11). — V 26 (7). 182 (15). 265 (19). 273 (13). 276 (12). — VI 36 (25). 353,11*. 505 (24). 547 (27). 590 (23). — Pālipotthakāni IV 134 (8). — VI 274 (22). — Pāḷinayena IV 447,8*. Pālivasena V 341 (7). 460 (22). atthato ca Pālito ca V 147 (6).

Pālita, aggasāvako Piyadassi-Buddhassa N 39,4.

Pālita, upaṭṭhāko Maṅgala-Buddhassa N 34,8.

Pāvāriya, rājā V 443,13. 20. — Pārivārika V 444,3.

Piṅgala, rājā Bārāṇasiyaṁ (= Devadatto) II 241*,9 (18). 19. 242,16 (cfr. Mahāpiṅgala).

Piṅgala, luddo (= Aḷāto) VI 227,8.

Piṅgalā dāsī. III 101*,6. 19 (22).

Piṅgiya, purohito Bārāṇasirañño (= Devadatto) III 159,10*. 160,24*. 161,27.

Piṅgiya, sunakho III 535,26*.

Piṅgiyānī, bhariyā Brahmadattassa V 444,12. 15.

Piṅguttara, māṇavo Mithilavāsī VI 347*,7. 25. 348,13*.

Piṭakāni, tīṇi N 30,10. 41,1. — I 118,7. 119,6. 17. — Piṭa

kāni VI 594,30. — Piṭakattayaṁ VI 594,16. 595,33. — Te-piṭakaṁ Buddhavacanaṁ IV 37,7.
Piṇḍola-Bhāradvāja, (thero) IV 263,11. 375,4. — Bhāradvāja IV 375,22.
pituposako upāsako IV 43,22.
Pipphalī, bodhi Dīpaṁkara-Buddhassa N 29,24.
Piyaketa, pāsādo Vidhurapaṇḍitassa (Bodhisattassa) VI 289*,10. 12.
Piyaṅgu-rukkha, bodhi Piyadassi-Buddhassa N 39,5.
Piyadassin, Buddho N 38,27. 28. 39,8. 44,7.
Pilindiyavaccha, (thero) III 363,28.
Piliya, seṭṭhi Bārāṇasiyaṁ (— Devadatto) I 466*,3. 5. 467,21*. 468*,12. 23. 27. 469,3*. 11.
Piliyakkha, rājā Bārāṇasiyaṁ VI 76,29*. 77,28*. 83,27*. 85,19*.
Pilotika (?) VI 478,18*.
Pīṭha-jātaka (337) III 118—121.
Pukkusa, amacco Maddava-mahārañño Bārāṇasiyaṁ III 337,24*. 338,6*. 339*,14. 17. 22. 340,9*. 341,8*. 17.
Pukkusa, paṇḍito dhammānusāsako Vedeharañño Mithilāyaṁ VI 330,4*. 343 (15). 353,28*. 368,20*. 369,10*. 370,6*. 380,10*. 383*,5. 8. 386,26*. 387*,11. 12 (17). 436,22*. 441*,12. 16. 478,17*.
Pukkusāti, kulaputto IV 180,19.
Pucimanda-jātaka (311) III 33—35.
Pucimanda-vagga III 33—70.
Puññalakkhaṇadevī, bhariyā Anāthapiṇḍikassa II 410,25. 31. 415,7. — Puññalakkhaṇadevī III 435,5.
Puṭadūsaka-jātaka (280) II 390—392.
puṭadūsako dārako II 390,26.
Puṭabhatta-jātaka (223) II 202—206.
Puṇḍarīka-rukkha, bodhi Sikhi-Buddhassa N 41,31.
Puṇṇa, (dāso?) II 381,21. — (brāhmaṇo?) IV 314,20.

Puṇṇaka, assataro VI 135,28*.

Puṇṇaka, (dāsanāma) VI 273,25*.

Puṇṇaka, yakkho senāpati, bhāgineyyo Vessavaṇamahārājassa VI 255,24. 265,13*. 266,18*. 267*,5 (7). 19 (25). 26. 268*,22. 26. 29. 270,34*. 271,3* (8. 14). 272,5 (15. 30). 273 (7). 25*. 274,17*. 280*,1. 7. 8. 21. 281*,9. 11. 14. 20. 282*,8. 9. 11. 18 (24). 31. 283*,12. 29. 284,10*. 285,22*. 288,1. 10. 20. 289 (7. 17). 23*. 301,18*. 24. 302*,1. 21 (28). 303*,10. 11. 304,20* (29). 306,28*. 307*,4. 5. 24. 308,21*. 309,3*. 8. 311,10*. 312,17*. 313*,4. 22. 27. 314 (1. 3. 6). 15*. 318 (26). 322 (29. 30). 323*,1. 4. 28. 29. 324,30*. 325,2. 28*. 326,15*. 327*,1. 5. 9. — — Puṇṇaka-rājā IV 182,19*. — Kaccāyano VI 273,29*. Kaccāno VI 283,11*. 286,3*. 301,28. 323,17*. Kātiyāno VI 293,22*. 306,4* (19). 308,29*. — Anūnanāmo VI 273,30*.

Punnaka-jātaka, (— Vidhurapaṇḍita-jātaka (545)) IV 14,24. 182,19*.

Punṇanadī-jātaka (214) II 173—175. — V 122 (6).

Puṇṇapāti-jātaka (53) I 268—270.

Puṇṇamukha, gahapati VI 135,5*.

Puṇṇamukha, phussakokilo V 419,15. 420*,12—28. 421*,2—28. 422*,1—18 (32). 423* (5). 24. 30. 32. 424,12*. 15. 16. 24—28. 425,11. 430 (33). 431 (18). 432,31. 433*,7—28. 434,8. 10. 20. 456,4*.

Puṇṇalakkhaṇadevī, bhariyā Anāthapiṇḍikassa III 435,5. — Puññalakkhaṇadevī II 410,25. 31. 415,7.

Puṇṇā, dāsī Sujātāya N 69,1. 2. 10.

Puṇṇikā, dāsī II 428,21* (25). 429,3* (6).

Puthujjana, rājā VI 99,10*.

puthujjanapucchako pañho I 405,28 (cfr. Jāt. (483)).

Punabbasu, chabbaggiya-bhikkhu, see: Assaji.

Punabbasumitta, seṭṭhi Vipassissa Bhagavato kāle N 94,10.

Pupphaka, pāsādo Sutasomarañño V 187*,3. 13 (17).

Pupphaka, suvo (— Bodhisatto) IV 431*,3. 4. 434,26*. 437,1. — Pupphasuvo IV 434,1*.
Pupphāratta-jātaka (147) I 499—500. — II 443,4.
Pupphavatī, — Bārāṇasī IV 119,29*. — VI 131,11*. 132,10. 145*,23—29. 146*,1—7 (10). 148,(2).
Pubbavideha-dīpa VI 279 (3) (cfr. Videhā).
Pubbārāma III 310,13.
pubbekatavādī amacco Bārāṇasi-rañño V 228*,21. 24. 238,26*. 241,11*.
Purāṇa-Kassapa, diṭṭhigatiko I 509,10. — V 246,11. — Purāṇa-sāvakā, Purāṇādayo V 262,20.
purāṇadutiyika-palobhanaṁ I 153,23. 210,15. 495,18. — II 113,14. 155,12. 167,15. 178,6. 443,3. — III 58,26. 219,18. 248,18. 275,4. 336,23. 461,16. — V 152,2. 193,8.
purāṇasanthavo II 449,15.
Purindada, — Sakko V 139,16*. 141,8. 317*,4. 8. — VI 482,26*.
puriso aññataro II 436,18.
purohito Kosalarañño III 104,18.
Pūtimaṁsa, sigālo III 532,19 24*. 534,1*. 21 (28. 29). 535,4*.
Pūtimaṁsa-jātaka (437) III 532—536.
Pūraṇa-Kassapa, see: Purāṇa-Kassapa.
Peṇṇākaṭa, — Bheṇṇākaṭa, (janapado?) VI 237 (89).
Peta VI 99,12* (16). 595,27. — Petabhavana VI 99,24*. — Petaloka VI 101,(38).
Peta-vatthu IV 78 (9).
pesuññasikkhāpadaṁ III 149,11.
Pokkharakkhī, bhariyā Candakumārassa (Bodhisattassa) VI 148,19*.
pokkharavassaṁ VI 479,8 (cfr. N 88,5—89,2.).
Poṭṭhapāda, (paribbājako?) VI 478,17*.
Poṭṭhapāda, suko (— Bodhisatto) I 495,27*. 496,21*. 30.
Poṭṭhapāda, suko, kaniṭṭhabhātā Bodhisattassa II 132,25*.

133,8*. 134,2* (7). 15. — III 97,25*. 98,26*. 99,3*. 100,2. — IV 129 (5).
Potali-nagara, Kāsiraṭṭhe II 155,18*. 156,9*. — Assakaraṭṭhe III 3*,4. 16.
Pottika, tunnakāra-putto IV 38,25*. 39*,1. 9. 20. 40,21*. 42*,22. 28. 43 (18). — Pottika-bhaṇḍāgāriko 43,10*. — Pottiyo 40,16*. 41*,1. 10. 16. 18. 42 (17). 43,1*.
Polajanaka, putto Mahājanakassa Videharañño VI 30*.21. 26. 31*,7. 15. 32,27*. 33,27*. 34*,15. 29

Ph.

Phaggunī, aggasāvikā Nārada-Buddhassa N 37,8.
Phagguṇi-puṇṇamā N 86,29.
Phandana-jātaka (475) IV 207—211. — V 414,14.
Phala-jātaka (54) I 270—272.
phalakusalo upāsako I 270,15.
Phalika, pabbato Himavante V 415,23. — Phalikaguhā II 6,17*. 7*,3. 8. 10. 12. 20. 22. 8*,11. 16.
Phārusaka, (vanaṁ Tāvatiṁsabhavane) VI 278,28*.
Phusatī, Maddarājadhītā, aggamahesī Sañjayassa Sivirañño VI 480*,9. 10. 481*,17. 25. 28. 482 (3) 26*. 483 (25). 484*,2. 7. 13. 16. 21. 26. 485,11*. 498,12* (22). 503 (24). 506,5*. 583,15*. 585,28*. 586 (12). 590,1*. 593,27.
Phussa, Buddho N 40,14. 29. 41,8. 20. 44,9.
Phussa-māsa N 86,23. — Phussa-nakkhatta V 476,4*. — Phussa-yoga V 477,11*.
Phussadeva, aggasāvako Dhammadassi-Buddhassa N 39,23.
Phussadeva, thero Kaṭakandhavāsī Tambapaṇṇidīpe IV 490,21. — VI 30,4.
Phussā, aggasāvikā Tissa-Buddhassa N 40,25.

B.

Baka, see: Baka-Brahman.

Baka, Bārāṇasi-rājā (— Kuṇalo sakuṇarājā — Bodhisatto) V 440,21. 443,17. 21. 26. 444,1. 3.

Baka-jātaka a) (38) I 220—224. — b) (236) II 233—234.

Bakabrahma-jātaka (405) III 358—363.

Baka-Brahman III 145,18. 358,20. 359,9. 10. 12. 360 (13). 363,17. — Bako III 360,2. 15. — IV 180,26. — Bakādayo brahmāno VI 329,25.

Badarikārāma, Kosambiyaṁ nissāya I 160,19. — III 64,3.

Bandhanamokkha-jātaka (120) I 437—440. (cfr. Jāt. 472).

bandhanāgāraṁ (Sāvatthiyaṁ) II 139,4.

Bandhanāgāra-jātaka (201) II 139—141.

Bandhumatī, nagaraṁ Vipassi-Buddhassa N 41,15. — VI 480,12*.

Bandhumatī, mātā Vipassi-Buddhassa N 41,16.

Bandhumā, rājā, pitā Vipassi-Buddhassa N 41,15. — VI 480,13*.

Bandhura, hatthimeṇḍo Bārāṇasirañño III 430,29*. 431*,2. 9.

Bandhula, senāpati Kosalarañño IV 148,10. 25. 149,18. 23. 27. 150,4. 9. 16. 19. 151,20. 23. — Bandhula-mallo IV 148,28. 149,8.

Babbu-jātaka (137) I 477—480.

Baladeva, Devagabbhāya putto dutiyo IV 81,5*. 82*,4. 10. 88*,13. 17. 19.

Bahukā, nadī V 388,24*. 389 (1).

Bahucintin, maccho I 427*,9. 16. 428,1 (8). 9.

Bahuputta(ka), rājā Bārāṇasiyaṁ IV 423,26*. 428 (19).

bahubhaṇḍo bhikkhu I 126,16. 206,17.

Bahusodarī, devadhītā Gandhamādanavāsinī VI 83,22*.

Bārāṇasī, nagaraṁ N 43. 81. 86. — *I 98. 100. 107. 120. 122. 124—5. 127. 133—4. 140. 149. 157. 159. 166. 173.

175. 178. 181. 184. 186. 189. 194. 196. 205. 208. 210. 216. 224. 231. 239—40. 242. 245. 247—8. 250. 252—3. 257. 259. 261—2. 264. 269—70. 272. 277—8. 280. 283—5. 289. 295. 299. 300—1. 303—4. 307. 310. 312. 314. 319—20. 323. 328. 333. 343. 349. 354. 356—8. 361. 365—6. 368. 370. 375. 378—9. 383. 388. 395. 404. 406. 409. 411—13. 415—16. 418—19. 421. 423. 425. 427. 429. 430—1. 434. 436—7. 441. 445—7. 450—2. 454—5. 459—61. 463. 466. 469. 471. 473—5. 478. 480. 482. 484. 487. 489. 491. 494—5. 497. 499. 502. 505. 510. — *II 2. 6. 10. 13. 15. 18. 19. 26. 30. 33. 36. 41. 43. 46—48. 50. 52. 57. 59. 64. 66. 68. 70. 72. 74. 76. 79. 82. 85. 87. 90. 94. 96. 98. 100—1. 104—5. 107—9. 112—13. 116. 118—19. 121. 125. 131—2. 134. 137. 139. 142 145. 149—51. 153. 158. 161—2. 165. 167. 173. 175—6. 178—9. 181. 184. 186. 197. 199. 200. 203—4. 206. 212. 217—19. 221. 225. 227. 229. 232. 234. 236. 238. 240. 243—4. 246. 247—50. 253. 257. 260. 262. 264—5. 267. 269. 272. 277—9. 283. 287. 292. 295. 297. 314. 316. 319. 322—3. 328. 335. 338. 341. 345—6. 349. 354. 356. 359. 361. 382. 385. 387. 388—9. 391. 394. 400. 402. 405. 411. 413. 417. 419. 421. 423. 427. 429. 431. 433—5. 437—8. 440—1. 445. 447. 450. — II 18.3. 194 (24). — *III 16. 18. 21. 23. 25. 27. 30. 31. 34. 36. 39. 45—6. 49. 51. 56. 59. 62. 64. 67. 73. 75. 82. 84. 87. 90. 93. 97. 102. 105. 107 110—12. 115—16. 119. 122. 126. 128. 133. 135. 137. 138. 140. 142—3. 145. 147. 149—50. 153. 155. 158—9. 162. 168. 171. 174. 178. 183. 187. 189. 191. 194. 198. 200. 202. 204. 208. 213. 215. 219. 225. 228—9. 232. 235. 238. 246. 248. 249. 254—5. 257—8. 265—7. 275. 277. 281. 286. 289. 292. 300—1. 303. 308. 310. 312. 314. 317. 321—2. 325. 329—30. 333. 337. 341—3. 352. 355. 362. 370. 376. 379. 383. 385. 388. 391. 397. 403. 406. 410. 416. 421. 424.

428. 435. 439. 444. 446. 463. 475. 497—8. 502. 505. 507. 517. 520. 527. 532. 537. — III 226 (20). 227 (1). 283 (28). 299,24. 312,16. 328 (26). 411 (21). 419 (16). 487,17. 508,14. — *IV 1. 7. 15. 22—3. 28. 39. 40. 44. 59. 62—3. 70. 74. 90—1. 96—7. 100. 114. 116. 119. 129. 131. 134. 153. 159. 168—9. 171. 176. 181. 189. 194. 197. 200. 202. 207. 212. 214. 220. 224. 237. 245. 248. 250—2. 255—7. 267. 269. 283. 289. 298. 305. 318. 333. 344. 351. 354. 370. 373. 376—8. 388. 413. 423. 437. 442. 456. 458—9. 468—9. 473. 475. 479. 486. 488. 490 2. — IV 70,9. 119 (24). 135 (18). 136 (8). 155 (1). 352 (29). 464 (16). 468 (12). — *V 1. 12—3. 53—4. 59. 65. 68. 75. 88. 95. 109. 112. 127—8. 135. 164. 177. 193. 201. 211. 227—8. 235—6. 247—8. 263. 312. 354. 357. 370. 382. 385—6. 457. 466. 505. 507—8. 511. — V 29 (17). 68,28. 96 (1). 112 (16). 114 (21). 261 (9). 380 (8). 426 (1. 18). 427 (28. 25). 428 (12. 23). 430 (30. 24). 437,25. 440,5. 22. 25. 465,8. — *VI 1. 2. 29. 71. 75—76. 95. 131. 158. 160—1. 163. 165. 170. 178. 186. 195. 198. 219. 257. — VI 17 (10). 19 (9). 99 (13). 100 (26). 111 (11). 119 (26). 120 (27). 123,5. 165. (10). 166,3. 6. 176 (16). 227,9.

Bārāṇasi-dvāragāmo V 288,19*.

Bārāṇasi-brāhmaṇo III 219,23*.

Bārāṇasi-maggo I 273,10*. 320,23* (B-gāmimahāmaggo). — IV 256*,22. 27. — V 386*,25. 26 (Bārāṇasigamamaggo).

Bārāṇasi-mahānadī I 79,26*.

Bārāṇasi-susānaṃ III 330,16*.

Bārāṇasi-seṭṭhi I 242,7*. 295,27. — Bodhisatto: 231,26*. 232,4*. 234,9. 252,23. 269*,16—17. 270,11. 365,27. 379,2. 413,22. 452,9*. 455,2. 458*,17. 19. 459,29. — II 50,24*. 51*,2—19. 52,17. 65,22 (— Bo.). 225,16*—226,22 (— Bo.). 232*,4. 9. 233,30. 237,18 (— Bo.). 361,22*. — III 119,24*.

121,8*. 18. 196,6—197,17 (— Bo.). 225,2*. 299,24. 314,30*. 475,4*. — IV 68,22*. 376,8*.

Bārāṇasi-kumāra, (— Brahmadatta-kumāro) V 458,10*.

Bārāṇasiggaha, (Kaṁso) II 403,2 (5).

Bārāṇasi-rajja I 126,3*. 178,25*. 262*,21. 23. 24. 263*,11. 18. — II 94,8*. 214 (21). 244,5*. 401*,3. 11. — III 168,28*. — IV 40,8*. 129,20*. 170,4*. 479,10*. — V 97 (9). 430 (15. 31). 507,9*. 508,20*. — Bārāṇasirajjasāmiko (Brahmadatto) II 3,10*.

Bārāṇasi-rāja I 446,21. — II 36,4*. 193 (28). 208,6*. — III 100,7*. 211,14*. 238,25*. — IV 39,4*. 315,31*. 316,16*. — V 39,26*. 40,5*. 58 (18). 164,23*. 177,6. 248,8*. — VI 101 (27). 202 (15).

— Bodhisatto: I 159,11. 261,20. 263*,2. 12. 295,16. 410,18. — II 5,8. 115,11. 207,23. 221,4. 229,3. 266,21. 351,18. 401,9*. 403,9. — III 8,20*. 13,8. 92,18*. 147,15. 153,10*. 155,5.

— Aṅgo: VI 203 (10). 204 (4. 21).

— Uggaseno: IV 446,14.

— Udayo: III 452,9*.

— Dhanañjayo: III 97,20*.

— Brahmadatto: I 134,25*. 149,25*. 159,11 (— Bo.). 178*,20. 23. 261,20 (— Bo.). 313,10*. 359,19*. 409,11*. 415,13*. 421,6*. 455,26. 486,27. — II 3*,8. 10. 4*,11. 27. 28. 5,8 (— Bo.). 94,16*. 104,7*. 119,23. 122,9*. 124,2*. 205,27*. 257,23 (— Bo.). 218,20. 229,28*. 266,21 (— Bo.). 278,10*. 315,2. 351,18 (— Bo.) 398,9*. 399,15*. 411,15*. 413,9*. 433,23*. — III 21,9*. 22,27. 23*,2. 9. 45,13*. 70,22. 92,13* (— Bo.). 115,15*. 116*,6. 12. 117,5*. 122,20*. 140,5*. 144,5*. 147,15 (— Bo.). 158,15*. 159,19*. 206,10. 215,23*. 292,18*. 303,16*. 304,15*. 325,4*. 326,1*. 370,22*. 391*,20. 22. 407,17*. 420,3*. 428,27*. 429,8*. 433,21*. 446,3*. 514,27*. — IV 24,21*.

131,16. 197,8*. 212,27*. 283,15*. 334,14*. — V 3,4*. 68,23*. 428 (35). 430, (3). — VI 159,10*. 162*,9. 14.
— Mahāsīlavo (Bo.): I 263*,2. 12.
— Vissaseno: II 346 (25).
— Saṁyamo: V 354,9*. 364,24*.
Bārāṇaseyyaka, adj. IV 352 (30) (Bārāṇaseyyakaṁ bhaṇḍaṁ).
Bāḷaka-loṇakāra-gāma III 489,30.
bālagāmikamanussā aññatarasmiṁ gāmake Magadharaṭṭhe I 246,18.
Bāveru-jātaka (339) III 126—128.
Bāveru-raṭṭha III 126,18—19*. 127,9*. 128,8 (Bāveru). 128 (11).
Bāhika, see: Bāhiya.
Bāhiya, Bāhika-raṭṭha-vāsī III 432,24* (25). — (bāhiyā, bahijanapade jātā itthī I 421,23* (25)).
Bāhiya-jātaka (108) I 420—422.
Bimbasundarī, (= Bimbādevī?) VI 478,12*.
Bimbādevī, therī II 392,11. 393,19. 394,2. 433,8.
Bimbisāra, rājā (Magadhesu) N 82,28. — II 237,18. 403,14. III 121,18. — IV 263,25. 342,28. — VI 129,21.
Biḷāra-jātaka (128) I 460—461.
Biḷārikosiya-seṭṭhi, IV 67,15*. — Biḷārikosiko IV 69,8*. — Biḷārikosiyo IV 69,12*.
Biḷārikosiya-jātaka (450) IV 62—69.
Bījaka, dāso VI 227,23. 228,4. 229,8. 9 (18. 15). 233,6 (10). 23 (32). 235,4 (16) 22. 237 (15). 255,7. — Bījaka-vatthu VI 233 (11).
Bīraṇatthambhaka-vagga II 164—196.
Bīraṇī, devadhītā VI 117,1*. 16.
Buddha N 75,5. 80,31. 84,26. 92,16. — I 96,4. 96,1. 184,9. 270,16. 408,8. 422,16. — II 23 (7). 130,6. 8. 145,4. 147,2*. 170,29. 286,12. 314,10. 331,25. 332,21. 345,7. 366,18. 390,27. — III 20,24. 51,12—16. 122,10. 126,7. 128,5. 7. 352,1. 363,4 (7). 364,5. 384,23. 470,1. — IV 15,5. 14. 17. 28,1. 5.

96,10. 112 (14). 113,29. 158,15. 167,12. 187,7. 200,4. 236,22. 289,15. 305,4. 315,9. 328*,15. 20. 28. 332 (13). 361,1. 368,8*. 25. 369,31. 406, (11). — V 56,6 (28). 109,17. 334,21. 415,9. — VI 129,26. 132,18*. 219,22. 220,21. 342 (10). 553 (3). — sabbaññū-Buddho I 177,27*. 366,7. — III 348,7. 349 (11). 406,20. — IV 10 (6). 271,22*. — V 66, (2). — VI 225,11*. Buddhā (pl.) I 105 (25). 277,7. 444,8. 508,11. — II 34*,10. 14. 35, (1). 45,24. 46,4. 54,12. 129,26. 130 (15). 140 (25). 191 (18). 259,28. 417,16–31. — III 178,10. 257,24*. 342*,4. 8. 354 (19). 360 (11. 28). 363 (7. 8). 406,18–22. 408,18*. 409 (1. 21). 411,10*. 473 (15). — IV 187,7. 228,18. 20. 233,15. 234 (3. 9). 263,28. 360 (7). — V 129,6. 147 (20). 224,9. 424,10*. 456,27. — VI 480,3. — Buddhā sabbā N 44,2.

Buddhādayo II 185 (18). 430 (11). — III 131 (19). 214 (20). 228,6. 234 (12. 15. 20). 354 (27). 367 (19). 412 (29). 473 (27). — IV 33 (29). 453 (11). 478 (8). 486 (5). — V 50 (20). 149 (4). 174 (23). 186 (6). 225 (27). 256 (30). 335,12. 30. 398 (7. 18). 411 (1). 483 (28). 484 (3). 510 (18). — VI 15 (6). 18 (19). 26 (23). 363 (9).

Buddhaṁkuro IV 328,4*. 14. 368,8*. — VI 331,9*.

Buddhānussati-kammaṭṭhānaṁ I 97,13. 18. 22.

Buddhāsanaṁ I 137,18. 501,26. — III 376,2. — IV 265,14. 17. — V 11,28.

Buddhupaṭṭhāko IV 59,6.

Buddhupaṭṭhānaṁ I 299,19. 21. 24. 404,12. 426,29. — II 64,4. 181,15. 259,18. 338,16. 445,2–4. — III 36,20–22. 28,8. 17. 299,13. — IV 59,8. 176,4. 8.

Buddha-paccekabuddhānaṁ uppatti V 175 (16).

Buddhuppādo I 381,4. — IV 238,3*. — V 210,2. — VI 262,10*. 481,14*. — Buddhuppādakālo VI 333,25*.

Buddhūpaṭṭhāyikā paridevatā V 88,10.

Buddhūpanissayasampadā IV 96,9.

Buddhovādako VI 158,6.

Buddhakārakadhammā X 19,33 etc. — III 242 (20).

Buddha-kālo III 178,9.

Buddha-kiccaṁ VI 97, (21. 24). 329,8*.

Buddha-gāravo I 381,24.

Buddha-guṇo I 149,9. 277,7. 349,12. — II 34,10*. 35,11*. 111,15. 16. 148,14*. 216,16. 259,34. — III 363,12. — IV 235,28*.

Buddha-ñāṇaṁ IV 360 (4). — VI 97,10* (21).

Buddha-tejo V 336,13.

Buddhattabhāvo IV 328,15*.

Buddha-dassanaṁ VI 70,7.

Buddha-Dhamma-Saṁgha-guṇā V 334,1. (cfr. II 147,2*.)

Buddha-Dhamma-Saṁgha-māmakā upāsakā V 334,18.

Buddha-Dhamma-Saṁgha-upaṭṭhānaṁ V 382,13.

Buddha-nāgo V 335,9.

Buddha-paṭikaṇṭako Devadatto II 239,24. 240,4.

Buddha-parisā I 106,9. 110,25. 145,12. 172,25. 178,10. 246,14. 261,20. 268,4. 272,14. 315,24. 319,12. 329,20. 332,22. 334,24. 363,8. 369,8. 371,24. 393,14. 401,24. 403,26. 432,23. 436,30. 472,29. — II 62,26. 73,22. 79,5. 86,22. 130,21. 132,12. 148,18. 186,12. — III 293,4. 351,18. 375,13. — IV 55,22. 89,16. 104,7. 130,19. 136,19. 143,5. 157,27. 180,6. 218,28. 282,13. 412,24. 437,1. 491,5. 499,24. — V 227,18. 277,5. 312,12. 332,24. 354,8. 382,6. 511,22. — VI 30,2. 129,16. 593,29.

Buddha-puttā I 105 (27). — V 224,9.

Buddha-balaṁ I 330,7. 469,22. — II 46,7. — IV 212,14. — V 335,25.

Buddha-mātā, Māyā devī VI 481,3*.

Buddha-ratanaṁ IV 369,5.

Buddha-līḷhā I 119,28. 149,9. 152,10*. 155,25*. 314 (9). 330,2. 491,1. 13. — II 81,21*. — III 289,2*. 290,10*. 301,23*.

342,8*. 343,28*. 348,10. 394,28*. 396,29*. — IV 13,13*. 75,19*. — V 64,26*. 65,14*. 64,14*. 115,24*. 124,22*. 333,17. 335,10. 423,24*. 466,8*. 29. 501,28*. — VI 256,2*. 292,7*. 298,21*. 309,29*. 311,18*.

Buddha-vacanaṁ, see: Tepiṭaka.

Buddha-vārano V 336,16

Buddha-vilāso III 292,10*.

Buddha-visayo IV 212,12. 266,24. 267,5. — V 58,9.

Buddha-veneyyo I 504,19.

Buddha-sarīraṁ I 106,25.

Buddha-sāvako II 23,7. 45,21. 141 (1). 191 (14). — III 354 (19). — V 125,25. 126,2. — VI 225,11*.

Buddha-paccekabuddha-ariyasāvakā V 368 (24).

Buddha-paccekabuddha-sāvakā II 82,14. — III 241 (21). 354 (19).

Buddha-paccekabuddha-sāvaka-bodhisattānaṁ paveṇi III 367 (22).

Buddha-sāsanaṁ N 85,4. — I 126,29. 349,1. 367,25. 497,6. — II 142,4. 366,13. — IV 96,10. 185 (6). 220,3. 297,25.

Buddha-sirī III 384,7. — V 414,3.

Buddha-seyyā I 119,20.

Buddha-halāhalaṁ N 47,21. 23. 48,8. 12.

Buddhadeva, bhikkhu N 1,18.

Buddhamitta, (thero) N 1,16.

Buddhavaṁsa N 1,13. 2,29. 3,11. 28,18. 90,5.

Buddhavagga, Dhammapade N 79,31.

Buddhija, upaṭṭhāko Kakusandha-Buddhassa N 42,26.

Bodhi-pūjā IV 236,16. (cfr. Mahābodhi-pūjā.)

Bodhi-maṇḍa IV 228,23. 233*,5. 10. 235 (2). 12*. 236,6 (11). (cfr. Mahā-bodhimaṇḍa.)

Bodhikumāra, udiccabrāhmaṇaputto Kāsiraṭṭhe, paribbājako (— Bodhisatto) V 227,26*. — IV 22,18*. — Bodhiparibbājako V 229*,23. 28. 230,22*. 231,8*. — N 46,5. — Mahābodhi-paribbājako V 235*,7. 16. 246,12. (cfr. Cūḷabodhi-tāpasa).

Bodhikumāra, putto Udenassa rañño III 157,23. 24. 158,4. 161,27.

Bodhisatta [in the times of the former Buddhas] —

Ajito brāhmaṇo, Sobhita-Buddhassa kāle N 35,16.

Atidevo brāhmaṇo, Revata-Buddhassa kāle N 35,8.

Atulo nāgarājā, Sumana-Buddhassa kāle N 34,17. — Vipassi-Buddhassa kāle N 41,12.

Arindamo rājā, Sikhi-Buddhassa kāle N 41,25.

isi, Nārada-Buddhassa kāle N 37,2.

Uttaro māṇavo, Sumedha-Buddhassa kāle N 37,31.

Kassapo māṇavo, Piyadassi-Buddhassa kāle N 38,30.

Khemo rājā, Kakusandha-Buddhassa kāle N 42,21.

cakkavatti-rājā, Sujāta-Buddhassa kāle N 38,12.

Jaṭilo Mahāraṭṭhiyo, Padumuttara-Buddhassa kāle N 37,16.

Jotipālo māṇavo, Kassapa-Buddhassa kāle N 43,16.

Pabbato rājā, Koṇāgamana-Buddhassa kāle N 43,3.

Maṅgalo tāpaso, Siddhattha-Buddhassa kāle N 40,5.

yakkhasenāpati, Anomadassi-Buddhassa kāle N 35,30.

Vijitāvī khattiyo, Phussa-Buddhassa kāle N 40,31. — cakkavattī, Koṇḍañña-Buddhassa kāle N 30,6.

Sakko devarājā, Dhammadassi-Buddhassa kāle N 30,23.

sīho, Paduma-Buddhassa kāle N 36,15.

Sujāto khattiyo, Tissa-Buddhassa kāle N 40,18.

Sudassano rājā, Vessabhu-Buddhassa kāle N 42,7.

Sumedha-tāpaso, Dīpaṁkara-Buddhassa kāle N 15,16.

Suruci brāhmaṇo, Maṅgala-Buddhassa kāle N 32,2.

Susīmo mahiddhikatāpaso Atthadassi-Buddhassa kāle N 39,11.

Bodhisatta, [in the Jātakas] —

Akitti brāhmaṇo (480).

akkhadhutto (91).

agghakārako (agghapāṇiko) Bārāṇasiraññe (5).

Ajjuna-kumāro Paṇḍurājaputto (536) V 426,10—427,15 (- Kuṇālo sakuṇarājā).

aṭaviārakkhika-jeṭṭhako (265).

Aṭṭhiseno, brāhmaṇo Bārāṇasiyaṁ (403).

Anitthigandha-kumāro, putto Brahmadattassa Bārāṇasi-rañño (263). (507).

Aparaṇṇo, gijjho (381).

amacco Bārāṇasi-rañño (26). (27). (92). (107). (108). (226). amacca-ratanaṁ (331). (345). (409). atthadhammānusāsako (25). (158). (183). (184). (186). (195). (215). (223). (247). (306). (336). (337). (396). (473). ovādadāyako (462, cfr. 8). vinicchayāmacco (218). (332). (333). sabbakiccakārako (320). sabbatthaka-amacco (176). — Senako, brāhmaṇa-kumāro (401). (402). — Vidhūro, amacco Koravya-rañño (495). Vidhurapaṇḍito, amacco Dhanañjayakorabbassa (545).

Ayoghara-kumāro, putto Brahmadattassa Bārāṇasi-rañño (510).

Ayyakākāḷako, go (29).

Arako, satthā, isi (169).

Arindamo, Bārāṇasi-rājā, putto Magadharañño (529).

Alīnacitta-kumāro, putto Bārāṇasi-rañño (rājā Bārāṇasi-yaṁ) (156).

Alīnasattu-kumāro, putto Jayaddisa-rañño Uttarapañ-cālanagare (513).

Asadisa-kumāro, putto Bārāṇasi-rañño (181).

assavāṇijo (254).

asso, ājaññasindhavo (24). bhojājānīyasindhavo (23). — Vātaggasindhavo (266).

ācariyo, disāpāmokkho Bārāṇasiyaṁ (41). (64). (65). (119). (123). (130). (150). (185). (200). (245). (287). (377). — Takkasilāyaṁ (61). (71). (97). (252). (338). (353). (373). — Rakkhito, brāhmaṇo, tāpaso (453).

ājīviko (94).

Ādāsamukha-kumāro, rājā Bārāṇasiyaṁ (257).

isi (66). gaṇasatthā (10). (43). (81). (117). (124). (161). (175). (180). (197). (203). (213). (271). tāpaso (76). (77). (87). (165). (166). (167). (173). (234). (244). (246). (253). (273). (281). (293). (301). (314). (319). (334). (348). (376). (380). (392). (414). (418). (426). ovādadāyako tāpaso (149). (312). kulūpaka-tāpaso (284). pañhavissajjanaka-tāpaso (17). brāhmaṇo, purohito Bārāṇasi-rañño (362). udiccabrāhmaṇo, pitā Isisiṅgassa (526). udiccabrāhmaṇo — Bārāṇasi-rājā (73). udiccabrāhmaṇo — Mahābrahmā (99). — Arako, satthā (169). — Kaṇhapaṇḍito, brāhmaṇakumāro (440). — Kappo, brāhmaṇakumāro (346). (405). — Kassapo, pitā Isisiṅgassa (523). Komāyaputto, brāhmaṇo (299). Takkapaṇḍito (63). Tirīṭavacchakumāro tāpaso (259). Brahmadatto, Bārāṇasirājā tāpaso (519). Lomasakassapo, purohitaputto (— Kassapo) (433). Vacchanakha-paribbājako (235). Saṁkiccapaṇḍito, purohitaputto (330). Sarabhaṅgasatthā (— Jotipālo, purohitaputto) (423). (522).

udakakāko, Vīrako (204).

Udayabhaddo, Kāsirājā (— Sakko) (458).

Udayo, Bārāṇasirājā (421).

udiccabrāhmaṇo, isi, gaṇasatthā (10). (81). (117). (124). tāpaso (77). (87). (149). pitā Isisiṅgassa (526). Bārāṇasirājā (73). — Mahābrahmā (99). — disāpāmokkhācariyo Bārāṇasiyaṁ (119). — nibbutaggi tāpaso (144). — Culladhanuggahapaṇḍito (80). — Bodhikumāro (Mahābodhi-paribbājako) (528).

Kaṭṭhavāhana-rājā Bārāṇasiyaṁ (7).

Kaṇha-paṇḍito, brāhmaṇakumāro, isi (440).

Kaṇhadīpāyano, tāpaso (444).

kapi (20). (208). (404). (407). (516). cfr. vānaro.

Kapilo, brāhmaṇo, purohito Cetiyarañño (422).

kaputo, see: pārāpato.
Kappo, brāhmaṇa-kumāro (māṇavo, isi) (346). (405).
kappako Illīsa-seṭṭhino (78).
kammāraputto (387).
kassako (56). (189).
kassaka-brāhmaṇo (389).
Kassapo, purohitaputto, isi (Lomasakassapo) (433). tāpaso, pitā Nāradassa (477) — (106). pitā Isisiṅgassa, mahāisi (523). — Akitti-brāhmaṇo (480).
kāko (140). — Supatto kākarājā (292).
Kāraṇḍiya-māṇavo (356).
Kāliṅgabhāradvājo, purohito (479).
kinnaro, Cando (485).
kukkuṭo (383). (448).
kukkuro (22).
kuṭumbiko (39). (288). brāhmaṇo (354). kuṭumbika-putto, Sujāto (352). °-dārako (367). (368).
Kuṇālo, sakuṇarājā (536).
Kuṇḍakumāro, brāhmaṇo, khantivāditāpaso (313).
Kuddālaka-paṇḍito, paṇṇikakula-putto (70).
kumbhakāro (178). paribbājako (408).
kuruṅgamigo (21). (206).
Kusa-rājā, Kusakumāro putto Okkākassa (531).
Komāyaputto, brāhmaṇo, isi (299).
Khadiravaniyo, rukkhakoṭṭha-sakuṇo (210).
gandhabbo, Guttilakumāro (243).
Garuḷo (536) V 428,31 (— Kuṇālo sakuṇarājā).
gahapati (199). pabbajitapuriso (201). Sakkadattiyarājā (194).
gijjho (164). (399). (427). Aparaṇṇo (381).
Guttila-kumāro, gandhabbo (243).
go, Ayyakākāḷako (29). Nandivisālo (28). Mahālohito (30). (286). Sārambho balivaddo (88).
godho (138). (141). (325).

Ghaṭa-kumāro, paṇḍito, putto Devagabbhāya (454).
Ghaṭa-kumāro, Bārāṇasi-rājā (355).
cakkavāko (434). (451).
caṇḍālaputto (179). (309). (474). Cittapaṇḍito (498). Mātaṅga-paṇḍito (497).
Cando, kinnaro (485).
Candakumāro, rājā Bārāṇasiyaṁ (542).
Campeyyo, nāgarājā (506).
Citta-paṇḍito, caṇḍālaputto (498).
Cullaka-seṭṭhi (4).
Culladhanuggaha-paṇḍito, udiccabrāhmaṇa-putto (80).
coro (279). (318).
Chaddanto, nāgarājā (514).
Chaḷaṅgakumāro (536) V 430 (18) — Kuṇālo sakuṇarājā.
Janako, rājā (52) — Mahājanako (539).
Janasandho, Bārāṇasi-rājā (468)
Jambuko, suko (521).
javanahaṁso (476).
Juṇha-kumāro, Bārāṇasi-rājā (456).
Jotipāla-kumāro, purohitaputto (— Sarabhaṅgasatthā) (423). (522).
Takka-paṇḍito, isi (63).
Takkāriya-paṇḍito, māṇavo (481).
tāpaso (cfr. isi, udiccabrāhmaṇo) (154). (162). (207). (251). (285). (323). (328). (435). (490). (496). (511). dibbacakkhukatāpaso (436). — Kaṇhadīpāyano (444). Kassapo (477) — (106). Kuṇḍakumāro, khantivāditāpaso (313). Mahākañcano (488). Mahādhanakumāro, seṭṭhiputto (425). Hārito (431). — dhammānusāsako amacco Bārāṇasirañño (337).
tittiro (37). (438).
Tirīṭavaccha-kumāro, tāpaso, isi (259).
tulāputto — Kuṇālo, sakuṇarājā (536) V 424,25. 428 (28).

Temiya-kumāro, putto Kāsirañño (— Mūgapakkhapaṇḍito) (538).
daliddakula-putto (415). (421).
Dīghāvukumāro, putto Kosalarañño (371). (428).
Duyyodhano, Magadharājā (— Saṁkhapālo nāgarājā (524).
devatā, ākāsattha-devatā (147). kusanāḷi-devatā (121). pabbatamatthaka-devatā (419). rukkha-devatā (18). (19). (38). (74). (102). (105). (113). (139). (187). (205). (209). (217). (272). (283). (294). (298). (361). (400). (437). (492). eraṇḍarukkha-devatā (109) (295). gaṇḍatindukarukkha-devatā (520). nimbarukkha-devatā (311). palāsarukkha-devatā (307). phandanarukkha-devatā (475). simbalirukkha-devatā (412). vanasaṇḍa-devatā (13). (227). samudda-devatā (146). (190). (296).
devaputto (104). (297). (326). (369) (449). Dhammo (457). devarājā (82). (439). Bhaddasāla-devarājā (465).
dhaññavāṇijo (249). (365).
dhataraṭṭhahaṁso (533). (534).
Dhanañjayo, Kururājā (276).
Dhammo, devaputto (457).
Dhammaddhajo, purohito Bārāṇasi-rañño (220).
Dhammapālo, putto Mahāpatāpassa Bārāṇasi-rañño (358).
Dhammapālo, brāhmaṇa-putto (447).
naṭaka-putto (212).
Nandiyo, migo (385). — vānaro (222).
Nandivisālo, go (28).
nāgo, see: hatthi.
nāgarājā (cfr. hatthi), Campeyyo (506). Mahādaddaro (304). Saṁkhapālo (524). Bhūridatto, putto Dhataraṭṭha-nāgarañño (543).
Nārado, Mahābrahmā (544).
Nigrodha-kumāro, seṭṭhiputto (445).
Nigrodha-migarājā (12).
Nimi, rājā Mithilanagare (541).

niyyāmako, Suppārako (463).
nīlamaṇḍuko (239).
nesādaputto, Suvaṇṇasāmo paṇḍito (540).
Pañcālacaṇḍo (— Kuṇālo sakuṇarājā) (536). brāhmaṇakumāro V 430 (82); purohito V 440,10.
Pañcāvudha-kumāro, putto Bārāṇasi-rañño (55).
Paṇḍito, vāṇijo (98).
paṇḍita-kumārako, putto sattavassiko Vasiṭṭhakassa (446).
paṇḍita-puriso (46). (49). (89). (242). (268). (280).
paṇṇikakula-putto, Kuddālaka-paṇḍito (70).
Padumakumāro, putto Bārāṇasi-rañño (193). (472).
pārāpato (42). (274). (275). (277). (395). kapoto (375).
pāsāṇakoṭṭakamaṇikāro (137).
Pupphako, suvo (503).
purohito Bārāṇasirañño (34). (86). (120). (214). (216). (241). (290). (330). (362). (487). Kapila-brāhmaṇo, purohito Cetiyarañño (422). Kāliṅgabhāradvājo (479). Dhammaddhajo, purohito Bārāṇasirañño (220). Vidhūrapaṇḍito, purohito Koravyarañño (413).
purohitaputto (163). (310). Kassapo — Lomasakassapo, isi (433). Jotipālakumāro — Sarabhaṅgasatthā, isi (423). (522). Saṁkiccapaṇḍito, isi (530). Susīmakumāro — Susīmarājā (411). Hatthipālo (509).
Poṭṭhapādo, suko (145).
Bako, Bārāṇasirājā — Kuṇālo sakuṇarājā (536) V 444,1.
balivaddo, see: go.
Bodhikumāro, udiccabrāhmaṇa-putto — Mahābodhi-paribbājako (528). brāhmaṇaputto paribbājako (443).
Brahmadatto, Bārāṇasi-rājā (14). (67). (225). (248). (459). isi (519). — Kuṇālo sakuṇarājā (536) V 444,23.
Brahmadattakumāro, putto Bārāṇasi-rañño, rājā Bārāṇasiyaṁ (50). (151). (415). putto Magadha-rañño, rājā Bārāṇasiyaṁ (378).

rāhmaṇo (cfr. udiccabrāhmaṇo, ācariyo, isi, tāpaso, purohito, māṇavo) (174). (250). Kassaka-brāhmaṇo (389). kuṭumbiko (354). — Akitti (480). Aṭṭhiseno (403). Saṁkho (442). antevāsiko Vedabbhabrāhmaṇassa (48). — brāhmaṇaputto (68). (155). (237). Kaṇhapaṇḍito (440). Dhammapālo (447). Bodhikumāro (443). Sambhavakumāro (515). Sonakumāro (532). Somadatto (211).
Bhaddasāla-devarājā (465).
Bharato, rājā Roruvanagare (424).
Bhallāṭiyo, Bārāṇasi-rājā (504).
Bhūridatto, putto Dhataraṭṭha-nāgarañño (543).
bherivādako (59).
Bhojanasuddhika-rājā Bārāṇasiyaṁ (260).
Makhādevo, rājā Mithilāyaṁ (9).
Magha-kumāro, māṇavo (Sakko) (31).
maccho (75). (236). Mitacintī (114).
Mandhātā, rājā paṭhamakappe (258).
Mahākañcano, brāhmaṇaputto, isi (488).
Mahājanako, rājā Mithilāyaṁ (539) — Janako (52).
Mahātuṇḍilo, sūkaro (388).
Mahādaddaro, nāgarājā (304).
Mahādhanakumāro, putto Bārāṇasi-seṭṭhino, tāpaso (425).
Mahānandiko (Nandiyo), vānaro (222).
Mahābodhi-paribbājako — Bodhikumāro udiccabrāhmaṇaputto (528).
Mahābrahmā (134). (135). udiccabrāhmaṇo, isi (99). Nārado (544).
Mahālohito, go (30). (286).
Mahāsīlavo, rājā Bārāṇasiyaṁ — Sīlavakumāro (51).
Mahāsudassano, rājā Kusāvatiyaṁ (95).
Mahiṁsāsa-kumāro, putto Brahmadattassa Bārāṇasi-rañño (6).

mahiso, sīlavamahisarājā (278).

Mahosadha-paṇḍito, putto Sirivaḍḍhaseṭṭhino (546).

māṇavo (cfr. brāhmaṇo) (305). (432). (467). (478). Kāraṇḍiyo (356). Takkāriya-paṇḍito (481). Maghakumāro (— Sakko) (31). Sutano, duggatagahapati-putto (398).

Mātaṅgapaṇḍito, caṇḍālaputto (497).

migo (11). (15). (16). (359). kuruṅgamigo (21). (206). rurumigo (482). sarabha-migo (483) — Nandiyo (385). Nigrodha-migarājā (12). Rohanto migarājā (501).

Mitacinti, maccho (114).

Mūgapakkha-paṇḍito — Temiyakumāro, putto Kāsirañño (538).

mūsika-rājā (128). (129).

moro (339). (491). suvaṇṇa-moro (159).

Yuvañjayo, putto Sabbadatta-rañño Rammanagare (460).

Rakkhita-kumāro, tāpaso, ācariyo (453).

rājā: Mandhātā, paṭhamakappe (258)

Kuru-rājā, Dhanañjayo (276).

Kusāvatī-rājā, Kusakumāro (531), Mahāsudassano (95).

Gandhāra-rājā (Takkasilāyaṃ) (229). (406). putto Bārāṇasi-rañño (96). (132).

Bārāṇasi-rājā (62). (100). (191). (230). (233). (262). (269). (282). (289). (302). (303). (327). (343). (347). (349). (351). (420). udiccabrāhmaṇo (73).

— Arindamo (529).

— Ādāsamukho (257).

— Udayo (421)

— Udayabhaddo (Sakko) (458).

— Kaṭṭhavāhana-rājā (7).

— Ghatakumāro (355).

— Candakumāro (542).

— Janasandho (468).

— Joṇhakumāro (456).

— Bako — Kuṇālo sākuṇarājā (536) V 444.).

— Brahmadatto (14). (67). (225). (248). (459). tāpaso (519). — Kuṇālo sakuṇarājā (536) V 444,23.
— Bramadattakumāro (50). (151). (378). (415).
— Bhallātiyo (504).
— Bhojanasuddhiko (260).
— Mahāsīlavo — Sīlavakumāro (51).
— Sakkadattiyarājā, gahapatiputto (194).
— Susīmakumāro, purohitaputto (411).
Magadha-rājā, Duyyodhano — Saṁkhapāla-nāgarājā (524). Sivi-rājā' Sivikumāro (499). (527). Sovīra-rājā, Bharato (424). Videha-rājā Mithilāyaṁ: (160), Makhādevo (9). Mahājanako (539) — Janako (52), Nimi (541), Sādhīno (494).
rājakumāro: putto Mahāpiṅgalassa Bārāṇasi-rañño (280). putto Brahmadattassa Bārāṇasi-rañño (416). bhāgineyyo Brahmadattassa Bārāṇasi-rañño, rājā (126).
Ajjunakumāro, putto Paṇḍurañño (536) — Kuṇālo sakuṇarājā V 426,27.
Anitthigandhakumāro, putto Bārāṇasi-rañño (263). (507).
Alīnacittakumāro, putto Bārāṇasi-rañño (156).
Alīnasattukumāro, putto Jayaddisa-rañño Uttarapañcālanagare (513).
Asadisakumāro, putto Bārāṇasi-rañño (181).
Ghatakumāro, putto Devagabbhāya (454).
Dīghāvukumāro, putto Kosalarañño (371). (428).
Dhammapālo, putto Mahāpapātassa Bārāṇasi-rañño (358).
Pañcāvudhakumāro, putto Bārāṇasi-rañño (55).
Padumakumāro, putto Bārāṇasi-rañño (193). (472).
Mahiṁsāsakumāro, putto Brahmadattassa Bārāṇasi-rañño (6).
Yuvañjayo, putto Sabbadatta-rañño Rammanagare (460).
Rāmapaṇḍito, putto Dasarathassa Bārāṇasi-rañño (461).
Vessantaro, putto Sañjayassa Sivirañño (547).
Sutasomakumāro, putto Koravyarañño, rājā (537).

Somakumāro (Sutasoma-rājā), putto Bārāṇasi-rañño (525).
Somanassakumāro, putto Reṇurañño Uttarapañcālanagare (505).
Rādho, suko (198). (329).
Rāma-paṇḍito, putto Dasarathassa Bārāṇasi-rañño (461).
rurumigo (482).
Rohanto, migarājā (501).
lamghaunaṭako (116).
lāpa-sakuṇo (168).
Lomasakassapo, isi — Kassapo purohitaputto (433).
Vacchanakha-paribbājako, isi (235).
vaṭṭaku (33). (35). (118). (394).
vaḍḍhakī (466).
vāṇijo (cfr. satthavāho) (44). (79). (324). assavāṇijo (254). kacchapuṭavāṇijo, Serivo (3). dhaññavāṇijo (249). (365). — Paṇḍito (98).
Vātaggasindhavo, asso (266).
vānaro (cfr. kapi) (57) — (224). (58). (177). (219). (342). — Nandiyo (Mahānandiko) (222).
vāraṇo, see: hatthi.
vālāhasso (196).
Vidhurapaṇḍito, amacco Dhanañjayakorabbassa (545).
Vidhūrapaṇḍito, amacco Koravyarañño (495). purohito Dhanañjayassa Koravyarañño (413).
Visayho, seṭṭhi (340).
visavejjo (69).
Vīrako, udakakāko (204).
Vessantaro, putto Sañjayassa Sivirañño (547).
sakuṇo (36). (115). (133). (384). — rukkhakoṭṭhasakuṇo (308). — Khadiravaniyo (210). Kuṇālo sakuṇarājā (536).
Sakko, devarājā (202). (228). (264). (300). (344). (372). (374). (386). (391). (393). (410). (417). (469). (489). (512).

— seṭṭhi (291). (450). (535). — Udayabhaddo Kāsirājā (458). — Maghakumāro māṇavo (31).
Saṁkicca-kumāro paṇḍito, purohitaputto (530).
Saṁkho, brāhmaṇo (442).
Saṁkha-seṭṭhi Rājagahe (131).
saṁkhadhamaka-putto (60).
Saṁkhapālo, nāgarājā — Duyyodhano Magadharājā (524).
satthavāho (cfr. vāṇijo) (1). (2). (54). (85). (256). (366). (493).
Sambhavakumāro, brāhmaṇaputto (515).
Sarabhaṅga-satthā, isi — Jotipālakumāro purohitaputto (423). (522).
sarabhamigo (483).
saso (316).
Sādhīno, rājā Mithilāyaṁ (494).
Sārambho, balivaddo (88).
sigālo (142). (148).
siṅgila-sakuṇo (321).
Sivikumāro Sivirājā (499). (527).
Sīlavakumāro, putto Bārāṇasi-rañño — Mahāsīlavarājā (51).
Sīlava-nāgarājā, hatthi (72).
sīho (152). (153). (157). (172). (188). (322). (335). (397). (486). — kesarasiṁho (143).
suko (suvo) (255). (429). (430). (484). — Jambuko (521). Pupphako (503). Poṭṭhapādo (145). Rādho (198). (329).
Suciparivāra-seṭṭhi (382).
Sujāto, kuṭumbikaputto (352).
Sutano, māṇavo duggatagahapati-putto (398).
Sutasomo (Somakumāro), putto Bārāṇasi-rañño, rājā (525). putto Koravyarañño, rājā (537).
supaṇṇa-rājā (360). (518).
Supatto, kākarājā (292).
Suppārako, niyyāmako (463).

Suvaṇṇasāmo paṇḍito, nesādaputto (540).
suvaṇṇahaṁso (32). (136). (270). (370). (379). (502).
Susīmakumāro, purohitaputto = Susīmarājā (411).
sūkaro, Mahātuṇḍilo (388).
seṭṭhi Bārāṇasiyaṁ (40). (45). (47). (53). (83). (84). (90). (93). (103). (125). (127). (171). (232). (238). (363). (390). — = Sakko (291). (450). (535). — Cullakaseṭṭhi (4). Visayho (340). Saṁkhaseṭṭhi Rājagahe (131). Suciparivāraseṭṭhi (382).
seṭṭhiputto (261). (315). (317). — Nigrodhakumāro (445). Mahādhanakumāro, tāpaso (425). Mahosadha-paṇḍito, putto Sirivaḍḍhaseṭṭhino (546).
Senako, amacco Janakassa Bārāṇasi-rañño (402). amacco Maddavassa Bārāṇasi-rañño (401).
Serivo, kacchapuṭavāṇijo (3).
Sonakumāro, brāhmaṇaputto (532).
Somakumāro (Sutasomo), putto Bārāṇasi-rañño (525).
Somadatto, brāhmaṇaputto (211).
Somanassakumāro, putto Reṇu-rañño Uttarapañcālanagare (505).
haṁso, javanahaṁso (476). dhataraṭṭhahaṁso (533). (534). suvaṇṇahaṁso (32). (136). (270). (370). (379). (502).
hatthācariyo (182). (231).
hatthi (vāraṇo, nāga-rājā) (122). (221). (267). (357). (455). — Chaddanto (514). — Sīlava-nāgarājā (72).
Hatthipālo, purohitaputto (509).
Hārito, tāpaso = Harittaca-kumāro brāhmaṇaputto (431).
Bodhisatta-cariyā III 73,27.
Bodhisatta-paveṇi VI 552 (38).
Bodhisatta-mātā N 51,29–31. 52,3–7. — III 91,29*–94,11* (hatthinī).
Bodhisattā (pl.) I 303,18. 24. — II 141 (1). — III 282,6*. 283,8*. 409 (20). 425,8*. — IV 65 (15). 341,16*. — V 147, (20).

262,$_{26}$*. 291,$_{6}$*. 358,$_{11}$*. — VI 401,$_{29}$*. 405,$_{28}$*. 431,$_{28}$*. 552 (32—33). — Mahābodhisattā VI 225,$_{11}$*.

Brahāchatta-jātaka (336) III 115—118.

Brahmadatta, brāhmaṇo, pitā Kassapa-Buddhassa N 43,$_{21}$.

Brahmadatta, rājā Bārāṇasiyaṁ *I 98. 107. 120. 124. 127. 134. 140. 149. 157. 159. 166. 173. 175. 178 181. 184. 186. 189. 194. 196. 208. 210. 216. 224. 231. 242. 245. 247. 248. 250. 252. 253. 257. 259. 262 269. 270. 272. 277. 278. 280. 283. 284. 285. 289. 295. 299. 301. 303. 307. 310. 312. 319. 323. 328. 333. 343. 349. 354. 356. 361. 365. 366. 368. 370 375. 378. 379. 383. 388. 395. 404. 406. 409. 411. 413. 415. 416. 418. 421. 423. 425. 427. 429. 430. 431. 434. 436. 437. 441. 447. 450. 451. 455. 460. 461. 463. 469. 471. 473. 474. 475. 478. 480. 482. 484. 487. 489. 491. 494. 495. 497. 499. 502. 505. 510. — *II 2—3. 6. 10. 13. 15. 18. 26. 30. 33. 41. 43. 50. 52. 57. 59. 64. 66. 68. 70. 72. 74. 76. 79. 82. 85. 87. 94. 96. 100. 101. 107. 108. 109. 113. 116. 121. 125. 131. 132. 134. 137. 139. 142—3. 145. 149. 151. 153. 158. 161. 162. 165. 167. 173. 175. 178. 179. 181. 184. 197. 199. 203. 206. 217. 221. 225. 229—30. 232. 234. 236. 238. 243. 246. 248. 257. 260. 262. 264. 265. 267. 269. 272. 277. 283. 287. 292. 295. 314. 319. 322. 323. 328. 335. 338. 341. 349. 356. 359. 361. 382. 385. 387. 391. 394. 400. 405. 411. 417. 419. 421. 423. 427. 429. 431. 433. 437. 438. 440. 441. 445. 447. 450. — *III 16. 18. 21. 23. 25. 27. 30. 34. 36. 45. 49. 51. 56. 59. 64. 67. 73. 75. 80. 82. 84. 87. 90. 93—4. 102. 105. 110. 112. 115. 119. 122. 126. 128. 133. 137. 140. 142. 145. 147. 149. 155. 158. 162. 168. 171. 174. 183. 191. 194. 198. 200. 202. 204. 208. 213. 215. 219. 225. 228. 232. 240—1. 246. 248. 255. 257. 265. 267. 281. 286. 299—300. 303. 308. 310. 312. 314. 317. 321. 325. 330 333. 352.

355. 370. 376. 388. 391. 397. 403. 406. 415. 424. 428. 435. 439. 444. 463. 475. 497. 502. 514. 520. 527. 532. 537. — III 452*.16. 20. 25 (28) (— Udayo Bārāṇasirāja (Bo.)). — III 487,17. 18. 489 (14). — *IV 7. 15. 22. 44. 50. 59. 62. 70. 90. 96. 100. 114. 131. 153. 159. 168. 176. 189. 197. 200. 207. 212. 220. 224. 237. 245. 255. 267. 283. 289. 298. 305. 316. 333. 370. 376. 413. 491. — *V 1. 12. 68. 75. 88. 109. 127. 177. 193. 227. 263—64—69. 382. 457. — V 102*.15. 21 (28). 103.21*. 104*.20. 24. 105* (6). 14. 19. 106*,12. 17 (— Pañcālo, rājā Uttarapañcālanagare). — V 425.2 (27). 428 (32). 430 (31). 444.12. 23. 26 (— Kuṇḍla-rājā (Bo.)). — V 475 (10). — *VI 158—195—96.

Brahmadatta, see: Cūḷani-Brahmadatta, Sāgara-Brahmadatta.

Brahmadatta-kumāra, putto Brahmadattassa Bārāṇasi-rañño I 259,10* (Bo.). — II 2,4* (Bo.). 87,7* (bhātā Bodhisattassa). 229,28*. 279,19*. — III 158.15*. 391.22*. 407,13* (Bo.). 475,4*. 514.25*. — IV 315.31*. — V 263.4*. 457*.9. 12. 15. 458*.1. 10 (Bārāṇasi-kumāro). — VI 159.19*.

Brahmadatta-kumāra, putto Magadharañño (— Bodhisatto) III 238,7*.

Brahmadatta-jātaka (323) III 78—81.

Brahmadeva, aggasāvako Revata-Buddhassa N 35.8.

Brahmadeva, aggasāvako Tissa-Buddhassa N 40.24.

Brahman (cfr. Mahābrahman) IV 452.24*. — V 53.1*. 228 (17). — VI 201.8* (13. 19). 207,18*. 208*,16. 29. 24. 210 (6. 20. 21 24). 220.25. 242 (31). 568,8. 571,12. — Brahmāno (pl.) III 363,15. — V 55 (25). Brahma-sahassaṁ III 363 (18). — IV 180,27.

Brahmā (Tudu-), see: Tudu-Brahman.

Brahmā (Baka-), III 358.23. 359,3. 12 (27). 360,4. 361 (17). 362 (30). (cfr. Baka-Brahman).

Brahmā Mahindo V 411,6*. (cfr. Mahinda).

Brahmā Sahampati N 81.9. (cfr. Sahampati).

Brahmattaṁ III 132,5*. — Brahmattabhāvo IV 377,22*.

Brahmissariyaṁ IV 10,14*.

Brahma-gutto (— Brahma-gopito, Brahma-rakkhito) II 14,14* (18. 19).

Brahma-tejo VI 243,8*.

Brahma-deyyaṁ VI 486,3*.

Brahma-patti III 359,20 (25).

Brahma-bhattā (pl.) IV 377,26*. 378,17*.

Brahma-manto II 33,20*. 35,12*.

Brahma-vihāro II 43,8*. — Brahmavihārā (cattāro) I 334,21*. — II 54,3*. 56,15*. 61,13. 19*. 69,24*. 132,8*. 148,16*. — III 519,24*. — V 246,7*. — VI 21,17*. 96*,8. 12. 129,4*. — Brahmavihārabhāvanā IV 490,12*.

Brahma-sampatti N 48,19.

Brahmaloka N 30,11. 34,6. 48,2. 72,17. 76,8. 9. — I 139,20*. 142,9*. 201,18*. 246,10*. 334,22*. 406,28*. 407,13*. 417,24*. 432,28. 433,4. 473,26*. 474,21*. 494,6*. — II 62,23*. 198,25 (27). 328,9*. 403 (7). — III 48,13*. 93,22*. 254,22*. 355,10*. 359,2 (28). 363 (10) 15. 474 (3). 487,1. — IV 22*,16. 21. 73,11. 78,26*. 104*,20. 24. 180,26. 224,3*. 242,22*. 244,30. 377,15*. 389,22*. 469,2*. 7. 9 (17). 490*,14. 15. — V 138 (18). 149 (25). 191 (28). 312*,22. 25. 484,13*. 502,17*. — VI 72*,7. 12. 96*,9. 13. 14. 98 (30. 34). 99,25*. 101 (37. 38). 141 (26). 183,23*. 242,25 (29). 255,2*. 256,26*. 486,18*. 547 (25). 556,2*. — Brahmaṁ ṭhānaṁ V 149,29*.

Brahmalokūpago II 43,4*. 45,7*. 61,6. 69,24*. 90,24*. 132,9*. 276,25*. — III 246,5*. 303,8*. 310,6*. — IV 314,14*. 401,5*. 453,29*. 471,30. 473 (6). — V 98,17*. 177,3*. 246,8*. 261,25*. — VI 95,5* 129,5*.

Brahmaloka-parāyano I 362,28*. 371,21*. 373,31*. 407,14*. 432,18*. 440,23*. 493,27*. 494,7*. 495,12*. — II 54,3*. 56,15*. 61,14. 23*. 65,20*. 73,19*. 141,20. 148,16*. 270,14*. 318,16*. 331,5*. 418,26*. 423,10*. 430,23*. 438,9*. — III

15,18*. 81,21*. 97,6*. 102,4*. 149,4*. 170,13*. 195,26*. 369,21*. 396,32*. 434,20*. 519,24*. 526,28*. — IV 8,8*. 27,19*. 36,25*. 119,6*. 123,13*. 175,21*. 332,19*. 423,13*. — V 10,30*. 152,21*. 192,1*. 332,20*. — VI 29,26*. 68,16*. 96,10*.

Brahmaloka-parāyanatā IV 499,19*.

Brahmaloka-parāyanattaṁ I 334 (18).

Brahmaloka-maggo I 334 (17).

Brahmaloka-sampattiyo cha I 105,29.

Brahmavaddhana, — Bārāṇasī IV 119,20*. — V 312,19*. 313,13*. 314,27*. 316,15*.

brāhmaṇo, aññataro II 137,7. — IV 167,3. mahallako Sāketanagaravāsī I 308,25. — II 234,25.

brāhmaṇakumāro, aññataro II 99,19.

Bh.

Bhagīrasa, rājā VI 99,9*.

Bhagu, thero I 140,6. — III 489,30.

Bhaggari, see: Bhaggiri.

Bhaggava, kumbhakāro, paribbājako (— Bodhisatto) III 382,14*.

Bhaggavī, bhariyā Bodhisattassa, paribbājikā III 381,21*. 382 (2).

Bhaggā, (janapado) III 157,22.

Bhaggiri, (vihāro?) Tambapaṇṇidīpe IV 490,23 (Bh-vāsi-Mahādevatthero). — VI 30,5 (Bhaggari-vāsī Mahātissatthero).

Bhaṇḍakucchi, dovāriko IV 382,14* (18).

bhaṇḍanakārakā (bhikkhū) Kosambiyaṁ III 211,4. 486,9.

Bhaṇḍukaṇṇa, nāṭako IV 324*,10. 12.

bhattabhuñjana-sunakho II 246,9.

Bhadda, aggasāvako Koṇḍañña-Buddhassa N 30,13.

Bhaddakāpilānī, (therī) IV 491,4. — VI 95,10. (cfr. Kāpilānī).

Bhaddaji, thero II 331,14. 17. 29 (Bhaddajikumāro). 333,1. 2. 4. 6. 7. 15. 20. 334,7 (21. 22. 25). 335,3. — IV 325,12. — VI 255,6. — °-therassa ānubhāvo II 331,18.

Bhaddavatikā, nigamo I 360,5. 11. 18.

Bhaddavatiya-hatthinī Udenassa rañño Kosambiyaṁ III 384,3. Bhaddavatikā 384,25. 27. 29. 385,2. 6. 18*. 388,14.

Bhaddasāla, aggasāvako Nārada-Buddhassa N 37,6.

Bhaddasāla V 81,29* (read: bhaddasāla?).

Bhaddasāla, devarājā (— Bodhisatto) IV 154,28*. 156*,13 (10). 22. 157,27.

Bhaddasāla-jātaka (465) IV 144—157. — I 133,24. 175,3. 484,13. — III 369,28.

Bhaddasāla-rukkha IV 156 (4). 157 (4).

Bhaddasena, vemātikabhātā Canda-kumārassa (Bodhisattassa) VI 134,6* (10). 157,22 (Candaseno, Cod. B[d]: Bhaddaseno).

Bhaddā, aggasāvikā Revata-Buddhassa N 35,9.

Bhaddiya, gahapati VI 135,5*.

Bhaddiya, thero N 82,16. — I 140,3. 5. 9. 15. 16. 142,11.

Bhaddiya-nagara II 331,16.

Bhaddiyavaggiya-kumārā tiṁsa N 82,27.

Bhaddiyaseṭṭhi, pitā Bhaddaji-kumārassa II 331,18. 332,12.

Bhaddekaratta-sutta IV 481 (30). 482 (1). — V 66 (27).

Bhadrakāra, māṇavo putto Vidhurabrāhmaṇassa V 60*,17. 21. 26. 28. 61*,4. 5. 62 (29). 67,25.

Bhadraghaṭa-jātaka (291) II 431—32.

Bharata, isi VI 99,28*.

Bharata, rājā Roruvanagare Sovīraraṭṭhe III 470,6*. 474,18.

Bharata, luddo III 432*,18. 23.

Bharata-kumāra, putto Dasarathassa rañño Bārāṇasiyaṁ IV 124,15*. 125*,15. 17. 27. 126*,11. 16. 127 (24). 128 (6. 23). 129 (10). 19*. 130,18.

Bharatūsabha, — Pañcālo rājā Uttara-pañcālanagare V 99,26*. 101 (3).

Bharu-jātaka (213) II 169—173. — V 101 (6). 118 (31).
Bharu-nagara II 171,5*.
Bharu-raṭṭha II 171,1*. 172*,11. 14 (23). — IV 137,8*.
Bharu-rājā II 171,1*. 172,13*. 18 (22. 24). 173 (2). — IV 137,8*. — V 118 (31).
Bharukaccha, (paṭṭanagāmo) III 188,13*. 190,2*. — IV 137*,8. 9. 138,20*. 139,12* (14). 140*,1. 11. 22. 141*,5. 25. 142,24*. — Bharukaccha-vāṇijā III 188,13*.
Bhallāṭiya, rājā Bārāṇasiyaṁ (— Bodhisatto) IV 437,16*. 438,12. 443,5. 444,5.
Bhallāṭiya-jātaka (504) IV 437—444.
Bhalluka, vāṇijo N 80,16.
Bhavagga VI 354,16.* 398 (32).
Bhāgīrathī, Gaṅgā (var. lect. Bhāgīrasī) V 93,1 (20). Bhāgīrasodakaṁ V 255,13*. — Bhāgīrasī VI 204,10*. Bhāgīrasīgaṅgā VI 204 (18).
Bhārata, — Pañcālo, rājā Uttarapañcālanagare IV 435,12*. (19). — — Bārāṇasi-rājā V 170,5* (20). — — Manojo Bārāṇasi-rājā V 317,9*. 326,9*.
Bhāradvāja, aggasāvako Kassapa-Buddhassa N 43,22.
Bhāradvāja, brāhmaṇavaḍḍhakī IV 210,20 (25).
— Kāliṅgabhāradvāja IV 235,13*.
— Piṇḍolabhāradvāja IV 375,22.
— Sucīrato V 58,13. 60,25. 61,28. 65,4. Bhāradvājagotto: V 59 (16).
— Jūjako VI 532,12. 18 (18). 574,24.
see: Aggika Bhāradvāja.
Bhāva-seṭṭhī, — Bījako VI 228,7 (22).
Bhāvitatta, aggasāvako Sumana-Buddhassa N 34,27.
Bhikkhāparampara-jātaka (496) IV 369—374.
bhikkhu aññataro I 471,11. — II 130,15. 144,21. 209,27. 444,19. — III 118,28. 246,11. 307,25. 490,14. — atibahuṁ bhuñjitvā ajīrakena kālakato II 291,26. — aparissāvanako I 198,10. — cīvara-vaḍḍhako I 220,16. — daḍḍhapaṇṇabālo

I 215,15. — bahubhaṇḍiko I 126,10. 206,17. — saddhivihāriko Sāriputtassa I 224,15.
bhikkhū bhaṇḍanakārakā Kosambakā III 211,4. 486,9.
Bhikkhudāsikā, dhītā Kikirañño VI 481,12*.
Bhiyyosa, aggasāvako Koṇāgamana-Buddhassa N 43,9.
Bhiruka-jātaka, see: Pañcagaru-jāt.
Bhisa-jātaka (488) IV 304—314. — V 275 (22). — VI 363 (11).
Bhisapuppha-jātaka (392) III 307—310.
Bhīmaratha, rājā V 135,21*. 137,3*. 149,30*.
Bhīmasena, tantavāyo I 356*,23. 25. 357*,7. 12. 17. 358*,11. 18. 21. 23. 25. 26. 28. 359*,3. 10. 15. 21. 26.
Bhīmasena, Paṇḍurājaputto V 424,20. 426 (11).
Bhīmasena-jātaka (80) I 355—359.
Bhummaja, chabbaggiya-bhikkhu, see: Mettiya.
Bhūridatta, — Datto, putto Dhataraṭṭhanāgarañño (— Bodhisatto) VI 168,30*. 171,21*. 173,11*. 175*,7. 24 (20). 176,6*. 12. 15. 177*,1. 5. 179*,8. 20. 23. 182*,10. 12. 183,4*. 184*,1. 27. 187,3. 188*,12. 14. 16 (18). 20—29. 189*,2. 6. 10—16. 21—26. 190*,3. 5 (6). 18. 22. 24. 191,8*. 196*,23. 28. 197*,18. 22. 198,15*. 201 (4). 219,27. — N 45,21. — Kāsiputto VI 175,7* (10).
Bhūridatta-jātaka (543) VI 157—219. — IV 182,20*. 456,27*.
Bhūripañha-jātaka (452) IV 72. — Bhūripañho V 147 (16). — VI 372,31*—376,5.
Bheṇṇākaṭa, (janapado?) VI 237,12 (33) (— Peṇṇākaṭa). 239 (23).
Bherivāda-jātaka (59) I 283—84.
Bherī, paribbājikā VI 467*,2. 5. 28. 468,25*. 469,4*. 478,11*.
Bhesakalā-vana, Suṁsumāragiriṁ nissāya Bhaggesu III 157,23.
Bhesajjasannidhikāra-sikkhāpadaṁ III 363,22.
Bhogavatī, mandiraṁ (nāga-rājadhānī) VI 269,3*. 270, (9).
Bhoja, brāhmaṇo N 56,4.
Bhoja, vejjo IV 491,7*. 498 (32).

Bhojanasuddhi(ka), rājā Bārāṇasiyaṁ (— Bodhisatto) II 319,6*. 321,4.

Bhojaputtā (pl.), (janapado) N 45,20.

Bhojājānīya-jātaka (23) I 178—181.

M.

Maṁsa-jātaka (315) III 48—51.

Makasa-jātaka (44) I 246—248.

Makkaṭa-jātaka (173) II 68—69.

Makkhaligosāla, diṭṭhigatiko I 509,13. — V 246,11.

Makhādeva (v. l. Māghadeva), yakkho III 325,20*.

Makhādeva, rājā Mithilāyaṁ Videharaṭṭhe (— Bodhisatto) I 137,25*. 138*,8. 18. 139,18*. 29. — Nimirājā VI 95,19. 21*. 96,14*.

Makhādevambavana, Mithilaṁ upanissāya VI 95,14.

Makhādeva-jātaka (9) I 137—139.

Makhilā, aggasāvikā Sikhi-Buddhassa N 41,31.

Magha-kumāra (Magha-māṇava), mahākulassa putto Rājagahe (— Sakko — Bodhisatto) II 199*,5. 6. 30.

Magadha-raṭṭha I 143*,10. 17. 154,5*. 199*,1. 8. 213,11*. 246,10. 373,9*. 444,15*. 466,1*. — II 55,8*. — III 479,20*. — IV 325*,24. 25. 454*,10. 11. 14. — V 316,19*. — VI 239 (28). 465 (14). — Māgadha VI 237,7. — Magadharajjaṁ VI 272 (9). — Magadhā (pl.) I 212,7—9. 246,17. — II 211,15* (20) — V 171,30*. 317,28*. — VI 236,30. 237 (18. 28). — Magadhakhettaṁ III 293,20*. — IV 276,18*. 277*,14. 18. — Magadhavāsino (-vāsikā) N 87,13. — 154*,6. 14. — II 211,1*. — Māgadhā saṁkhā VI 465,13. — (cfr. Māgadha.)

Magadha-rāja N 83,29. — I 143,10*. 154,5*. 162,23*. 199,1*. 373,2*. 444,15*. 446,21. 466,1*. — III 288,5*. — IV 276,11*. 454,16* (Magadho). 454*,13. 14. 27. 28. — V 161,25*. 247,7*.

316,13* (Magadho). — VI 220,1. 4. — Magadha-mahārājā IV 37,14*.

Maghavā Sujampati, devānaṁ indo III 146,30*. — IV 403*,27. 28. — V 137,27*. 139,17* (27). — VI 102,17. 481,1*. 573,21. Maghavā VI 212*,13. 16. — Maghavā Sakko V 141,8. — Maghavā devakuñjaro V 158,10. — VI 98,6.

Maṁgaṇa, (vihāro?) Sīhaladīpe VI 30,3 (Maṁgaṇa-vāsī Khuddakatissa-thero).

Maṁgala-jātaka (87) I 371—374.

Maṅgala, tāpaso Siddhattha-Buddhassa kale (— Bodhisatto) N 40,5. — Maṅgalabodhisatto IV 13 (8).

Maṅgala-Buddha, N 30,17. 18. 31,5. 34,6. 14. 30. 44,5.

Maṅgala-sutta IV 73,17.

Macala-gāmaka, Magadharaṭṭhe I 199,3-4*.

Maccha-jātaka, a) (34) I 210—212. — b) (75) I 329—332. — c) (216) II 178—179.

Maccha-raṭṭha VI 280 (28). — Macchā VI 280,24* (28). 281 (2).

Maccharikosiya, seṭṭhi asītikoṭivibhavo, tāpaso V 383*,14. 22. 384,5*. 386*,16. 26. 389,18*. 390,12*. 392,13. 16*. — Kosiyo V 387,21*. 388,8*. 389*,19. 22. 30. 390,2*. 391*,15. 24. 395*,20. 22. 28. 396,6*. 397,19*. 399,16*. 400,27*. 401,1*. 402,24*. 403,28*. 405,13. 406,34*. 407*,7. 15. 408,10*. 15. 16 (18). 409,11. 13. 411*,5. 13. 14. 23. 412 (4). 9. — Kosiko V 396,10*.

Maccharikosiya, seṭṭhi Sakkhare Rājagahanagarassa avidūre I 345,20.

maccharīseṭṭhi I 345,18.

Macchuddāna-jātaka (288) II 423—26.

Majjhantika, thero V 142 (28).

Majjhimadesa, janapado N 49,7-8. 80,17. — III 115*,25. 26. — V 134,2*.

Majjhimapadesa III 364,11*. 463,21*.

Majjhimapaṇṇāsaka (— Jāt. (51) — (100).) I 410,19.

Majjhimapadesa, see: Majjhimadesa.
Mañjerika-nāgabhavana N 72,14. — VI 264 (4).
Maṭṭakuṇḍali-jātaka (449) IV 59—62. — Maṭṭhakuṇḍali-vatthu (sic!) IV 79,5.
Maṭṭhara, see: Māṭhara.
Maṇi-pabbata, Himavante II 92,27. — V 415,23. Maṇipassa-pabbato V 38,10*.
Maṇikaṇṭha, nāgarājā II 283*,14. 18.
Maṇikaṇṭha-jātaka (253) II 282—286. — III 78,24. 351,24. 353 (10).
Maṇikuṇḍala-jātaka (351) III 153—155.
Maṇikuṇḍala-vagga III 153—190.
Maṇikhaṇḍa, Vidhurapaṇḍitajātake VI 279,32.
Maṇikhandha-jātaka, see: Khandhaka.
Maṇicora-jātaka (194) II 121—125. — IV 77 (28).
Maṇipassa, see: Maṇi.
Maṇimekhalā, devadhītā samuddarakkhikā IV 17,10*. — VI 35,5*.
Maṇisūkara-jātaka (285) II 415—418.
Maṇḍa-kappa N 38,24. 39,19. 30. 41,7. 42,16.
Maṇḍavya (v. l. Maṇḍabba), tāpaso, Dīpāyanassa gihisahāyo IV 28*,18. 23. 29*,17. 25. 30*,7. 9. 18. 20. 33,6*. 34*,1. 17. 27. 36*,5. 13. 15. 24. 28. — Aṇimaṇḍavyo IV 30,18*. Āṇimaṇḍavyo 30,24*. 37,1 (?).
Maṇḍavya, putto Diṭṭhamaṅgalikāya IV 379*,1. 8. 24 380,28*. 381,17*. 383,18*. 386,13*. 387*,1. 5 (17). 388,6*. 390,2.
matakabhattaṁ I 166,7.
Matakabhatta-jātaka (18) I 166—168.
matapitika-kuṭumbiko III 155,9. — IV 123,25.
mataputtaka-kuṭumbiko III 162,3. — IV 59,5.
matabhariya-kuṭumbiko III 92,20.
Matabhariya-Matapitika-vatthu III 162,4.
Matarodana-jātaka (317) III 56—58.

Madda-raṭṭha IV 230,20*. — V 40,3*. 283,26*. — VI 280 (28). 471 (20). 473 (8). 474 (20).

Maddā VI 280,24* (28). 281 (8).

Madda-rāja IV 230*,21. 25. — V 283,27*. 284,17*. 285*,7. 9. 15. 22. 28. 290,23*. 294,10*. 296,2* (9). 300*,20. 29. 303,23*. 30. 304,5*. 309,28*. 30. 310,3*. 311,6*. — VI 471 (25). 484,5*.

Maddakulaṁ V 306,15*. 309,4*. Maddarājakulaṁ V 39,25*. 309 (9). — VI 486,26*. Maddarājadhītā (— Candādevī) VI 1,16*. (— Phusatī) VI 480,9*. 498 (20).

Maddakucchi, migadāyo (Rājagahaṁ nissāya) IV 430,11. 16.

Maddava, mahārājā Bārāṇasiyaṁ III 337*,1. 4. (cfr. Māgadha.)

Maddi-pabba, Vessantarajātake VI 568,19.

Maddī, aggamahesī Vessantarassa, dhītā Maddarañño N 77,13. — VI 486*,27. 30. 494,10*. 14. 20. 26* (28). 495*,8. 13. 22. 498,10*. 500*,10. 12. 502 (1). 505,8*. 506,7*. 25. 29. 507,10. 12. 14. 508 (31). 509,23. 28. 510,23*. 27. 30. 511 (5). 27. 28. 512,2*. 8*. 18. 513,1*. 3. 20*. 27. 514 17*. 26 (25). 515,1*. 520*,10. 16. 20. 24. 28. 521,4*. 527,8*. 540*,17. 22. 25. 541*,2. 5. 7. 8. 555,5. 556,4* (23). 32*. 562,1 (3). 34. 566,7 (9. 12). 16*. 25*. 567,6. 8. 9. 13 (16). 22*. 32*. 568,11. 568*,1. 7. 19. 23—25. 569*,25. 30. 570,9. 12. 13 (15). 18. 20 (23). 28*. 572,1—3. 573*,25. 31. 582,10*. 15 (24). 586,5—10 (12—18). 587,11. 588,22*. 589,1. (14). (18). 590,6. 8. 12 (31). 591,6. (8). 593,28.

Maddha, (vihāro?) Sīhaladīpe VI 30,9 (Maddhavāsī Mahānāgatthero).

Madhuvat (?), (— seṭṭhavānaro) IV 314,23.

Manoja, rājā Bārāṇasiyaṁ V 312,20*. 314,24*. 316*,8. 9. 22. 319,18*. 320,13*. 322,22. 323,14*. 324,28*. 332,28.

Manoja, sīho, putto Bodhisattassa III 321*,24. 26. 322*,5. 8. 323*,8. 21. 28. 324 (15). 21.

Manoja-jātaka (397) III 321—324.

Manojava, isi VI 99,26*.

Manosilā-tala, Himavante N 12,22. 50,12. — I 95,18. 232,6*. — II 65,27. 92,28 — III 379,10*. — V 392*,23. 27.

Mantidatta, thero IV 343,10. — Datta-thero IV 343,12. 16. (— Utta-thero(?) II 403,28. 404,3. 6. Cod. B.)

Mantin, brāhmaṇo N 56,3.

Mandhātar, rājā paṭhamakappe (— Bodhisatto) II 311,12*. 312*,10. 16. 22. 313,6*. 16 (24. 28). 314,15. — III 454*,16. 17.

Mandhātu-jātaka (258) II 310—314.

Mayūra, pāsādo Vidhurapaṇḍitassa VI 269*,10. 12.

Mayha(ka), sakuṇo III 301*,22. 25.

Mayhaka-jātaka (390) III 299—303.

maraṇabhīruka-bhikkhu III 286,10.

Mala-raṭṭha (v. l. Mallaka-, Malaya-, Codd. B), IV 327,20*. — Malata(?) IV 331,3*. (cfr. Malla-).

Malimahādeva, thero Tambapaṇṇidīpe IV 490,22. — Maliya-mahādeva-thero VI 30,9. (cfr. Mahāmaliyadeva.)

Malla, Malla-putta, see: Dabba, Pukkusa, Bandhula, Roja. (cfr. Cāṇura, Muṭṭhika).

Malla-giri IV 438,28* (the text: Mallaṁgiriṁ). 439 (3). — Mallā-giri 439 (4).

Malla-raṭṭha V 278,22*. (cfr. Mala-).

Mallaka-raṭṭha, see: Mala-raṭṭha.

Mallika, Kosalarājā II 3*,3. 8. 12. 23. 4* (8). 26. 28. 5,9*. 7.

Mallikā, devī Pasenadi-Kosalarañño, dhītā mālakārajeṭṭha-kassa Sāvatthiyaṁ I 335,23. — III 20,16. 19. 22,27. 44,13. 405,16. 406,16. 20. — IV 437,4. 13. 444,4. — V 88,6. 12. 98,18. 19.

Mallikā, bhariyā Bandhulassa senāpatino Kosalarañño IV 148,10. 149,5. 16. 150,4. 27. 151,14.

Masakkasāra, bhavanaṁ Vāsavassa Sinerupabbate V 167,12*. 168 (14. 15). — VI 271,31. 272 (10—11). 289,15*. — Masak-kasāra-ppabhavā devatā (— Āsā) V 400,28* (31).

mahallaka-thero I 188,30. — II 9,12. 106,24. — III 197,23 (— mahāthero II 266,24). — III 213,9. 388,18.
dve mahallakā therā I 426,22. — IV 342,28 (— Dhanuggahatissa & Mantidatta, cfr. II 403—4).
mahallaka-bhikkhu III 36,8.
mahallakā bhikkhū I 497,8.
Mahānāthapiṇḍika I 148,4.
mahābhinikkhamanaṁ IV 119,13.
Mahāvīci, nirayo V 266,14*. 271 (12) (cfr. Avīci).
Mahā-assāroha-jātaka (302) III 8—13.
Mahāukkusa-jātaka (486) IV 288—297. — IV 77 (24).
Mahā-ummagga-khaṇḍa, Mahāummagga-jātake VI 466,18.
Mahā-ummagga-jātaka (546) VI 329—478. — II 83,2. 115,13. — III 197,20. 281,14. — IV 412,27. 473,12. — V 57,6. 75,8. 227,22. (cfr. Ummagga-jātaka.)
Mahā-ummaggassa vaṇṇanā VI 478,9*.
Mahosadha, paṇḍito, — Osadha-kumāro, putto Sirivaḍḍhaseṭṭhino Mithilāyaṁ (— Bodhisatto) N 46,6. 63,21. 30. — VI 334*,3. 8. 338 (23 Mahosadhabuddhaṁkuro). 339 (15. 27). 340 (35). 341 (10). 342 (9. 10. 32. 36). 343 (6. 10). 344,15*. 345,24*. 346,21*. 348,30*. 351,21*. 356*,24. 28. 357*,14. 15. 358,8*. 363,17*. 368*,15. 25. 369,16*. 370,5*. 371,4*. 372*,8. 13. 20. 374,6*. 384*,10. 25 (29). 385,9*. 386,14*. 393*,4. 21. 23. 394,29*. 395*,17. 20. 396*,22. 26. 397,8*. 398 (32). 399,18*. 401,2*. 402*,3. 28. 403*,8. 27. 404*,9. 14. 409*,4. 11. 410,3*. 412,30*. 414*,5. 7. 415*,22. 29. 424 (21). 425,25. 427,15. 428,6*. 429,10*. 430,4*. 431*,8. 11. 22. 25. 435,23*. 437 (12). 439,9*. 440,17*. 441 (1. 26. 28). 442,7*. 443,2. 445,2. 20. 446,11*. 447*,17 (20). 24. 451*,27. 30. 456*,3. 14. 458,7*. 459,21*. 462,19*. 463*,21. 28. 465,3. 7. 467*,3. 8. 28. 468*,1. 4. 7. 8. 12. 21. 469 (26). 470,5* (9). 476,19*. 477*,9. 12. 478,14*.
Mahākaṁsa, rājā Asitañjana-nagare Kaṁsabhoge Uttarāpathe IV 79,9*

Mahâ-Kaccâyana, see: Kaccâyana.

Mahâkañcana-kumâra, putto brâhmaṇamahâsâlassa Bârâṇasiyaṁ, tâpaso (— Bodhisatto) IV 305*,8. 12. 26. 306,7*.

Mahâkaṇha, sunakho IV 181,26*. 182*,12. 16. — Kaṇho IV 183*,12 (14). 21. 185 (4). 186 (4).

Mahâkaṇha-jâtaka (469) IV 180—186. — I 259,5. — III 145,22. 303,11. — IV 182,20*. — V 115 (6).

Mahâkapi-jâtaka a) (407) III 369—375 (v. l. Râjovâda-jât. B). b) (516) V 67—74. — Vevaṭiyakapi-jâtaka III 178,7.

Mahâkappina, (thero) IV 180,20.

Mahâkammâsadamma, Sutasoma-mahâsattena porisâdassa damitapadeso V 36,1*. (cfr. Kammâsadamma).

Mahâkassapa, see: Kassapa.

Mahâkâla, nâgarâjâ, see: Kâla.

Mahâkâla, pabbato Himavante V 38,8*.

Mahâkâliṅga, putto Kâliṅgassa, râjâ Dantapura-nagare Kâliṅgaraṭṭhe IV 230,7*. 231,27*.

Mahâkosala, pitâ Kosala-rañño II 237,17. 403,14. 22. — IV 342,26.

Mahâgaṅgâ II 117*,3. 8. — VI 436,6*.

Mahâgotamo III 44,25. (cfr. Gotamo).

Mahâgovinda, (brâhmaṇo — Bodhisatto) N 45,14. 46,5.

Mahâgovinda-sutta III 469,26.

Mahâcûlani, râjâ, pitâ Cûlani-Brahmadattassa VI 470 (20). 474 (10).

Mahâjanaka, râjâ Mithilâyaṁ Videharaṭṭhe VI 30*,20. 28.

Mahâjanaka, putto Ariṭṭhajanakassa Videharañño, râjâ Mithilâyaṁ (— Bodhisatto) III 489 (24). — VI 33,11*. 35,9*. 40,7*. 42,22*. 53 (27). 54 (21). 56,16*. 57 (7). 67,27*. 68,22. (cfr. Janaka).

Mahâjanaka-jâtaka (539) VI 30—68. — N 46,13. — I 268,9. — III 238,27*. — IV 40,4*.

Mahâtakkâri-jâtaka (— Takkâriya-jât. (481)) II 175,10.

Mahātissa, thero Bhaggari-vāsī, Sīhaladīpe VI 30,5.
Mahātuṇḍila, sūkaro (— Bodhisatto) III 287*,4. 18. 288*,1. 9 293,4.
mahāthero aññataro II 266,24.
Mahādaddara, nāgarājā, putto Sūradaddararañño (— Bodhisatto) III 16*,7. 10. 17,4*. 25. — Daddaro III 16,24*.
mahāduggato manusso I 422,6.
Mahādeva, thero Bhaggiri-vāsī Tambapaṇṇidīpe IV 490,22.
Mahādhana-kumāra, putto Bārāṇasi-seṭṭhino, tāpaso (— Bodhisatto) III 475,5*.
Mahādhanaka, seṭṭhiputto Bārāṇasiyaṁ (— Devadatto) IV 255,27*.
Mahādhammapāla, see: Dhammapāla.
Mahādhammapāla-jātaka (447) IV 50—55. — N 92,11. — IV 282,22.
Mahānandika — Nandiya, vānaro (— Bodhisatto) II 202,21.
Mahānāga, thero Kāḷavallimaṇḍapavāsī Tambapaṇṇidīpe IV 490,24. — thero Maddha-vāsī, Sīhaladīpe VI 30,9.
Mahānāma, thero N 82,16.
Mahānāma Sakka, pitā Vāsabhakhattiyāya I 133,24. 134,3. — II 79,5. — IV 145,7. 17. 23. 28. 29. 146,5. 7. 147,17.
Mahānāradakassapa-jātaka (544) VI 219—255. — N 83,28. — V 177,11.
Mahānipāta (XXII) VI 1—593.
Mahānirayā, aṭṭha I 168 (17). — III 473 (11).
Mahānīpa-rukkha, bodhi Sumedha Buddhassa N 38,6.
mahānekkhammaṁ I 137,15. — II 86,27. — III 238,2. 391,10. — IV 491,8. — VI 1,8. 30,15.
Mahāneru, — Sinerupabbato III 210,3* (6).
Mahāpajāpatī Gotamī, (bhaginī Māyāya) II 202,21. 392,13. Mahāpajāpatī III 182,4. Gotamī VI 481,15*.

Mahāpatāpa, rājā Bārāṇasiyaṁ, pitā Bodhisattassa III 178,19*. 179,16* (20). 180*,7. 12. 18. — Mahāpatāpano V 113 (32).

Mahāpadāna N 59,8.

Mahāpaduma-kumāra, — Padumakumāro (Bodhisatto) IV 191*,16. 25. 194*,4. 16.

Mahāpaduma-jātaka (472) IV 187—196. — I 437,4.

Mahāpanāda, putto Surucino[2], rājā Mithilāyaṁ Videharaṭṭhe II 333,4. 20. 23*. 334 (21. 22. 24). 335,3. — IV 323*,5. 20. 25. 324*,18. 25. 325*,3 9. 12. (cfr. Panāda).

Mahāpanāda-jātaka (264) II 331—335. — IV 325,9*.

Mahāpanthaka, bhātā Cullapanthakassa I 115,3. 24. 116,22. 26. 29. 118,14. 119,13. 120,4. — Panthako I 114,28.

Mahāpalobhana-jātaka (507) IV 468—473. (cfr. Cullapalobhana-jāt. (263)).

Mahāpiṅgala, rājā Bārāṇasiyaṁ, pitā Bodhisattassa (— Devadatto) II 240*,10. 18. 21. 241,18*. (cfr. Piṅgala).

Mahāpiṅgala-jātaka (240) II 239—242.

Mahābodhi, rukkho Bodhisattassa N 54,7. — IV 228,20. 28. 229,5. 17. 21.

Mahābodhi-jātaka (528) V 227—246. — II 76,15.

Mahābodhi-paribbājaka, see: Bodhikumāra.

Mahābodhi-pūjā IV 228,6. 236,18*. (cfr. Bodhi-pūjā).

Mahābodhi-maṇḍa IV 228,28. 229,23. 230,4. 232,20*. 233,2*. 235,29*. (cfr. Bodhi-maṇḍa).

Mahābrahman N 53,16. 68,28. 72,11. 17. — I 407,16 (— Bodhisatto). 473,28 (— Bo.). 474,23 (— Bo.) 494,7*. — II 43,27*. — III 359 (27). 362 (20. 31). — IV 175,2*. 245,6. 377*,12. 16. — VI 200,17*. 201 (20). 204 (17. 20). 205 (6). 210 (5). 216 (5. 18. 24). 486,17*. 528,22. — Mahābrahmāno (pl.) N 48,17. 52,28. — VI 72,17*. 241,32*. — Mahābrahma-bhariyā IV 378,19*. — Nārada-Mahābrahmā (Bo.) VI 242,4*. 255,11. — Vasi Mahābrahmā VI 201 (20). — Sahampati Mahābrahmā IV 245,9. (cfr. Brahman, Ghaṭikāra, Nārada, Vasin).

Mahâmaṅgala-jâtaka (453) IV 72—79.
Mahâmaṅgala-sutta IV 72,18.
mahâmattâ dve II 359,8. (cfr. II 12—13; 52,21).
Mahâmalīyadeva, thero Kâḷavela-vâsī, Sīhaladīpe VI 30,7. (cfr. Malimahâdeva).
Mahâ-Mittavinda(ka)-jâtaka, — Catudvâra-jâtaka (439), I 363,9. — III 206,15.
Mahâmeru, see: Meru.
Mahâmora-jâtaka (491) IV 332—342.
Mahârakkhita, tâpaso Himavante IV 444*,11. 21. 28. 445*,7. 10. — Rakkhito IV 454,2.
Mahârakkhita, thero Uparimaṇḍakamâlavâsī, Sīhaladīpe (— Mahâsaṁgharakkhito IV 490,22.) VI 30,5.
Mahâraṭṭhiya, see: Jaṭila.
Mahârâja-pabba, Vessantarajâtake VI 582,3.
Mahârâjâ, cattâro I 229,27. (cfr. Câtummahârâjâ.)
Mahâli, Licchavi andho, Vesâliyaṁ IV 148,20. 149,9.
Mahâlohita, go (— Bodhisatto) I 196,27*. 198,5. — II 419*,11. 21. 420,23.
Mahâvaṁsaka, thero Sīhaladīpe VI 30,4.
Mahâvagga, (Saṁyutta-Nikâye) II 58,25.
Mahâvattanī, M.-maggo I 429,10*. °-mahâmaggo I 429,14*. — Mahâvattani-aṭavī I 270,30*. 395,25*. — III 200,11*. — V 22,19*. (cfr. Vattani-).
Mahâvana, Vesâliyaṁ upanissâya N 77,5. — I 420,17. 504,6. — II 6,2.
Mahâvanavaṇṇanâ, Vessantarajâtake VI 540,14.
Mahâvâṇija-jâtaka (493) IV 350—354.
Mahâvihâra, Tambapaṇṇidīpe N 85,11. — °-vâsino N 1,21.
Mahâveḷu-rukkha, bodhi Sujâta-Buddhassa N 38,20.
Mahâvessantara-jâtaka — Vessantara-jât. (547) VI 481,20*.
Mahâvessantara-dhammadesanâ VI 482,1*. — Vessantara-dhammadesanâ VI 593,24.

Mahāsaṁgharakkhita, thero, Uparimaṇḍalakamalaya-vāsī Tambapaṇṇidīpe IV 490,22. (— Mahārakkhito VI 30,5).
Mahāsattassa pariyesana-khaṇḍa, Bhūridattajātake VI 200,18.
Mahāsamaya-sutta V 456,16.
Mahāsammata, rājā paṭhamakappe I 132 (5). — II 311,8*. — III 454,18*.
Mahāsammata-khattiyavaṁsa N 90,2.
Mahāsammata-paveṇī II 438,17.
Mahāsammata-rāja-kula IV 192 (23).
Mahāsāgara, rājā Uttaramadhurāyaṁ Uttarāpathe IV 79,21*. 80,6*.
Mahāsāra-jātaka (92) I 381—387. — II 23,28 (v. l. B. Mahāsāṭaka-jāt.)
Mahāsineru, pabbato IV 462 (28). (cfr. Sineru).
Mahāsirīsa-rukkha, bodhi Kakusandha-Buddhassa N 42,27.
Mahāsiva, see: Mahāsīva.
Mahāsīlava, rājā Bārāṇasiyaṁ (— Sīlavakumāro — Bodhisatto) I 262,8*.
Mahāsīlava-jātaka (51) I 261—268. — II 401,6*. — III 13,17*.
Mahāsīva, thero, Vāmanta-pabbhāra-vāsī Tambapaṇṇidīpe IV 490,23. — Mahāsivatthero Vāmattapabbhāra-vāsī VI 30,6.
Mahāsuka-jātaka (429) III 490—494.
Mahāsutasoma-jātaka (537) 456—511. — N 46,21.
Mahāsudassana, rājā Kusāvatiyaṁ (— Bodhisatto) N 45,13. I 392*,3. 7. 393,8*. 14. (cfr. Sudassana).
Mahāsudassana-jātaka (95) I 391—393.
Mahāsudassana-sutta I 392,2.
Mahāsupina-jātaka (77) I 334—345.
mahāsupinā soḷasa Kosalarañño I 334,23.
Mahāsubhaddā, aggamahesī hatthi-nāgarañño (Bodhisattassa) Himavante V 37,10*. 39*,4. 19.
Mahāsubhaddā, seṭṭhidhītā N 93,1.
Mahāsoṇa, kūṭa-asso Bārāṇasirañño II 31*,1. 6. 16. (cfr. Soṇa).

Mahāsoṇa-rukkha, bodhi Nārada-Buddhassa N 37,8.
Mahāhaṁsa-jātaka (534) V 354—382. — IV 424,12*. — V 147 (26). 431 (22).
Mahiṁsaka-raṭṭha I 356,17*. — V 145 (9). 162,7*. 337,20*.
Mahiṁsāsa-kumāra, putto Brahmadattassa Bārāṇasiraññо (— Bodhisatto) I 127,18*. 133,19.
Mahiṁsāsaka-vaṁsa N 1,17.
Mahinda, (Sakko) V 397,2*. 411,8*. — Brahmā Mahindo V 411,6*.
Mahinda, thero N 7,28.
Mahilāmukha, maṅgalahatthi Brahmadattassa Bārāṇasiraññо I 186,26*. 187,17*. 188,10* (14. 16). 28.
Mahilāmukha-jātaka (26) I 185—188. — I 487,5. — II 98,4. — III 321,19 (Mahilāmukhata-jāt.).
Mahisa-jātaka (278) II 385—387.
Mahosadha, see: Mahā-osadha.
Māgadha, — Maddava-rājā Bārāṇasiyaṁ III 339*,4 (7). 26. 340,16*.
Māgadhā, saṁkhā VI 465,18 (14).
Māgha, isi VI 99,28*.
Māghadeva, see: Makhādeva.
Māṭhara, suvapaṇḍito (v. l. B Mādhara) VI 418,18. 20. 423,6*. 424,12*. 425,24. — Maṭṭharo VI 418,18.
Mātaṅga-paṇḍita, caṇḍālo (— Bodhisatto) IV 376*,2. 8. 12. 377,12*. 379,15*. 383,7. 384,8*. 387,3*. 389,27*. 390,2. — V 114 (10). 267,10*. 273 (4. 5).
Mātaṅga-jātaka (497) IV 375—390. — III 384,5. — V 101 (6). 114 (9). 273 (5).
Mātali, devaputto, sārathi (saṅgāhako) Sakkassa I 202*,28. 29. 203*,3. 8 (12). 20. 206,13. — II 254*,12. 19. 257,4*. — III 222*,10. 11. 18. 19. — VI 63*,7. 14. 18. 65,19*. 68*,27. 28. 69,24. 181,22*. 186,16*. 18. 355*,16. 19. 356,3*. 11*. 14 (31). 358,15*. — V 383,13*. 388,22*. 389*,9. 18. 390,21*. 396,2*.

11 (15). 397*, 1. 4 (11). 20. 23. 398,16*. 28. 408,11*. 18. 409,3. 10. 410,2*. 411*,8. 14. 25. 412,10. — VI 103*,6. 10. 18. 28 104,2. 10*. 18. 27—29*. 105,8 (10). 30*. 33. 106,2. 5. 16*. 24. 27. 107,17. 20. 108,2. 5 (12). 26. 29. 109,7. 10 (19). 32. 110,1. 22. 25. 111,7. 10. 28. 31. 112,14. 17. 113,4. 7. 114,2. 6 (18). 34. 115,8. 20*. 27. 31. 116* (8). 11. 12. 17. 18. 27. 117,4*. 11. 14. 118,4*. 15. 119,13. 17. 120,8. 11. 121,8. 11. 122,6. 9. 33. 123,3. 20. 23. 124,2*. 9. 12. 125*,3. 12. 126,2. 4. 22—27*. 31. 33. 128,14. 128*,13. 19. 22. 24. 129,16.

mātiposaka, see: mātuposaka.

mātu-vilokanaṁ Buddhassa N 49,25.

mātugāmo, eko Sāvatthiyaṁ I 463,3.

Mātuposaka-jātaka (455) IV 90—95.

mātuposaka-bhikkhu II 50,12. — III 270,9. 324,26. 330,12. — IV 90,8. 276,3. — V 21,2. 312,15. — VI 66,25. — mātuposako III 422,5.

Mātuposaka-sutta VI 70,11.

Mādhara, see: Māṭhara.

Mānusiya, padumasaro Sakuḷanagaraṁ nissāya V 337,24*. — 338*,1. 8. 347 (29).

Māyā, mātā Gotama-Buddhassa N 15,22. 16,9. — II 381,25. — VI 481,8*.

Mahāmāyā N 49,27. 50,2. 5 (Mahāmāyāya supinaṁ). 52,3. — I 136,7. 309,12. — II 23,22. 50,7. 141,23. — III 490,10. — IV 95,8. 160,18. 464,3. 491,3. — VI 157,20. 478,12*. 481,16*. 593,28.

Māyāvī, sigālī III 333,14*. 335,28*. 336 (6).

Māra, (devaputto) N 63,17. 21. 23. 71,27. 31. 72,2. 10. 29. 73,26. 31. 74,1. 13. 14. 17. 75,1. 6. 10. 14. 18. 78,18. — I 231,20. 232*,12. 24—26. 29. 30. 233,27*. 234,3. — II 60,5. — III 298,22. 532,17. — IV 123 (17. 18 — maccu). — Mārā tayo II 84 (21). — Mārattaṁ V 53,1*. — Mārassa soḷasa lekhā N 78,17.

Mārāvaṭṭana- III 494,26.
Māra-ghosanā N 71,30.
Māra-dhītāro tisso N 78,29. 79,8. — I 469,21. 25. — Māra-dhītānaṁ palobhanasuttanto I 469,15.
Māra-parisā N 72,4. 74,6. 16. 30.
Māra-bandhanaṁ I 400 (18).
Māra-balaṁ N 71,29. 30. 72,11. 23. 74,15. 27. 33. 75,28.
Māra-Brahma-Cakkavatti-sampatti N 48,19.
Māra-senā N 71,31.
(cfr. Kilesa-Māro, Namuci, Vasavatti).
Mālāgiri, pabbato (cfr. Mallagiri) VI 204,18* (25). 212,19*.
mālāpūjakārakā bhikkhū II 321,9.
Māliya, sunakho III 535,26*. 536 (1).
Māluta, vāto I 165,15* (21). — IV 222,23*. — VI 263,12*. — māluto VI 14,24*.
Māluta-jātaka (17) I 164—166.
Migadāya, Bārāṇasiyaṁ N 81,20.
Migapotaka-jātaka (372) III 213—215.
Migasammatā, nadī Himavantato Gaṅgaṁ pattā VI 72*,25. 26. 30. 75,19*. 76,1*. 79,30* (33). 80,4*. 83,28*. 84,8*. 86 (1. 29). 87,10* (12).
Migācira, uyyānaṁ Bārāṇasiyaṁ V 68,21*. 29. 69 (16). 476,8*. 506,14*. 507 (1). — Migāciruyyānaṁ Koravyassa rañño VI 256,15*.
Migājina, tāpaso VI 58,29*. 59*,11 (13). 20 (27). 60*,18. 24. 26. 61 (8). 19*. 68,11*. 20.
Migāra-mātā — Visākhā IV 314,28.
Migālopa, gijjho, putto Bodhisattassa III 255*,11. 17 (23). 256,7* (21). 27.
Migālopa-jātaka (381) III 255—56.
Miṅgala, mahāmaccho V 462,18*.
micchātapo ājīvikānaṁ I 493,17.
Mitacinti-jātaka (114) I 426—428.

Mitacintin, maccho (— Bodhisatto) I 427*,9. 11. 18. 27. 428,2 (4—6). 10.

Mitta, (purisanāma?) IV 478 (27).

Mittaka, see: Mittavindaka.

Mittagandhaka, upāsako IV 288,25. 289,10. 18.

Mittavindaka, duggatakulaputto I 238,30*. 239*,6. 14. 15. 18. 28. 30. 240*,7. 12. 19. 20. 241,3* (18). 10*. 23. 241,0* (12) (Mittako).

Mittavindaka, putto asītikoṭivibhavassa seṭṭhino Bārāṇasiyaṁ I 363,24*. 27. 414,19. — III 206,16*. 207*,8 (19). 24. 208,2. — IV 1,10*. 2*,21. 28. 3,18*. 4*,1. 4. 6,4* (13). 23. — Mittavindo IV 6,10*.

Mittavinda-jātaka a) (82) I 363. — I 413,26. — b) (104) I 413—414. — c) (369) III 206—208. — d) Mahā-Mittavinda(ka)-jātaka — Catudvāra-jātaka (439) IV 1—6. — I 363,9. — III 206,15. (cfr. Losaka-jātaka (41).)

Mittāmitta-jātaka a) (197) II 130—132. — b) (473) IV 196—199.

Mithilā, nagaraṁ Videharaṭṭhe I 137,25*. 139,21*. — II 39*,5. 18. 28. 40 (4. 5). 28*. 333,22*. — III 365,7*. 366,1*. 378,14*. 381 (25). — IV 315,28*. 316,25*. 355,6*. 358,16*. — V 164,12*. — VI 30,20*. 31,6*. 32,26*. 33,28*. 34,27*. 35*,13. 17. 46*,19. 22—30. 47*,1—4. 54*,10. 29. 55 (3). 62,2*. 68,13*. 95,18. 21*. 96,18*. 102,22*. 103,7*. 104 (7. 8). 128*,20. 23. 24. 220,28*. 227 (27). 228 (24). 246,18*. 330*,8. 27. 347*,7. 25. 392,19*. 393*,20. 27. 32. 394,29*. 395*,5. 10. 21. 28. 396,10*. 397,5*. 409,24*. 410,15*. 411*,5. 8. 9. 425,19*. 427,21*. 440 (9. 31). 446,29*. 447,30*. 449,19*. 450 (17). 453,17*. 458,27*. 459 (27). 463,8* (9). 465 (30. 31). — Mithilaggaho — Videha-rājā II 40,1* (4). — IV 319,26*. — VI 104,3 (7). 16. 127,28. 129,7. 346,29*. — Mithila-rajjaṁ VI 393,24*. — Mithila-vaṇṇanā VI 46,21*.

Missaka, (vanaṁ Tāvatiṁsabhavane) VI 278,22*.

Mucalinda, saro Himavante VI 518,18. 519,28*. 534,27*. 30 535,10. 536,7. 537 (17). 539,20. 24. — N 80,2 (?). Su-mucalinda-saro VI 582,5*.

Mucalinda, nāgarājā N 80,3.

Mucalinda, rājā VI 99,9*.

Mujalinda, rājā Bārāṇasiyam VI 202,23* (25. 26). (— Mucalindo?)

Muṭṭhika, mallo IV 81*,21. 25. 82*,8. 13. 88,16*. (cfr. VI 277,7* (10) muṭṭhikā: mallā.)

Muṇika, sūkaro I 197*,2. 15 (17. 19). 23. 25. 26. 198,8.

Muṇika-jātaka (30) I 196—198.

Muditā, dhītā Candakumārassa (Bodhisattassa) VI 134,26*.

Mudupāṇi-jātaka (262) II 323—327.

Mudulakkhaṇa-jātaka (66) I 302—306. — V 117 (26).

Mudulakkhaṇā, aggamahesī Bārāṇasi-rañño I 304*,11. 14. 19. 305*,6. 7. 9. 306,8* (10). 23.

Musila, Musila, see: Mūsila.

Mūgapakkha-jātaka (— Temiya-jātaka) (538) VI 1—30. — N 46,25. — VI 30,10. 73,2*. — Mūgapakkha-samāgamo IV 490,24. — VI 30,7.

Mūgapakkha-paṇḍita, — Temiyakumāro, putto Kāsirañño (— Bodhisatto) VI 30,2.

Mūlapariyāya-jātaka (245) II 259—262.

Mūlapariyāya-suttanta II 259,14. 21. 23. Mūlapariyāya-desanā II 260,3.

Mūsika-jātaka (373) III 215—219.

Mūsikā, dāsī III 217*,3. 8. 11 (14. 16). 25. 218 (8).

Mūsila (v. l. Musila, Musila), jeṭṭhagandhabbo Ujjeniyaṁ (— Devadatto) II 248,28*. 249*,2. 6. 11. 28. 250*,2. 26. 251*,9. 16. 18. 252 (9). 20*. 253*,17. 23. 254,6*. 257,10.

Meghiya, Bhagavato anibaddhaupaṭṭhāko IV 95,15.

Mejjhārañña III 310,22*. 311,18*. — IV 389,23*. — V 267,11*.

Mejjha-raṭṭha IV 388,6*. 389,25.

Mejjha-rāja IV 388,6*. 389,13*. — V 114 (10).
Mejjho IV 389,27*. — V 267,9*.
Meṇḍaka-jātaka (471) IV 186.
Meṇḍaka-pañha, Ummaggajātake VI 355,21. — IV 186,24.
Meṇḍissara, isi Pajakaraññ̄o vijite Lambacūḷakaṁ nissāya III 463,18*. 464,7*. 469,21. jeṭṭhantevāsī Sarabhaṅgassa V 133*.10. 19. 151,28.
Metta-sutta II 60,27.
Mettiya, chabbaggiya-bhikkhu II 387,11 (Mettiya-Bhummajakā).
Metteyya-lokanātha VI 594,9.
Medhaṁkara-Buddha N 44,9.
Meru, Mahāsinerupabbato IV 462,22*. — Mahāmeru N 25,22. — IV 498 (1). (cfr. Neru, Sineru).
Meḷa-mātā, eḷikā III 533,1*. 534,10* (14).
Moggallāna, paribbājako Rājagahe, thero N 85,15. 18. — I 220,12. 327,21. 346,34. 349,17. 354,9. 12. — II 5,7. 10,1. 155,8. 358,23. — III 56,5. 90,11. 193,17. 341,17. 469,22. 479,4. 17. 543,5. — IV 69,24. 218,27. 265,25. 266,7. 297,17. 314,19. 332,28. 491,4. — V 67,25. 127,10. 151,26. 192,7. 412,11. — VI 68,20. 157,22. 219,28. 255,7. 329,16. — Kolito V 151,30 (cfr. III 469,22). — (cfr. Kolita).
Mahā-Moggallāna N 85,21. — I 161,12. 346,34. 349,5. 391,22. 408,8. — II 9,16. 93,22. 393,7. 447,5. — III 88,9. 22. 191,11. 16. 310,14. — IV 228,27. 265,22. — V 127,7.
Mahā-Moggallānattherassa parinibbānaṁ V 125,20 (cfr. I 391,21).
Mora-jātaka (159) II 33—38. — IV 414,11*.
Molinī, nagaraṁ (= Bārāṇasī) IV 15,20*. 20,24*. 21 (2). 11*. 120,1* [1]).

Y.

Yaññadatta, brāhmaṇo, pitā Koṇāgamana-Buddhassa N 43,8.

Yaññadatta-kumāra, putto Maṇḍavya-tāpasassa IV 30,25*. 31*,7. 15 (19). 21. 32*,5. 24 (28). 33,5*. 36,8*.

Yaññabhedavāda, Bhūridattajātake VI 205,29*.

Yama II 318 (1). — III 472,12*. — IV 273,17* (20. 21). 405 (16) — V 425,22. 432 (9). — VI 201,26*. 457 (29). 568,9. 571,18 (cfr. Vesāyin).

Yamakkhayo (= nirayo, Yamanivesanaṁ) V 268,24*. 274 (13) 304,19*. 305 (3).

Yama-niddesakārino (nirayapālā) VI 249,21* (23).

Yama-nivesanaṁ V 274 (14). 305 (4).

Yama-visayo II 318 (2).

Yama-sādanaṁ (codd. Yamasādhanaṁ) IV 405,12 (16) (Yamassa āṇāpavattiṭṭhānaṁ). — V 267,18*. 273 (6) (= nirayo) 304,14* (27) (= maccubhavanaṁ). — VI 457,28* (28). 505,15.

yamakapāṭihāriyaṁ I 193,22.

Yamadaggi, see: Yāmataggi.

Yamunā, nadī II 151,21*. — VI 158*,13. 14. 161,29*. 162,5*. 163,4*. 164,8* (13). 169,16*. 170,10*. 172*,8 (18). 16. 176 (16). 179*,6. 10. 197*,17. 21. 198,4*. 200,4* (8). 217,28*. — Yamunodakaṁ V 496 (3). — VI 412 (20). 415 (31).

Yava-kumāra, putto Brahmadattassa Bārāṇasiraññō III 215,24*. — Yavarājā III 218 (8).

Yavamajjaka, gāmo (Mithilaṁ nissāya) VI 365,26*. 366 (7). (cfr. VI 330,28*).

Yasa, kulaputto N 82,19. 21.

Yasapāṇi, rājā Bārāṇasiyaṁ II 186,19*.

Yasavat, rājā, pitā Anomadassi-Buddhassa N 36,4.

Yasavatī, mātā Vessabhu-Buddhassa N 42,12.

Yasavatī, bhaginī Akitti-brāhmaṇassa (Bodhisattassa) IV 237,7*.

Yasodharā, mātā Anomadassi-Buddhassa N 36,5.

Yāma-bhavana IV 475*,5. 7. — Yāmā (devā?) VI 279,9*.

Yāmataggi, porāṇaka-rājā (v. l. B Yamadaggi) VI 251,15* (27).

Yāmahanu, isi VI 99,27* (31).

Yāmuna, (adj. — Yāmuneyya) II 152,1* (Yāmunā macchā). — VI 200,5* (8) (Yāmuno giri — Himavanto).

Yāmuneyya, (adj.) II 151*,21. 26. 27.

Yugandhara, pabbato I 119,26. 322,1* (Sineru-Yugandharādayo). — IV 213*,18. 21. 214,6*. 265,17. — VI 125,18 (20. 21). — Yugandhara-sāgaro N 64,10. — VI 43,5*.

Yudhañjaya, see: Yuvañjaya.

Yudhiṭṭhila, Paṇḍurājaputto V 424,21. 426 (11).

Yudhiṭṭhila, Yudhiṭṭhilagotto Dhanañjayarājā III 400,18*. 401,7. — V 59,22* (26). 61,2*. 26. 65,17*. 66,10* (23). (cfr. Dhanañjaya). — Yudhiṭṭhilagotto Koravyarājā IV 361*,4. 15 (cfr. Dhanañjaya).

Yudhiṭṭhila-kumāra, putto Sabbadatta-rañño Ramma-nagare (Bārāṇasiyaṁ), kaniṭṭho Bodhisattassa IV 122,12*. 123,9*. 15 (18). 22.

Yuvañjaya, jeṭṭhaputto Sabbadatta-rañño Ramma-nagare (Bārāṇasiyaṁ) (— Bodhisatto) IV 120*,3. 27. 121,15. 31*. 122,29*. 123,15 (17). 23. (v. l. B Yudhañjaya).

Yuvañjaya-jātaka (460) IV 119—123. — IV 120,1*.

R.

Rakkhita, — Mahārakkhita-tāpaso IV 454,8.

Rakkhita-kumāra, tāpaso Himavante, ācariyo (— Bodhisatto) IV 44*,2. 22.

Ragā, dhītā Mārassa N 78,29. — I 469,17.

Rajata-guhā, Himavante II 67,1*.

Rajata-pabbata, Himavante N 50,16. 19. — II 6,10*. 7*,9. 18 8 (24. 25). 92,27. (cfr. Daddara.)

Raṭṭhapāla, thero I 156,14.

Ratanaghara-cetiya N 78,3. 6. 9.

Ratanacaṁkama-cetiya N 78,2.

Ratanattayaṁ N 1,5.

ratanāni tīṇi N 85,2. — II 147,2*.

Rativaddhana, pāsādo Rammanagare IV 122,16*. — (pāsādo Mithilāyaṁ) VI 231 (3). 232 (12).

Rattakuravaka-rukkha, bodhi Dhammadassi-Buddhassa N 39,28.

Rathakāra, daho Himavantapadese V 415,24.

Rathalaṭṭhi-jātaka (v. l. B Rathayaṭṭhi-) (332) III 104—106.

Rathavatī, kimpurisā (kinnarī) VI 422,5* (16).

Ramma, nagaraṁ Dīpaṁkara-Buddhassa N 11,10. 12. 13,33. 26,1. 30. 31. 28,8. 10. — Rammakaṁ nagaraṁ N 11,9. — Rammavatī N 29,19.

Ramma, nagaraṁ (= Bārāṇasī) IV 119,26*. 120,1*. 122,23*. 123 (5). — Rammakaṁ IV 122,23*. 123 (5)

Rammavatī, nagaraṁ Koṇḍañña-Buddhassa N 30,12. (cfr. Ramma).

Rājakārāma, Jetavana-samīpe Pasenadi-raññā kārito II 15,3. 4.

Rājagaha, nagaraṁ Magadharaṭṭhe N 66,1. 3. 83,1. 84,4. 6. 18. 21. 85,1. 15. 28. 86,22. 27. 87,15. 18. 92,13. 16. 29. — I 96,8. 114,9. 11. 115,8. 16. 142,16. 143,10*. 145,17. 147,29. 154,5*. 156,10. 19. 157,12. 162,28*. 186,3. 217,9. 345,19. 346,24. 350,25*. 372,1. 373,9. 13. 18. 391,27. 444,15*. 446,12*. 466*,1. 8. 26. 468,24*. 469,7*. 489,14*. 508,26. — II 55*,6. 21. 56,22. 196,16. 18. 197,7. 387,11. — III 33,9. 20. 71,5. 6. 72,24. 238,5*. 293,17*. 363,23. 479,23*. — IV 37,14*. 38*,1. 16. 18. 72,19. 152,5. 276,11*. — V 125,22. 161,25*. 247,7*. 334,24. 35. 335,4. 6. 7. — VI 236,30. 237 (18). 271,23*. 24. 479,4 — Rājagaha-seṭṭhi IV 37,15*. 263,10.

Rājagiri, hatthi VI 135,28*.
Rājavasati-khaṇḍa, Vidhurapaṇḍita-jātake VI 298,22.
Rājāyatana, (rukkho) N 80,6. 16.
Rājovāda-jātaka a) (151) II 1—5. — b) (334) III 110—112. (cfr. Mahākapi-jāt. (407).)
Rājovāda-sutta III 439,6.
rājovādo II 1,5. — III 317,4. — V 98,22. (cfr. V 109,4.)
Rādha, suko, kaniṭṭho Bodhisattassa I 495,25*. 496*,4. 11. 19. 25. 496,20.
Rādha, suko (= Bodhisatto) II 132,24*. 133*,9. 11. 17. 25. — — III 97,24*. 98*,15. 21. 99*,5. 12. 100,2.
Rādha-jātaka a) (145) I 495—496. — b) (198) II 132—134. (cfr. Kālabāhu-jātaka (329).)
Rāma, paṇḍito, jeṭṭhaputto Dasaratha-mahārañño Bārāṇasiyaṁ (= Bodhisatto) IV 124,9*. 125*,8. 11. 18. 23. 25. 28. 126*,18. 21. 26. 129*,18. 19. 130,12. 19. — VI 557,30. 558 (21—22).
Rāma, brāhmaṇo N 56,3.
Rāma, (mātiposako Bārāṇasivāsī) V 29,2* (17. 26).
Rāma-putta, see: Uddaka.
Rāmā, aggasāvikā Paduma-Buddhassa N 36,25. — aggasāvikā Sumedha-Buddhassa N 38,8.
Rāhu, (asurindo) I 183,26. 274,27*. — III 364*,19. 21. 24. 365*,17. 18. 20. 21. 26. 377,15*. 477,23*. — IV 330,28*. — V 34,2* (8). 253 (30). 453,6. 482,5*. — VI 426,8*. 443,5. 7. 551,21*.
Rāhula, **Rāhulakumāra**, putto Gotama-Buddhassa N 60,22. 24. 62,21. 92,1 — I 139,20. 161,4. 5. 23. 28. 162,2. 6. 7. 13. 14. 19. 20. 164,21. 23. 393,13. — II 67,25. 69,26. 109,14 (Rahulo). 141,24. 270,20. 393,11. — III 64,5. 8. 66,17. 168,6. 383,26. — IV 37,1. 297,17. — V 192,6. 261,29. — VI 68,21. 157,21. 329,16. 593,28. — Rāhulo dāyajjaṁ yācati N 91,18—30. Rāhulatthero I 160,20. — III 64,3. — IV 158,9. Rāhulasāmaṇero II 392,23. 393,25. Rāhulabhaddo I 161,10. 17. — II 433,6.

Rāhula-mātā, devī N 54,6. 58,18. 60,20. 62,18. 15. 89,16. 90,24. 91,18. — I 145,12. 393,14. — II 125,8. 141,21. 381,25. 392,17. 394,4. 400,2. 433,15. 436,14. — III 97,9. 132,15. 286,6. 324,22. 383,23. 397,2. 414,25. 454,4. 474,18. 524,9. — IV 27,22. 72,13. 113,18. 119,10. 130,18. 252,18. 23. 28. 283,2. 288,22. 468,22. — V 36,6. 192,5. 312,12. — VI 68,21. 157,21. 329,15. 593,28.

Rukkhadhamma-jātaka (74) I 327—329. — V 414,23.

Ruci, see: Suruci.

Rucira-jātaka (275) II 365.

Rujā, dhītā Aṁgati-rañño Mithilāyaṁ VI 220,29*. 230,25. 31. 231 (9). 35. 232,4. 24. 31. 233,8. 18 (24). 239 (35). 241,11. 25*. 248,28. 255,9.

Ruru(miga)-jātaka (482) IV 255—263.

Ruhaka, purohito Bārāṇasi-rañño II 113,22*. 114,22* (24). 115,1*. 10.

Ruhaka-jātaka (191) II 113—115.

Ruhaka-vagga II 113—138.

Reṇu, rājā Uttarapañcālanagare Kururaṭṭhe IV 444,10*. 447,1* (20. 21).

Revata, Buddho N 30,18. 35,1. 12. 24. 44,5.

Revata, upaṭṭhāko Siddhattha-Buddhassa N 40,9.

Roja, Mallo, gihisahāyo Ānandassa II 231,15. 23. 24. 27. 233,20.

Roja, rājā paṭhamakappe, putto Mahāsammatassa II 311,9*. — III 454,14*.

Romaka-jātaka (v. l. Pārāpata-jāt.) (277) II 382—384.

Roruva, nagaraṁ Sovīraraṭṭhe III 470,6*.

Roruva, nirayo III 299,10. — VI 237,9. 238 (4). 239 (24). — Roruvā, dve nirayā V 266,18*. 271 (6. 11). (cfr. Jāla-roruva, Dhūma-roruva.)

Rohaṇa (v. l. B) = Rohanta.

Rohanta, migarājā (= Bodhisatto) IV 413,14*. 415*,18. 22. (24). 416*,13. 17. 419,19*. 420,7*. 423,20.

Rohanta, saro Himavante IV 413,16*.
Rohantamiga-jātaka (501) IV 413—423.
Rohiṇī, dāsī Anāthapiṇḍikassa I 248,14.
Rohiṇī, dāsī seṭṭhino (Bodhisattassa) I 248,27*.
Rohiṇī, nadī I 327,27. IV 207,22. — V 412,16. — VI 576,6 (8) (?).
Rohiṇī-jātaka (45) I 248—49.
Rohiṇeyya, amacco Vāsudeva-rañño IV 84,19*. 85,3. 89,16.

L.

Lakuṇṭaka-bhaddika, thero II 142,3. 144,16. — Lakuṇṭaka-bhaddiyo II 142,14. — Lakuṇṭako nāmanero II 142,6.
Lakkhakhaṇḍa, Vidhurapaṇḍita-jātake VI 292,8.
Lakkhaṇa, putto Dasaratha-mahārañño Bārāṇasiyaṁ III 124,9*. 125*,8. 21. 126*,6 (7). 17. 129,21*. 130,18.
Lakkhaṇa, brāhmaṇo N 56,3.
Lakkhaṇa, migo, putto Bodhisattassa I 143,13*. 144*,8. 15. 20 (28). 145,12.
Lakkhaṇa-jātaka (11) I 142—145.
lakkhaṇapaṭiggāhakā, aṭṭha brāhmaṇā N 56,8–7.
Lakkhī II 413,25. — III 262*,4 (6). 12 (= Siri). 306,13* (17). — V 112,30*.
Laṭukika-jātaka (357) III 174—177. — V 414,21.
Laṭṭhivana, Rājagahanagarūpacāre N 84,5. — III 282,20. — Laṭṭhivanuyyānaṁ N 83,1. 84,6. 85,4. — VI 219,29. 220,21. — Laṭṭhimadhukavanaṁ N 68,12.
Lambacūḷaka, nigamo Pajaka-rañño vijite (Avantiraṭṭhe) III 463,13*. — Caṇḍapajjota-rañño vijite V 133,15*.
Lābhagaraha-jātaka (287) II 420—423.
Lāḷudāyin, thero I 123,12. 124,1. 126,19. 446,25. 447,2. 5. 449,16. — Udāyi I 123,14. 27. 124,6. — II 164,16. 165,2. 167,9. 11. 263,18. 20. 23. 25. 264,27. — VI 478,20*.

Licchavi-kumāra, duṭṭho I 504,8. 13. 505,11. 508,4. 6.
Licchavi-kumārikā II 5,19. 24. 9,7.
Licchavi-rāja I 420,17. 18. 24. — Licchavi-rājāno III 1,6. — IV 149,7.
Licchavī (pl.), Vesāliyaṁ III 1,7. 10. — IV 148,26. 149,1. 7. 20. — Licchavi-sippaṁ III 1,21. (cfr. Mahāli, Sunakkhatto.)
Litta-jātaka (91) I 379—380.
Litta-vagga I 379—410.
Lumbini-vana, Kapilavatthu-Devadaha-nagarānaṁ antare N 52,15. 19. 54,5.
lokatthacariyā I 259,5. — III 145,21. 303,11. — V 180,9.
Lokantara-niraya VI 247*,2 (8). 18. — Lokantarika-nirayo VI 46,17*.
Lokabyūhā, kāmāvacaradevā N 47,24.
Lomasakassapa, tāpaso — Kassapo, purohitaputto (— Bodhisatto) III 515*,8. 24. 516,2*. 517,1*. 518*,1. 5. 519,27. — V 455 (4). (cfr. Kassapa).
Lomasakassapa-jātaka (433) III 514—519.
Lomahaṁsa-jātaka (94) I 389—391. — N 47,6 (— Cariyāpiṭ. III 15,1.).
Lola-jātaka (274) II 361—364.
lolabhikkhu I 241,27. — II 318,23. 361,16. 365,3. — III 224,28. 312,12. 314,17. 520,3. — IV 70,2.
lolamakkaṭo II 385,3.
Lolavatthu III 224,23.
Lolā, Licchavi-dārikā, paribbājikā III 1,14.
Losaka-jātaka (41) I 234—246.
Losakatissa, thero I 234,14. 235,20. 30. 236,3. 13. 16. 241,24. — Losako I 235,34. 236,1. 6. 20. — Tisso I 236,9. 11.
Lohakumbhi-jātaka (314) III 43—48. — III 428,11.
Lohakumbhi-niraya IV 493,7*.
Lohitaka, chabbaggiyabhikkhu, see: Paṇḍuka.

V.

Vaṁsa-bhūmi, VI 236,34. 237 (22) (= Vaṁsa-raṭṭhaṁ).
Vaṁsa-raṭṭha IV 28,8*. — VI 237 (22).
Vaṁsa-rāja, see: Udena.
Vaka-jātaka (300) II 449—451.
Vaṁka-pabbata V 31,8. — VI 491,15*. 505,18. 507,14. 511,4. 513,11*. 515,26. 516,9 (13). 517,18. 520*,1. 19. 523,22*. 524,10*. 525,16. 18 (20). 23*. 28. 526 (3. 6. 8). 527,14. 16. 534 (28). 566 (9). 580,14*. 581,17. 23. 592 (20). — Vaṁkata-pabbato VI 513,14. 16. — Vaṁka-giri VI 589 (16). 592,5*. (cfr. Giribbaja.)
Vaṁka, rājā Sāvatthiyaṁ III 168,28*. 169*,1. 11 (24). 170,15.
Vaccha, tāpaso Himavante VI 422,5* (7. 22).
Vaccha Kisa, see: Kisavaccha.
Vacchanakha, paribbājako, isi Himavantapadese (= Bodhisatto) II 232*,14. 17. 233,20.
Vacchanakha-jātaka (235) II 231—233.
Vajirakumārī, dhītā Pasenadi-Kosalarañño II 404,20.
Vajji-raṭṭha VI 239 (16). 240 (8). — Vajjī (pl.) VI 238,20. 239 (11—12).
Vaṭṭaka-jātaka a) (35) I 212—215. — I 172,10*. — b) (118) I 432—435. — c) (394) III 312—314. — V 414,27 (= Sammodamāna-jāt. (32).)
Vaḍḍhakisūkara-jātaka (283) II 403—409.
Vaṇṇāroha-jātaka (361) III 191—193.
Vaṇṇāroha-vagga III 191—210.
Vaṇṇupatha-jātaka (2) I 106—110.
Vattani-mahāmagga I 429,18*. — III 201 (22). (cfr. Mahāvattanī).
vattasampanno brāhmaṇo I 449,20.
Vatra, asuro V 153 (4).
Vatrabhū, Indo Vatrabhū V 153,2 (4).

vadhāya parisakkanaṁ Devadattassa, see: Devadatta.

Vanappavesana-khaṇḍa, Bhūridatta-jātake VI 177,14. — Vessantara-jātake VI 521,6.

Vappa, thero N 82,13. 14.

Vammīka-sutta I 148,31.

Varakalyāṇa, putto Kalyāṇassa, rājā paṭhamakappe II 311*,10. 11. — III 454*,15. 16.

Varaṇa-jātaka (71) I 316—319.

Varaṇa-vagga I 316—359.

Varamandhātar, putto Mandhātussa, rājā paṭhamakappe III 454,17*.

Vararoja, putto Rojassa, rājā paṭhamakappe II 311,9*. — III 454,14*.

Varuṇa, aggasāvako Revata-Buddhassa N 35,8.

Varuṇa, upaṭṭhāko Anomadassi-Buddhassa N 36,5.

Varuṇa, upaṭṭhāko Paduma-Buddhassa N 36,25.

Varuṇa, tāpaso V 12,20*. 13,2*.

Varuṇa, (deva-)rājā V 28,25*. — VI 201,24*.

Varuṇa, nāgarajā VI 164,8* (12). 257*,4. 16. 261,26*. 266 (7). 267*,3. 18. 268,11*. 269,21*. 307,7*. 308*,17. 20. 322*,4. 6. 12 (20). 323,1*. 325,30*. 329,16.

Varuṇadeva, Devagabbhāya putto chaṭṭho IV 81,6*.

Vaḷabhāmukha-samudda IV 141,18*. 142,1*. — Vaḷabhāmukhī IV 141,25*.

Valāhassa-jātaka (196) II 127—130.

Valāhassa-rājakula IV 232,18*. — VI 440 (7).

Vasavattin, Māro N 63,21. 81,11. — I 232,24* (Vasavatti Māro). — III 359,19 (24). — Paranimmita-Vasavatti N 48,17.

Vasavattin, rājā Pupphavatiyaṁ (Bārāṇasiyaṁ) VI 131,12*. — pitā Candakumārassa VI 137,17 (19).

Vasiṭṭha(ka), putto ekassa kulassa aññatarasmiṁ Kāsigāme (pitā Bodhisattassa) IV 44,31*. 45*,20. 27. 29. 47*,23. 27. 48*,18. 25. (v. l. B Saviṭṭhako).

Vasin, — Mahābrahmā VI 201,12* (19—20).

vāṇijā Sāvatthi-vāsino II 294,20. — IV 350,30.

Vātaggasindhava, maṅgalasso Bārāṇasirañño (— Bodhisatto) II 338,22*. 339*,8. 16. 22. 340,23. Vātaggo II 340,17.

Vātaggasindhava-jātaka (266) II 337—340.

Vātamiga-jātaka (14) I 156—159.

Vānara-jātaka (342) III 133—134.

Vānarinda-jātaka (57) I 278—280. (cfr. Kumbhila-jāt. (224).)

Vāmagotta, see: Sūra Vāmagotta.

Vāmatta-pabbhāra, see: Vāmanta-pabbhāra.

Vāmanta-pabbhāra, Tambapaṇṇi-dīpe IV 490,28 (Vāmanta-pabbhāra-vāsī Mahāsīvatthero). — VI 30,6 (Vāmattapabbhāra-vāsī).

Vāyu, Vāyussa putto III 528,1*. 529,13* (17). 530,2*.

Vāruṇi-jātaka (47) I 251—252.

vāruṇidūsako gahapati I 251,21.

Vāruṇī VI 500,25* (read: vāruṇī, cfr. VI 586,11.)

Vālodaka-Jātaka (183) II 95—97.

Vāsabhakhattiyā, dhītā Mahānāma-Sakkassa ca Nāgamuṇḍāya dāsiyā ca, aggamahesī Kosalarañño I 134,2. 8. — IV 145,7. 19. 146,15. 147,2. 13. 17. 18. 24. 148,2. Vāsabhakhattiyāya vatthu I 133,28 (cfr. Jāt. 465).

Vāsava, — Sakko N 65,9. — III 131,14*. 215,6*. 306,14*. 357,16*. 391,2*. — IV 240,2*. 274,16*. 309,27*. 311 (10). 314,4* (8). 356,25. — V 139,28*. 160,26*. 167,12*. 392,4*. 393,17. 394 (1. 3). 396,22* (30). 407,18*. — VI 98,7. 10. 16 (25). 127,24. 203,32*. 205,11* (14. 15. 17). 271,31. 289,15*. 483,1* (15). 484,2*. 492,14.

Vāsudeva, Devagabbhāya jeṭṭhaputto, rājā Dvāravatiyaṁ IV 81,4*. 82,17*. 84*,11. 20. 87,15*. 88*,13. 20. 22. 89,16. — Vāsudevo Kaṇho VI 421,20* (22). — Vāsudeva-kulaṁ IV 87,25*. — V 114 (12). (cfr. Kaṇha, Kaṇhāyanagotta, Kesava.)

Vāsula, putto Candakumārassa VI 143,14*. 17. 24*. 153 (9). 157,21.
Vāseṭṭha, upaṭṭhāko Nārada-Buddhassa N 37,7.
Vāseṭṭha, brāhmaṇo — Dhūmakāri III 401,24*. 402 (8).
Vāseṭṭhī, brāhmaṇī, bhariyā purohitassa Esukāri-rañño (mātā Bodhisattassa) IV 483,27* (28).
Vikaṇṇaka-jātaka (233) II 227—229.
vikatthiko (vikatthito) bhikkhu I 355,25. 451,14. 458,15.
Vighāsa-jātaka (393) III 310—312.
vighāsādā pañcasatā II 95,26.
Vijaya, amacco Aṁgatissa Videharañño VI 221,3*. 16. 222,10. 16. 17 (82. 83). 230,14. 255,7.
Vijayuttara, saṁkho Sakkassa N 72,7. 16. — VI 157 (3).
Vijitāvin, khattiyo Phussa-Buddhassa kāle (— Bodhisatto) N 40,31.
Vijitāvin, cakkavattī Koṇḍañña-Buddhassa kāle (— Bodhisatto) N 30,6.
Viḍūḍabha, putto Vāsabhakhattiyāya ca Kosalarañño ca I 133,27. — IV 146,19. 21. 147,4. 15. 148,3. 152,1. 5. 10. 16. 17. 152,29 (Viḍūḍabharājā).
vitthāravyākaraṇaṁ Dhammasenāpatino I 473,4.
Vidūra-jātaka, see: Sucira-jātaka.
Videha-, cfr. Vedeha.
Videha, rājā Videharaṭṭhe Mithilāyaṁ (cfr. Videha-rājā) II 39,5* (pitā Bodhisattassa). — III 364,11*. — Videha-tāpaso 365*,14. 17. (cfr. Vedeha, Vedeha-tāpasa). — VI 416 (18). 461,29*. 478,30* (— Vedeho).
Videha-raṭṭha, Majjhimapadese I 137,25*. — II 39*,5. 17 333,22*. — III 364,11*. 365,7*. 366*,1. 27. 378,13*. — IV 355,18*. — V 164,11*. 167 (23). — VI 30,20*. 42,21*. 57 (8). 62 (3). 95,21*. 122 (20). 220,28*. 459 (26). 463,15*.
Videhā (pl.) III 381,17* (26). — IV 321,25*. — VI 62,1*. 97,16 (26) — Videhavāsino. 102,31*. 164,18*. 219,29. 221,11.

278,15*. 279 (8) — Pubbavidehadīpo. 412,15*. 423,28* (31). 459,20* (22. 28).

Videhaputto (Aḷāro) V 166*,4. 16. 167 (23). — Videharaṭṭhissaro II 40 (40). — Videhissaro VI 231 (30). — Videhanarindo VI 410,16*. — Videhaseṭṭho VI 354,24*.

Videha-rāja II 38*,24. 26. 40,1* (4). 28 (— Videho — Bodhisatto). — III 365,4*. 366,2* (— Videho). — VI 51 (27) (— Somanassa). — VI 229 (30) (— Aṅgāti). — VI 394*,17. 20. 395*,11. 20. 31. 396,8*. 398 (20). 400,10*. 411,5*. 424 (1). 426,4*. 427 (1). 430,7*. 447,25*. 454 (25). 455,6* (— Vedeho). — Videharājaputto VI 164 (22).

Vidhavā, nadī anto-Himavante III 467,12.

Vidhātar, devarājā VI 201,24*.

Vidhura, brāhmaṇo V 58*,14 (19). 24. 59*,9. 13. 24 (26). 60,21*. 62 (22). 67,25.

Vidhura-paṇḍita (Vidhūra), amacco Dhanañjayakorabbassa (— Bodhisatto) VI 255,23 (Vidhura-kumāro). 255,28*. 259,18*. 262,5* (Candabrāhmaṇaputto). 262,18*. 263*,4 (7). 13. 14 (15). 22. 264*,8—10. 12. 13. 16. 265 (10). 20* (26). 268 (3). 6*. 270,2*. 271*,18. 20. 283,16*. 284*,17. 19 (20. 28). 285 (28). 286*,18. 27. 287 (12). 288,8*. 289,8. 292,11. 298,21*. 299,2. 300,32. 301,2. 4. 302,25. 303 (9). 18. 20. 22. 323,9. 324,20*. 326*,13. 17. 329,17. (cfr. Dhammapāla.)

Vidhūrapaṇḍita-jātaka (546) VI 255—329.

Vidhūra, aggasāvako Kakusandha-Buddhassa N 42,26.

Vidhūra-paṇḍita, putto purohitassa Dhanañjayassa Koravyarañño (— Bodhisatto) N 46,4. — III 400,23*. 401,3*. 7. 402,29. — amacco Yudhiṭṭhilagottassa Koravyarañño (— Bodhisatto) IV 361*,5. 10. 14—16. 362*,3. 18. 22. 363*,3. 15. 25. 364*,8. 18. 26. 365,10*. 367*,18. 22. 28. 368,7*. 21.

Vinataka, pabbato VI 125,14 (23. 26).

Vinaya N 49,15. — II 449,15 (cfr. Vin. vol. I, 59). — III 27,12.

Vinīla(ka), putto suvaṇṇarājahaṁsassa ca kākiyā ca (— Devadatto) II 39*,11. 16. 22. 25. 40,2* (6). 16* (18). 28.

Vinīlaka-jātaka (160) II 38—40.

Vindaka, assataro VI 135,20*.

vipakkhasevī (-sevako) bhikkhu (cfr. Jāt. (26)) I 487,4. — II 98,8. 101,14. — III 321,18

Vipassin, Buddho N 41,9. 21. 42,8. 44,9. 94,9. — VI 480,11*. 481,18*. — Vipassi-kālo I 409,28.

Vipula, khattiyo, pitā Revata-Buddhassa N 35,8.

Vipula, pabbato VI 518,9. 519,21*. (cfr. Vepulla.)

Vipulā, mātā Revata-Buddhassa N 35,8.

Vimalā, devī, bhariyā nāgarājassa (Varuṇassa) VI 262*,8. 10. 24 (20). 263*,22. 23. 266 (6). 267,10*. 269,23*. 304,22*. 308*,16. 19. 318,8* (12). 18. 326*,9. 28.

Vimāna-vatthu IV 78 (3). — Vimānāni III 409 (17).

Virukkha, see: Virūpakkha.

Virūpakkha, mahārājā Cātummahārājika-devaloke, pitā Kālakaṇṇiyā III 257,20*. 258,12*. 259,11*. — VI 168*,23—24 (Virukkha, read: Virūpakkha).

Virūpakkhā, Virūpakkha-nāgarājakulaṁ II 145,19* (22).

Virūḷha, (mahārājā Cātummahārājika-devaloke) III 258,18*.

Virocana-jātaka (143) I 490—493.

Vivara-vagga III 1—33.

Visayha, seṭṭhi Bārāṇasiyaṁ (— Bodhisatto) N 45,15. — III 128,27*. 129,9*. 130,18*. 132,15.

Visayha-jātaka (340) III 128—132.

Visavanta-jātaka (69) I 310—311.

visavāruṇī I 268,19.

Visākhā, dhītā Dhanañjaya-seṭṭhino (cfr. Migāramātā) I 148,4. 9. 10. — II 287,1. — III 119,1. 5. 520,4. — IV 144,8. 12. 188,20. 228,25. 229,4. 315,4. 11. 13. 17. 19. 21. 23. 26. 325,11. 18. — V 11,5. 8. 16. 19. — VI 481,16*. — Visākhāya aṭṭha varā

IV 314,29. — Visākhāya sahāyikā surāpāyikā pañcasatā itthiyo V 11,5.
Visākhā, (nakkhattaṁ) N 18,22. 94,8.
Visākhā-puṇṇamā N 68,11. 16.
Visākhā, brāhmaṇī mātā Kakusandha-Buddhassa N 42,35.
visuddhasaṁkileso IV 468,25. (cfr. Jāt. (263).)
Vissakamma, devaputto N 7,5. 8,17. 60,2. 3. — I 314,20*. 315,11*. — IV 265,10. 30. 323,10*. 325,18. 489*,3. 16. 499,16*. — V 132,5*. 190,20*. 191,8*. — VI 12,14*. 21,2*. 29,9*. 72*,28. 29. 332,29*. 519,31*. 520,2*.
Vissasena, rājā Bārāṇasiyaṁ II 345,19*. 346,24* (25).
Vissāsabhojana-jātaka (93) I 387—389.
vissāsabhojanaṁ I 387,23. — III 141,22.
Vīṇāthūṇa-jātaka (232) II 224—226.
Vīticcha-jātaka (244) II 257—259.
Vīraka, udakakāko (— Bodhisatto) II 149*,3. 8. 10. 15. 21. 150*,2. 5 (7). 10. 23.
Vīraka-jātaka (204) II 148—150.
Vīsatinipāta (XV) IV 375—499. — VI 363,23 (— Jāt. 500). 379,14 (— Jāt. 508).
Vejayanta, pāsādo Sakkassa I 203*,27. 28. — IV 357,7*. — V 126,23 (read: Vejayantakampanasamatthā). 386,1*. — VI 132,1*. 169,2*. 174 (13). 28*. 232 (12). 278,24*.
Vejayanta-ratha, Sakkassa I 202,28*. — II 254*,13. 20. — IV 355,17*. — V 408,21*. 409 (15). — VI 103*,8. 19. 21.
Veṇī, sigālī III 532,24*. 534,9* (11). 535,4*.
Vetaraṇī, nadī niraye III 472,12*. 473 (11). — IV 273,17* (20. 21). 26*. — V 269*,12. 14. 275 (5. 8). 276 (2). — VI 105,6*. 8 (10. 11. 13). 20*. 106,4. 10. 16 (Vetarani-nirayo). 250*,11. 13.
Vetaraññe — Vetaraṇī-udake 250,19* (20).
Vetaraṇī, vejjo IV 496,7*. 498 (82).
Vettavatī, nagaraṁ Mejjharaṭṭhe IV 388,7*.
Vettavatī, nadī Mejjharaṭṭhe IV 388,8*.

Vedabbha, brāhmaṇo I 253*,18. 21. 256,7* (10. 11). 26.
Vedabbha, manto I 253,5*. 256 (10).
Vedabbha-jātaka (48) I 253—256.
Vedā (pl.) III 195,1*. 237,3*. — IV 385,22*. 477,18*. — VI 594,30 etc. — Vedā tayo II 43,21*. 46,28*. — III 237 (6). — IV 386 (6—7) etc. — Vedattayaṁ V 399 (29). — Veda-catukkaṁ V 451 (10). — vedamado IV 385,21*. 386 (6). — Veda-vedaṅga-kusalo V 476,3*.
Vedeha-, cfr. Videha-.
Vedeha, — Videho, rājā Mithilāyaṁ: III 366,21*. 367,17*. 369 (1). 24. Vedeha-tāpaso III 366,17*. 367,20*. 369*,15. 19. — Kāsirājā IV 94,18*. — Suruci IV 319,26*. — Sādhīno IV 355,29*. 356 (2). 15. 24. — Somanassa VI 47*,5. 7. 9. — Nimirājā VI 102,18. 103,24*. 104,16. 127,28. 129,7. — Aṁgati VI 222,22. 223,17. 21. 224,12. 14. 225,19. 227,30. 228,4. 10. 229,30. 230,16. 24. 231,35. 232,8. 26. 233,18. 237,9. 238,11. 17. 20. 23. 27. 239 (14). 240 (1). 242,27.
Vedeha, rājā Mithilāyaṁ VI 330,3*. 346*,15. 29. 403*,5. 6. 13. 14. 406,15*. 407,5*. 410,2*. 411,28*. 415,12*. 418,12. 424* (2). 13. 17. 426*,29. 30. 427 (1). 17. 428,4*. 433,7 (27) 434,5* (8). 10*. 16. 435,28*. 443,3. 444,2*. 445,8. 19. 448*,25. 27. 449,8*. 450 (15). 19*. 451,2*. 452*,22. 31. 453,6—29. 454*,2—20. 455,13* (16). 458*,15. 17. 20. 27. 462*,4. 7. 463,8. Vedeharājā VI 333,26*. 393,18*. 410*,1. 10. 411,25*. 434,29*. 435,2*. 445,9*. 466*,13. 20.
Vedeha-putta, — Vedeharājadhītāya putto V 90,8* (12).
Vedeha-rajja VI 393*,18. 20. 23.
Vedeha-raṭṭha VI 411,22*. 462 (22).
Vedeha-rāja, (— Aṁgati) VI 223 (31). (cfr. Vedeha.)
Vedehi, — Kosaladevī II 403,14 (v. l. B).
Venateyya, — Garuḷo V 424,27. (cfr. Garuḷa).
Venasāra-jātaka, see: Dhonasākha-jāt.
Vepacittiya, asurindo I 205,23*.

Vepulla, pabbato I 445*,1. 4. — IV 232.14*. — VI 271.23*. 272,5 (15. 16). 326.18*. (cfr. Vipula.)

Vebhāra, nagaraṁ Siddhattha-Buddhassa N 40.8.

Vebhāra-pabbata N 37.15.

Verañja, brāhmaṇo III 494.25.

Verañja-kaṇḍa III 494.21.

Verañjā, (nagaraṁ) III 494.22.

Veri-jātaka (103) I 412—413.

Verocana, maṇi V 310,17. 18 (29). 311,22.

Velāma, (brāhmaṇo?) I 228.19.

Velāma(ka)-sutta I 228.24.

Veḷuka, āsīvisapotako I 245*.13. 23. 246.5*.

Veḷuka-jātaka (43) I 244—246.

Veḷuka-pitar, tāpaso I 245*,14. 24. 246.14.

Veḷuvana, uyyānaṁ Rājagahaṁ nissāya N 85.4. 7. 10. 12. 14. 24. 27. — I 142.17. 143,1. 156,10. 11. 15. 173.8. 185.25. 186,14. 278,11. 280,23. 319.15. 322,25 371,27. 372,26. 29. 33. 424,23. 444,2. 465,19. 482.17. 487,8. 489.6. 490,24. 491,6. 508,9. — II 38,21. 70.2. 98,2. 101.13. 121.14. 152.22. 162,12. 186,15. 196,17. 199,8. 206,6. 221.5. 237.16. 242.24. 248,5. 382,2. — III 33,12. 97,12. 112,16. 121,16. 133.2. 174,6. 177,25. 202,12. 215,14. 293,7. 321,17. 414.28. — IV 37,4. 55,26. 256,15. 413,2. 423.22. — V 67,29. 125.19. 23. 127,6 (Veḷuvana-dvāra-koṭṭhaka). 333,3. 334.25. 28. 337.10. 354,6.

Vevaṭiyakapi-jātaka (v. l. Mahākapi-jāt.) III 178,7. (cfr. Mahākapi-jāt. (516)).

Vesāyin, — Yamo II 317.18*. 318 (1).

Vesālī, nagaraṁ N 77.5. — I 217.9. 389,15. 24. 420.16. 504,6. 8. — II 5,12. 259,26. 262.7. 392.18. — III 1,6. 8. 20. — IV 148,21. 24.

Vesālika, (adj.) Vesāliko duṭṭha-Licchivikumārako I 504,7.

Vessantara, ulūkaputto V 110,24*. 111*,14. 16. 17. 21. 24. 25. 112*,1. 2. 6. 11. 114 (30). 115*,23. 27. 29. 116 (12). 120 (17). 125,10.

Vessantara, putto Sañjayassa Sivirañño, rājā (= Bodhisatto) VI 485*,18. 21 487*,15. 19. 30. 489 (20) (Vessantara-mahārājā). 490*,7. 27. 491*,1. 10. 29. 492,2. 12. 15. 494 (22) 25*. 495,15*. 498,20. 24. 26. 28. 499 (18). 500,4. 502 (1. 3). 8. 10. 18. 20. 22. 33. 503,4. 8. 16 (25. 28. 30. 34). 504 (9. 13. 33). 505,1*. 506,11*. 28. 508,24. 33. 510,25*. 511,1. 8 (10. 12). 512,27. 513,29. 514,17*. 515,1*. 516,7*. 517,8* (20). 519*,15. 19. 523,22*. 524 (11). 525,9*. 18. 526,11. 13. 16. 18. 21. 24. 27. 30. 527 (2). 7*. 528,10* (16). 23. 529,3 (7. 17). 530,26. 531 (20). 25*. 533 (11. 30). 28. 539,31. 540 (10). 18 (14). 19*. 542,5*. 544,19*. 545*,3. 22. 551,25. 552 (16). 553 (4). 556,5*. 558 (7. 24). 561 (9. 28). 565 (10). 566 (14). 26*. 568*,17. 21. 571 (25). 573,22 (28). 575,9. 11. 18*. 17. 579,6. 581,29. 582 (3). 13. 583,11. 586,5 (32). 587,7. 11. 588,14. 23*. 589,2 (14. 17). 591,17. 19. 21. 24. 27. 29. 592,4*. 9. 11. 13. 15. 17 (20. 24). 593 (4). 6* (Vessantara-mahārājā). 593,20. 21. 29. 596,14. — Vessantarattabhāvo N 2,6. 31,8. 44,23. 47,13 (cfr. Cariyā-piṭ. I 9,38.). 53,21. 30. 74,21. 24. — Vessantarakālo N 45,15. — Vessantaradānaṁ N 74,29. — Vessantarabodhisatto IV 13 (9).

Vessantara-jātaka (547) VI 479—593. — N 89,2. — III 340 (22). — IV 282,21. — Mahā-Vessantara-jātaka VI 481,26*.

Vessantara-dhammadesanā VI 593,24. — Mahā-Vessantara-dhammadesanā VI 482,1*.

Vessantara-pañha, Tesakuṇa-jātake V 115,31.

Vessantara-vaṇṇanā VI 373,30. 593,30.

Vessabhū. Buddho N 41,22. 42,5. 17. 29. 44,9. 94,14. — III 474 (10) (Vessabhūdasabalādayo).

Vessavaṇa, mahārājā Cātummahārājika-devaloke I 128*,13. 14. 328*,12. 13. 14. — II 16,3*. 17,5*. 397,17*. 398,7*. 399*,5. 11. 12. 20. — III 258,18*. 325,20*. 502,23*. — IV 324,15*.

492,16*. — V 21,27*. — VI 265,13*. 268,28*. 270*,31. 32. 271,1*. 313,9*. 326,15. 568,9. 571,18. — Vessavaṇo Kuvero VI 269,2*. 271,9. — Vessavaṇa-ambo IV 324,15.
Vessāmitta, porāṇaka-rājā VI 251,14*.
Vehapphalā, (devā) III 358,24.
Vyaggha-jātaka (272) II 356—358.

S.

Saṁyama, rājā Bārāṇasiyaṁ V 354,9*. 364,24*. — Saṁyama-rājaputtā V 381,27*.
Saṁyutta, Saṁyutta-suttanto (cfr. Mahávagga, Saṁy. Nik. XLVI.) II 58,25. — Saṁyuttaṭṭhakathā V 56,4*.
Saṁvara, ājīviko V 87,24 (27).
Saṁvara, māyākārapuriso asurindo ca V 452,31. 454 (34).
Saṁvara-kumāra, putto kaniṭṭho Brahmadattassa Bārāṇasi-rañño, mahārājā IV 131*,18. 23. 29. 132*,24. 25. 27. 133*,3. 22. 23. 25. 27. 134*,5. 17. 135,28*. 136 (1). 9*. 17.
Saṁvara-jātaka (462) IV 130—136. — I 136,12. — II 17,26.
Sakuṇa-jātaka (36) I 215—217.
Sakuṇagghi-jātaka (168) II 58—60.
Sakuṇovāda-sutta II 58,23.
Sakula, nagaraṁ Mahiṁsakaraṭṭhe V 337,20*. (v. l. B Sāgala.)
Sakula, rājā Sakulanagare V 337,20*. 348 (25). 353,18*.
Sakka, see: Mahānāma. (cfr. Sākiya, Sakya).
Sakka, devarājā N 7 (5). 32,18. 33,9. 18. 39,23 (— Bodhisatto). 48,16. 52,22. 59,28. 65,4. 68,21. 72,7. 15. 80,11. 13. 81,10. 84,13. 28. — I 199,3*. 202*,8. 10. 21. 28. 202,17* (jara-Sakko). 203*,24. 28. 204* (11). 21. 26. 205*,2. 10. 18. 16. 206*,1. 5. 206,14 (— Bodhisatto). 229,28. 230,21. 314,25*. 328,12*. 330,11. 350,16*. 351,19*. 352*,25. 30. 353*,1. 8. 22. 24. 25. 354,5*. 12. — II 93,2. 102*,5. 12. 17. 123*,28. 27. 124*,12. 15. 125,4*. 8.

142,22* (— Bodhisatto). 143*,4. 12. 17. 144,17. 188*,16. 19. 22. 189*,11. 20. 27. 190*,13. 19. 191*,19. 24. 28. 192,4*. 212*,17. 27 (— Bodhisatto). 213*,13. 18. 21. 214,24*. 216,1*. 5. 251*25. 26. 252*,3. 12. 253*,1. 16. 20. 254*,10. 16. 19. 22. 255,7*. 257,10. 312*,11. 16. 19. 20. 25. 334,8 (20. 26). 335,3 (— Bodhisatto). 344*20. 21. 380*,23. 25. 27. 394,15*. 395,15*. 396*,5. 11. 431,19*. 432,2*. 28 (— Bodhisatto). 450*,5. 12. 19. 27 (— Bodhisatto). 451,9. — III 4*,23. 25. 7*,9. 12. 18. 40,6*. 53,8*. 55*,9. 17. 19. 20. 23 128,24. 129*,8. 11. 130,15*. 131,4*. 132*,4. 7. 10. 137,25*. 139,18 (— Bodhisatto). 146*,8. 18. 19. 22. 147,15. 163,27*. 165*,1. 21. 166,12*. 167*,1. 24. 26. 213,28*. 214*,6. 10. 25. 26. 215,9*. 11 (— Bodhisatto). 222*,8. 10. 224,7*. 19 (— Bodhisatto). 249,13*. 252*,11. 16 (24). 258*,14. 15. 277,24*. 280,17*. 281,11 (— Bodhisatto). 303,15*. 304,18*. 305,12*. 306*,3. 11. 20. 307,15*. 22 (— Bodhisatto). 310*,21. 25. 312,10 (— Bodhisatto). 389,24*. 390*,4. 8. 20. 21. 391,4*. 6 (— Bodhisatto). 392,5*. 410,16*. 413 (14). 425,8*. 426*,4. 25. 427,7. 15. 428 (2) 7 (— Bodhisatto). 491*,10. 16. 492,26*. 493,21*. 494*,6. 7. 9. 18. 495,23*. 496,21. 515*,10. 17. 19. 20. 26. 516,31*. — IV 8*,28. 29. 9*,3. 17. 10*,1. 21 (31. 32). 11,3*. 12 (29). 13*,12. 18. 22. 14*,1—3. (7). 13. 15. 21. 63,4. 11. 23. 64*,5. 16. 65,5*. 68*,20. 25. 69*,5. 16. 24 (— Bodhisatto). 73,12. 19. 106*,1. 30. 108,1*. 109,18*. 110,15*. 113,18 (— Bodhisatto). 170,1*. 181,16*. 182*,9. 22. 24. 183,19*. 186,10*. 18 (— Bodhisatto). 188,27. 233,8*. 238*,17. 18. 26. 239*,6. 12. 289,22 (bhūtapati). 240*,1—28. 241*,7—24. 242,20*. 24. 264,16. 265,30. 266,8. 272*,9. 13. 20. 273,11* (18. 19). 274,11*. 275,1*. 288*,2. 7. 13. 306,30*. 308,9. 312,13*. 313* (6). 8. 26. 314,1* (10). 13*. 24. 318,9*. 319,7*. 321,19*. 322 (5). 13*. 323,18*. 324,24*. 325,13 (— Bodhisatto). 355,14*. 356,24. 357* (1). 6. 10. 30. 358,16*. 360,20. 403,1*. 406*,2. 22. 409,4. 6—26*. 411,3*. 412,23. 455,15*. 474,28*. 475*,8. 13. 15. 489,21*. 499,16*. — V 14,10*.

15,16°. 19,30°. 20*,12. 17. 25. 20,29 (— Bodhisatto). 33,15°. (24). 92*,2. 13. 94*,15. 18. 113,7°. 115 (1) (— Indo). 132*,5. 11. 136,6°. 137*,16. 25. 138* (1). 9. 21 (29). 139,3°. 139 (24—26) (Sakkassa gaṇanāmāni). 140,18°. 141,6°. 8. 142*,12. 16. 20. 143,6°. 145 (32). 146,2°. 147 (27). 149 (8. 23). 151,2°. 152,24°. 153,16°. 154,7°. 158 (27. 28. 30). 161*,12. 18 (14). 190,20°. 193,17°. 194*,4. 6. 201,13°. 216,1° (32). 260,1. 5. 7. 276 (24). 279,28°. 280*,4. 11. 12. 23. 281*,5—27. 300,18°. 309,10°. 310 (29). 314,23°. 317*,4. 8. 383,11°. 385,27°. 386,27°. 388*,2. 13. 390*,10. 22. 392*,5. 13. 21 (Sakassa catassa dhitaro). 393 (22. 26). 394 (22. 30). 395,17°. 407,19°. 408 (4. 7). 9°. 411,25°. 412,11 (— Bodhisatto). 468 (29. 31). 469 (1. 4). 474,4°. 511,21. — VI 2*,2. 8. 12*,11. 27. 13*,13. 17. 31,26°. 32*,9. 19. 72,28°. 73*,7. 16. 21. 27. 95,9. 97,32°. 98,8 (26). 99 (2). 103*,5. 9. 21. 104 (24). 116,11°. 124*,2. 24. 127*,17. 23. 30. 128*,18. 19. 28. 129,15. 155,10b (28). 157 (2). 168,25°. 169,1°. 171,14°. 174*,4 (5). 17 (22. 24). 204 (3). 236,26. 239 (30. 32). 256*,10. 23. 257*,2. 12. 14. 258*,14. 28. 259,15°. 260 (25). 261,25°. 262*,1. 7. 329,16. 25. 331,7°. 338 (22. 27. 28. 32. 37). 339 (3. 5. 8). 340 (7). 362,8°. 383,21°. 388,5°. 404,11°. 481*,20. 22. 482*,14. 21. 483,28°. 484*,15. 19. 486,16°. 519,30°. 520,11°. 568,21°. 31. 569,24°. 571*,5. 32. 572,20. 29. 573,18°. 583 (5). 586,29°. 593,9°. 27. (cfr. Inda, Kosiya, Gandhabbarāja, Purindada, Maghavat, Mahinda, Vatrabhū, Vāsava, Sahassacakkho, Sahassanetta, Sujampati).

Sakkā (pl.) I 203,22° (aññehi cakkavāḷehi Sakkā āgacchanti). 204 (9) (Sakkānaṁ satasahassaṁ). — II 311,9; 312,23°; 313,9° (chattiṁsa Sakkā, chattiṁsā Sakkānaṁ).

Sakkattaṁ I 353,27°. — II 101,24°. 124,1°. — III 131,6°. 132,5°. 137,21°. 213,20°. 219,28°. 275,11°. 388,28°. — IV 105,21°. 238*,20. 28. — V 58,1°. 152,25°.

Sakkattabhāvo II 143,10. 450,19°. — IV 274,11°.

Sakkattarajjāni I 315,13°.

Sakkânubhāvo III 132,9*. 307,15*. 427,19*. 515,13*. — IV 170*,9. 14. 411,2*. — VI 339 (5).
Sakkissariyaṁ IV 10,14*.
Sakkaṭṭhānaṁ IV 242 (17).
Sakka-dattiyo (adj.) VI 21,15*. — Sakka-dattiko rājā (— Bodhisatto) I 124,25*. 125,9 (Sakka-dattiya-rājā). — V 300 (6) (Sakkadattiya-kusaṭinasamānanāmo rājā — Kusarājā). — Sakka-dattiyaṁ Kaviṭṭhaka-assamaṁ III 463,7*. (cfr. Kaviṭṭha). — Sakkadattiyaṁ assamaṁ IV 489,20*. — VI 29,6*. 529 (7). 572,25*. — Sakkadattiya-bhāvo VI 21,8*. 73,7*.
Sakka-dassanaṁ VI 155 (29).
Sakka-brāhmaṇo (jarāpatto andhabrāhmaṇo — Sakko) IV 410,25*.
Sakka-bhavanaṁ N 33,9. 61,27. — II 188,16*. 394,14*. — III 129,6*. 491,10*. 515,10*. — IV 7,7. 306,29*. 318,9*. 455,17*. — V 92,1*. 152,24*. 193,16*. 279,28*. — VI 2,2*. 12,11*. 31,26*. 46,19*. 72,27*. 97,32*.
Sakka-bhāvo II 450,21*. — III 515,11*. — IV 239,26*. 272,15*.
Sakka-līḷhā VI 170,24*. 196,16*. 450,29*.
Sakka-vilāso VI 432,30*.
Sakka-visayo VI 251,18* (28).
Sakka-sampatti N 48,19. — IV 239 (25). — VI 169,3*.
Sakka-siri-sadiso VI 43,7*.
Sakka-pabba, Vessantara-jātake VI 573,24.
Sakkhara, nigamo Rājagahanagarassa avidūre I 345,20 346,17. 347,1.
Sakya, (cfr. Sakka, Sākiyā). Sakya-kulāni (v. l. sekhakulāni) IV 144,19. — Sakya-dhītā IV 144,20. — Sakya-putto (Upanando) II 441,16. — III 332,5. — samaṇā Sakya-puttiyā II 15,13. 416,20. — IV 263,18. — Sakya-rājakulāni IV 158,9. — Sakya-rājadhītā (— Vāsabhakhattiyā IV 146,12. — Sakya-rājāno IV 148,23. — VI 479,9.

Sagga, gandhabbo Tambarañño Bārāṇasiyaṁ III 188*,9. 25. 189*,1. 24. 190,1*.

Sagga-loka I 152,9*. — VI 132,12. etc. 151,28*.

Saṁkappa-jātaka (251) II 271—277. — V 117 (26).

Saṁkappa-vagga II 271—321.

Saṁkassa, nagaraṁ I 193,25. 473,2. 474,2. — IV 265,24. 25. 26. 28. 32.

Saṁkicca-kumāra, paṇḍito, purohitaputto (— Bodhisatto) V 263*,5. 23. 264,11*. 19. 23. 31. 265 (6. 13). 27. 277,6.

Saṁkicca-jātaka (530) V 261—277.

Saṁkicca-sāmaṇera-vatthu VI 14 (28).

saṁkileso I 302,29.

Saṁkha, brāhmaṇo Molinī-nagare (— Bodhisatto) N 45,13. — IV 15,21*. 17*,14. 25. 19*,11. 16. 20,12*. 21,17. 22,8.

Saṁkha, seṭṭhi Rājagahe (— Bodhisatto) I 466,3. 7. 9. 18. 37. 468*,12. 22. 469,3*. 11.

Saṁkha-jātaka (442) IV 15—22. — Saṁkhabrāhmaṇa-jātaka IV 120,1*(?).

Saṁkhadhamana-jātaka (60) I 284.

Saṁkhapāla, nāgarājā (— Bodhisatto) V 162*,11. 18. 22. 28. 167 (13. 28). 169,16*. 170 (11. 18). 171 (15). 175 (8. 17) 177,7. — Saṁkhapāladhammadesanā V 174 (27).

Saṁkhapāla, rājā Ekabalaraṭṭhe VI 390*,24. 29.

Saṁkhapāla-jātaka (524) V 161—171. — N 45,24 (— Cariyā-piṭ. II 10,7). — IV 456,27*.

Saṁkhapāla-daha, Mahiṁsakaraṭṭhe V 162,7*.

Saṁkhabrāhmaṇa-jātaka, see: Saṁkha-jātaka.

Saṁgāmāvacara-jātaka (182) II 92—95.

Saṁgīti-kārakā I 345 (14).

saṁgha II 147,8*.

Saṁghadāsī, dhītā Kikissa rañño (Kassapadasabalassa kāle) VI 481,13*.

Saṁghabhedaka-khandhaka VI 129,20. (cfr. Vin. vol. II 180—206).
Saṁghabhedaka-jātaka III 211,11. (— Sandhibheda-jātaka (349) (?) cfr. Kosambi-jātaka (428).)
Saṁghāta, nirayo V 266,13*. 270 (29).
Saṁghānussati-kammaṭṭhāna I 97,14.
Saccaka, nigaṇṭha-putto Vesāliyaṁ III 1,15. 20. — VI 478,18* (?).
Saccaṁkira-jātaka (73) I 322—327.
Saccatapāvī, seta-samaṇī V 424,24. 427 (23. 26. 29. 32).
Saccā, Licchavi-dārikā, paribbājikā III 1,14.
Sañjaya, uyyānapālo Brahmadattassa Bārāṇasi-rañño I 157*,20. 22. 158,23*. 159,11.
Sañjaya, (paribbājako?) N 85,20.
Sañjaya-belaṭṭhiputta, (diṭṭhigatiko) I 509,14.
Sañjaya-kumāra, bhātā kaniṭṭho Bhadrakārassa, putto Vidhura-brāhmaṇassa V 61*, 6. 13. 20. 23. 27. 28. 62 (28). 27*. 67,25.
Sañjaya, Sivirājā Jetuttaranagare (pitā Vessantarassa (Bo.)) VI 480,8*. 484*,10. 14. 16. 21. 487,15*. 490,27*. 503 (24). 505,12. 533,2. 544 (24). 574,5*. 26. 579,15. 581 (32). 583,15*. 589,3. 26. 591,12*. 592,1*. 593,27.
Sañjīva, aggasāvako Kakusandha-Buddhassa N 42,26.
Sañjīva, nirayo V 266,13*. 270 (24). 272 (2).
Sañjīva, māṇavo matavyagghupaṭṭhāko I 510,16. 23. 25. 29. 511 (9. 11).
Sañjīva-jātaka (150) I 508—511. — V 241 (20).
Sañjīvika, vyaggho (cfr. Sañjīva-māṇavo) I 511,2* (9. 10).
Saṭṭhi-nipāta (XIX) V 247—277.
Satadhamma, māṇavo Bārāṇasiyaṁ II 82,18. 24*. 84,11. 19 (21. 23). — Santadhamma 84 (22).
Satadhamma-jātaka (179) II 82—85.
Satapatta-jātaka (279) II 387—390. — V 147 (20).
Sataporisa, nirayo V 269,7*. 274 (29).
Sattati-nipāta (XX) V 278—332.

Sattadāraka-pañha, Mahāummaggajātake VI 339 (10).
Satta-nipāta III 317—421. — Sattanipātavaṇṇanā III 421,14.
Sattasuriya-sutta IV 498 (4).
Sattigumba, suvo (— Devadatto) IV 431*,2. 4. 25. 27. 432,28*. 433,17*. 434,29*. 435 (4). 436,30.
Sattigumba-jātaka (503) IV 430—437. — VI 86 (1).
Sattisūla, nirayo V 143,27*. 145 (16).
Sattuka, coro Bārāṇasiyaṁ III 435,31*. 437*,16. 27. 438*,12. 16 (23. 24).
Sattubhasta-jātaka (v. l. Sattubhatta-) (402) III 341—351. — N 46,7. — V 122 (6). 147 (6).
saddo bhiṁsanako, Kosalarañño aḍḍharattasamaye suto III 428,10. (cfr. III 43,18).
Saddhā, dhītā Sakkassa V 392,21*. 393,12. 398,18*. 23. 402*,6. 16 (20). 403,7* (24). 408,16 (19). 409,18. 410,3* (7).
saddhivihāriko dhammasenāpatissa, suvaṇṇakārapubbako bhikkhu I 182,10. — saddhivihāriko Sāriputta-therassa I 224,15. — II 160,25 (daharabhikkhu). 420,27.
saddho upāsako II 111,3.
Santa, aggasāvako Atthadassi-Buddhassa N 39,15.
Santadhamma, see: Satadhamma.
Santikenidāna, N 77—94. — N 2,1. 9.
Santusita, (devaputto Tusita-bhavane) N 48,16. 81,11.
Santhava-jātaka (162) II 43—45.
Santhava-vagga II, 41—63.
Sandhibheda-jātaka (349) III 149—152. — Saṁghabhedaka-jātaka III 211,11 (?).
Sabala, suvāno Lokantaraniraye VI 247,16*.
Sabbakāma, aggasāvako Sumedha-Buddhassa N 38,5.
Sabbadatta, rājā Rammanagare (Bārāṇasiyaṁ), pitā Bodhisattassa IV 119,26*. 120,3*. 122,29*.
Sabbadassin, aggasāvako Piyadassi-Buddhassa N 39,4.

Sabbadāṭha, sigālarājā (= Devadatto) III 244*,1. 3. 10. 13. 14. 23. 245,7*.
Sabbadāṭha-jātaka (241) II 242—246.
Sabbanāmā, aggasāvikā Dhammadassi-Buddhassa N 39,27.
sabbaparikkhāradānaṁ III 51,11. — IV 15,2.
Sabbamitta, upaṭṭhāko Kassapa-Buddhassa N 43,23.
Sabbamitta, rājā Sāvatthiyaṁ V 13,18*. 14,17*. 18,17.
Sabbasaṁhāraka-pañha (110) I 424,11–14.
Sabhiya, upaṭṭhāko Phussa-Buddhassa N 41,4.
Sabhiya, paribbājako VI 329,24.
Samaṇaguttaka, coro V 126,4.
Samaṇā, dhītā Kikissa rañño (Kassapadasabalassa kāle) VI 481,12*.
Samaṇī, dhītā Kikissa IV 481,12*.
Samālā, aggasāvikā Vessabhu-Buddhassa N 42,18.
Samiddhi, thero II 56,23. 24. 57,1. 11. 314 (7).
Samiddhi-jātaka (167) II 56—58.
Samugga-jātaka (436) III 527—531. — = Karaṇḍaka-jātaka V 455 (2).
Samudda, isi VI 99,28*.
Samudda-jātaka (296) II 441—442.
Samuddajā, dhītā Brahmadatta-kumārassa ca nāgamāṇavikāya ca, mātā Bhūridattassa (Bo.) VI 160,2*. 162,29*. 163*,17. 31. 164,18* (22. 28). 165,28. 166,32*. 167,24*. 171,30*. 190,1*. 196,19*. 219*,14. 16. 19.
Samuddavāṇija-jātaka (466) IV 158—166. — I 142,30.
Samuddavijayā, aggamahesī Bharatarañño Roruvanagare Sovīraraṭṭhe (Bo.) III 470,10*. 474,18.
Samuddā, aggasāvikā Koṇāgamana-Buddhassa N 43,9.
Sambala, aggasāvako Siddhattha-Buddhassa N 40,9.
Sambula-jātaka (519) V 88—98. — IV 77 (28).
Sambulā, aggamahesī Sotthisenassa rañño Bārāṇasiyaṁ V

88*,17. 24. 90*,6. 7. 22. 91*,1. 4 (21. 25). 92,13* (23). 93 (8). 95*,13. 16. 18 (27). 97*,28* (30). 98,4* (11). 10.

Sambhava, aggasāvako Sikhi-Buddhassa N 41,30.

Sambhava, upaṭṭhāko Revata-Buddhassa N 35,9.

Sambhava, upaṭṭhāko Tissa-Buddhassa N 40,24.

Sambhava-kumāra, paṇḍito, kaniṭṭhabhātā Sañjaya-kumārassa, putto Vidhura-brāhmaṇassa (= Bodhisatto) V 62,8*. 10. 27*. 63*,1. 2. 6. 7. 24—26 (29). 64 (3. 7. 10). 21*. 65*,4. 19. 21. 66 (29). 67,26.

Sambhava-jātaka (515) V 57—67. — V 122 (7).

Sambhūta, paṇḍito, caṇḍālo (mātucchāputto Bodhisattassa) IV 390,17*. 391*,14. 25. — Uttarapañcālarañño putto 392*,22. 24. 393*,2. 8. 394,7* (17). 395 (1. 8). 401,8. — Pañcālo 398*,8. 12. 16. 20.

Sammāsambuddha N 44,17. — I 276,34. 348,6. 349,2. 407,24. 422,19. 469,30. 504,18. 505,12. 20. 508,23. 28. 509,8. 20. — II 24,7. 137,12. 173,15. 199,11. 239,25. 248,7. 8. 14. 257,16. 259,17. 286,11. 332,6. 392,12. 20. 393,8. 415,9. — III 44,25. 26. 178,11. 293,12. 369,29. 536,24. — IV 159,1. 189,4. 10. 360,1*. 369,20. 406 (14). — V 11,10. 262,4. — VI 70,8. 131,1. 8. 304 (7). — Sammāsambuddhā (pl.) II 147,25*. — Sammāsambuddha-sāvako II 313,21. 314 (10). — Sammāsambuddha-sāsanaṁ VI 124,15. — Sambuddho III 409 (9). — IV 22,12.

Sammillabhāsinī, brāhmaṇa-dhītā Kāsiraṭṭhe III 93,24*. 94,2. 4. 8. 13. 95,14*. 97,9.

Sammodamāna-jātaka (33) I 208—210. — Vaṭṭaka-jātaka V 414,27. 97,9.

Sayha (v. l. B Seyha, Seyya), amacco Bārāṇasi-rañño III 31,22*. 32*,7 (19). 29. 33,4. — III 516*,1. 10. 18. 517*,4. 7. 519,27.

Sayha-jātaka (v. l. B Seyya-jāt.) (310) III 30—33.

Saraṇa, aggasāvako Sumana-Buddhassa N 34,26.

Saraṇa, aggasāvako Sumedha-Buddhassa N 38,5.

Saraṇa, nagaraṁ Dhammadassi-Buddhassa N 39,25.

Saraṇa, rājā, pitā Dhammadassi-Buddhassa N 39,26.

Saraṇaṁkara, Buddho N 44,2.

Sarabhaṅga, satthā (isi) (— Bodhisatto) III 464*,9. 25. 466,11*. 467,3*. 469*.13. 16. 22. — V 135*.5. 27. 136*,8. 10. 137 (10). 140*.2. 4 (8. 9). 144 (18). 151 (17). 31. (cfr. Koṇḍañña, Jotipāla.)

Sarabhaṅga-jātaka (522) V 125—151. — N 58,29. — I 406,1 (read: Sarabhamiga-jātake). — V 101 (6). 114 (8). 122 (7). 272 (8).

Sarabhamiga-jātaka (483) IV 263—275. — I 193,23. 406,1 (in stead of Sarabhaṅga-jātaka).

Salalavatī, nadī Majjhimadese N 49,10.

Saviṭṭhaka, kāko (— Devadatto) II 149*,7. 16. 150*.3. 6. 14. 28.

Saviṭhaka, see: Vasiṭṭhaka.

Sasa-jātaka (316) III 51—56. — Sasa-paṇḍita-jātaka N 45,17 (— Cariyāpiṭ. I 10,28).

sahajātā satta N 54,9.

Sahadeva, Paṇḍurājaputto V 424,21. 426 (11).

Sahampati, Mahābrahmā IV 245,9. — Sahampati Brahmā IV 266,4.

Sahassacakkhu, — Sakko V 394,27 (90).

Sahassanetta, — Sakko III 426,7* (10). — VI 174*,3 (13). 27.

Sākiyā (pl.), Sākiya-rājakulaṁ N 88,4. 13. — IV 145,8. 10. 16. 147,6. 10. 23. 152.11. 24. 27. 29. — V 413,7. — VI 479,14. — Sākyā IV 151,25. — Sākiyo eko N 88,28. — eka-Sākiyo VI 479,30. — Sākiyakammakarā V 413,3. — Sākiya-Koliyā V 412,15. 413,10. — Sākiya-gaṇo IV 423,19. — Sākiya-bhikkhu IV 219,6. 430,8. (cfr. Sakka, Sakya.)

Sāketa, nagaraṁ Kosalaraṭṭhe I 308,24. 26. 27. — II 234,24. — III 270,15*. 272*,3. 6 (8). 11. — V 13,17*. — VI 228,7 (Sāketā). 228 (30).

Sāketa, brāhmaṇo II 234,25. (cfr. I 308,27: Sāketanagaravāsi-mahallakabrāhmaṇo).
Sāketa-jātaka a) (68) I 308—310. — b) (237) II 234—235. — II 82,8 (?).
Sākyā, see: Sākiyā.
Sākha, migo (— Devadatto) I 149,24*. 150*,7. 22. 151*,3. 4. 152*,13. 17. 18 (21. 24). 153,17.
Sākha-kumāra, seṭṭhiputto Rājagahe (— Devadatto) IV 38,23*. 39*,24. 25. 40*,15. 18. 20. 24. 41*,2. 7. 16. 19. 20. 25. 27. 29. 42*, (1. 2). 7—8 (18). 21. 22. 26. 43*,6. 14. 16. 18.
Sāgata, upaṭṭhāko Dīpaṁkara-Buddhassa N 29,22.
Sāgata, see: Sāgala.
Sāgata, thero I 360,4. 12. 19. 21. 32. 361,3. 5. 6. 13.
Sāgara, upaṭṭhāko Sumedha-Buddhassa N 38,5.
Sāgara, rājā VI 99,9* (14). — VI 203,7* (?).
Sāgara, rājā, pitā Atthadassi-Buddhassa N 39,14.
Sāgara, rājā Uttaramadhurāyaṁ, putto Mahāsāgarassa IV 79*,22. 23.
Sāgara-Brahmadatta, putto Brahmadatta-kumārassa ca nāgamāṇavikāya ca VI 159,31*. 217*,10. 26. 219*,10. 18.
Sāgala, Bhagavato anibaddhaupaṭṭhāko IV 95,14. (v. l. B Sāgato).
Sāgala-nagara, Maddaraṭṭhe IV 230,21*. — V 283,26*. 285,6*. 289,16*. 290,9*. — VI 471 (21). 473 (8).
sāṭakalakkhaṇa-brāhmaṇo I 371,28.
sāṭakasahassapaṭilābho Ānandattherassa II 23,27. (cfr, II 314,20).
Sātāgira, yakkho (?) IV 314,22. — VI 440 (8).
Sātodikā, nadī Suraṭṭhajanapade III 463,12*. — V 133,20*.
Sādhīna, rājā Mithilāyaṁ (— Bodhisatto) IV 355*,6. 15. 17. 356,19. 358,16*. 360,20. — Vedeho 355,29*. 356 (2). 15. 24.
Sādhīna-jātaka (494) IV 355—360.
Sādhusīla-jātaka (200) II 137—138.

Sānu-pabbata, Himavantapadese V 415,23.

Sāma, nesādaputto — Suvaṇṇasāmo (Bodhisatto) VI 75,4*. 76,1*. 78*,11 (30). 30. 79,19*. 80,18* (31). 82 (7). 14. 28*. 28. 83 (9. 13). 84*,4. 6. 8 (10). 86*,15. 24. 25. 27. 87*,3. 4. 6 (7). 25. 88 (1. 3. 20. 21). 24—26* (29). 89*,9. 11. 13. 15. 29. 90,7—25. 91,14—29. 92,3*. 7—13. 18—25 (29). 93*,2—4. 15 (16). 18. 94*,6. 9.

Sāma, rājā Bārāṇasiyaṁ II 98*,7. 20 (22).

Sāma, suvāno Lokantaraniraye VI 247,16*.

Sāma-jātaka (540) VI 68—95. — II 50,18. — III 324,26. — Sāmajātaka-vatthu IV 90,3. — IV 276,4. — V 21,3. 312,10.

Sāmaññaphala-suttanta I 509,32.

Sāmā, aggasāvikā Kakusandha-Buddhassa N 42,26.

Sāmā, gaṇikā Bārāṇasiyaṁ III 59*,17. 26. 60*,5. 7. 17. 22. 62*,9. (11. 12). 16. 20 (24). 63*,3. 9 10 (15). 24.

Sārambha, balivaddo (— Bodhisatto) I 375,2. 14.

Sārambha-jātaka (88) I 374—375.

Sāriputta, thero, dhammasenāpati N 7 (9). 8 (26. 36). 88,16. 16. 22. 23. 91,34. 92,1. — I 133,19. 142,24. 143,2. 6. 145,7. 12. 161,11. 162,5. 7. 181,2. 182,22. 26. 27. 217,7. 14. 18. 19. 218,8. 220,18. 224,15. 26. 226,18. 310,6. 16. 21. 311,17. 19. 322,22. 327,21. 345,13. 389,26. 27. 390,1. 9. 391,21. 406,3. 6. 407,16. 408,13. 446,21. 473,28. 474,23. 482,14. 491,2. 12. 14. — II 5,8. 9,21. 24. 23,23. 38,26. 39,2. 50,8. 52,17. 93,19. 25. 107,6. 108,6. 113,8. 148,23. 24. 155,8. 158,15. 160,25. 170,25. 196,9. 24. 25. 26. 202,20. 246,6. 286,10. 19. 287,11. 291,23. 296,23. 356,4. 10. 14. 358,12. 381,21. 384,22. 392,11. 394,1. 6. 400,3. 420,26. 421,9. 433,3. 15. 436,14. — III 2,5. 23. 8,13. 20,13. 33,4. 35,25. 43,18. 48,15. 19. 49,8. 51,7. 56,6. 90,12. 112,23. 145,18. 170,18. 174,2. 191,11. 13. 18. 20. 193,17. 237,23. 274,24. 281,11. 341,17. 351,18. 400,2. 434,25. 469,20. 543,6. — IV 37,1. 55,22. 69,23. 79,1. 89,16. 95,20. 130,19. 136,18. 166,27. 196,19. 218,26. 228,2. 244,4. 20. 22. 245,11. 263,8. 265,23. 266,6. 7. 16. 19. 24. 30. 267,1. 2. 11.

275,4. 6. 297,18. 314,19. 332,22. 354,26. 369,18. 374,4. 406 (14). 423,18. 430,8. 454,3. 468,22. 491,5. — V 36,5. 67,25. 88,8. 125,16. 20. 127,6. 151,28. 177,7. 192,5. 227,17. 332,23. 335,23. 25. 354,8. 382,6. 412,11. 456,11. 511,21. — VI 30,1. 68,20. 157,22. 219,26. 236 (23). 255,7. 258 (12). 329,16. 487,13*. 593,26.

Sāriputta-Moggallānā II 107,6. 108,6. 356,4. 10. 14. — IV 245,12. (cfr. aggasāvakā dve).

Sāriputtattherassa Bimbādevītheriyā ambarasadānaṁ II 392,11. (cfr. II 433,3.).

Sāriputtattherena dinnarasapiṇḍapāto III 48,10. — Dhammasenāpatino vitthāravyākaraṇaṁ I 473,8. — IV 263,8.

Sāriputtassa (dhammasenāpatissa) saddhivihāriko (dahara-) bhikkhu I 182,10. 224,15. — II 160,25. 420,27.

Sāriputtattherassa senāsanapaṭibāhanaṁ I 217,7.

Sāla, aggasāvako Paduma-Buddhassa N 36,25.

Sālaka, makkaṭo II 268,1* (4).

Sālaka-jātaka (249) II 266—268. — III 197,23.

Sālakalyāṇī, bodhi Koṇḍañña-Buddhassa N 30,15.

Sālarukkha, bodhi Padumuttara-Buddhassa N 37,22. — bodhi Vessabhu-Buddhassa N 42,14.

Sālikā, read: sālikā (?) VI 478,19*.

Sālikedāra-jātaka (484) IV 276—282.

Sālittaka-jātaka (107) I 418—420.

Sālindiya, brahmaṇagāmo Rājagahassa pubbapasse III 293,17* (Sālindiyaṁ). 298,17*. — IV 276,12* (Sālindiyo). 276,14*. 279,15*.

sālibhattaṁ II 433,4. (cfr. II 392,11.)

Sāliya, balivaddo V 104*,18. 16 (17). 105,2* (10).

Sāliya-jātaka (367) III 202—203.

Sāliyā-vacana VI 425,25 (26).

Sālissara, isi, jeṭṭhantevāsiko Sarabhaṅgassa (Bodhisattassa) III 463,11*. 464,7*. 469,20. — V 133*,10. 18. 151,28.

Sālūka, sūkaro II 419,15*. 420,1*. 4* (5. 10) 18*. 22.

Sālūka-jātaka (286) II 419—420.

Sāvatthiya-nagara, see: Sotthivati-nagara.

Sāvatthī, nagaraṁ N 77,4. 92,19. 29. — I 95,6. 96,7. 106,18. 15. 110,30. 156,16. 23. 31. 189,1. 198,10. 217,6. 10. 235,10. 31. 32. 246,19. 257,3. 268,19. 276,2. 303,2. 311,24. 330,3. 4. 331,7*. 333,7. 349,2. 366,4. 367,26. 374,29. 377,20. 27. 31. 378,1. 404,3. 412,27. 413,1. 422,6. 432,26. 433,1. 463,3. 474,27. 477,6. 497,4. 501,3. — II 12,18. 45,12. 63,8. 76,9. 79,9. 85,7. 92,8. 95,25. 99,10. 130,24. 197,7. 216,10. 224,21. 229,7. 257,15. 271,6. 286,11. 295,2. 310,23. 331,14. 337,11. 341,8. 12. 385,8. 387,13. 390,26. 392,16. 19. 22. 393,14. 436,18. — III 2,1. 7. 20,22. 30,18. 36,3. 43,10. 22. 48,22. 51,11. 66,23. 72,24. 74,22. 82,5. 115,16*. 118,28. 155,11. 168,26*. 182,8. 11. 299,3. 14. 375,18. 400,12. 403,4. 18. 405,17. 414 (10. 14). 461,16. 490,1. 7. 494,28. 501,22. 502,4. — IV 15,3. 59,6. 11. 123,28. 144,7. 146,6. 147,22. 148,24. 150,5. 152,2. 23. 158,14. 167,5. 27. 187,12. 200,6. 264,3. 6. 13. 19. 22. 26. 27. 265,28. 267,7. 8. 288,26. 314,27. 351,5. 437,8. — V 11,6. 13,18*. 36,10. 209,22. 262,3. 278,5. 382,10. 413,18. 28. — VI 68,26. 69,25. 70,4. 5. 19. 70,9 (Sāvatthimaggo) 128,25 (34. 35) (Kassapabuddhakāle). 157,25.

Sāvatthi-vāsino I 257,17. 316,5. — II 416,25. — IV 187,27. 228,7. — Sāvatthivāsi-upāsako I 299,14. 332,26. 411,9. — Sāvatthivāsi-kuṭumbiko I 126,17. 270,16. — II 202,25. 236,3. — Sāvatthivāsi-kuladhītā IV 219,3. — Sāvatthivāsi-kulaputto I 276,4. 302,29. 414,23. 418,4. 435,20. 449,21. — II 271,5. — III 139,21. 286,10. — IV 130,23. 219,7. — V 278,4. — Sāvatthivāsino dve kulaputtā II 151,4. — Sāvatthivāsinī kuladhītā I 428,13. — Sāvatthivāsī dānapati IV 236,21. — Sāvatthivāsī brāhmaṇo IV 167,3. — Sāvatthivāsino dve bhikkhū II 366,1. — Sāvatthivāsino vāṇijā II 294,20. — IV 350,19. — Sāvatthivāsino dve vāṇijā II

181,8. — Sāvatthivāsino pañcasatā sahāyakā Tathāgatassa IV 113,21. — Sāvatthivāsī sirilakkhaṇa-brāhmaṇo II 410,7.

Sikhin, Buddho N 41,22. 28. 42,4. 44,9. 94,11.

Sigāla-jātaka a) (113) I 424—426. — b) (142) I 489—490. — c) (148) I 501—504. — d) (152) II 5—9.

Sigāla-jātaka — Guṇa-jātaka II 314,21.

Sigāla-vagga II 242—270.

sigālo udapānadūsako II 354,7.

Siñgāla, gahapati VI 135,5*.

sitapātukammaṁ VI 96,14.

Siddhattha, Buddho N 40,2. 27. 44,8.

Siddhattha (Siddhattha-kumāra), — Gotamo Buddho N 56,29. 58,20. 28. 59,3. 60,3. 61,11. 66,18. 71,28. 72,30. 30. 73,22. 29. 74,10. 18. 28. 75,1. 77,19. 88,14. 89,14. — IV 50,11. 328,16*. — VI 479,15.

Sineru, pabbato N 48,1. — I 202*,12. 18. 204 (12). 212,18. 19. 229,11. 303,30. 322,1*. 501,28. — II 271,20. 313 (28). — III 210 (6) (— Mahāneru). — IV 265,18. 32. 333,2. 483 (10). — V 11,22. 168 (16). 314,18*. 332,15*. — VI 125,1. 126 (17. 18). 165 (6). 174,18*. 259 (30). 272 (11). 278*,18. 19. 279 (5). 362,28*. 432,30*. 486*,18. 24. 511,30. 547 (24). 575,28*. 586,28*. (cfr. Neru, Meru.)

Sindhava-raṭṭha V 260 (22).

Sindhu-nadī V 260 (22).

Sibba, (— Sivirājā) V 219,18*. 220*,21. 30. 224 (18).

Sibbi, — Sivi, rājā Dvāravatiyaṁ, putto Vāsudevassa Kaṇhassa VI 421,19*. Sivi: 421 (28).

Simbali-niraya V 275 (12).

Simbali-vana, (Tāvatiṁsabhavane) I 202*,26. 28. 203*,1. 8 (12).

Siri-jātaka (284) II 409—415.

Sirikāḷakaṇṇi-jātaka a) (192) II 115,12—14. — b) (382) III 257—264.

Sirikāḷakaṇṇi-pañha, Mahāummagga-jātake VI 349,18. — V 122 (6).
siricorabrāhmaṇo II 409,29.
Sirimanda-jātaka (500) IV 412.
Sirimanda-pañha, Mahāummagga-jātake VI 363,23. — IV 412,26. — VI 356*,5. 8.
Sirimā, mātā Phussa-Buddhassa N 41,3.
Sirimā, mātā Sumana-Buddhassa N 34,26.
Sirivaḍḍha, seṭṭhi Sikhissa Bhagavato kāle N 94,12.
Sirivaḍḍha(ka), seṭṭhi Mithilāyaṁ, pitā Osadhakumārassa (Bodhisattassa) VI 331*,1. 18. 30. 334*,2. 8. 339 (27). 343 (6). 404,9*.
Sirī, dhītā Dhataraṭṭha-mahārājassa Cātummahārājika-devaloke III 257,21*. 258,7*. 261,22*. 262*,2. 4 (6). 263,9*. 264*,15. 19. 20. 24. (cfr. Lakkhī). — V 112,30*. 114 (24). — dhītā Sakkassa V 392,21*. 393,12. 398,17*. 23. 399,1. 7 (18). 23*. 408,16 (19). 409,13. 410,2*.
Sirīsavatthu, yakkhanagaraṁ Tambapaṇṇidīpe (v. l. B Sirīsavatthu) II 127,23*.
Silesaloma, yakkho I 273*,10. 12.
Siva, — Sivirājā III 468,4 (12).
Sivi, mahārājā Ariṭṭhapuranagare (pitā Bodhisattassa) IV 401,27*. — V 210,18*.
Sivi, mahārājā Jetuttaranagare (pitā Sañjayassa) VI 480,7*. 484,9*.
Sivi, rājā Dvāravatiyaṁ VI 421 (28). (cfr. Sibbi.)
Sivi-kumāra, Sivi-rājā, putto Sivimahārañño Ariṭṭhapuranagare (— Bodhisatto) N 45,15. — IV 401,27. 28*. 403,2*. 408,6. 409,16*. 412,24. — V 210,19*. 216,3*. 221,21*. 224 (18). 227 (5). 18.
Sivi-jātaka (499) IV 401—412. — N 83,15.
Sivi-raṭṭha III 467,24. — IV 401,27*. 411*,18. 28. — V 218,18*

— VI 419 (11). 27*. 424,29*. 480,7*. 489 (32). 499, (19). 579,6 (9). (cfr. Sovīra-raṭṭha).

Siviraṭṭhavāsino VI 490 (31). 504 (9). — Sivī VI 480,29* (30). — Sivayo: IV 405,1* (6. 7). 411,28*. 412,7*. — VI 490,5*. 491*,18. 22. 492,3. 6. 8. 20. 23. 25. 30*. 493*,13. 10 (24). 495,15*. 515,25 (28). 516,27. 517,11. 528,4. Sivīhi: VI 533,2. 17 (21). Sivīnaṁ: IV 405,24*. 408,28. 411,4*. — V 223*,8. 10. 227 (2. 6). — VI 488*,4. 14. 489,15. 30 (32). 490*,26. 28. 491*,3. 7. 19. 499,8* (13). 16* (18). 502,16. 25. 28. 30. 33. 504,16. 505,17. 32*. 506,28. 508,29. 510,1. 515,7. 18. 516,18. 517,14. 525,5 (7). 545,5. 547,16. 22. 567,25. 570,10. 591,22. 25. 27. 592,11—17. 32. 593,20. — Sivikaññā (pl.) VI 502,6. 503 (24). 589,1.

Sivi-rāja III 467,24. 30. (cfr. Siva). — VI 419*,28. 30. 421 (21). 424,30*. 425,2*. 492,9. 503 (25). 510 (32). 533,6. 17. 548,10. 554,8 (17). 561 (7). 563 (28. 29). 574,5*. 589 (6). — Sivi-puttā (Jāli Kaṇhājinā ca) VI 563,10. 14 (28). — Sivi-maggo VI 510,31 (32). — Sivi-vāhinī (senā) VI 581,16. 21. — Sivi-seṭṭho VI 511,29. 579,11 (13) (— Sivis' uttamo). 584,30. 585 (8).

Sivī (— Sivi?), porāṇakarājā VI 251,16* (28).

Sivira-jātaka, see: Sovīra-jātaka.

Sīta-vana, Rājagahaṁ nissāya N 92,18.

Sītā, devī, dhītā Dasarathassa Bārāṇasi-rañño IV 124,10*. 125*,3. 21. 126*,6 (7). 17. 129,21*. 130,5*. 18. — VI 557,30. 558 (22—28).

Sīdantara, samuddo VI 125 (19—21. 24—26). (cfr. Sīdā-mahā-samudda).

Sīdā, nadī Uttarahimavante VI 100,3* (14. 17). 101 (14. 20. 23. 28).

Sīdā, mahāsamuddo VI 125 (8. 10). — Sīdantarā nagā (pabbatā) VI 125,5 (8). 15. (cfr. Sīdantara.)

Sīrisavatthu, see: Sirīsavatthu.

Sīla-khaṇḍa, Bhūridatta-jātake VI 184,22.

Sīla-vagga I 142—172.

Sīlava-kumāra, putto Brahmadattassa Bārāṇasi-rañño, mahārājā (= Bodhisatto) I 262,6*. 263*,14. 25. 264*,5. 18. 17. 18. 20. 265,20*. 266,22*. 267*,6. 11. 268,4. — Mahāsīlava-rājā I 262,8*.

Sīlava, nāgarājā (hatthī) (= Bodhisatto) N 45,21. — I 320,4*. 322,23.

Sīlavatī, aggamahesī Okkākassa rañño Kusāvatiyaṁ V 279*,1. 22. 25. 280,18*. 285,8*.

Sīlavanāga-jātaka (72) I 319—322.

sīlavīmaṁsako brāhmaṇo I 369,7. — II 429,17. — III 100,6. 193,22.

Sīlavīmaṁsa-jātaka a) (330) III 100—102. — b) (362) III 193—195.

Sīlavīmaṁsana-jātaka a) (86) I 369—371. — II 429,18. — b) (290) II 429—430. — c) (305) III 18—20.

Sīlānisaṁsa-jātaka (190) 111—113.

Sīvaka, vejjo Sivi-rañño IV 404,18*. 406*,20. 21 (25). 29. 30. 408,6. 412,23.

Sīvali, Sīvali-kumāro, Sīvali-thero, putto Suppavāsāya I 408,12. 14. 21. 26. 31. 410,17.

Sīvali-vatthu VI 14 (27).

Sīvalī, aggasāvikā Maṅgala-Buddhassa N 34,9.

Sīvalī, aggasāvikā Siddhattha-Buddhassa N 40,9.

Sīvalī, devī, dhītā Polajanakassa VI 37*,20. 23. 38,5* 40*,12. 25. 26. 30. 44,10*. 52,29*. 54,5*. 55*,6. 19. 56,17*. 61,20*. 62 (3). 63,26*. 64*,13. 16. 17. 65,11* (22). 66,3*. 67*,7. 8. 20. 24 (26). 68,21.

Sīveyyaka, (adj.) Sīveyyako uttarāsaṁgo IV 401,17. — Sīveyyaka-vatthaṁ IV 401,20.

Sīha, senāpati (Vesāliyaṁ) II 262,8.

Sīha-jātaka, see: Guṇa-jātaka.

Sīhakoṭṭhuka-jātaka (188) II 108—109.

Sīhacamma-jātaka (189) II 109—110.

Sīhapura, nagaraṁ Upacarassa rañño tatiyena puttena māpitaṁ III 460,26*.

Sīhappapāta, daho Himavantapadese V 415,24.

Sīhala-dīpa VI 30,8. (cfr. Tambapaṇṇidīpa.)

sīho rājā catuppadānaṁ paṭhamakappe I 207,1*. — II 352,9*.

Suṁsumāra-jātaka (208) II 158—160.

Suṁsumāragiri, Bhaggesu III 157,23. — Suṁsumāragira III 157,25.

Suka-jātaka (255) II 291—294.

Sukhavihāri-jātaka (10) I 140—142.

Sugata (— Buddho) II 15,6.

Sugata-pasatthaṁ dānaṁ III 472,18*. 473 (24).

Sugata-mahācīvara I 119,22. 330,23.

Sugatālaya I 490,24. 491,2. 18. — II 38,22. 28. 148,22. 24. 162,13. 14. — III 112,17.

Sugatovāda I 119,9. 349,3. — II 9,14. 13,1. 46,2. — III 368,10*.

Sucandaka, pāsādo Rāma-paṇḍitassa IV 130,8*.

Suciparivāra, seṭṭhi Bārāṇasiyaṁ (— Bodhisatto) III 257,14*. 258,17*. 264,24. — V 114 (22).

Suciparivāra, seṭṭhi asītikoṭidhanavibhavo Bārāṇasiyaṁ III 444,19*.

Sucira-jātaka (v. l. B Vidūra-jāt.) IV 360,24 (— Āditta-jātaka (424) o: Sovīra-jātaka?)

Sucīrata, brāhmaṇo Bhāradvājagotto, purohito Dhanañjayakorabyassa Indapattanagare V 57*,8. 11. 14. 17. 58*,11. 25. 59 (15). 60,21*. 61,18*. 62,8. 10. 13*. 64*,21. 27. 66*,9. 11 (10. 28). 67,10*. 24. (cfr. Bhāradvāja).

Succa-jātaka (320) III 66—70.

Sujampati, — Sakko III 146,30* (devānaṁ indo Maghavā Sujampati). — IV 9,20*. 403,27*. 409,4. — V 137,30*. 139,17* (27). — VI 102,17. 484,1*. 573,21.

Sujā, asurakaññā, bhariyā Sakkassa III 227,28*. 491,18*. 494,2*. — V 139 (27). — VI 157 (4). — Sujātā III 494,10*.
Sujāta, aggasāvako Padumuttara-Buddhassa N 37,21.
Sujāta, kuṭimbiko Bārāṇasiyaṁ V 465,4* (8. 12. 16). 468,16* (20). 469 (14).
Sujāta, kuṭumbikaputto Bārāṇasiyaṁ (— Bodhisatto) III 155,17*. 156*,3. 8. 157*,8. 14 (15). 20.
Sujāta, khattiyo, isi (— Bodhisatto) N 40,17.
Sujāta, Buddho N 37,27. 38,10. 24. 39,7. 44,7.
Sujāta-jātaka a) (269) II 347—351. — b) (306) III 20—22. — c) (352) III 155—157.
Sujātā, aggasāvikā Piyadassi-Buddhassa N 39,5.
Sujātā, aggasāvikā Sobhita-Buddhassa N 35,22.
Sujātā, itthī gehe Bodhisattassa I 201*,3. 28. — bakasakuṇikā 204,31*. 205,2*. — dhītā kumbhakārassa Bārāṇasiyaṁ 205,28*. — dhītā Vepacittiyassa asurindassa 206*,2. 4. — aḍḍhatiyānaṁ nāṭakakoṭīnaṁ jeṭṭhikā devanagare 206,7*.
Sujātā, devī, mātā Koṇḍañña-Buddhassa N 30,13.
Sujātā, devī Brahmadattassa Bārāṇasi-rañño III 21,19*. 22,18*. 27.
Sujātā, Dhanañjayaseṭṭhidhītā Visākhāya kaniṭṭhabhaginī II 347,7. 13. 19. 349,1. 12. 16. 18. 22. 351,13.
Sujātā, dhītā Senāni-kuṭimbikassa N 68,7. 21. 32. 69,15. 82. 88.
Sujātā, Bārāṇasi-kuladhītā, bhariyā Bodhisattassa II 121,23*. 122*,2. 8. 11. 123*,7. 11. 124,11*. 125,11.
Sujātā, bhariyā Sakkassa III 494,10*. (cfr. Sujā).
Sujātā, mātā Padumuttara-Buddhassa N 37,20.
Sutanā, migapotikā, kaniṭṭhabhaginī Bodhisattassa IV 413,13*. 417,1*. 419,29*. 421,16*.
Sutanu (Sutano), māṇavo, duggata-gahapatiputto (— Bodhisatto) III 325,2*. 329*,8 (12). 28.
Sutano-jātaka (398) III 324—330. (v. l. Cdd Sutanu-jāt.).
Sutasoma, putto Brahmadattassa Bārāṇasirañño, rājā (— Bodhisatto) V 177,16*. 179*,4. 8. 19. 25. 180 (24). 181*,12. 16.

183,12* (16). 184,13 (16). 185,23*. 186,8*. 187,20*. 190*,20. 30. 192,7. — Somakumāro V 177,15*.

Sutasoma, putto Koravyassa rañño Indapattanagare, rājā (— Bodhisatto) V 457*,5. 10. 13. 25. 458,4*. 473,22*. 474*,8. 11. 475 (20. 21). 27*. 476,4*. 478*,6. 16. 17. 19. 479*,1 (6. 7). 9. 481,9*. 482,6*. 483,10*. 485*,2. 13. 486,16*. 487,30*. 489,16*. 490 (28). 491,16*. 493,1* (24). 494*,3. 19. 497,5*. 498*,7. 28. 499,4*. 500 (4). 501*,24. 28. 502*,14. 21. 22. 27. 30. 506,19*. 507*,11. 16. 25. 508*,24. 29. 510,24*. 511,22. — Koravyaseṭṭho V 479*,2. 31. — Sutasoma-mahāsatto V 35,28*.

Sudatta, brāhmaṇo N 56,4.

Sudatta, rājā, pitā Sumana-Buddhassa N 34,26.

Sudatta, rājā, pitā Sumedha-Buddhassa N 38,4.

Sudattā, aggasāvikā Tissa-Buddhassa N 40,26.

Sudattā, mātā Sumedha-Buddhassa N 38,5.

Sudassana, aggasāvako Sujāta-Buddhassa N 38,19.

Sudassana, cakkavatti-rājā (— Bodhisatto) I 391,30. (cfr. Mahāsudassana).

Sudassana, devanagaraṁ II 214 (13).

Sudassana, nagaraṁ Sumedha-Buddhassa N 37,27. 38,4.

Sudassana, nagaraṁ (— Bārāṇasī) IV 119,28*. — V 177,19*. 186 (2). 191,18* (25).

Sudassana, nāgarājā IV 182,30*.

Sudassana, putto Dhataraṭṭha-nāgarañño VI 167,29*. 171,21* (25. 26). 187*,5. 19. 188,9*. 190*,4 (6). 15. 191*,5. 21. 28. 29. 192*,5. 17. 193*,4. 18. 194*,3. 15. 195 (5). 11*. 196*,6. 16. 17. 27. 219,25.

Sudassana, pabbato VI 125,13 (17. 18). 126,7. 126 (17) — Sinerugiri. — Sudassanagiri II 214 (12. 14).

Sudassana, mahāvihāro (Ramma-nagaraṁ upanissāya) N 11,10. 12. 12,5.

Sudassana, rājā Vessabhu-Buddhassa kāle (— Bodhisatto N 42,7.

Sudassana-siluccaya N 29,5.

Sudassanā, mātā Atthadassi-Buddhassa N 39,14.

Sudāṭha, migarājā III 192*,18 (20). 21. 23.

Sudinna, rājā, pitā Piyadassi-Buddhassa N 39,8.

Sudeva, aggasāvako Maṅgala-Buddhassa N 34,8.

Suddhodana, mahārājā, pitā Gotama-Buddhassa N 15,28 16,10. 49,24. 52,9. 54,11. 14. 19. 55,16. 56,20. 60,21. 67,18. 85,25. 29. 87,9. — I 136,7. 309,11. — II 23,22. 50,8. 141,23. — III 490,9. — IV 50,8. 55,20. 130,17. 491,2. — VI 478,11*. 593,27. — Suddhodana-putto N 72,19.

Sudhaññavatī, nagaraṁ Revata-Buddhassa N 35,7.

Sudhamma, nagaraṁ Sobhita-Buddhassa N 35,19.

Sudhamma, rājā, pitā Sobhita-Buddhassa N 35,20.

Sudhammā, aggamahesī Reṇu-rañño Uttarapañcālanagare IV 445,19*. 448 (4). 452*,15. 29.

Sudhammā, aggasāvikā Atthadassi-Buddhassa N 39,16.

Sudhammā, itthī gehe Bodhisattassa I 201*,2. 3. 14. — pādaparicārikā Sakkassa 204,22*.

Sudhammā, devamaṇisabhā (Tāvatiṁsabhavane) I 204,24*. 205,4*. — IV 322,12*. 355,12*. 356,18. — V 153,3 (7). 386,2*. — VI 97,8*. 102 (19). 104,8. 126,26*. 127,1. 16*. 278,26*. 333,14*. 432,26*.

Sudhammā, dhītā Kikissa rañño (Kassapa-dasabalassa kāle) VI 481*,13. 17.

Sudhammā, mātā Sobhita-Buddhassa N 35,20.

Sudhābhojana-jātaka (535) V 382—412. — IV 186,21.

Sunakkhatta, (Licchaviputto) satthu upaṭṭhāko I 389,16. 17. 27. 390,9. — Bhagavato anibaddhaupaṭṭhāko IV 95,14. — VI 219,29. 255,8.

Sunakha-jātaka (242) II 246—248.

Sunakha-mahāniraya V 145 (2).

sunakho, bhattabhuñjana- II 246,9.

Sunanda, khattiyo, pitā Koṇḍañña-Buddhassa N 30,12.

Sunanda, sārathi Kāsirañño VI 10,26*. 11,8*. 15,14*. 18,3*. 21,18*.

Sunanda, sārathi Sivirañño V 213*,19. 23. 214,28*. 227,17.

Sunandā, aggasāvikā Dīpaṁkara-Buddhassa N 29,23.

Sunandā, bhariyā Bārāṇasi-rañño VI 134,31*.

Sunandā, mātā Dhammadassi-Buddhassa N 39,26.

Sunāma, amacco Aṁgati-rañño Mithilāyaṁ VI 221,3*. 16. 222,4. 10. 29 (33). 230,14. 255,6.

Sunimmita, (devaputto) N 81,11.

Sunetta, aggasāvako Sobhita-Buddhassa N 35,21.

Sunetta, upaṭṭhāko Dhammadassi-Buddhassa N 39,27.

Sundarī, aggasāvikā Anomadassi-Buddhassa N 36,6.

Sundarī, (paribbājikā) II 415,21. 22. 416,8. 11. 18. 24. 417,3. 6. 10. 12. — Sundarī-māraṇaṁ II 415,12. [Sundarī-māraṇa-vatthu II 415,12—417,16 — Dhammapadassa atthavaṇṇanā v. 306. (cfr. Paramattha-jotikā 41., Paramattha-dīpanī p. 228.)]. — Sundarī(?) VI 478,16*.

Supaṇṇa-bhavana III 91,4*. 187,21*. — VI 256*,14. 19. 287,7* etc. — Supaṇṇa-rājā III 91,2*. 188,2* (— Bodhisatto). — VI 257,6*. etc.

Supatta, kāka-rājā (— Bodhisatto) II 433,19*. 435,15*. 436,7*. 14. Supattakākovādo 436,12*.

Supatta, gijjharājā (putto Bodhisattassa) III 484,5*.

Supatta-jātaka (292) II 433—436.

supinā, soḷasa mahāsupinā (Kosalarañño) I 334,28.

Suppatiṭṭhita, titthaṁ Nerañjarāya tīre N 70,6.

Suppatīta, rājā, pitā Vessabhu-Buddhassa N 42,12.

Suppavāsā, Koliyarājadhītā (Koliyadhītā), upāsikā I 407,20. 408,1. 2. 5. 9. 11. 16. 18. 409,2. 410,2. 18.

Suppāraka, paṇḍito, niyyāmaka-jeṭṭhako Bharukacche (— Bodhisatto) IV 137,11*. 138*,22. 24. 139*,9. 20. 140*,9. 19. 141*,2. 22. 143,5.

Suppāraka-jātaka (463) IV 136—143.

Suphassā, kākī, bhariyā Supattassa (Bo.) II 433*,20. 22. 25. 435*,3. 9. 16. 436,14.
Suphassā, mātā Siddhattha-Buddhassa N 40,8.
Subāhu, vyaggho III 192,16 (18). 23. 24. — III 540,19* (23).
Subhakiṇṇā, devā III 358,25.
Subhaga, putto Dhataraṭṭha-nāgarañño VI 168,1*. 189,22*. 27. 190*,23. 30. 197*,16. 24. 198*,7. 11. 199,3*. 200*,1. 16. 23. 201,6*. 203 (18. 19). 219,26.
Subhaga-vana, Ukkaṭṭhaṁ nissāya II 259,14.
Subhadda, aggasāvako Koṇḍañña-Buddhassa N 30,18.
Subhaddā, aggasāvikā Revata-Buddhassa N 35,9.
Subhaddā, devī Mahāsudassanassa rañño Kusāvatiyaṁ (Bo.) I 392,7* (21). 393 (4). 18.
Subhaddā, dhītā Madda-rañño, aggamahesī Bārāṇasi-rañño V 39,25*. 40*,4. 10. 42,12*. 47,17*. 48 (18). 50 (9. 14). 51,10*. 53,9*. 54*,1. 10. (cfr. Cullasubhaddā.)
Sumaṅgala, aggasāvako Dīpaṁkara-Buddhassa N 29,21.
Sumaṅgala, uyyānapālo Bārāṇasi-rañño III 439*,11. 19. 21. 23. 25. 440*,1. 9. 21. 441*,2. 8. 12. 443,11*. 444,8.
Sumaṅgala, nagaraṁ Sujāta-Buddhassa N 38,18.
Sumaṅgala, seṭṭhi Kassapassa Bhagavato kāle N 94,21.
Sumaṅgala-jātaka (420) III 439—444.
Sumana, upaṭṭhāko Padumuttara-Buddhassa N 37,31.
Sumana, Buddho N 30,18. 34,17. 30. 35,12. 44,5.
Sumanā, aggasāvikā Anomadassi-Buddhassa N 36,6.
Sumanā, devī, bhariyā Sirivaḍḍhakassa, mātā Osadhakumārassa (Bo.) VI 331*,1. 6.
Sumanā, nāgamāṇavikā, aggamahesī Campeyya-nāgarājassa IV 455,14*. 456,14*. 459,1*. 461,27*. 468,22.
Sumitta, aggasāvako Siddhattha-Buddhassa N 40,9.
Sumukha, senāpati Supattassa kākarañño II 433,20*. 434,2*. (436,14).
Sumukha, haṁsasenāpati IV 424*,10. 13. 17. 21. 425*,1. 7. 8.

16. 426*,4. 14. 427,12*. 430,4*. 8. — senāpati Dhataraṭṭhahaṁsarañño V 337,28*. 338,19*. 339,6*. 341 (15). 342 (11 17). 343,9*. 344*,16. 24. 345,2*. 348*,4. 5. 349*,13. 16. 350,28*. 351*,3 (6). 7. 353*,17. 19 (26). 354,8. — V 357*,23. 27. 358,2*. 359*,25. 29. 360* (3). 6. 26. 30. 361,16. 30*. 362,21*. 24. 363*,7. 22. 364*,9. 29. 365*,16. 23. 366,2. 6*. 9. 10. 12. 21*. 368,9* (28. 29. 30). 369,21*. 370,1*. 371,12*. 373*,2. 4. 5. 9. 11. 15. 28. 374,17*. 375*,8. 11. 14 (19). 21. 376,28*. 378,17. 379*,9. 27. 381*,3. 12. 26. 28. 382,6.

Sumucalinda-sara VI 582,5*. (cfr. Mucalinda).

Sumedha, khattiyo, pitā Dīpaṁkara-Buddhassa N 29,19.

Sumedha, khattiyo, pitā Nārada-Buddhassa N 37,6.

Sumedha, Buddho N 37,27. 28. 38,3. 8. 44,7.

Sumedha (Sumedhapaṇḍita), brāhmaṇo Amaravati-nagare, tāpaso N 2,14. 23. 3,15. 19. 6,7. 7 (3. 6). 8 (17). 10,32. 11,2. 23. 12,3. 7. 13. 14. 23. 15 (9). 11. 18. 16,17. 18. 32. 20,3. 22. 21,5. 24. 22,7. 24. 23,7. 26. 24,11. 28. 26,10. 27,6.

Sumedha, (— Brahmadatto — Bo.) III 245,17 (19. 20). (read: sumedhaṁ?).

Sumedhakathā, N 2,28. 28,5.

Sumedhā, janiyā Dīpaṁkara-Buddhassa N 29,20.

Sumedhā, devī, dhītā Brahmadattassa Bārāṇasi-rañño, aggamahesī Suruci[2]-mahārañño Mithilāyaṁ IV 316*,11. 19. 28. 317,16*. 318*,5. 8. 9. 319,14*. 325,13.

Sumbha-raṭṭha I 393,17.

Suyāma, (devaputto) N 48,16. 53,17. 81,10. — IV 266,3.

Suyāma, brāhmaṇo N 56,4.

Sura, vanacarako V 12,1*. 13,2*.

Surakkhita, aggasāvako Phussa-Buddhassa N 41,4.

Suraṭṭha-janapada III 463,11*. — V 133,20*.

Suraṁmukha, assataro VI 135,28*.

Surāpāna-jātaka (81) I 360—363.

Surāmā, aggasāvikā Siddhattha-Buddhassa N 40,10.

Surâmâ, aggasâvikâ Sumedha-Buddhassa N 38,6.
Suriya-kumâra, putto Bârâṇasi-rañño, bhâtâ Candakumârassa (Bo.) VI 134,6* (9). 137*,8. 29. 144*,24–28. 145*,2–8 (10). 147,25*. 148*,11. 20 (22). 149*,3. 9. 154*,2–15. 157,22.
Suriya-kumâra, putto Brahmadattassa Bârâṇasi-rañño (vemâtikabhâtâ Bodhisattassa) I 127,24*. 128*,7. 11. 18. 21. 133,11*. 18.
Suriya, devaputto IV 63*,6. 14. 18. 65,6*. 68*,28. 28. 69,24.— V 383,12*. 386,9*. 388,14*. 389,10*. 390,20*. 412,10. 427 (25). — VI 89*,3. 11. 90,10. 201,25*. 247,4. 263,12*. 278,17*. 279 (5). 443,7. 459,12*.
Suriyadeva, Devagabbhâya catuttho putto IV 81,6.
Suriyapassa-pabbata, Himavante V 38,9*.
Suruci-jâtaka (489) IV 314—325. — II 333,28.
Suruci, brâhmaṇo (= Bodhisatto) N 32,2. 14.
Suruci[1]), râjâ Mithilâyaṁ IV 315,28*.
Suruci[2]), râjâ Mithilâyaṁ, putto Surucino[1]) II 333,22*. — IV 315,29*. 316*,1. 9.
Suruci[3]), râjâ Mithilâyaṁ, putto Surucino[2]), pitâ Mahâpanâdassa II 333,23*. — IV 316*,9. 11. 27. 317,5*. 319*,25. 28. 320 (24. 28). 324,2*. = Ruci IV 319,24*. 320 (24).
Surundhana, nagaraṁ Kâsiraṭṭhe IV 104,15. 18*. 113,3* (9). 119,27*. (= Bârâṇasî).
Sulasâ, nagarasobhanî Bârâṇasiyaṁ III 435,30*. 436*,7. 15. 16. 437*,19 26. 438*,12. 16 (28. 25). 28.
Sulasâ-jâtaka (419) III 435—439.
Suvakhaṇḍa VI 425,28 (cod. B[d]).
Suvaṇṇa-pabbata, Himavante N 50,19. 55,28. — II 92,27. — V 35,24*. (cfr. Suvaṇṇapassa-).
Suvaṇṇakakkaṭaka-jâtaka (389) III 293—298.
Suvaṇṇagiritâla, pabbato VI 514,1*.
Suvaṇṇaguhâ, Cittakûṭapabbate Himavanta-padese III 208,18*. — V 337,28*. 469 (28). — VI 56,12*.

Suvaṇṇapassa-pabbata, Himavante V 38,10*. 42,23*. 47,19*. 24. 48 (15. 16). (cfr. Suvaṇṇa-pabbata).
Suvaṇṇabhūmi, (janapado) III 188,14*. — IV 15,27*. — VI 34*,8. 10. 11. 44 (5).
Suvaṇṇamiga-jātaka (359) III 182—187.
Suvaṇṇavīthi, Tāvatiṁsabhavane) V 386,1*.
Suvaṇṇasāma, nesādo paṇḍito, putto Dukūlakassa ca Pāriyā ca (— Bodhisatto) VI 74,2*. 76,20*. 79,28*. 83,30*. 84,25*. 95,10. (cfr. Sāma.)
Suvaṇṇahaṁsa-jātaka (136) I 474—477.
suvaṇṇahaṁso, rājā sakunānaṁ paṭhamakappe (— Bodhisatto) I 207,2*. — II 353,24*.
Susīma, putto purohitassa Bārāṇasi-rañño, rājā Bārāṇasiyaṁ (— Bodhisatto) III 391,21*. 393*,14. 21. 397,3.
Susīma, mahiddhika-tāpaso (— Bodhisatto) N 39,11.
Susīma, rājā Bārāṇasiyaṁ II 46,18*. 48*,14. 23 (25). 49,7*. 50,8.
Susīma-jātaka a) (163) II 45—50. — b) (411) III 391—397.
Sussondī-jātaka (360) III 187—190. (cfr. Jāt. 327.)
Sussondī (v. l. Sussoṇī) aggamahesī Tambarañño Bārāṇasiyaṁ III 187*,18. 24. 188*,6. 27. 189,15*.
Suhanu, kūṭa-asso Bārāṇasi-rañño II 31*,11. 17. 24. 25. 32 (3. 4. 6. 7. 9).
Suhanu-jātaka (158) II 30—32.
Suhemā, pākahaṁsarājadhītā V 366,12 (17).
Sūkara-jātaka (153) II 9—12.
Sūci-jātaka (387) III 281—286.
Sūradaddara, nāgarājā Daddarapabbatapāde Himavantapadese III 16,6*.
Sūra Vāmagotta, putto Bārāṇasi-rañño, vemātikabhātā Candakumārassa (Bo.) VI 134,6* (10). 157,21.
Sūrasena, (— Dhanañjaya-korabbo) VI 280,23*. 281 (2).
Seggu, dhītā ekassa paṇṇika-upāsakassa II 180,4* (8).

Seggu-jātaka (217) II 179–180.
seṭṭhi, Anāthapiṇḍikassa sahāyo III 196,8.
senibhaṇḍanaṁ II 12,8. 52,21. (cfr. II 359,8.)
Setakaṇṇika, nigamo dakkhiṇāya disāya N 49,11.
Setaketu, māṇavo, udiccabrāhmaṇa-putto I 401 (17). — III 232,24*. 233*,17. 22. 234*,1. 5. 235,16*. 236*,1. 26. 237,19*. 23.
Setaketu-jātaka (377) III 232–237.
Sedaka, see: Desaka.
Senaka, paṇḍito, dhammānusāsako Vedeharañño VI 330*,4. 18. 334*,11. 12. 335 (4). 339 (8. 9. 28). 342 (7. 8. 11. 14. 19). 343,15*. 344,31*. 345*,8. 22. 23. 348*,24. 27. 349,9*. 351*,14. 18. 20. 22. 352*,15. 24. 353*,13. 14. 23. 24. 356*,7. 11. 14. 357*,14. 16. 358* (2). 4. 17. 359,6*. 360*,5. 19. 26. 361*,8. 17. 362*,2. 11. 28. 29. 368*,14. 23. 369*,4. 8. 28. 370*,6. 24. 30. 372,6. 27. 28. 378*,28. 29. 379,20*. 380,4*. 381*,11. 12. 29. 382*,1. 4. 10. 12. 22. 386*,26. 28. 29. 387 (7. 8). 9*. 415*,6. 7. 417 (22). 435,3*. 436,20*. 438 (7. 8). 31. 33. 440*,10. 26. 29. 32. 441,3*. 442*,2. 8. 443,31*. 444*,15. 18. 22. 445,2. 447*,13. 16 (20). 21. 463*,15. 25. 29. 465*,1. 4. 478,18*.
Senaka-kumāra, paṇḍito, brāhmaṇaputto, amacco Janakassa Bārāṇasi-rañño (— Bodhisatto) N 46,8. — III 341,24*. 343,25*. 344,16*. 345,6*. 348,27* (28). 351,6*. 19.
Senaka-kumāra, paṇḍito, brāhmaṇaputto, amacco Maddava-rañño Bārāṇasiyaṁ (— Bodhisatto) III 337*,2. 5. 340*,6. 10. 13. 341,9*. 17.
Senaka, rājā Bārāṇasiyaṁ III 275*,10. 11. 276,6*. 278,20. 279 (1). 7* (12).
Senaka, vānaro, bhāgineyyo Bodhisattassa II 78*,18. 19. 20. 79,5.
Senaka-vagga III 275–316.
Senāni, kuṭimbiko, pitā Sujātāya N 68,6. — Senāni-nigamo N 68,6.
senibhaṇḍanaṁ, see: seṇibhaṇḍanaṁ.
Seyya, rājā Bārāṇasiyaṁ V 354,9 (read: Saṁyama).
Seyya-jātaka (282) II 400–403. — III 13,11 (Seyyaṁsa-jāt.).

Seyya-, Seyha-, see: Sayha.

Seriva, kacchapuṭa-vāṇijo Seriva-raṭṭhe (— Bodhisatto) I 111,6*. — Serivavāṇijo (v. l. Seri-vāṇijo) I 111,2.

Seriva-raṭṭha I 111,5*.

Serivat, lola-kacchapuṭa-vāṇijo (— Devadatto) I 111,6*. 113,16 (23. 24).

Serivāṇija-jātaka (3) I 110–114.

Seruma-dīpa, — Nāgadīpo III 187,20*. 189,23* (25). (v. l. Serūma-).

Sela, rājā VI 99,9*.

Selā, kumārī, kaniṭṭhabhaginī Candakumārassa VI 143 (6). 8. 157,21.

Soṇa, aggasāvako Vessabhu-Buddhassa N 42,12.

Soṇa, kūṭa-assa Bārāṇasi-rañño II 31*,24. 25. 32 (2. 4. 6–8). — Mahāsoṇo II 31*,1. 6. 16.

Soṇa, thero Kuraraghare VI 15 (12) (Kuraraghariya-Soṇatthero).

Soṇadinna, devaputto VI 118,4. 119,1*. — Soṇadinno, gahapati aññatarasmiṁ Kāsiraṭṭha-nigame Kassapadasabalassa kāle VI 118,17 (28. 29).

Soṇananda-jātaka, see: Sona-Nanda-jātaka.

Soṇarukkha, bodhi Paduma-Buddhassa N 36,27.

Soṇā, aggasāvikā Sumana-Buddhassa N 34,27.

Soṇuttara, see: Sonuttara.

Sotumbarā nadī VI 507,8 (21).

Sotthija, upaṭṭhāko Koṇāgamana-Buddhassa N 43,9.

Sotthiya, tiṇahārako N 70,30.

Sotthiya, seṭṭhi Vessabhussa Bhagavato kāle N 94,14.

Sotthivati-nagara, Cetiyaraṭṭhe (v. l. B Sāvatthiya-nagara) III 454,19*.

Sotthisena, rājā Bārāṇasiyaṁ, putto Brahmadattassa V 88*,16. 20. 89,7*. 90,6*. 93 (8). 24*. 94,10*. 95*,9. 12. 18. 97,18. 98,10.

Sona-kumāra, paṇḍito, brāhmaṇaputto Bārāṇasiyaṁ (— Bodhisatto) V 312*,24. 29. 313,26*. 318,19* (23. 25. 29). 319 (9). 30*. 320,21*. 321,2*. 324 (18). 325 (16. 30). 328*,12. 17. 332,19*. 24.

Sonaka, purohitaputto Rājagahe V 247,10* (Sonakumāro). 247,18*. 248*,8. 21. 30. 249*,4. 8. 250*,19. 20 (21). 27. 28. 251,5. 9. 12-14. 251,31. 252,13*. 254,30*. 257,22. — Sonaka-paccekabuddho V 249,15*. 251 (23). 254,23*.

Sonaka-jātaka (529) V 247—261.

Soṇa-Nanda-jātaka (532) V 312—332. — IV 119,28* (Soṇanandajātaka).

Sonuttara, nesādo V 36,28. 42,16*. 43,21*. 45,30*. 46*,4. 11. 50 (19). 54,17*. 55 (2). 56 (19. 26). (v. l. Soṇuttara.)

Sobhavati, nagaraṁ Koṇāgamana-Buddhassa N 43,7.

Sobhita, upaṭṭhāko Piyadassi-Buddhassa N 34,4.

Sobhita, nagaraṁ Atthadassi-Buddhassa N 39,14.

Sobhita, Buddho N 30,18. 35,14. 24. 36,9. 44,5.

Soma, (deva-)rājā V 28,25. — VI 201,25*. 568,9. 571,18.

Soma-kumāra, see: Sutasoma.

Somadatta, kaniṭṭhabhātā Sutasomassa V 185*,12. 18. 192,7.

Somadatta, putto Bārāṇasidvāragāmavāsi-brāhmaṇassa VI 170*,3. 7. 172,29*. 173*,4. 8. 176*,18. 20. 26. 28. 179,18*. 182*,13. 17. 23 (27). 183*,1 (13). 15. 20. 28. 219,15.

Somadatta, brāhmaṇaputto (= Bodhisatto) II 166*,2. 7. 18. 167*,6*. 11.

Somadatta, hatthicchāpo III 389*,3. 12.

Somadatta-jātaka a) (211) II 164—167. — b) (410) III 388—391.

Somanassa, Videharājā VI 47,5*. 51 (27).

Somanassa-kumāra, putto Reṇu-rañño Uttarapañcālanagare (= Bodhisatto) N 45,28. — IV 445,27*. 447,6*. 452,16*. 453 (20). 454,8.

Somanassa-jātaka (505) IV 444—454.

Somayāga, isi VI 99,27*.

Sorūma, see: Seruma.

Soḷasanipāta, I 142,30 (read: Dvādasa-nipāta). — (cfr. Tiṁsa-nipāta).
Sovīra-jātaka (v. l. B Sivira-jāt.), (— Āditta-jāt. (424)) IV 401,12. (— Sucira-jāt. IV 360,24?)
Sovīra-raṭṭha (v. l. B Sivi-raṭṭha) III 470,6*.

H.

Haṁsa-jātaka (502) IV 423—430.
haṁsaghātaka-bhikkhu II 365,25.
haṁsapaharaṇako bhikkhu I 418,8.
Haṁsavatī, nagaraṁ Padumuttara-Buddhassa N 37,20.
Haṁsivagga I 424—440.
Hatthipāla, putto purohitassa Esukāriraññno Bārāṇasiyaṁ (— Bodhisatto) N 45,28. — IV 476*,2. 18. 20. 477*,9. 16. 27. 479*,12. 20. 26. 481,1*. 482,7*. 483,18*. 484,5*. 485,4*. 486*,19. 22. 488* (9). 25. 27. 489*,2. 10. 490*,5. 6. 17. 491,5. — Hatthipālasamāgamo IV 490,25. — VI 30,8.
Hatthipāla-jātaka (509) IV 473—491. — I 315,5*. — V 191,10*. 192,2*.
Hatthipura, nagaraṁ Upacarassa rañño paṭhamena puttena māpitaṁ III 460,10*.
Hatthimatta, muṇḍapabbatako I 303,21.
Haritaca-jātaka, see: Hārita-jātaka.
Haritamāta-jātaka (v. l. B Haritamaṇḍuka-) (239) II 237 —239.
Harittaca-kumara, brāhmaṇa-putto (— Bodhisatto) II 497,9*. (cfr. Hārita-tāpaso).
halāhalāni tiṇi N 47,22.
Haliddirāga-jātaka (435) III 524—526. (v. l. Haliddhi(ra)-jāt.).
Hārita, brāhmaṇaputto, tāpaso (— Bodhisatto) III 498*,17. 26 (28). 499,20*. 500*,4. 8. 501,14. 18. — V 455, (3). — Harittaca-kumāro III 497,9*.

Hārita-jātaka (431) III 496—501. (v. l. B Haritaca-jāt.) — III 534 (27). — V 117 (26).

Hiṅgula-pabbata, Himavantapadese V 415,23.

Himavat, (— Himavanto). Himavā: VI 204,13*. 212,19*. 579,23. 580 (8). (cfr. V 63,18.) Himavato: IV 287*,3. 5. 7. 8. 9. 11. — V 392,18*. 419,18*. — VI 56,12*. Himavati: II 396,16*. — III 377,15*. — V 37,1*. 316,21*. 423,33*. 432 (15).

Himavanta I 6,11. 23. 24. 7 (4). 27,17. 50,12. 55,24. 26. 128,9*. 140*,21. 24. 28. 141*,3. 7. 142,7*. 207,5*. 233,27*. 245,6*. 304,1*. 306*,4 (16). 18. 314*,17. 23. 315,10*. 319,23*. 320*,1. 6. 325,19*. 328,31*. 333,17*. 361,30*. 362,11*. 371,20*. 373*,12. 13. 406,11*. 415*,12. 17. 429,9*. 431,26*. 440,22*. 450,8*. 505,29*. — II 44,19*. 45,5*. 68,14*. 72*,12. 18. 73,19*. 86,19*. 129,10*. 139,18. 140,10*. 158,10*. 162,18*. 171*,4. 13. 172,11*. 176*,6. 24. 200,7*. 230,1*. 258,2*. 262,20*. 269,8*. 272*,12. 19. 273,18*. 276*,21. 25. 341,21*. 397,7*. 402,26*. 430,21*. 437,9*. — III 31,16*. 37*,6. 8. 10. 11. 39,30*. 42,24*. 45,12. 79*,5. 12. 81,30*. 94*,19. 21. 97,5*. 119,22*. 121,9*. 134,25. 136,20*. 143*,4. 13. 15. 16. 23. 26. 146,3*. 147,24*. 183,17*. 195,24*. 213,31*. 229,2*. 246,2*. 250,19*. 303,2*. 362 (22). 366,8*. 369,18*. 388,29*. 393,16*. 401,18*. 428,24. 434,19*. 450,18*. 452,6*. 467,11. 479,22*. 491,4*. 497,14*. 501,11*. 515,6*. 520,14. 18*. 527,10*. — IV 27,18*. 74*,9. 18. 22. 78,23*. 95,3*. 123,10*. 125,6*. 175,20*. 194*,10. 13. 220,17*. 252,4*. 253*,6 (21. 22). 277,10*. 283,17*. 286,11*. 306,1*. 333*,20. 21. 335*,16. 22. 377,17. 379,15*. 386,23*. 392,27*. 400,30*. 413*,15. 18. 423,12*. 437,19*. 442,33*. 444*,12. 21. 445,8*. 449,11*. 453,25*. 488,29*. 489,1*. 493,13*. 499,15*. — V 12,2*. 13,9*. 68,9*. 72 (15). 93,3 (25). 94,30*. 144 (26). 152,10*. 157 (9). 176,2*. 195,14*. 199,22*. 200 (7. 8). 228,2* 246,6*. 261 (7). 263,30*. 264,7*. 313,2*. 320,12*. 355,27*. 389,21*. 395*,19. 21. 396 (8). 414,16. 415,12. 21. 27. 30. 416,1. 5. 419 (21). 427 (14). 456,2*. 465 (9. 23). — VI

46,20*. 68,7*. 72*,24. 25. 29. 75,21*. 76*,13. 15. 79,1*. 100 (24). 177,16*. 183,22*. 190*,17. 23. 24. 200 (9). 203 (22. 23). 204,10* (18). 256,5*. 265,1*. 278,19*. 326,21*. 401,5*. 422 (9). 432,21*. 519,30*. 562 (3). — anto-Himavante III 467,11. — sakala-Himavanto V 423,32*. — VI 197,15*. 547 (26). (cfr. Yāmunā, Uttara-Himavanta.)

Himavantābhimukho IV 401,2*. 453,23*. 488,27*. — V 190,28*.

Himavantāraññaṁ V 318 (20). 325 (10).

Himavantokāso V 235,3*.

Himavanta-guhā III 112,27*.

Himavanta-cārikā II 92,18. — V 415,18.

Himavanta-padeso I 280,26*. 303,32*. 315,1*. 319,23*. 320,2*. 325,19*. 328,4. 16*. 343,12*. 361,21*. 431,23*. 491,17*. — II 6,8*. 10,13*. 36,1*. 41,11*. 53,3*. 55,10*. 57,17*. 61,20*. 65,19*. 66,28*. 76,21*. 85,20*. 101,23*. 108,16*. 131,16*. 145,10*. 149,2*. 156,5*. 158,24*. 162,18*. 171,3*. 176,2*. 184,17*. 197,13*. 199*,18. 20. 229,27*. 232,3*. 234,2*. 292*,9. 10. 352,10* 359,9*. 385,19*. 394,10*. 411,12*. 417,27*. 447*,19. 20. — III 16,6*. 25,29*. 37,8*. 64,12*. 73,11*. 110*,10. 16. 133,6*. 170,12*. 174,14*. 208,18*. 240,1*. 247,1*. 248,23. 249*,2. 24. 301,3*. 352,9*. 365*,4. 9. 370,7*. 371,4*. 403,28*. 432,17*. 470,14*. 537,7. — IV 8,6*. 23,2*. 28,12*. 74,5*. 90,8*. 194,18*. 206 (16). 207,27*. 283,13*. 393,7*. 413,11*. — V 2,10*. 51 (20). 152,22*. 164,25*. 191,2*. 193*,10. 15. 194,9*. 227,29*. 313,14*. 412 (4). 415,17. 22. 424,7*. — VI 77,2*. 177,23*. 264 (26). 302 (29). 390,6*. 496,9*. 561 (11). 568,5.

Himavanta-pabbato II 92,28. — V 216 (14). — VI 272,4 (14) (Himavaṁ pabbataṁ). — Himavantapabbatapādo II 128 (8)

Himavanta-passaṁ I 218,18*. — III 510,9. 532,22*. — V 396,6* (Himavanta-passmani). 423,30*.

Himavanta-pādo I 8,18.

Himavanta-matthako II 103,17*. — VI 177,21*.

Himavanta-vásiko II 273,18*. — Himavanta-vásí IV 370,14*. Himavanta-vásiní VI 498,10*. — Himavanta-vásiní-devatáyo VI 556,3*.

Himavanta-vaṇṇanā, Vessantara-jātake VI 498,11*.

Hiraññavatí, (nagaraṁ — Bhogavatí) VI 269,4*. 270 (10. 11).

Hiri-jātaka (363) III 196—197.

Hirí (Hiri), Hiri-deví, Hiri-devatá, dhītá Sakkassa V 392,21*. 393,12. 398,19* (23). 403,29*. 404,15* (20). 405,14. 406,34*. 407,5* (26). 408,17 (19). 409,14. 410,6 (11). 28. 411*,7 (9). 28. 412 (4). 9.

Hemavataka, (adj.) I 506*,10. 14. — IV 437,29*. 477,10*.

Hemavatá, nadí IV 438,30 (26). cfr. 437,29*.

II

ALPHABETICAL LIST

OF

ALL THE INTRODUCTORY GATHAS TO THE JATAKAS.

Akakkasaṁ (387).
Akataññussa posassa (72).
Akarambhase te kiccaṁ (308).
Akāsi yoggaṁ (211).
Akittiṁ disvāna sammataṁ (480).
Akilāsuno vaṇṇupathe (2).
Akkhī bhinnā paṭo naṭṭho (139).
Agārā paccupetassa (372).
Agghanti macchā (288).
Aṅgārajātā (421).
Acetanaṁ brāhmaṇa (307).
Accuggatā aṭibalatā (117).
Accheraṁ vata lokasmiṁ (541).
Ajjāpi me taṁ manasi (252).
Aññamaññehi titthehi (25).
Aññe socanti rodanti (355).
Añño uparimo vaṇṇo (212).
Aṭṭhakkhuraṁ Kharādiye (15).
Atikaraṁ akarācariya (116).
Atikkamma ramaṇakaṁ (82).
Attānaṁ saṁkamaṁ katvā (407).
Atthi me puriso deva (225).
Ath' abravī (523).
Adamha te vāri bahūtarūpaṁ (174).
Adassanena morassa (339).
Adāsi dānāni (340).
Adeyyesu dadaṁ dānaṁ (302).
Addhā Pādañjalī sabbe (247).
Addhā hi nūna migarājā (280).
Anikkasāvo kāsāvaṁ (221).
Aniccā vata saṁkhārā (95).
Anutīracāri bhaddan te (400).
Anuttare kāmaguṇe samiddhe (303).
Anupāyena yo atthaṁ (48).
Apacantāpi (450).
Apaṇṇakaṁ ṭhānam eke (1).
Apāyimha anaccimha (81).
Api ataramānānaṁ (8).
Api Kassapa mandiyā (312).
Api nū hanukā santā (146).
Api passena semāno (23).
Api Ruhaka-cchinnāpi (191).
Api Vīraka passesi (204).
Api hantvā hato brūti (332).
Appakena pi medhāvī pābhatena (4).
Appamādo (amatapadaṁ) (520).
Appossukko dāni tuvaṁ kapoṭa (490).
Abaddhā tattha bajjhanti (120).
Abbhantaraṁ nāma dumo (281).
Abbhuto vata lokasmiṁ (494).

Abhijjamāne vārismiṁ (263).
Abhitthanaya Pajjunna (75).
Abhutvā bhikkhasi bhikkhu (167).
Amātāpitarisaṁvaddho (119).
Amittahatthatthagatā (368).
Amb' āham addaṁ vanamantarasmiṁ (408).
Ambho ko nām' ayaṁ rukkho (210).
Ayaṁ Assakarājena (207).
Ayaṁ isī upasamasaṁyame rato (250)
Ayam eva sā aham pi so anañño (193).
Araññā gāmam āgamma (348).
Ariyāvakāso si (524).
Alam etehi ambehi (208).
Alaṁkatā kuṇḍalino suvatthā (522).
Alaṁkato maṭṭakuṇḍalī (449).
Alīnacittaṁ nissāya (156).
Avadhī vata attānaṁ (215).
Avasiṁha tavāgāre (343).
Asakkhiṁ vata attānaṁ (342).
Asaṁkiyo 'mhi gāmamhi (76).
Asantaṁ yo paggaṇhāti (150).
Asabbatthagāmi-vācaṁ (123).
Asamekkhitakammantaṁ (152).
Asampadānen' itarītarassa (131).
Asātaṁ sātarūpena (100).
Assa Inda-samo rāja (433).
Assaṁ gavaṁ rajataṁ jātarūpaṁ (488).
Ahaṁ eva dubbhāsitaṁ bhāsiṁ bālo (481).
Aham eva dūsiyā bhūnahatā (358).
Ahañ ce Daḷhadhammāya (409).
Ahaṁ dasasataṁvyāmaṁ (412).
Ahāsi me ambaphalāni pubbe (474).

Āgamissati me pāpaṁ (416).
Ādittasmiṁ (424).
Āmantayāmi nigamaṁ (525).
Āyatiṁ dosaṁ ñāññāya (85).
Āraññakassa isino (271).
Ārogyam icche paramañ ca lābhaṁ (84).
Āsā lokitthiyo nāma (61).
Āsāvatī nāma latā (380).
Āsiṁseth' eva puriso (51). (483).
Āsīvisaṁ mamaṁ santaṁ (239).
Āhu rājā Videhānaṁ (541).

Iṁgha ekapadaṁ tāta (238).
Iṅgha vaddhamayaṁ pāsaṁ (206).
Itthī siyā rūpavatī (192). cfr. VI 348.
Idaṁ tad ācariyavaco (222).
Idan te raṭṭhaṁ (531).
Idaṁ pure ninnaṁ āhu (418).
Idaṁ suvaṇṇakāyūraṁ (419).
Idāni kho 'mhi (375).
Idh' uragānaṁ pavaro paviṭṭho (154).
Idh' eva haṁsa nipata (476).
Idha ce hi naṁ virādhesi (3).
Imāni maṁ (304).
Isīnam antaraṁ katvā (213).

Ukkaṭṭhe sūram icchanti (92).
Ukkā milācā bandhanti dīpe (486).
Ucce viṭabhiṁ āruyha (187).
Ucce sakuṇa omāna (297).
Ucchānge deva me putto (67).
Uṭṭhehi Kaṇha (454).
Uṭṭhehi cora (311).
Uḍḍayhate janapado cāpi (526).
Uttamaṁgaruhā mayhaṁ (9).
Udumbarā c' ime pakkā (298).
Udet' ayaṁ cakkhumā (159).
Upanīyatīdam maññe (485).
Upasāḷhakanāmānaṁ (166).
Ubhayaṁ me na khamati (199)
Ubho khañjā (78).
Ummujjanti nimujjanti (463).
Urago va tacam jiṇṇaṁ (354).
Usabhass' eva te khandho (295).

Ekacintito va ayam attho (232).
Ekapaṇṇo ayaṁ rukkho (149).
Ekaputtako bhavissasi (249).
Ekā icchā pure āsi (66).
Ekā nisinnā (458).
Eko araññe (356).
Etaṁ hi te durājānaṁ (142).
Ete yūthā patīyanti (501).
Ete haṁsā pakkamanti (502). (534).
Etha Lakkhaṇa Sītā ca (461).
Evam akkhāyati (536).
Evam eva nūna rājānaṁ (160).
Evañ ce sattā jāneyyuṁ (18).
Evaṁbhūtassa te rājā (371).

Odātavatthā (417).

Kaṇho kaṇho ca (469).
Kaṇho vatāyaṁ puriso (440).
Kamatthaṁ abhisandhāya (278).
Kare sarikkho (121).
Kalyāṇadhammo (171).
Kalyāṇarūpo vatāyaṁ (324).
Kalyāṇim eva muñceyya (88).
Kasanti vapanti te janā (466).
Kasmā tuvaṁ (537).
Kassa gāmavaraṁ dammi (482).
Kassa sutvā sataṁ dammi (529).
Kāyaṁ balākā rucirā (275).
Kāyam balākā sikhinī (274).
Kā tvaṁ suddhehi vatthehi (465).
Kā nu kāḷena vaṇṇena (382).
Kā nu vijju-r-ivābhāsi (506).
Kā vedhamānā (519).
Kākolā kākasaṁghā ca (379).
Kāni kammāni kubbāni (473).
Kāmaṁ kāmayamānassa (467).
Kāmam patāmi nirayaṁ (40).
Kāmaṁ yahiṁ icchasi tena gaccha (234).
Kāyena yo nāvahare (326).
Kāḷamigā setadantā tava ime (163).
Kāḷāni kesāni pure ahesuṁ (411).
Kāle nikkhamanā sādhu (226).
Kāḷe vā yadi vā juṇhe (17).
Kālo ghasati bhūtāni (245).
Kāsāyavatthe (434).

Kim agghati taṇḍulanālikā (5).
Kiṁ aṇḍakā (306).
Kin te jaṭāhi dummedha (138).
Kiṁ te vataṁ (447).
Kin nu daṇḍaṁ kim ajinaṁ (528).
Kim nu santaramāno va (352).
Kin nu socasi (514).
Kiṁ su naro (453).
Kiṁchando kimadhippāyo (511).
Kuṭhārihattho puriso (475).
Kuto nu āgacchatha (436).
Kuto nu āgacchasi rammavāsi (497).
Kūlāvakā (31).
Kusalūpadese dhitiyā daḷhāya (132).
Kohiṁ gatā kattha gatā (373).
Ko 'yaṁ bindussaro (294).
Ko 'yaṁ majjhe samuddasmiṁ (539).
Ko 'dha jāgarataṁ sutto (414).
Ko taṁ hiṁsati heṭheti (505).
Ko n' āyaṁ (296).
Ko nu uddhitabhatto vā (273).
Ko nu kho bhagavā hetu (237).
Ko nu maṁ usunā vijjhi (540).
Ko nu saddena mahatā (172).
Ko nu santamhi pajjote (364).
cfr. VI 372.
Ko pātur āsī (512).
Kodhanā akataññū ca (63).
Ky' āhaṁ devānam akaraṁ (369).

Khamanīyaṁ yāpanīyaṁ (426).
Kharājinā jaṭilā paṁkadantā (487).
Khuddānam lahucittānaṁ (464).
Khemaṁ yahiṁ (133).

Gaṅgā kumudinī (425).
Gajaggameghehi (229).
Gavañ ce taramānānaṁ (334).

Catudvāram idaṁ nagaraṁ (439).
Catuppado ahaṁ samma (153).
Catubbhi aṭṭh' ajjhagamā (104).
Candābhaṁ (135).
Cirassaṁ vata passāma (395).
Cirassaṁ vata me (513).

Janittaṁ me bhavittaṁ me (178).
Jarudapānaṁ khaṇamānā (256).
Jānanto no mahārāja (462).
Jino rathassamaṇikuṇḍalā ca (351).
Jīva vassasataṁ Gagga (155).
Jīvakañ ca mataṁ disvā (97).

Ñātam etaṁ kuruṅgassa (21).

Tath' eva kassa kalyāṇaṁ (126).
Tath' eva puṇṇapātiyo (53).
Tadeva me tvaṁ (333).
Tañ ca appañ ca (179).
Tayo giriṁ (228).

Na takkaḷā santi na ālupāni (446).
Na taṁ jitaṁ sādhu jitaṁ (70).
Na taṁ daḷhaṁ bandhanam āhu dhīrā (201).
Na te kaṭṭhāni bhinnāni (477).
Na te pīṭham (337).
Na tvaṁ Rādha vijānāsi (145).
Na maṁ umhayate diavā (197).
Na pāpajanasaṁsevī (141).
Na maṁ sītaṁ na maṁ uṇhaṁ (34).
Na m' āyaṁ aggi tapati (216).
Na me ruccaṁ (381).
Na vissase avissatthe (93).
Na ve anatthakusalena (46). (47).
Na vāham etaṁ jānāmi (445).
Na santi devā pavasanti nūna (194).
Na santhavaṁ kāpurisena kayirā (161).
Na santhavasmā param atthi pāpiyo (162).
Na hi vaṇṇena sampannā (269).
Nakkhattaṁ patimānentaṁ (49).
Naguttame (535). cfr. V 393,1.
Name namantassa (223).
Narānaṁ ārāmakarāsu (341). cfr. V 435,22.
Navachandake (388).
Nānacchandā mahārāja (289).
Nigrodham eva seveyya (12).
Niccaṁ ubbiggahadayā (140).
Nivesanaṁ kassa nu 'daṁ Sunanda (527).

Paṁko ca kāmā (378).
Pañca paṇḍitā samāgatā (508) cfr. VI 379.
Pañcālo sabbasenāya (546)
Paññāy' upetaṁ siriyā vihīnaṁ (500) cfr. VI 356.
Paṇītaṁ bhuñjase bhattaṁ (394).
Paṇḍū kisiyāsi dubbalā (545).
Panādo nāma so rājā (264).
Pabbatūpatthare ramme (195).
Parapāṇarodhā jīvanto (300).
Parisaṁkupatho nāma (427).
Parosataṁ ve pi samāgatānaṁ (101).
Parosahassam pi samāgatānaṁ (99).
Pavāsā āgato tāta (198).
Passa saddhāya sīlassa (190).
Pāṇi ce muduko c' assa (262).
Puṭṭhassa me aññatarena (293).
Puṇṇaṁ nadiṁ (214).
Putto ty-āhaṁ mahārāja (7).
Puthusaddo (428).
Purāṇacorāna vaco nisamma (26).
Pure tuvaṁ (299).

Pharusā vata te vācā (315).
Phusati varavaṇṇābhe (547).

Bahucinti Appacintī ca (114).
Bahunnaṁ vijjati (328).
Bahum p' etaṁ asabbhi Jātaveda (144).
Bahum p' etaṁ vane kaṭṭhaṁ (105).

Bahum pi so vikattheyya (125).
Bahussutaṁ (432).
Bahussuto (442)
Bārāṇassaṁ ahū rājā (516).
Bārāṇassaṁ mahārāja (292).
Bālo vatāyaṁ dumasākhagocaro (176).
Bālo vatāyaṁ sunakho (242).
Brahā pavaddhakāyo so (335).
Brahmalokā cavitvāna, (507).

Bhaddako vat' ayaṁ pakkhī (236).
Bhallāṭiyo nāma ahosi rājā (504).
Bhutvā tiṇaparighāsaṁ (254).
Bhus' amhi kuddho (420).

Maññe sovaṇṇayo rāsi (39).
Matamatam eva rodatha (317).
Madhuvaṇṇaṁ madhurasaṁ (366).
Manuññam eva bhāseyya (28).
Manussassēva te sīsaṁ (321).
Manussindaṁ jahitvāna (346).
Mam' annapānaṁ (253).
Mahesī Rucino bhariyā (489).
Māssu kujjhi bhūmipati (376).
Mā tāta kujjhi, na hi sādhu kodho (377).
Mā paṇḍicciyaṁ (538).
Mā Muṇikassa (30).
Mā Sālūkassa pihayi (286).
Mā su nandi: icchati maṁ (64).
Migan tipallatthaṁ (16).
Migaluddo mahārājā (503).
Mittāmaccaparibbūḷhaṁ (460).
Mitto mittassa (459).
Mitto have sattapadena hoti (83).

Yato yato garu dhuraṁ (29).
Yato vilutta ca hatā ca gāvo (79).
Yatth' eko labhate babbu (137).
Yattha verī nivasati (404).
Yattha verī nivisati (103).
Yathannu puriso hoti (109).
Yathāpi kītā (231).
Yathōdake avile appasanne (185).
Yathā kesā ca massu ca (261).
Yathā cāpo ninnamati (397).
Yathā nadī ca pantho (65).
Yathā māṇavako pantho (279).
Yathā vācā va bhuñjassu (130).
Yad esamānā vicarimha (492).
Yadā yadā (24).
Yaṁ annapān' assa (329).
Yaṁ ussukā saṁgharanti (284).
Yam ekarattim paṭhamaṁ (510).
Yaṁ etaṁ (392).
Yaṁ kiñci ratanaṁ atthi (543).
Yañ ca aññe na rakkhanti (10).
Yan taṁ vasantasamaye (318).
Yan te pavikatthitaṁ pure (80).
Yaṁ nissitā (36).
Yan nu gijjho yojanasataṁ (164).
Yaṁ passati na taṁ icchati (244).

Yaṁ brāhmaṇo (62).
Yaṁ laddhaṁ tena tuṭṭhabbaṁ (136).
Yasaṁ laddhāna dummedho (122).
Yasokaro puññakaro 'ham asmi (457).
Yasmiṁ mano nivisati (68).
Yass' atthā dūram āyanti (260).
Yass' ete caturo dhammā (57). (224).
Yass' ete tayo dhammā (58).
Yassa maṁgalā samūhatā (87).
Yā-y-aññam anusāsati (115).
Yāvatā candimasuriyā (258).
Yāvaṁ so mattaṁ aññāsi (255).
Ye 'me ahaṁ na jānāmi (403).
Ye kukkurā (22).
Ye na kāhanti ovādaṁ (196).
Ye vaddham apacāyanti (37).
Ye saññino (134).
Yenāsi kisiyā paṇḍu (266).
Yena mittena saṁsaggo (272).
Yena sattubilaṅgā ca (112). cfr. VI 365.
Yenakāmaṁ paṇāmeti (157).
Yo atthakāmassa (41). (42). (43).
Yo 'yaṁ sāliyachāpo (367).
Yo alīnena cittena (55).
Yo indriyānaṁ (423).
Yo kopaneyyo (441). cfr. VI 257.
Yo te imaṁ visālakkhiṁ (443).
Yo te puttake (438).
Yo te hatthe ca pāde (313).
Yo dukkhapuṭṭhāya bhaveyya tāṇam (102).
Yo nīliyaṁ maṇḍayati (344).
Yo pahaṭṭhena cittena (56).
Yo pubbe katakalyāṇo (90).
Yo pubbe karaṇīyāni (71).
Yo maṁ pure paccudeti (410).
Yo ve kāle asampatte (331).
Yo ve dhammadhajaṁ katvā (128).
Yo ve mettena cittena (169).
Yo ve sabbasametānaṁ (268).

Rajjañ ca paṭipann' asmā (515).
Rājā apucchi Vidhūraṁ (413).
Rājā avoca Vidhūraṁ (495).
Rājā Kāliṅgo cakkavatti (479).
Rājā te bhattaṁ (398).
Rājāsi luddakammo (542).
Rudam manuññaṁ (32).

Lasī ca te nipphalitā (143).
Lāpūni sīdanti (77).
Littaṁ paramena tejasā (91).

Vaṇṇagandharasūpeto (186).
Vaṇṇavā abhirūpo si (451).
Vaṇṇāroheṇa (361).
Vanaṁ yad' aggi dahati (345).
Vandāmi taṁ kuñjara saṭṭhihāyanaṁ (357).
Varaṁ varaṁ tvam (283).
Vassāni paññāsa (277).

Vācā va kira te āsi (89).
Vāṇijā samitiṁ katvā (493).
Vāti gandho timirāṇaṁ (360).
Vāti cāyaṁ tato gandho (327).
Vāyameth' eva puriso (52). (124).
Vālodakaṁ apparasaṁ (183).
Vikiṇṇavācaṁ (518).
Vikkama re mahāmiga (359).
Viditaṁ thusaṁ (338).
Vibbhantacitto (402).
Virūpakkhehi me mettaṁ (203).
Vivaratha imāsaṁ dvāraṁ (301).
Vutto 'mhi (365).
Vessantaraṁ taṁ pucchāmi (521).

Sakuṇo Mayhako nāma (390).
Saṁkapparāgadhotena (251).
Saṁgāmāvacaro sūro (182).
Sace brāhmaṇa gacchasi (385).
Sace muñce (19).
Sace vo vuyhamānānaṁ (517). cfr. VI 469.
Sace hi ty-āhaṁ dhanahetu gahito (491).
Saccaṁ kira (452). cfr. VI 373.
Saccaṁ kir' evam āhaṁsu (73). (386).
Saṭhassa sāṭheyyam idaṁ (218).
Satta me rohitā macchā (316).
Sattatantiṁ sumadhuraṁ (243).
Sattāham evāhaṁ (444).
Saddabāsi sigālassa (113).
Santi pakkhā (35).
Santi rukkhā (430).
Sandhiṁ katvā amittena (165).
Sabbakāmadadaṁ kumbhaṁ (291).
Sabbam idaṁ carimavataṁ (309).
Sabbaṁ narānaṁ saphalaṁ suciṇṇaṁ (498).
Sabbaṁ bhaṇḍaṁ (374).
Sabbasaṁhārako n' atthi (110) cfr. VI 336.
Sabbāyasaṁ (347).
Sabbesu kira bhūtesu (175).
Sabbehi kiṁsuko diṭṭho (248).
Sabbehi kira ñātihi (270).
Sabbo jano (240).
Sabbo loko (217).
Samaṇaṁ taṁ maññamāno (325).
Samatittikaṁ anavasesakaṁ (96).
Sampannaṁ sālikedāraṁ (484).
Sammodamānā (33).
Sarīradavyaṁ (200).
Sasamuddapariyāyaṁ (310).
Sādhu kho Paṇḍito nāma (98).
Sādhu kho sippakaṁ nāma (107).
Sādhu sambahulā ñātī (74).
Sikkheyyā sikkhitabbāni (108).
Sigālo mānatthaddho va (241).
Siṅgī migo āyatacakkhunetto (267). (389).
Sīlaṁ kir' eva kalyāṇaṁ (86). (290). (330).
Sīlaṁ seyyo (362).
Sīhaṅgulī sīhanakho (188).
Sukhaṁ jīvitarūpo si (220).

Sukhaṁ vata mam jīvantaṁ (106).
Sukhā gharā Vacchanakha (235).
Sukhumālarūpaṁ disvā (496).
Sucittapattacchadana (383).
Succajaṁ vata na-ccaji (320).
Suṇohi mayhaṁ vacanaṁ janinda (456).
Sutaṁ m' etaṁ mahābrahme (431).
Sutitikkhaṁ (435).
Sumukha (533).
Susukhaṁ vata jīvanti (393).
Susukhaṁ vata jīvāmi (319).
Sūro sūrena saṁgamma (227).
Seno balasā patamāno (168).
Seyyaṁso seyyaso hoti (282).
Seyyo amitto (44). (45).
Sotatto sosīto (94).
Sobhanti macchā gaṅgeyyā (205).

Haṁsā koñcā mayūrā (202).
Haṁsi tuvaṁ evaṁ maññasi (111) cfr. VI 343.
Haṁso palāsam avaca (370).
Hanti hatthehi pādehi (350).
Hantvā jhatvā vadhitvā (246).
Hitvā gāmasahassāni (406).
Hiraññam me suvaṇṇam me (219).
Hiriottappasampannā (6).
Hirin tarantaṁ (363).
Hoti sīlavataṁ attho (11).

III

INDEX OF GĀTHĀS

OR PARTS OF GĀTHĀS WHICH MORE THAN ONCE OCCUR

IN THE JĀTAKAS AND THE COMMENTARY.

Akataññussa posassa 1,71. — 9,108.
Akāle vassatī tassa 2,84. — 8,48.
Akkocchi maṁ avadhi maṁ 5,108. 109. — 9,12. 18.
Akkodhano niccapasannacitto 6,116. — 13,151. (cfr. 8,88.)
Akkhehi no t' āyaṁ mudhā nu laddho 22,1398. 1422.
Agārā paccupetassa anāgārassa 5,111. (cfr. 7,107.)
Agārino annadapānavatthadā I 401 (15). — 6,9.
Aggi yathā tiṇakaṭṭhaṁ ḍahanto 21,414. (cfr. 10,45.)
Aggiṁ dvārato dema, gaṇhāmase vikattanaṁ 22,1588. 1589.
Aghaṁ taṁ patisevissaṁ vane 22,1848. 1850. (cfr. 1984.)
Aṅgam etaṁ manussānaṁ bhātā loke pavuccati 4,58. — VI 297 (22).
Acintitam pi bhavati, cintitaṁ pi vinassati 13,180. — 22,139.
Accāhitaṁ kamma karosi luddaṁ 10,69*. (cfr. 17,70.)
Accenti kālā tarayanti rattiyo 15,317. 318. 319.
Accharāsahassāhaṁ pavarā II 255,24. — III 409 (18).
Acchariyarūpaṁ vata yādisañ ca 15,217. — 22,1080.
Acchecchuṁ vata bho rukkhaṁ 22,1824. 1825. 1826.
Accheraṁ vata lokasmiṁ 22,1909. (cfr. 22,411. 1908.)
Ajaññam jaññasaṁkhātaṁ 3,128. — III 244 (6).
Ajānīyā va jātiyā sindhavā 19,46. — 22,201. (cfr. 22,170.)
Ajinamhi haññate dīpī 22,299. 300.
Ajjāpi me taṁ manasi 3,4. — 5,77.
Ajja ce me imaṁ rattiṁ 22,880. (cfr. 22,2252.)
Ajj' eva pabbajissāmi, ko jaññā 19,37. 42. 45. 48. 51. 58. 55.
Ajjhāyakaṁ mantaguṇūpapannaṁ 22,881. 919.

Ajjhenaṁ ariyā paṭhaviṁ janindā 22,870. 896.
Añño nu te ko 'dha naro pathavyā 18,75. 81. 84.
Aṭṭhaṁsā sukatā thambhā 22,569. 760.
Atikkamma ramaṇakaṁ sadāmattañ ca 1,81. — 5,96.
Aticiraṁnivāsena piyo bhavati appiyo 13,87. — 18,136.
Atīthismiṁ yo nisinnasmiṁ 21,195. 197. 200. 202.
Atītaṁ mānusaṁ kammaṁ 22,1523. 1528. 1531.
Attano ce hi vādassa aparādhaṁ 18,141. 147. 151. 150.
Attānam eva paṭhamaṁ patirūpaṁ 'nivesaye II 441,21. — III 333,6.
Atthi me pānīyaṁ sītaṁ ābhataṁ 22,394. (cfr. 15,152. — 20,137. — 22,388. 2048. 2126. 2303.)
Athāparo paṭinandittha suvo 15,150. (cfr. 20,135.)
Athāyaṁ isinā satto antalikkhacaro 19,98 (cfr. 8,56).
Ath' ettha vattati saddo tumulo 22,1711. 1712. 1713. — VI 504 (11).
Ath' ettha sakuṇā santi 22,2101. 2102. 2106. 2108. 2109. 2110. 2111. (cfr. 22,2082.)
Ath' ettha sāsapo bahuko 22,2088. 2113.
Atha tvaṁ kena vaṇṇena 22,1636. 1673. 2127. 2304.
Atho ārogaṁ yoggaṁ me 22,80. 2420. (cfr. 22,70. 2419).
Atho ubho arogā 22,2302. (cfr. 20,180. 182. — 22,2041. 2048. 2119. 2121. 2296. 2298. 2300. 2409)
Atho ḍaṁsā ca makasā ca 20,188. — 22,2044. 2122. 2299. 2368. (cfr. 20,181. — 22,2042. 2120. 2297. 2361. 2410.)
Atho pi me amaccesu doso 15,129. — 21,61. 167. (cfr. 15,128. — 21,60. 166.)
Atho me sādisī bhariyā 15,131. — 21,63. 169. (cfr. 15,130. — 21,62. 168.)
Adāsi ujubhūtesu vippasannena 22,523. 532. 541. 548. (cfr. 14,114. — 22,515.)
Adiṭṭhapubbaṁ disvāna macco 22,1390. 1404.
Addhā tuvaṁ katte hitesi mayhaṁ 18,94. 96.
Addhā pajānāmi aham pi etaṁ 13,145. (cfr. 22,1372.)
Addhā Pādañjalī sabbe paññāya atirocati 2,192. — V 122 (12).

Addhā piyā mayha janinda esā 18,76. 82.
Addhā sataṁ bhāsasi nāga dhammaṁ 22,1397. 1421.
Addhā have sevitabbā sapaññā 6.115. — 15,219. 259. 260. — 17,180. 190. (cfr. 21.396.)
Addhā hi tāta satān' esa dhammo 14,53. (cfr. 16,76.)
Addhā hi dubbissasam etam āhu 15.234. 237.
Addhā hi me taṁ dukkharūpaṁ III 340 (25). — 22,2188.
Addhā hi saccaṁ bhaṇasi 17,98. — 22,1296.
Addhā hi saccaṁ vacanaṁ tav' etaṁ 14,152. — 15,45. 299.
Addhā hi no bhakkho ayaṁ manāpo 17.148. — 21,456. 463.
Addhā hi so socati rājaseṭṭho 22.1396. 1420.
Adhammo nirayaṁ neti, dhammo pāpeti suggatiṁ 15.845. — 19.81.
Adhicca laddhaṁ pariṇāmajan te 17.167. — 22,1386. 1410.
Anariyarūpo puriso janinda 22,1463. 1517.
Analā mudusambhāsā duppūrā 3,35. — 15,289. — 21,345.
Anāgāriyupetassa vippamuttassa 7,107. (cfr. 5,111.)
Anāsavā vītarāgā santacittā samāhitā N 77. 79.
Anikkasāvo kāsāvaṁ yo vatthaṁ 2,140. — 16,122.
Anekarūpaṁ ruciraṁ nānācitraṁ 22,558. 562.
Annañ ca pānañ ca pasannacitto 17,171. (cfr. 22,1389. 1413.)
Annena pānena upetarūpaṁ 22,1375. (cfr. 10,52.)
Annena pānena pasannacitto 16,50. (cfr. 17,171 etc.)
Api ataramānānaṁ phalāsā 1,7. — 22,30. 41. (cfr. 22,31. 42.
Api ataramānānaṁ sammadattho 22,31. 42. (cfr. 1,7. — 22,30. 41.)
Api ce pattam ādāya anāgāro paribbaje 3,111. — 4,30. 40. — 9,64. 65.
Api ce maññatī poso 13,33. 58. 130.
Api jīvam mahārāja purisaṁ 22,396. 397.
Apet' ayaṁ cakkhumā ekarājā 2,17[b]. (cfr. 2,17.)
Apetā te brāhmaññā 14,228. 232. 236. 240. 245. 249. 253. 257. 261. 265.
Appassa kammassa phalaṁ mamedaṁ 8,41. — III 446,11.)
Apposukko nirāsaṁkī asoko akutobhayo 10,126. — 14,161.
Abaddhā tattha bajjhanti 1.116. — II 192 (96).

Abbahi vata me sallaṁ 5,11. 116. — 7,112. — 10,107. 161.
Abbhakūṭasamā uccā 22,1110. 1114.
Abbhuto vata lokasmiṁ uppajji 14,202. — 22,483.
Abhave nandati tassa bhave 12,80. (cfr. 12,86.)
Abhijjamāne vārismiṁ sayaṁ 3,37. — 15,287.
Amitte tassa bhajati mitte 12,78. (cfr. 12,84.)
Ambā ca sālā tilakā ca jambuyo 15,258. — 18,20. (cfr. 22,1166.)
Ammā ca tāta nikkhantā 22,2155. 2158
Ayam assa asokavanikā 17,227. 228.
Ayaṁ assa pāsādo 17,229. 234. (cfr. 22,668.)
Ayam assa pokkharaṇī sañchannā 17,237. 238. — 22,670.
Ayaṁ ekapadī eti 22,2087. 2114. 2206.
Ayaṁ ekapadī rāja 20,112. (cfr. 22,319.)
Ayaṁ dvedhāpatho bhadde 22,281. 289.
Ayan nu macco kim akāsi sādhuṁ 22,498. 510. 528. 544.
Araññā gāmam āgamma 4,185. — 9,80.
Arahante sītibhūte sakkaccaṁ 22,514. 522. 531. 540. 547.
Ariyassa ariyena sameti sakkhi 21,449. 450.
Ariyavatt' asi vakkaṅga yo piṇḍam II 280) (22). — 21,106.
Ariyāvakāso si anariyo cāsi 16,259. (cfr. 22,1848.)
Ariyāvakāso si pasannanetto II 281 (1). — 17,140.
Alam etehi ambehi 2,114. — 4,162. (cfr. V 122 (20).)
Alaṁkatā suvasanā mālinī 4,172. — 22,1149.
Alaso gihī kāmabhogī na sādhu 4,127. — 5,4. — 15,200. — VI 375,28.
Avasī tuvaṁ mayha tīhaṁ agāre 22,1830. (cfr. 1868.)
Avyāpajjhaṁ kathaṁ assa 22,1248. (cfr. 22,1250)
Avhayant' eva gacchantaṁ 22,2015. 2068.
Asaṁvihitakammantaṁ bālaṁ dummantamantinaṁ 16,313. — VI 361,28.
Asaṁsayam imaṁ disvā haṁsarājaṁ 21,39. 53.
Asanthutaṁ maṁ cirasanthutena 4,77. — 5,124.
Asassataṁ sassatan no tavedaṁ 22,1385. 1409.

Asā lokitthiyo nāma, velā tāsaṁ na vijjati 1,60. — 21,332.
Asicammaṁ gahetvāna khaggaṁ 12,58. — 14,356.
Asmā ratyā vivasane 22,1731. 1739. (cfr. 22 (1728).
Assatthassêva taruṇaṁ pavāḷaṁ 20,150. — 22,346.
Assatthā panasā cême nigrodhā 22,2172. 2192. 2268.
Assamo sukato mayhaṁ N 39. — I 7 (10).
Ahañ ca kho sāmiko câpi mayhaṁ 22,1418. (cfr. 17,171. — 22,1889.)
Ahañ ca bhariyā ca manussaloke 22,1889. (cfr. 17,171. — 22,1418.)
Aham pi purimaṁ jātiṁ sare 22,992. (cfr. 22,990.)
Aham pi samma bhuñjāmi 10,126. (cfr. 14,161.)
Aham hi kuñjaraṁ dajjaṁ 22,1917. (cfr. 22,1717.)

Ākiṇṇaluddo puriso dhāticelam 6,120. — 9,107.
Āgañchu dovārikā khaggabaddhā 15,107. 318.
Ācariya samanuññātā tayā anumatā 21,186. (cfr. 21,83.)
Ācariyānaṁ vacanā ghātessaṁ 22,598. 608. (cfr. 22,595.)
Ādāya dantāni gajuttamassa 16,181. 185. — (cfr. 16,128.)
Ādāya beluvaṁ daṇḍaṁ aggihuttaṁ kamaṇḍaluṁ 22,1965. (cfr. 22,2128. 2300.)
Ādittaṁ vata maṁ santaṁ 5,10. 115. — 7,111. — 10,108. 150.
Ādu cāpaṁ gahetvāna khaggaṁ bandhitvā III 340 (28). — 22,2187.)
Ādu paññā kimatthikā 9,43. (cfr. 22,1554.)
Ānando ca pamâdo ca sadā 20,177. 178.
Āmantayassu te putte 22,2136. 2186.
Āyatiṁ dosaṁ nâññāya yo kāme 1,84. — V 432 (21).
Āraññakassa isino ciraratta tapassino 3,61. — 14,276. — 22,795.
Āruyha selaṁ bhavanaṁ kinnarānaṁ 16,106. 115.
Ārūḷhā gāmaṇīyehi illiyācâpadhārihi 19,47. — 22,171. 202. 1885. 2331.
Ārūḷhā gāmaṇīyehi cāpahatthehi vammihi 19,50. — 22,173. 175. 177. 179. 181. 183. 185. 187. 189. 204. 206. 208. 210. 212. 214. 216. 218. 220. 1837.

Ārūḷhā gāmaṇīyehi tomaraṁkusapāṇibi 19,44. — 22,169. 200. 1833. 2379.
Ālambarā mutiṅgā ca naccagītā 22,509. 585.
Āḷāra nāññatra manussalokā 17,182. (cfr. 15,258.)
Āḷārikā ca sūdā ca 22,2888. (cfr. 22,1108.)
Āvaṭṭanī mahāmāyā brahmacariyakopanā 3,38. — 15,288. — 21,346.
Āveṭhitaṁ piṭṭhito uttamaṅgaṁ 15,11. 16.
Āsanaṁ udakaṁ pajjaṁ 15,33. 298.
Āsāya Saddhā-Siriyā ca Kosiya 21,274. 280.
Āsiṁseth' eva puriso 1,50. — 13,134. 136. — 22,134. 135.
Āhaññantu sabbaviṇā bheriyo 22,1641. 2389.

Iṁgha Maddi nisāmehi 22,1807. 1809. 2390.
Icc-ete kusale dhamme ṭhite passāmi 6,74. — 21,177.
Icc-ete soḷasākārā 12,81. 87. (cfr. 2,60.)
Icc-eva mantayantānaṁ ariyānaṁ 21,18. 98.
Iti Maddī varārohā 22,2285. 2294. (cfr. 22,2258.)
Ito ujuṁ uttarāyaṁ disāyaṁ 16,105. — 18,19. (cfr. 16,115.)
Itthāgāraṁ pi te dammi 22,92. 109.
Itthiyā kāraṇā rājā bandhāpesiṁ II 192,22. 193 (8).
Itthī siyā rūpavatī II 115,13. — VI 348,29.
Itthīsahassaṁ bhāriyānaṁ 22,1320. 1324. 1385. 1389.
Idam assa ambavanaṁ supupphitaṁ 17,235. 236. — 22,600.
Idam assa uyyānaṁ supupphitaṁ 17,229. 230. — 22,665.
Idam assa kaṇikāravanaṁ supupphitaṁ 17,231. 232. — 22,667.)
Idam assa kūṭāgāraṁ sovaṇṇaṁ 17,225. 226. — 22,664.
Idam assa pāṭalivanaṁ supupphitaṁ 17,233. 234. — 22,668.
Idañ ca paccayaṁ laddhā 22,2487. 2488. 2489.
Idañ ca me sattubhattaṁ madhunā 22,2085. (cfr. 22,1977.)
Idañ ca sutvāna amānusānaṁ 15,187. 188. 189.
Idaṁ tad ācariyavaco Pārāsariyo 2,142. — 5,16.

Idaṁ te raṭṭhaṁ sadhanaṁ sayoggaṁ 20,1. — 21,416. (cfr. 16,72.)
Idaṁ (pi) dutiya(ka)ṁ sallaṁ kampeti hadayaṁ mama 22,314. 2251.
Idam pi pānīyaṁ sītaṁ ābhataṁ 15,162. — 20,187. — 22,336. 2048 2126. 2303. (cfr. 22,304.)
Idaṁ vatvāna pakkāmi 19,35. — 20,113.
Idaṁ vatvāna pakkāmi accharā 17,108. 119.
Idaṁ vatvāna Maghavā devarājā Sujampati 22,429. 1697. 2382.
Idaṁ sutvā brahmabandhu 22,2090. 2116.
Idh' evāhaṁ vasissāmi 14,161. (cfr. 10,126.)
Indaṁ hi so brāhmaṇaṁ maññamāno 16,98. (cfr. Jāt. (316).)
Imaṁ gale gahetvāna nāsetha 22,1471. 1520.
Imaṁ tvam tatiyaṁ tāva daḷhaṁ katvā N 137. — III 242 (22).
Imaṁ mayhaṁ hadayasokaṁ paṭimuñcatu 14,23. 24. — 22,682. 683. 684. 685.
Imamhi naṁ padesamhi puttakā 22,2229. 2230. 2231.
Imasmiṁ [me] samaṇa hatthe 22,277. 278.
Imassa daṇḍañ ca vadhañ ca datvā 13,9. (cfr. 15,8.)
Imā [tā] pokkharaṇiyo rammā 14,216. — 22,2276. (cfr. 167. 1222.)
Imā nu nariyo kiṁ akaṁsu 22,482. 505.
Imās' āhaṁ dhammaṁ sutvā II 257,1. (cfr. 14,214. — 22,675.)
Ime kumāre passanto (disvāna) mañjuke 22,1760. 1761. 1762. 1763. 1764. 1765. 2138. 2140.
Ime te jambukā rukkhā vedisā 22,2171. 2191. 2267.
Ime tiṭṭhanti ārāmā ayaṁ sītodakā nadī 22,2173. 2198. 2269.
Ime nu maccā kiṁ akaṁsu pāpaṁ 22,442. 445. 448. 451. 454. 457. 461. 464. 467. 470. 473. 477. 485. 489.
Ime nu maccā kiṁ akaṁsu sādhuṁ 22,511. 551.
Ime no hatthikā assā balivaddā ca 22,2176. 2178. 2179. 2190. 2272.
Ime sudaṁ yanti disodisaṁ pure 3,98. — 14,169.
Isiñ ca dāni pucchāmi 14,277. (cfr. 14,288. — 22,1704.)
Isinaṁ antaraṁ katvā Bhararājā 2,124. (cfr. V 118 (31).)
Issatthe c' asmi kusalo daḷhadhammo 22,295. 316. 336. 350.

Ukkāmukhe pahaṭṭhaṁ va 20,120. — 22,933.
Uggā ca rājaputtā ca vesiyānā ca brāhmaṇā 22,1714. 1730. 1741.
Uṭṭhānapāricariyāya 20,146. (cfr. 22,318.)
Uṭṭhāhakañ ce pi alīnavuttiṁ 21,324. (cfr. 21,313.)
Uṭṭhehi Kaṇha (cora), kiṁ sesi 4,41. — 10,139. (cfr. 11,11.)
Uttamañgaruhā mayhaṁ ime jātā 1,8. — VI 96,4
Udet' ayaṁ cakkhumā ekarājā 2,17. (cfr. 2,17ᵇ.)
Upanīyat' idaṁ maññe 17,219. 220. (cfr. 14,18.)
Upanīyatī jīvitaṁ appamāyu 15,41. 42. 43. 44.
Upaman te karissāmi 19,34. — 22,1087.
Upayācitakena puttaṁ labhanti 22,696. 697.
Upari dumapariyāyesu 22,2014. 2057.
Uparivisālaṁ duppūraṁ 5,93. — 10,6.
Upalepabhayā dhīro n' eva 15,163. — 22,1049–50.
Upahacca manaṁ Mejjho 15,24. — 19,96.
Upetaṁ annapānehi naccagītehi 22,518. 528. (cfr. 22,504.)
Uposathañ ca upavasi sadā 22,503. 534. 538. 542. 549. (cfr. 14,114.
— 22,516.)
Uppajjanti ca me bhogā II 255,14. 28. — III 409 (15).
Ubbedhati me hadayaṁ mukhañ ca 22,1510. 1544.
Ummattikā bhavissāmi bhūnahatā 22,679. 680.
Usabhā rukkhā gāviyo gavā ca I 336,11. — 1,78.
Usūhi sattīhi ca tomarehi 22,404. (cfr. 22,1108.)

Ekarattiṁ vasitvāna pāto 22,2130. 2131.
Etañ ca te ruccati 8,7. 8.
Etan te anumodāma 18,118. (cfr. 21,182.)
Etasmiṁ te sulapite patirūpe subhāsite 10,13. 20. 22. — 13,85.
87. 89. 93. 97. 100.

Ete asapparisā loke bālā 18,156. 161. 163.
Ete c' aññe rājāno 22,421. (cfr. 22,1123.)
Ete nīlā padissanti nānāphaladharā 22,2012. 2056.
Ete bhavanti ākārā 2,90. (cfr. 12,81. 87.)
Ete bhutvā pivitvā (vamitvā) ca pakkamanti vihaṅgamā 14,4 — 15,121. 310.
Ete haṁsā pakkamanti vakkaṅgā 15,118. 120. — 21,89.
Ete hanatha bandhatha 14,199. — 15,165.
Etena saccavajjena putto uppajjataṁ ise 14,103. 106. 109. 111. 113. 115.
Evam āpajjati poso 7,12. — 20,48.
Evam etaṁ yathā brūsi saccaṁ 22,1388. 1407.
Evam eva ahaṁ Kāja bhutvā bhakkhaṁ 21,379. 387.
Evam eva imaṁ kāyaṁ N 33. 35.
Evam eva tuvaṁ rāja Cūlanīyassa 22,1468. 1515.
Evam eva tuvaṁ rājā dipadinda 21,384. 389.
Evam eva naro pāpaṁ thokathokaṁ 22,1039. (cfr. 22,1044.)
Evam eva manussesu yo hoti seṭṭhasammato 4,134. 136. — 18,105. 107. 169. 171.
Evam eva mahārāja paṇḍitehi sukhāvahaṁ 22,1568. 1640.
Evam evaṁ manussesu 2,100. 181.
Evam evaṁ manussesu vivādo yattha jāyati 7,38. — 13,24.
Evaṁ karonti sappaññā 5,13. — 10,158.
Evaṁ kicchā bhato poso 20,173. 174.
Evaṁ ce te laddham idaṁ vimānaṁ 22,1392. 1416.
Evañ ce no viharataṁ antarāyo na hessati 13,39. — 18,138.
Evañ ce yācamānānaṁ añjaliṁ 13,38. — 18,137. (cfr. 20,153.)
Evaṁ taṁ anugacchāmi 19,58. — 22,1759.
Evaṁ tuvaṁ nāga asampadosaṁ 22,1395. 1419.
Evam pi idha vaddhānaṁ 6,39. — 9,9.
Evam pi dahar' āpeto 16,160. 162. 164. 167. 169.
Evaṁ mittavataṁ atthā sabbe honti 21,88. 191.
Evaṁbhūtassa te rāja (me tāta) 5,106. 108.

Evaṁ yakkha sukhī hohi saha sabbehi ñātibhi 7,21. (cfr. 9,28. 38.)
Evaṁ luddaka nandassu saha sabbehi ñātibhi 5,54. — 7,28. — 15,98. 125. — 21,35. 49. (cfr. 9,28. 38.)
Evaṁ Sakka sukhī hohi saha sabbehi ñātibhi 9,28. 38. (cfr. 5,54 etc. — 7,21.)
Es' asmākaṁ kule dhammo 4,147. 148.
Esa selo mahābrahme (mahārāja) pabbato Gandhamādano 22,1838. 2010. 2054.
Esā te upamā rāja atthasandassanī katā 7,89. — 19,33.
Eh' imaṁ ratham āruyha 14,204. — 22,435.
Ehi taṁ anusikkhāmi yathā tvaṁ api 21,36. 50.
Ehi taṁ paṭinessāmi rājaputta 12,71. — 22,22.

Opānabhūtaṁ me gharaṁ tadāsi 17,171. — 22,1389. 1418. (cfr. 10,52.)
Orabbhikā sūkarikā macchikā 19,128. — 22,469.
Orodhā ca kumārā ca vesiyānā ca brāhmaṇā 22,25. 66. 1321. 1325. 1336. 1340. 1447. 1642. 2462.
Osadhehi ca dibbehi disā bhāti 22,2377. (cfr. 16,168.)
Ohāya maṁ ñātigaṇā ekaṁ pāsavasaṁ gataṁ 15,114. — 21,90.

Ka nv' ajja chātā tasitā 22,2181. 2182.
Kacci ārogaṁ yoggan te 22,79. 2419. (cfr. 22,80. 2420.)
Kacci ubho ārogā 22,2290. (cfr. 20,130. 132. — 22,2041. 2048. 2119. 2121. 2290. 2298. 2362. 2409.)
Kacci te sādisī bhariyā 15,130. — 21,62. 168. (cfr. 15,131. — 21,63. 169.)
Kacci daṁsā ca makasā ca 20,131. — 22,2040. 2120. 2297. 2361. 2410. (cfr. 20,133. — 22,2044. 2122. 2299. 2363.)

Kacci nu tâta kusalaṁ kacci tâta anâmayaṁ 22,75. 2417. (cfr. 15,126 etc.)
Kaccin nu bhoto kusalaṁ kacci bhoto anâmayaṁ 15,128. — 20,130. — 21,58. 164. — 22,2041. 2119. 2296. (cfr. 22,75. 2417. — 22,2360. 2362. — 22,2048. 2121. 2298.)
Kacci bhoto amaccesu doso 15,128. — 21,60. 166. (cfr. 15,129. 21,61. 167.
Katañûumhi ca posamhi sîlavante III 12 (22). — 10,63.
Katâ me kalyâṇâ anekarûpâ 21,431. 432.
Kato mayâ saṁgaro brâhmaṇena 21,398. 420. (cfr. 16,69. 70. — 21,404. 405.)
Katth' acchatî kattha-m-upeti ṭhânaṁ 16,111. (cfr. 16,118.)
Kathañ ca kira puttakâmâyo 22,631. 632.
Kathan nâma sâmasamasundarehi 22,674. 675. 676. 677.
Kathaṁ no abhivâdeyya 22,1382. 1384. 1406. 1408.
Kathan no kuñjaraṁ dajjâ 22,1717. (cfr. 22,1917.)
Kathaṁ samuddaṁ patari 4,106. (cfr. 4,107. — 5,56.)
Kathaṁkaro kintikaro kim âcaraṁ 14,158. — 17,81.
Kadalîmigâ bahucitrâ bijârâ 22,1206. (cfr. 21,267.)
Kadâ antepuraṁ rammaṁ 22,158. 159. 160.
Kadâhaṁ ajarathe sannaddhe 22,184. (cfr. 22,215.)
Kadâhaṁ ariyagaṇe vatthavante 22,194. (cfr. 22,225.)
Kadâham assagumbe 22,170. (cfr. 22,201. — 19,48. — 22,1834.)
Kadâhaṁ assarathe sannaddhe 22,178. (cfr. 19,49. — 22,209.)
Kadâhaṁ assârûhe 22,191. (cfr. 22,222.)
Kadâhaṁ oṭṭharathe sannaddhe 22,180. (cfr. 22,211.)
Kadâhaṁ kuṭâgâre vibhatte 22,161. 162. 163. 164.
Kadâhaṁ goṇarathe sannaddhe 22,182. (cfr. 22,213.)
Kadâhaṁ dhanuggahe 22,192. (cfr. 22,223.)
Kadâhaṁ pokkharaṇî rammâ 22,167. (cfr. 14,216. — 22,1222. 2276.
Kadâhaṁ migarathe sannaddhe 22,188. (cfr. 22,219.)
Kadâhaṁ Mithilaṁ phîtaṁ 22,145. 146. 147. 148. 149. 151. 152. 153. 154. 155.

Kadâhaṁ meṇḍarathe sannaddhe 22,186. (cfr. 22,217.)
Kadâhaṁ râjaputte 22,193. (cfr. 22,224.)
Kadâhaṁ rathaseṇiyo 22,172. (cfr. 19,49. — 22,203. 1886.)
Kadâhaṁ Vedehe phīte 22,156. 157.
Kadâhaṁ sajjhurathe sannaddhe 22,176. (cfr. 22,207.)
Kadâhaṁ sovaṇṇe rathe 22,174. (cfr. 22,205.)
Kadâhaṁ hatthārūhe 22,190. (cfr. 22,221.)
Kadâhaṁ hatthigumbe 22,168. (cfr. 19,43. — 22,199. 1882.)
Kadā sattasatā bhariyā 22,195. 196. 197. (cfr. 22,226. 227. 228.)
Kanditena have brahme 7,110. (cfr. 5,114.)
Kammārānaṁ yathā ukkā anto jhâyati 22,825. 1511. 1545.
Kammâsapādena viheṭhitattā 21,471. (cfr. 21,472.)
Karomi te taṁ vacanaṁ 20,104. — 22,247.
Kasiraṅ ca parittañ ca 22,90. (cfr. 11,68.)
Kassa aṁkaṁ pariggayha vālavījanim 20,122. — 22,935.)
Kassa kañcanapaṭṭena puthunā 20,119. — 22,932.
Kassa jambonadaṁ chattaṁ sasalākaṁ 22,934. (cfr. 20,121.)
Kassa paggahitaṁ chattaṁ sasalākaṁ 20,121. (cfr. 22,934.)
Kassa bherī mutiṅgā ca saṁkhā 20,118. — 22,931. (cfr. 22,1199.)
Kassa sutvā sataṁ damami V 249,7. — 19,1.
Kâyaṁ balākā sikhinī corī 3,70. — 5,131. (cfr. 3,71. 73.)
Kā nu vijju-r-ivâbhāsi osadhī 15,220. — 17,108.
Kāni kammāni kubbānaṁ kathaṁ viññū 12,78. 82.
Kāmaṁ kāmayamānassa 12,25. 26.
Kāmaṁ janapado māsi 13,132. — 22,1723. 1724. (cfr. 13,133.)
Kāḷā migā setadantā mama ime 2,25. 26.
Kāsikasucivatthadharā kuṇḍalino 22,647. 648. 649. 722. 723. 724. (cfr. 22,650. 725. 726. 727.)
Kāsiyāni ca dhâretvā khomakodumbarāni ca 22,1801. 1886.
Kicchā laddho piyo putto 22,347. 348.
Kim idaṁ appasaddo va 22,2243. 2244. (cfr. 22,2245–46. 2279–80. 2282–83.)
Kim idaṁ tuṇhībhūto si 22,2245. 2246. (cfr. 2248 etc.)

Kim eva disvā Uruvelavāsi N 282. — VI 220,8.
Kiṁ kammaṁ akarī pubbe 16,30. (cfr. 16,185.)
Kin te jaṭāhi dummedha 1,134. — 4,98.
Kin te vataṁ kim pana brahmacariyaṁ 10,77. — 17,160. — 22,1388. 1412. (cfr. 17,172. — 22,1391. 1416.)
Kin nu ummattarūpo va 10,141. (cfr. 15,144.)
Kin nu t' āyaṁ dijo hoti 15,122. — 21,20. 103.
Kin nu te akaraṁ bālo (dhīro) 13,91. 95.
Kin nu rurū garahasī migānaṁ 13,124. (cfr. 22,442 etc.)
Kiṁsīle kiṁsamācāre purise 6,42. 51.
Kuṇālakā bahucitrā sikhaṇḍī 22,1198. (cfr. 21,285.)
Kuto nu samma āgamma kassa vā pahito tuvaṁ 22,306. 1479.
Kumbhīla makarā c' ettha 22,1208. (cfr. 10,130.)
Kurarī hatachāpā va suññaṁ 22,823. 1811. 1812. 1813 (cfr. 22,821. 1808 etc.)
Kulaputto va jānāti kulaputte pasaṁsituṁ 3,131. 134.
Kusalañ c' eva no (me) brahme 22,2048. 2121. 2298. (cfr. 15,126 etc.)
Kusalaṁ c' eva no rāja atho rāja 20,132. (cfr. 15,126. — 20,130. — 22,2360. 2362.)
Kusalaṁ c' eva me putta 22,78. 2418. (cfr. 22,2048 etc.)
Kusalañ c' eva me samma 22,1478. 1916. (cfr. 22,76 etc.)
Kusalaṁ c' eva me haṁsa 15,127. — 21,60. 166. (cfr. 15,126 etc.)
Kusalaṁ paṭinandāmi Bhūridatta 22,779. 781.
Kusalā naccagītassa sikkhitā 22,98. 110.
Kena te tādiso vaṇṇo II 255,13. (cfr. II 255,25. — III 409 (14).)
Kevalo cāpi nigamo Sivayo 22,1715. 1790. 1738.
Kesesu jāṭaṁ bandhitvā 22,2958. (cfr. 22,2011 etc.)
Ko nu santamhi pajjote III 197,19. — VI 371,11.
Koso ca tuyhaṁ vipulo, koṭṭhāgārañ ca 17,212. 213.

Khaṇant' ālukalambāni 14,279. — 22,2904.
Khattiyamantā ca tayo ca vedā 22,927. 928.

Khattiyassa pamattassa raṭṭhasmiṁ 16,308. — 17,5.
Khattiyā brāhmaṇa vessā suddā 5,68. — 13,8. — 14,72. 73. 74.
Kharājinā jaṭilā paṁkadantā 6,10. — 14,62.
Khippaṁ anteporaṁ gantvā (netvā) rañño dassehi 21,37. 51. (cfr. 21,40.)
Khīrodanaṁ aham adāsiṁ III 409 (11). (cfr. II 255,22.)
Khuddānaṁ lahucittānaṁ akataññuna 21,311. (cfr. IV 144 (8).)

Gacchatha bho gharaṇiyo 22,634. 635.
Gatito ca ratto ca adhimucchito ca 6,16. (cfr. 9,28.)
Gandho isīnaṁ ciradakkhitānaṁ 17,54. 55.
Gambhīrapañhaṁ manasâbhicintayaṁ 17,76. (cfr. 10,69*.)
Gavañ ce taramānānaṁ ujuṁ gacchati 4,135. — 18,106. 170.
Gavañ ce taramānānaṁ jimhaṁ gacchati 4,133. — 18,104. 168.
Gāthā imā atthavatī suvyañjanā 17,91. — 21,445.
Gāme vā yadi vāraññe 5,32. — 6,2. 5. (cfr. 2,54.)
Gāvo bahitiṇassêva omasanti varaṁ varaṁ 21,320. 329.
Guyham atthaṁ asambuddhaṁ 16,209. — VI 388,25.
Guyhañ ca tassa n' akkhāti 12,79. (cfr. 12,85.)
Guyhassa hi guyham eva sādhu VI 381,5. 388,17.

Gharaṁ āvasamānassa gahaṭṭhassa 22,1240. (cfr. 1242.)

Caṁkamaṁ tattha māpesiṁ N 40. — I 7 (11).
Caje cajantaṁ, vanathaṁ na kayirā 2,145. — 4,131.
Catukkaṇṇaṁ va kedāraṁ 6,35. (cfr. 9,3. 5.)
Catubbhi aṭṭh' ajjhagamā 1,103. — 5,98. (cfr. 10,4-5.)

Cando ca suriyo ca ubho sudassanā 14,149. 150.
Cammavāsī chamā seti jātavedaṁ namassati 22,2011. 2016. 2034-2038. 2055. 2059. 2116. 2268.
Cātuddasiṁ pannarasiṁ (pañcadasiṁ) 14,114. — 22,502. 515—16. 523—24. 532—33. 541—42. 548—49. (cfr. 15,226. — 17,176. — 22,1006. 1059.)
Cittakūṭo ti yaṁ āha devarājapavesanaṁ 22,381. (cfr. II 210 (12).)
Cirassaṁ vata passāma 6,183. (cfr. 15,294—95.)
Cirānuvuttham pi piyaṁ manāpaṁ 21,318. (cfr. 21,324.)
Coriyo kaṭhinā h' etā vāḷā I 295,11. — 21,331.
Corīnaṁ bahubuddhīnaṁ yāsu saccaṁ I 296,7. — 16,295. — 21,344.

Janinda nāññatra manussalokā 15,258. (cfr. 17,182.)
Jayo hi Buddhassa sirimato ayaṁ N 274. 275. 276. 277.
Jātarūpamayā kaṇṇā 22,1161. 1173.
Jātimado ca atimānitā ca 15,6. 7.
Jivhā tassa dvidhā hoti 8,50. (cfr. 8,52.)
Jīranti ve rājarathā sucittā 21,409. 443.

Ñātīnañ ca piyo hoti mittesu 3,120. — 16,177.
Ñātīsu mittesu katā me kārā 21,485. 486.

Ḍayhamānena gattena niccaṁ 19,90. 106.
Ḍayhamāno na jānāti 5,20. 22. 24. 26. 28.

Tagarañ ca palāsena yo naro 15,184. — 22,1031.
Taggha te ahaṁ akkhissaṁ yathāpi kusalo tathā 16,172. 181. (cfr. 22,1935.)

Tato kumāre ādāya 22,2147. 2148.
Tato khomañ ca kāyūraṁ 22,2444. 2445.
Tato ca kho so gantvāna Māṭharo 22,1476. 1494.
Tato [ca] rājā taramāno yuttam āruyha sandanaṁ 19,71. — 22,71.
Tato ca rājā pāyāsi senāya 19,6. — 20,107. — 22,1500.
Tato cat' ahaṁ Vedeha 22,1001. (cfr. 22,1061. 1064—67.)
Tato tāta nivattassu, māssu etto paraṁ gami 6,35. — 9,8. 5.
Tato ratyā vivasane 19,124. — 21,188. 372. — 22,1011. 1728. 1820. 2295. 2328. (cfr. 22,1731. 1789.)
Tato vātātape ghore N 295. (cfr. 20,96. 170.)
Tato Vessantaro rājā dānaṁ datvāna khattiyo 22,1898. 2180. 2469.
Tato saṭṭhisahassāni yudhino cārudassanā 22,2374. 2496. 2461.
Tato so rajjum ādāya 22,2152. 2198.
Tato have dhitimā rājaputto 16,78*. 90. 95.
Tatth' addasā kuñjaraṁ chabbisāṇaṁ 16,116. (cfr. 16,107.)
Tatth' addasā pokkharaṇiṁ adūre 16,117. (cfr. 16,112.)
Tatth' ev' ete vattapadā IV 422 v. 11. — 17,48. (cfr. 17,13. 25.)
Tatth' eva sā pokkharaṇī adūre 16,112. (cfr. 16,117.)
Tattha kā nandi kā khiḍḍā 15,37. — 22,115.
Tattha-ppadhānaṁ padahiṁ N 44. — I 10 (80).
Tattha pakkhī sanniratā khemino 21,365. (cfr. 22,1193. 1198.)
Tattha pānāya-m-āyanti nānāmigagaṇā 21,368. (cfr. 22,1204.)
Tattha bindussarā vaggū nānāvaṇṇā 22,1945. 2308.
Tath' acchatī kuñjaro chabbisāṇo 16,107. (cfr. 16,116.)
Tath' eva tvaṁ sabbabhave passa N 139. — III 242 (26).
Tadāsi yaṁ bhiṁsanakaṁ 22,1708. 1709. 1843. 1844. 2149. 2150 2306.
Taṁ abravī mahārājā Sivīnaṁ 22,1856. 1858.
Taṁ abravī rājaputtī Maddī 22,1749. 1754. 1855. 1866. 1882. 1891.
Tañ ca disvāna āyantaṁ jalantaṁ 20,117. — 22,74.
Tañ ca disvāna āyantaṁ pitaraṁ 22,2407. (cfr. 22,2422.)
Taṁ taṁ Kaṇhājinā voca 22,2190. (cfr. 22,2347.)
Taṁ taṁ vadāmi Kosiya: dehi dānaṁ 21,194. 196. 198.
Taṁ tvaṁ bhattaṁ paṭiggayha 14,271. 274. 283.

Taṁ devā paṭinandiṁsu 14,306. — 22,570. (cfr. 15,160 etc.)
Taṁ n' ussahe jīvikattho pahātuṁ 6,15. — 9,23.
Taṁ nāgakaññā caritaṁ gaṇena 15,248. — 22,1874.
Tam me vataṁ taṁ pana brahmacariyaṁ 17,172. — 22,1391. 1415. (cfr. 10,77. — 17,160. — 22,1388. 1412.)
Taṁ lobhā pakataṁ kammaṁ 9,68. (cfr. 9,48.)
Taṁ vo vadāmi, bhaddaṁ vo 7,104. — 13,25. — 16,221.
Taṁ saṁgaraṁ brāhmaṇassa-ppadāya 16,67. 69. 70. — 21,397. 398. 405. 420.
Tasmā phalapuṭassêva ñatvā 15,105. — 22,1062.
Tasmā satañ ca asatañ ca 2,58. — 10,114. — 22,2317.
Tasmā hi chandāgamanaṁ 2,125. — 8,59. — 19,99.
Tasmā hi dhīrassa bahussutassa 11,91. (cfr. 16,258.)
Tasmā hi paṇḍito poso N 296. — 14,200.
Tasmiṁ me Sivayo kuddhā 22,1930. (cfr. 22,1923. 1934.)
Tassânujaṁ dhītaraṁ kāmayāmi 22,1851. (cfr. 1439.)
Tassâvidūre pokkharaṇī 22,2027. 2069.
Tassa taṁ dadato dānaṁ 22,432. (cfr. 22,412.)
Tassa taṁ vacanaṁ sutvā pasādam 21,47. 68.
Tassa te anumodanti ubho Nārada-Pabbatā 22,2203. 2315.
Tassa pāde gahetvāna katvā ca naṁ padakkhiṇaṁ 17,180. — 22,49.
Tassa puṭṭho vyākāsi Mātali 22,443. 446. 449. 452. 455. 458. 462. 465. 468. 471. 474. 477. 480. 486. 490. 495. 499. 506. 512. 520. 529. 538. 546. 552. 566.
Tassa puttā ca dārā ca 6,38. — 9,8.
Tassa rajjass' ahaṁ bhīto 22,86. (cfr. 22,61.)
Tassā me passa vimānaṁ II 255,23. — III 409 (12).
Tassā sumajjhāya piyāya hetu 22,1861. 1440. — VI 327,5.
Tā ca sattasatā bhariyā 22,236–241.
Tālā ca mūlā ca phalā ca 15,199. (cfr. 18,21.)
Ticīvarañ ca patto ca N 273. — III 377,10.

Tiṇalatāni (tiṇalatā ca) osadhyo pabbatāni vanāni ca 16,289. — 22,2303.
Tiṇḍukāni piyālāni madhuke kāsumāriyo 16,151. — 20,186. — 22,337. 396. 2047. 2125. 2309.
Tirokuḍḍaṁ tiroselaṁ samatiggayha pabbataṁ 15,79. 81.
Tumhehi brahme pakato 22,1982. 1988. 1990. 2000.
Tulā yathā paggahitā samadaṇḍā 22,1268. 1269. (cfr. 22,1043.)
Tuvan nu seṭṭho tvaṁ anuttaro si 18,90. — VI 261,10.
Te andhakaraṇe kāme 9,48. (cfr. 9,68.)
Te aroge anuppatte disvāna parame dije 21,83. 189.
Te gantvā dīgham addhānaṁ 22,1911. (cfr. 22,2367. — 11,101.)
Te nūna puttakā mayhaṁ kapaṇāya 22,2217—21.
Te patitā pamuttena bhattunā 21,87. 190.
Te su mattā kilantā ca sampatanti 22,1828. — VI 504,17.
Te hi nūna marissanti 15,86. 90. 96.
Ten' amhi evaṁ jalitānubhāvā II 255,27. — III 409 (16).
Tena me tādiso vaṇṇo II 255,25. — III 409 (14). (cfr. II 255 (18).)
Tesaṁ sokavighātāya tayā anumatā 21,83. (cfr. 21,186.)
Tvaṁ lohitakkho vihatantaraṁso 15,256. — 17,180.)

Thiyā guyhaṁ na saṁseyya 16,288. — VI 388,23.

•

Dajjemu kho te sutanuṁ sunettaṁ 22,1854. (cfr. 22,1155. 1157.)
Dadato ca me na khīyetha 13,99. — 22,2329.
Dadāmi te gāmavarāni pañca 11,24. — 16,61. (cfr. 11,15.)
Dadāmi te brāhmaṇa rohiṇīnaṁ 3,90. — 4,92. — 7,60.
Dadāmi dāni te bhariyaṁ 22,1508. (cfr. 22,2319.)
Dadāmi na vikampāmi 22,1706. (cfr. 22,2306.)
Dadāhi dāni me bhariyaṁ 22,1502. 1505. (cfr. 22,1506. 2319.)

Dadāhi me gāmavarāni pañca 11,15. (cfr. 11,24. — 16,61.)
Dammi nikkhasataṁ ludda 15,110. 230.
Dammi nikkhasahassan te 22,1630. (cfr. 1688)
Daharo c' asi dummedha paṭhamuppattito susu 5,120. (cfr. 22,96.)
Dānaṁ sīlaṁ pariccāgaṁ ajjavaṁ 6,78. — III 320 (6). 412 (20). — 21,176.
Dānāni dehi Koṇḍañña, ahiṁsā 22,597. 602. 604.
Dāsakammakarā beṭṭhā uddhaṁ I 401 (7). — III 234 (24).
Dinnaṁ nikkhasahassam me 22,1688. (cfr. 1630.)
Dinnaṁ me dānaṁ bahudhā bahunnaṁ 21,437. 438.
Divā vā yadi vā rattiṁ 22,1270. 1271.
Disā catasso vidisā catasso I 401 (10). — 16,104.
Disvā khurappe dhanuveganunne 3,43. 44.
Disvāna nāgassa gatiṁ ṭhitiñ ca 16,118. (cfr. 16,111.)
Dīpaṁkaro lokavidū āhutīnaṁ paṭiggaho N 70. 85.
Disvāna patitaṁ Sāmaṁ 22,362. 363. 364. 365. 376. 384.
Dīpā atho pi veyyagghā 19,49. — 22,203-5. 207. (cfr. 22,172 etc.)
Dukkatañ ca hi no putta 22,2370. 2431.
Dukkhaṁ kho me janayatha 22,609. 624. (cfr. 641.)
Dukkhūpanīto pi naro sapañño 13,138. — 22,138.
Duddadaṁ dadamānānaṁ dukkaraṁ kamma 2,57. — 10,118. — 22,2316.
Dunniggahassa lahuno I 312,15. 400 (12).
Dumapphalān' eva patanti mānavā 15,229. — 17,188.
Dulladdham me āsi Sutasoma 17,194. 196. 201. 202.
Devatā nu si gandhabbo ādu Sakko 19,68. — 20,98. — 22,7.
Devaputto mahiddhiko Mātali 14,208. — 22,434.
Devavāhavahaṁ yānaṁ assaṁ āruyha 22,1162. 1174.
Devā na jīranti yathā manussā 11,47. 48.
Deviddhipatto mahānubhāvo 15,257. — 17,181.
Doso rajo na ca pana reṇu vuccati I 118,1. (cfr. I 117,30. 118,2.)
Dvayaṁ yācanako tāta (rāja) 2,121. — 4,89.

Dve ca sādisiyo bhariyā 15,111. 231.
Dve me goṇā mahārāja II 165,28. 166,10.

Dhataraṭṭhā mahārāja haṁsādhipatino 21,38. 41. 52.
Dhan' āpi (dhanam pi) dhanakāmānaṁ nassati 20,175. 178.
Dhanuṁ adejjhaṁ katvāna 6,76. — 13,120.
Dhame dhame nātidhame 1,58. 59.
Dhammaṁ cara mahārāja 17,38—47. — 18,114—122. — 22,401—410. — I 177,28. — IV 401—422 (Cod. B).
Dhammena kira jātassa pitā puttassa makkaṭo 4,151. (cfr. Jāt. (58).)
Dhammena mocehi (mocemi) asāhasena 15,228. 229.
Dhammo patho mahārāja adhammo pana uppatho 19,81. (cfr. 15,343.)
Dhammo have pātur ahosi pubbe 11,28. — III 29 (4).
Dhammo have rakkhati dhammacāriṁ N 224. — 10,86. 87. — 15,342.
Dhavassakaṇṇā khadirā sālā 22,2018. 2056.
Dhārento brāhmaṇaṁ vaṇṇaṁ āsadañ ca 22,2011. 2016. 2034. 2038. 2055. 2069. 2115. (cfr. 2308.)
Dhi-r-atthu kāme subahū 9,89. (cfr. 11,64.)
Dhi-r-atthu taṁ āturaṁ pūtikāyaṁ 3,120. — III 244 (8).
Dhi-r-atthu taṁ yasalābhaṁ 3,110. — 4,36. 38. — 9,68.

•

Nāccāhitaṁ kamma karosi luddaṁ 17,70. (cfr. 10,66*.)
N' atthi citte pasannamhi I 228,12. — III 409 (9).
Nādhicca laddhaṁ na pariṇāmajam me 17,168. — 22,1387. 1411.
N' amhi devo na gandhabbo na pi Sakko 19,84. — 20,94. — 22,8.
Nāyam pure uṇṇamati II 63,2. — VI 346,20.
Nāssa sīlaṁ vijānātha 2,48. 171. — 6,96.

Nâhaṁ evaṁgataṁ jâto 22,510. 536.
Nâhaṁ dukkhapareto pi dhataraṭṭha 15,116. — 21,92. 93.
Nâhaṁ balâkâ sikhinî 3,71. (cfr. 3,74.)
Nâhaṁ Rohanta gacchâmi 15,85. 87. 89. 91.
Na idha santi samaṇabrâhmaṇâ va 22,1393. 1417.
Na kir' atthi anomadassisu I 228,14. — 7,142.
Na kho no deva passâmi 22,2279. 2280. 2282. 2283. 2284. (cfr. 22,2248–49.)
Na guyham atthaṁ vivareyya 16,237. — VI 388,21.
Na c' amhi vyamhito nâga 22,1381. 1405.
Na câyaṁ brâhmaṇo tâta 22,2200. 2248. (cfr. 22,2100.)
Na câham etaṁ icchâmi 14,218. — 22,574.
Na ca mayhaṁ chinnaṁ hadayaṁ 17,200. (cfr. 17,193. 199. 215.)
Na taṁ varaṁ arahati jantu dâtuṁ 21,448. 464.
Na tâdisî arahasi âsanûdakaṁ 21,240. 248. 253.
Na te kaṭṭhâni bhinnâni 13,40. — 18,25. — 22,2277.
Na dhanena na vittena labbhâ 22,1155. 1157. (cfr. 1364.)
Na naṁ umhayate disvâ 2,89. — 12,77.
Na paṇḍitâ attasukhassa hetu V 147 (12). — VI 374,31.
Na pâpajanasaṁsevî 1,137. — 7,12.
Na puttahetu na dhanassa hetu 15,255. — 17,179.
Na Migâjina jâtucca ahaṁ kañci kudâcanaṁ 22,260. 263.
Na me idaṁ tathâ dukkhaṁ 16,282. 294. — 22,309. 310. 2163. 2164.
Na me dessâ ubho cakkhû (puttâ) VI 406 (17). — 22,2311.
Na me piyaṁ appiyaṁ vâpi hoti 16,258. (cfr. 11,91.)
Na me sutaṁ vâ diṭṭhaṁ vâ 5,53. (cfr. 21,102.)
Na ve anatthakusalena atthacariyâ 1,45. 46.
Na ve dissanti sappaññâ 7,58. — (cfr. 20,96.)
Na ve piyaṁ me ti janinda tâdiso 6,83. — 21,457.
Na ve rudanti matimanto sapaññâ 21,306. (cfr. 6,115. — 16,219. 250. 290. — 17,189. 190.)
Na santi devâ, pavasanti nûna 2,83. — 16,288.
Na santhavasmâ param atthi seyyo 2,24. (cfr. 22,21. 28.)

Na so mitto yo sadā appamatto 5,64. 72.
Na ha nūn' imassa rañño 5,47. 48. — 22,713. 714.
Na h' ete ettakā yeva Buddhadhammā N,130. 135. 140. 145. 150. 155. 160. 165. 170.
Nā h' eva vedā aphalā bhavanti 6,18. — 14,65.
Na h' eva sabbattha balena kiccaṁ 5,42. — V 121 (28).
Na hi dhammo, adhammo ca 15,348. (cfr. 19,81.)
Na hi verena verāni 5,110. — 9,14.
Na hi sabbesu ṭhānesu puriso 8,22. 23.
Naggā nadī anodikā I 307,13. — 22,1874.
Nanu Maddī varārohā 22,2253. (cfr. 22,2285. 2294.)
Nanu maṁ samma jānāsi 3,74. (cfr. 3,71.)
Nabhā ca dūre paṭhavī ca dūre 21,410. 444.
Name namantassa, bhaje bhajantaṁ 2,144. — 4,130.
Namo te Kāsirāj' atthu 22,830. 854. (cfr. 15,283.)
Narānam ārāmakarāsu nārisu 21,307. (cfr. III 132,19.)
Nigrodham eva seveyya 1,11. — 10,68.
Niccaṁ ubbiggahadayā 1,136. (cfr. 6,132.)
Niccaṁ ubbegino kākā vaṁkā 6,132. (cfr. 1,136. — 10,125.)
Ninnāditā te paṭhavī 22,2292. 2314.
Niyyamāne pisācena kin nu tāta udikkhasi 22,2160. 2200. 2343.
Nivesanāni māpetvā Vedehassa yasassino 22,1497. 1499.
Nivesanesu sobbhesu rathiyā 22,754. 757.
Nisamma khattiyo kayirā 4,128. — 5,5. — 15,210. — VI 376,1.
Nīce c' olambate suriyo 22,2216. (cfr. 22,2201.)
Nekkhaṁ gīvan te kāressaṁ 20,14—18.

Paṁko ca kāmā palipo ca kāmā 6,14. — 15,302. (cfr. 15,312.)
Pañcamaṁ bhadraṁ adhanassa 19,16. (cfr. 19,12 etc. — 22,245.)
Paññā hi seṭṭhā kusalā vadanti III 348,18. — 17,80.
Paññāy' upetaṁ siriyā vihīnaṁ IV 412,23. — VI 356,9.

Paññö vajjho Mahosadho ti VI 384,26. — VI 386,14.
Paṭiggahītaṁ yaṁ dinnañ [ca] sabbassa 20,138. — 22,1923. 1984. 2040. (cfr. 1920.)
Paṭirājūhi te kaññā ānayissaṁ 22,94. 111.
Paṇḍukambalasañchannaṁ pabhinnaṁ 22,1716. 1918.
Pat' eva patataṁ seṭṭha 15,116. — 21,91.
Pattī' assu mayaṁ bhoto vara taṁ bhaññaṁ icchasi 20,98. (cfr. 7,58.)
Panādo nāma so rājā yassa yūpo suvaṇṇayo 3,40. — IV 325,7.
Pabhāsati idaṁ vyamhaṁ phalikāsu 22,504. 517. 625.
Pabhāsati idaṁ vyamhaṁ veḷuriyāsu 22,508. 634.
Parassa vā attano vāpi hetu VI 360,20. 361,10.
Paripakko me (te) gabbho 17,203. 204.
Parūḷhakacchanakhalomā paṁkadantā 14,228. 277. — 22,1704
Parosātaṁ khattiyā te (me) gahitā 21,453. 454.
Parosataṁ jānapadā mahāsālā 20,106. 140.
Parosataṁ ve (parosahassam) pi samāgatānaṁ 1,98. 100.
Paläsädä (pälasatä) ca gavajā ca mahisā 21,997. — 22,1205.
Pass' ettha pokkharaṇiyo 22,1222. (cfr. 14,218. — 22,167. 2276.)
Passa: toraṇamaggesu nānādijagaṇā 22,1192. (cfr. 21,285.)
Passa: pabbatapādesu nānāmigagaṇā 22,1204. (cfr. 21,286.)
Passa bherī mutiñgā ca 22,1199. (cfr. 20,118. — 22,931.)
Passāmi vo 'haṁ dahariṁ kumāriṁ 7,117. — 15,306. (cfr. 22,40.)
Pahūtabhakkhaṁ bahuannapānaṁ 17,164. 172. — 22,1176. 1235.
Pāṭihāriyapakkhañ ca 14,114. — 22,502. 516. 623. 633. 642. 549.
Pāṭhīnaṁ pāvusaṁ macchaṁ vālajaṁ 10,130. (cfr. 22,1208.)
Pāṇātipātā viratassa brūhi (brūmi) 14,146. 147.
Pāṇātipātā virato nu s' ajja 14,145. 167.
Pātheyyaṁ me karohi tvaṁ saṁkulyā 22,1977. (cfr. 22,2085.)
Pāpāni kammāni karitvāna rāja 6,11. (cfr. 14,68.)
Pitā ca mātā ca upaṭṭhitā me 21,483. 484.
Piyaṁ kho āḷi me (te) hotu 9,101. 102.
Puṇṇaṁ nadiṁ yena ca peyyam āhu 2,128. (cfr. V 122,5.)

Paṇṇaṁ pi ce 'maṁ (o' etaṁ) paṭhaviṁ dhanena 21,323. — 22,1369.
Pūtimacchaṁ kusaggena yo naro 15,182. — 22,1060.
Puthulomamacchākiṇṇaṁ supatitthaṁ 22,1940. 1947.
Puna p' āpajjasī samma 3,72. 76. — 5,135.
Puppharukkhehi sañchannaṁ 22,1944. 2005.
Pubbe va kho si vutto: dukkaraṁ 22,610. 625. 642.
Pubbe va dānā sumanā bhavāma III 300,18. — 10,80.
Purimaṁ sarām' ahaṁ jātiṁ 22,34. (cfr. 22,50.)

Phalānam iva pakkānaṁ niccaṁ 11,85. — 22,117.

Bahujjano pasanno 'si disvā 22,1450. 1845.
Bahum idaṁ mūlaphalaṁ 14,160. — 22,2226.
Bahussutā ye bahuṭhānacintino 6,115. — 15,219. 259. 260. — 17,189. 190. — 21,306.
Bahū janapadā c' aññe negamā ca samāgatā 22,27. (cfr. 13,181. — 22,68. 1323. 1327. 1338. 1342. 1449. 1644.)
Bahūni c' assa (vassa-) pūgāni assame 20,184. — 22,2045.
Bālo tuvaṁ elamūgo si rāja 22,1519. (cfr. 22,1470.)
Bāḷhaṁ kho si .... Sāma 22,336—71.
Bilasataṁ maṁ katvā yajassu 22,716. 717.
Brahāvāḷamigākiṇṇaṁ 22,356. 357. 358. 359.

Bhaṇaṁ kaṇṇasukhaṁ vācaṁ 15,100. 101.
Bhaddako vat' ayaṁ pakkhī dijo 2,170. — 6,85. — 14,13. — 15,154.
Bhamarā pupphagandhena 22,2062. 2067. 2081. (cfr. 22,2108.)
Bhayaṁ hi maṁ vindati sūta disvā 13,124. — 22,442. 445. 448. 451. 454. 457. 461. 464. 467. 470. 473. 477. 482. 489. (cfr. 22,494 etc.)

Bharāmi mātāpitaro 7,24. (cfr. 7,27.)
Bharukacchā payātānaṁ vāṇijānaṁ 5,57. — 11,106. 108. 110. 112. 114. 116.
Bhave ca nandati tassa 12,88. (cfr. 12,80.)
Bhūmindharo Varuṇo nāma nāgo 22,1350. 1499.
Bhogī hi te santi idh' ūpapannā 22,1394. 1418.

Maṁsarasabhojanā nahāpakasunahātā 22,650. 725. 726. 727.
Maṇayo saṁkhamuttañ ca vatthakaṁ 21,184. — 22,224.
Maṇī mama vijjati lohitaṁko 17,186. — VI 274 (22).
Mataṁ marissaṁ rodanti 5,113. — 7,100.
Maddī ca sirasā pāde 22,2408. (cfr. 2423.)
Manussattaṁ liṅgasampatti N 69. — I 44,20.
Manussassêva me sīsaṁ 4,81. 82.
Manussindaṁ jahitvāna 4,177. — III 362 (24).
Manoharo nāma maṇī mamāyaṁ 22,1184. (cfr. 17,186.)
Mayam eva bāl' amhase elamūgā 22,1470. (cfr. 22,1519.)
Maraṇaṁ vā tayā saddhiṁ jīvitaṁ vā 21,3. — 22,1730.
Mahāmattā ca me atthi 11,101. (cfr. 22,1911.)
Mahārājass' ahaṁ dhītā 6,41. (cfr. 6,50.)
Mahārukkhassa phalino āmaṁ chindati 18,172. (cfr. 18,174.)
Mahārukkhūpamaṁ raṭṭhaṁ adhammena 18,173. (cfr. 18,175.)
Mā tavaṁ Cande rodi 14,27. (cfr. 17,206. — 22,710.)
Mā tvaṁ bhāyī mahārāja 22,1547—53.
Mā naṁ rūpena pāmesi 20,21—33.
Mā no deva avadhi, dase no dehi 22,605—8. 620—28. 690—93.
Mā putta saddahesi: sugatī kira hoti 22,598. 601.
Mā [ca] putte mā ca patiṁ addakkhi 14,35. 36. — 22,686—89.
Mā bāḷhaṁ paridevesi 22,315. (cfr. 22,349.)
Mā bhāyi patataṁ seṭṭha, na hi bhāyanti 21,100. 127.
Mā me janapado āsi 13,133. (cfr. 13,132. — 22,1723—24.)

Mâtaraṁ pitarañ câpi jiṇṇake 12,44. 55. 56.
Mâtaraṁ pitaraṁ mayhaṁ vatto vajjâsi vandanaṁ 22,48. 821.
Mâtâpitâ disâ pubbâ âcariyâ I 401 (5). — III 234 (22).
Mâtâpitâ samaṇabrâhmaṇâ ca 11,35. 38.
Mâtâpettibharaṁ jantuṁ kule I 202,3. — 22,1786.
Mâyâ c' esâ marîci ca soko rogo c' upaddavo I 288 (18). — II 330 (19). — 21,118. — V 431 (28).
Mâlañ ca gandhañ ca vilepanañ ca 22,1390. 1414.
Mâlâgirî Himavâ yo ca Gijjho 22,890. 916.
Migânaṁ vighâsam anvesaṁ 22,817. 851.
Mitte tass' eva bhajati amitte 12,84. (cfr. 12,78.)
Mutto Campeyyako nâgo 15,228. (cfr. 22,820. 884.)
Mutto tuvaṁ porisâdassa hatthâ 21,400. 426. 480. (cfr. 16,71. — 21,406.)
Musâ tâsaṁ yathâ saccaṁ saccaṁ tâsaṁ I 295,9. — 21,329. (cfr. 21,320.)
Moho rajo na ca pana reṇu vuccati I 118,2. (cfr. I 117,30.)

Yakkhâ pisâcâ athavâpi petâ 15,331. (cfr. 15,332.)
Yajassu yaññaṁ khâda maṁ porisâda 21,427. 438. (cfr. 430.)
Yato sarâmi attânaṁ yato patto 'smi viññutaṁ 8,30. — 11,117. — 22,302.
Yattha posaṁ na jânanti jâtiyâ vinayena vâ 3,11. — 4,15.
Yattha verî nivisati (nivasati) 1,102. — 7,61.
Yathâ andaghare puriso ciravuttho N 138. — III 242 (24).
Yathâpi bîjaṁ aggismiṁ ḍayhati III 12, (21). — 10,52.
Yathâpi maccho balisaṁ vaṁkaṁ 22,1467. (cfr. 22,1514.)
Yathâpi himavâ brahme pabbato Gandhamâdano 16,183. (cfr. 22,2376—77.)
Yathâ âraññakaṁ nâgaṁ poto anveti 19,57. (cfr. 22,1758.)
Yathâ nadî ca pantho ca 1,64. — 21,319.

Yathâ pita vâ athavâpi mâtâ 21,473. 474.
Yathâ yâcitakaṁ yânaṁ yathâ 14,212. — 22,578.
Yathâ ye keci Sambuddhâ N 191—93.
Yathâ vârivaho pûro 22,2128. 2305. (cfr. 22,106. 107.)
Yad esamânâ vicaranti loke 14,91. (cfr. 14,159.)
Yadâ ca sarasampanno moro 4,151. (cfr. 4,156.)
Yadâ dakkhisi naccante kumâre 22,1766. 1767.
Yadâ dakkhisi mâtaṅgaṁ kuñjaraṁ 22,1768. 1769.
Yadâ dakkhisi hemante puppbite 22,1779. 1781.
Yadâ parâbhavo hoti poso 2,28. — 7,28. — 15,119. — 21,23.
Yadâ morîhi parikiṇṇaṁ 22,1776—78.
Yadâ hemantike mâse 22,1780. 1782.
Yadi kira yajitvâ puttehi 22,627. 628.
Yadi te suto Puṇṇako nâma yakkho 22,1350. 1488.
Yadi sakuṇi maṁsaṁ icchasi 22,655—62.
Yaṁ âhu devesu Sujampatîti 15,56. — 17,52.
Yaṁ etâ upasevanti chandasâ 3,98. 99. — 15,290. — 21,347.
Yaṁ kiñc' atthi kataṁ puññaṁ 22,353. 886. 2442.
Yaṁ kiñci ratanaṁ atthi 21,188. (cfr. 22,747.)
Yan taṁ Kaṇhâjinâ voca 22,2347. (cfr. 22,2199.)
Yaṁ tv-eva jaññâ sadiso maman ti 2,22. (cfr. 22,1518.)
Yaṁ nissitâ jagatiruhaṁ vihaṁgamâ 1,35. — 9,56.
Yan nu gijjho yojanasataṁ kuṇapâni 2,37. — 7,25.
Yaṁ yaṁ hi râja bhajati 15,160. — 22,1047.
Yaṁ hi kayirâ taṁ hi vade 4,78. — 5,71. — 6,31.
Yasmiṁ mano nivisati 1,67. (cfr. 13,34.)
Yass' ete caturo dhammâ 1,50. — 2,146. — V 122 (20). (cfr. 1,57.)
Yassa kâyena vâcâya manasâ 4,187. — 9,82.
Yassa pubbe anîkâni 22,1794—95. (cfr. 1792—93.)
Yassa pubbe dhajaggâni 22,1792—93. (cfr. 1794—95.)
Yassa ratyâ vivasane 22,101. (cfr. 19,124 etc.)
Yassa rukkhassa châyâya nisîdeyya 14,196. — 18,153. — 22,10. 1365. — VI 375,11.

Yassā hi dhammaṁ puriso (manujo) vijaññā 21,487. — VI 375,19.
Yā te sā bhariyā anariyarūpā 10,75. 76.
Yā daliddī daḷidassa aḍḍhā 4,80. — 22,1876.
Yādisaṁ kurute mittaṁ 15,161. — 22,1048.
Yānanāvā ca me hotha acalā 22,2144. 2146.
Yāni karoti puriso tāni attani passati 2,143. — 5,16.
Yāvatā candimasuriyā pariharanti I 132 (1). — 3,22.
Yāvanto purisass' atthaṁ guyhaṁ 16,240. — VI 388,27.
Yuvā ca daharo cāsi paṭhamuppattito susu 22,95. (cfr. 5,120.)
Yuvā care brahmacariyaṁ 22,96. 97.
Y' assu pubbe hatthivaradhuragate 22,651. (cfr. 22,652—54.)
Ye kec' ime maccharino kadariyā 21,207. — 22,447.
Ye khattiyā ye idha bhūmipālā 21,451. 452.
Ye na (ca) kāhanti ovādaṁ 2,87. 88.
Ye jīvalokasmiṁ asādhukammino 22,468. 487.
Ye jīvalokasmiṁ supāpadhammino 22,450. 459.
Ye brāhmaṇā vedagū sabbadhamme 2,18. 18[b].
Ye maṁ pure paccudenti araññā 22,2236. (cfr. 7,106.)
Ye vuddhā ye ca daharā 22,1827. 2325.
Yena saccen' ayaṁ Sāmo 22,377—82. 385. (cfr. 729.)
Yena sattu bilaṅgā ca I 424,20. — VI 365,21.
Yesaṁ pubbe khandhesu 22,719—20.
Yesaṁ rāgo ca doso ca avijjā ca virājitā 7,139. — 15,23.
Yesaṁ vo ediso dhammo adhammo 3,63. 90.
Yo atthakāmassa hitānukampino 1,40. 41. 42. — 6,16.
Yo alīnena cittena 1,54. (cfr. 1,56.)
Yo icche puriso hotuṁ jātijātiṁ punappunaṁ 22,1076. 1077.
Yo kopaneyye na karoti kopaṁ IV 14,24. — VI 257,21.
Yo ca { 'dha / ve } uppatitaṁ atthaṁ 4,163. 164. — 6,62. 63. — 8,25.
26. — 10,96. 97.
Yo ca etāni ṭhānāni 12,48. (cfr. 12,64. — 16,176.)
Yo ca yācanajīvāno kāle 7,56. 57.

Yo ca rājā addhammaṭṭho 18,180. (cfr. 19,108.)
Yo ca vantakāsāv' assa sīlesu 8,141. — 16,123.
Yo cajetha mahārāja bhattāraṁ 22,1628. 1629.
Yo taṁ (te) vissāsaye tāta vissāsañ ca 4,188. — 9,81.
Yo te (me) kato saṅgaro brāhmaṇena 21,404. 405. (cfr. 16,69. 70. — 21,398. 420.)
Yo disvā bhikkhuṁ caraṇūpapannaṁ 6,112. 113.
Yo dukkhaphuṭṭhāya bhaveyya tāṇaṁ 1,101. — 2,133.
Yo pahaṭṭhena cittena 1,55. (cfr. 1,54.)
Yo pubbe katakalyāṇo 1,89. — 7,102–3. (cfr. 4,8.)
Yo maṁ pure paccudeti araññe 7,105. (cfr. 22,2236.)
Yo mātaraṁ pitaraṁ vā 10,72–73. (cfr. 22,398–99.)
Yo m' issaro tattha ahosi rājā 22,1309. 1423.
Yo yācataṁ gatī āsi savantīnaṁ 22,1900. 2340.
Yo yācataṁ patiṭṭhāsi bhūtānaṁ 22,1989. 2339.
Yo ve dassan ti vatvāna 15,62. 63.

Rañño 'haṁ pahito dūto 16,146. 149. 153. 171.
Raṭṭhe vilumpamānamhi 19,17. — 22,247.
Rattimhi corā khādanti 16,319. 324. 328. 333. 338.
Ramassu bhikkhācariyāya putta 15,316. (cfr. 17,84.)
Rāgo rajo na ca pana reṇu vuccati I 117,20. (cfr. I 118,2.)
Rājaputti ca no mātā rājaputto ca no pitā 22,2227. 2350. (cfr. 2349.)
Rājā apucchi (avoca) Vidhūraṁ 7,128. — 14,222.
Rājāhaṁ asmi Kāsīnaṁ 22,294. 334.
Rājā ca pabbajjam arocayittha 15,314–16.
Rājā ca paṭhaviṁ sabbaṁ sasamuddaṁ 21,340. (cfr. 12,29.)
Rājā pasayha paṭhaviṁ vijetvā 12,29. (cfr. 21,340.)
Rājā me so dijo mitto (dijāmitta) sakhā 15,123. — 21,21. (cfr. 21,104.)

Rājā sabba-Videhānaṁ adā dānaṁ 22,412. (cfr. 22,421.)
Rūpe ca sadde ca atho rase ca N 283. — VI 220,18.
Roditena have brahme 5,114. (cfr. 7,110.)

Lakkhī vata me udapādi ajja 6,114. — 14,10.
Laṁghī samuddaṁ pakkhandi 10,4. (cfr. 1,108. — 5,98.)
Laddho piṇḍo na pīṇeti 6,182. (cfr. 10,125.)
Lāpūni sīdanti silā plavanti I 336,14. — 1,78.
Lābhā vata me anapparūpā VI 355,10. (cfr. 22,1628.)
Lābho alābho ayaso yaso ca 4,114. — IV 129 (2).

Vaṇṇārohena jātiyā balā 5,60. 61.
Vandāmi taṁ kuñjara 5,39. (cfr. 5,40.)
Vayhāhi pariyāyitvā sivikāya rathena ca 22,1802. 1886. (cfr. 1918.)
Varañ ce me ado Sakka 10,14. 21. 28. — 13,86. 88. 90. 94. 98. 101. — 17,139. — 22,1689. 2328.
Vāti gandho timirānaṁ 5,55. (cfr. 4,105.)
Vāti cāyaṁ tato gandho 4,105. (cfr. 5,55.)
Vāpitaṁ ropitaṁ dhaññaṁ N 43. — I 10 (28).
Vāyameth' eva puriso 1,51. 120. — 13,136. 187. — 22,136. 187.
Vicittavatthābharaṇā āmuttamaṇikuṇḍalā 14,188. — 22,1068.
Vicinanto tadā dakkhiṁ N 126. 131. 136. 141. 146. 151. 156. 161. 166. 171.
Vitti hi maṁ vindati sūta disvā 22,494. 498. 505. 511. 519. 528. 537. 544. 551. 559. 561. (cfr. 22,442 etc.)
Viditāni te mahārāja āvāsaṁ pāpakamminaṁ 22,492. 554.
Vidhura vasamānassa gahaṭṭhassa 22,1242. (cfr. 1249.)
Vibbhantacittā kupitindriyāsi 7,48. (cfr. 15,222.)
Virate methunā dhammā 14,223. 229. 233. 237. 241. 246. 250. 254. 258. 262. 266.

Vivādamanto dutiyo, ken' eko 22,279. 287.
Vivicca bhāseyya divā rahassaṁ 16,241. — VI 388,29.
Vividhāni pupphajātāni asmiṁ upari pabbate 22,2174. 2194. 2270.
Vividhāni phalajātāni asmiṁ upari pabbate 22,2175. 2195. 2271.
Vīsatiṁ c' eva vassāni tahiṁ rajjam akārayiṁ 22,85. 60.
Vehāsayaṁ agamā bhūripañño 15,14. (cfr. 16,85. — 17,51.)
Vyākāsi Āyuro (Pukkuso) pañhaṁ 7,41. 43.

Sa Puṇṇako Kurunaṁ kattuseṭṭhaṁ 22,1358. 1376. 1432. 1486.
Sa rājā isinā satto antalikkhecaro 8,58. (cfr. 19,98.)
Sa rājā paridevesi bahuṁ 22,328. 331.
Sa vītarāgo pavineyya dosaṁ 17,84. (cfr. 15,216.)
Saṁvāsena have Sakka 5,112. — 7,108.
Sakid eva Sutasoma sabbhi hotu 21,407. 441.
Sakuṇī hataputtā na suññaṁ 22,821. 822. 1808. 1809. 1810. (cfr. 22,823. 1811 etc.)
Sakko 'ham asmi devindo 15,72. — 22,2322.
Sakko pi paṭinanditvā 14,207. — 22,571.
Saṁkappam etaṁ paṭiladdha pāpaṁ 10,69*. (cfr. 17,76.)
Saṁketh' eva amittasmiṁ 2,90. — 16,252.
Saṁkeyya saṁkitabbāni rakkheyya 4,44. — 7,127.
Saṁgākako sakhilo saṇhavāco 6,53. — 11,50. (cfr. 17,78.)
Sace gacchasi Pañcālaṁ khippaṁ 22,1409. 1516.
Sace pi (hi) vāto girim āvaheyya 15,235.* — 21,402.
Sace maṁ vitanitvāna vedhayissasi 22,1606—9.
Sace maṁsañ ca pātabbaṁ sūle 22,1602—5.
Sace me dāsaṁ dāsiṁ vā 22,1067. 1973.
Sace me hatthe [ca] pāde ca 22,1598—1601.
Sace vo vuyhamānānaṁ satannaṁ V 75,2. — 22,1646.
Sace hi dhānakāmo si 22,801. 804.
Sace hi saccaṁ bhaṇasi 8,47. 49. 51. 53. 55. 57.

Sace hi so issaro sabbaloke 22,900—2.
Saccaṁ kir' evaṁ āhaṁsu narā ekacciyā idha 1,72. — 13,128. 22,2180. (cfr. 6,78.)
Saccaṁ kira tvaṁ api bhūripañño IV 72,15. — VI 372,1.
Saccaṁ te paṭijānāmi 20,71. 74.
Saṭṭhi assasahassāni 19,46. (cfr. 22,170. 1834.)
Saṭṭhi nāgasahassāni 19,48. (cfr. 22,168. 1832.)
Saṭṭhi rathasahassāni 19,49. (cfr. 22,172. 1836.)
Satta assasate datvā 22,1834. (cfr. 19,46. — 22,170.)
Satta no māse vasataṁ araññe 22,2123. 2130. (cfr. 22,1985.)
Satta rathasate datvā 22,1836. (cfr. 22,172. 176. 178. — 19,49.)
Satta hatthisate datvā 22,1832. (cfr. 22,168. — 19,48.)
Satthā ca me hosi sakhā ca me si 21,469. (cfr. 21,470.)
Saddhāhaṁ devī manujesu pūjitā (21,250. (cfr. 21,236. 243.)
Saddho mudū saṁvibhāgī vadaññū 11,60. — 17,78
Santi vehāsayā nāgā iddhimanto 22,1524. (cfr. 22,1525—27.)
Sandhiṁ katvā amittena aṇḍajena 2,29. — 16,251.
Sabbaṁ narānaṁ saphalaṁ suciṇṇaṁ 15,25. 26. 27.
Sabbamhi tamhi araññamhi 22,2454—50.
Sabbalokaviraddho si dhaṁka 10,198. (cfr. 6,132.)
Sabbasaṁkārako n' atthi suddhaṁ I 424,12. — VI 336 (16).
Sabbā nadī vaṁkagatā (vaṁkanadī) sabbe kaṭṭhamayā vanā I 289,20. — V 435,16. — VI 281,25.
Sabbā sīmantiniyo gacchatha 22,687. 688.
Sabbe vajanti sugatiṁ ye yajanti 22,611. 626. 643. (cfr. 630.)
Sabbesu bhūtesu nidhāya daṇḍaṁ 15,216. — 17,84.
Sabbesu vippamuttesu ye ca tattha samāgatā 22, 730. 738—46.
Sabbhir eva samāsetha 2,78. — 21,408. 442.
Samaṇaṁ brāhmaṇaṁ vāpi upāsemu 22,667. 660.
Samaṇe tuvaṁ (mayaṁ) brāhmaṇe addhike ca 10,52. 81. (cfr. 14,112. — 17,171 etc. — 22,1876.)
Samaṇe brāhmaṇe cāpi sīlavante bahussute 12,46. — 22,1264—67.
Samaṇe brāhmaṇe nūna 22,1959. 2266.

Samatittiyaṁ anavasesaṁ 1,95. — III 235 (1).
Samāgatā janapadā negamā samāgatā 13,181. — 22,68. 1828. 1837. 1838. 1842. 1440. 1644. (cfr. 22,27.)
Samuddhato me si tuvaṁ papātā 22,1359. (cfr. 22,1360.)
Sampassato lokam imaṁ 11,91. — 16,258.
Sammaddat' eva gandhena 22,2081. 2081.
Sasamuddapariyāyaṁ mahiṁ sāgarakuṇḍalaṁ 4,37. — 9,82. — 22,1669.
Sasetacchattaṁ saupatheyyaṁ 22,1719. 1919.
Sahassayuttaṁ hayavāhiṁ dibbaṁ yānaṁ 22,563. 563.
Sahassavedo pi na taṁ paṭicca 6,12. — 14,64.
Sā Kosiyenānumatā jutīmatā 21,250. 272.
Sā devatā antarahitā pabbate Gandhamādane 22,328. 887.
Sā nūnāhaṁ ito gantvā rañño muttā nivesanā 8,13. 14.
Sā nūna kapaṇā ammā 22,311. 2165. 2167. 2169.
Sā nūna cakkavākīva pallalasmiṁ 22,824. 1814–16.
Sā senā mahatī āsi 22,2391. 2394.
Sākaṁ bhisaṁ madhuṁ maṁsaṁ 14,280. (cfr. 22,1922.)
Sādūni ramaṇīyāni santi 4,178. — III 362 (27).
Sādhu kho si anuppatto 14,208. — 22,572.
Sādhu bhāsat' ayaṁ yakkho 11,68. (cfr. 22,80.)
Sādhu sakkhi kataṁ hoti 9,24. 34.
Sādhu sambahulā ñātī api rukkhā araññajā 1,73. — 14,176.
Sāmā ca soṇā ca balā ca gijjhā 19,110. (cfr. 22,445.)
Sāyam eke na dissanti 11,80. — 22,118.
Sālā va sampamathitā 22,826. 1319. 1819.
Sālīnaṁ bhojanaṁ (odanaṁ) bhuñje sūciṁ 4,34. 179.
Siṅgī migo āyatacakkhunetto 3,49. — 6,96.
Sir' āhaṁ devī manujesu pūjitā 21,298. (cfr. 21,348. 350.)
Sīlaṁ kir' eva kalyāṇaṁ 1,85. — 3,118. — 4,117.
Sīsaṁnahāte sucivatthe 22,2358. (cfr. 22,2434. 2449.)
Sīhavyagghā ca dīpī ca 16,262. (cfr. 21,303. — 22,1904.)
Sukiccharūpaṁ paridevayavho 15,170–2.

Sukhaṁ jīvitarūpo 'smi 2,139. (cfr. 2,188.)
Suññaṁ mātā rathaṁ disvā 22,50. 68.
Suṇantu me jānapadā negamā ca samāgatā 9,59. (cfr. 15,201.)
Suṇasī Sīvali gāthā 22,280. 288.
Suṇohi etaṁ (mêtaṁ) vacanaṁ: passas' etaṁ mahabbhayaṁ 22,1532. 1534. 1586. 1588.
Sudassanassa girino dvāraṁ h' etaṁ pakāsati II 214 (12). — 22,561.
Subhāsitan te anumodiyānaṁ 17,68. 74. 79. 81.
Surabhī taṁ vanaṁ vāti 22,2031. (cfr. 22,2067. 2081.)
Suvassa ca varaṁ datvā 9,29. 89.
Suvijānaṁ sigālānaṁ sakuntānaṁ 13,32. 57. 129.
Susukhaṁ vata jīvāma 22,245 (cfr. 19,16). 247 (cfr. 19,17.) 248.
Susukhaṁ vata saṁvāso paṇḍitehi 22,1567. 1689.
Sevamāno sevamānaṁ samphuṭṭho 15,182. — 22,1049.
Sv' ājj' evaṁ gate kāle na kiñci-m-abhibhāsati 22,925. (cfr. 22,906 etc.)
So 'haṁ abbūḷhasallo 'smi 5,12. 117. — 7,118. — 10,108. 132.
So 'ham evaṁ pajānāmi 22,116. (cfr. 15,88.)
So 'haṁ gantvā manussesu 14,214. — 22,575. (cfr. II 257,1.)
So 'haṁ sataṁ aññataro 'smi haṁsa 9,21. (cfr. 6,15.)
So ahaṁ su-ppajānāmi 15,88. (cfr. 22,116.)
So karassu ānubhāvaṁ, vītivattassu sīliyaṁ 4,84. — 10,127.
So ce attho ca dhammo ca kalyāṇo 18,140. 143. 146. 150. 155.
So codito brāhmaṇiyā brāhmaṇo 22,1984. (cfr. 22,1848. 1850.)
So te karissāmi yathānubhāvaṁ 4,27. 182.
So te suva varaṁ dammi 9,25. 85.
So ūna kapaṇo tāta 22,312. 2166. 2168. 2170.
So patīto pamuttena bhattunā 21,34. 48.
Soḷas' itthisahassāni āmuttamaṇikuṇḍalā 15,227. — 22,1671. (cfr. 19,54.)
Soḷasāhi ca battiṁsa 1,102. — 5,98. — 10,5.
Sovaṇṇamayaṁ maṇīmayaṁ 10,101. 142.

Svāgatan te mahārāja (mahābrahme), atho te adurāgataṁ 15,150. — 20,135. — 22,82. 336. 392. 1921. 2046. 2124. 2301. (cfr. 14,206. — 22,570.)

Sv-ādhippāgā Bhāradvājo 16,144. 148. 152. 170.

Haṁsā koñcā mayūrā ca 21,265. — 22,1192. (cfr. 2,99.)

Hāṁsi tuvaṁ evaṁ maññesi seyyo I 424,17. — VI 343 (83).

Hatthānīkaṁ rathānīkaṁ asse pattī ca 22,91. 108. (cfr. 22,1188.)

Hatthārūhā anīkaṭṭhā rathikā pattikārikā 11,100. — 16,312. — 20,80. — 22,26. 67. 1322. 1336. 1337. 1341. 1448. 1643. 1714. 1730. 1738. 1741. 2463. (cfr. 16,98.)

Hatthārohe anīkaṭṭhe rathike pattikārike 22,1189. 1285. 1572.

Hatthī assarathā pattī gacch' evādāya 18,4. — 22,1632.

Hatthī assā rathā patti senā tiṭṭhanti 22,1507. 1508.

Hatthī gavāssā maṇikuṇḍalā ca 22,1232-38. — VI 361,18.

Hatthīhi assehi rathehi pattihi 13,323. 324.

Hanti hatthehi pādehi VI 370,28. 376,14. (cfr. III 152,8)

Handa ca maṁ upagūha 22,699-701.

Haliddirāgaṁ kapicittaṁ purisaṁ 4,188. — 9,84.

Himavā yathā Gandharo pabbato Gandhamādano 22,2376. (cfr. 16,163.)

Hīnena brahmacariyena khattiye upapajjati 8,75. — 22,418.

LIST OF QUOTATIONS

FROM OTHER WORKS BY THE EDITOR.

Abhidhāna, ed. by Subhūti
637 .... Jāt. VI 564.

Attanagalu-vaṁsa, ed. by d'Alwis
47 .... Jāt. VI 1.
167 .... — VI 68.

Buddhavaṁsa, ed. by Morris
II v. 11-12.. Jāt. I 4,11.13.16.
— 38 ... — I 11,29.
— 63 ... — I 13,16.
— 66 ... — I 16,8.
— 88 ... — I 17,28.
— 100 ... — I 19,18.
— 124 ... — I 20,33.
— 125 ... — I 21,1.
— 176 ... — I 27,2.
— 192 ... — I 28,21.
VIII v. 1. .. — I 36,10.

Cariyā-piṭaka, ed. by Morris
I 8 v. 16... Jāt. IV 406 (17).
I 9 v. 66... — I 47,14.
I 10 v. 21.. — I 45,18.
II 10 v. 7.... — I 45,27.
III 6 v. 18.... — I 46,33.
III 9 v. 11.... — I 215,1.
III 11 v. 11-12. Jāt. IV 31,9.
III 13 v. 8..... — I 47,8.
III 15 v. 1..... — I 47,7.
page 73...... — IV 230,19.
— IV 242,25.
— 74...... — IV 15,1.
— 76...... — VI 95,12.
— 77...... — VI 129,15.
— 78...... — VI 479,1.
— 82...... — III 51,9.
— 85...... — IV 464,5.
VI 157,24.
— 86...... — IV 22,4.
— 87...... — IV 255,14.
— 88...... — IV 375,2.
— 89...... — IV 100,12.
— 90...... — V 21,1.
— 91...... — V 161,20.
— 92...... — IV 119,12.
— 94...... — IV 491,7.
IV 304,26.
— 96...... — VI 1,2.
— 99...... — IV 27,24.
— 100...... — V 456,18.
— 101...... — VI 68,24.
III 13,8.

Dhammapadam ed. V. Fausbøll

v. 3-5 ..... Jât. III 212,8.
488,5.
9-10..... — II 198,8.
V 50,27.
21 ...... — V 99,28.
33 ...... — I 400,26.
35 ...... — I 312,15.
400,12.
36 ...... — I 400,15.
37 ...... — I 400,18.
38 ...... — I 400,20.
39 ...... — I 400,23.
49 ...... — I 349,14.
54-56.... — III 291 (18).
61 ... .. — III 73,4.
66 ...... — III 291 (29).
67 ...... — III 291 (32).
69 ...... — III 291 (27).
76-77.... — III 367 (25).
79 ...... — III 442,1.
97 ...... — III 78 (17).
98 .... III 169,14. 229,18
103 ...... Jât. I 314,11.
116 .. ... — IV 490,27.
119-20.... — I 231,5.
121 ...... — III 169,14.
125 ...... — III 203,16.
130 ...... — III 292 (3).
146 ...... — V 11,25.
151 ...... — V 483,15.
153-54.... — I 76,23.
158 ...... — II 441,21.
— III 333,6.
168 ...... — III 268,7.
179-80.... — I 79,23.
186-87.... — II 313,18.
188-92.... — I 97,11.
v. 200 ...... Jât. VI 54,27.
205 ...... — III 196,22.
285 ...... — I 183,16.
306 ...... — II 416,30.
325 ...... — III 243,16.
328-30.... — III 488,16.
337 ...... — V 72,9.
363 ...... — II 350,17.
371 ...... — IV 422 ²).
394 ...... — I 481,28
— III 85,13.
page 90,3 ... — IV 496,17.
95,23... — IV 60,5.
96,22... — III 157,12.
103 ... — III 486
108,7 ... — III 488,16.
116 ff.... — I 2.
118,3 ... — I 60,30.
126,20... — I 31,31.
IV 54,30. 496,13.
146,8 ... — I 144,19.
146,25... — II 163,22.
147,12... — I 483,29.
148,11... — IV 158,22.
149,11... — III 539,11.
149,25... — II 241,9.
186 ff.... — I 198.
211 ff.... — IV 144.
215,24... — III 144,8.
215,28... — III 29,9.
216 ... — I 133.
275,4.... — II 97,5.
304 ... — I 170.
317 ff.... — II 164.
327 ff.... — I 145.
329,27... — I 152,17.
— IV 43,13.
[338 ff.... — IV 187.]

page 341,$_{1}$ ... Jāt. IV 192,$_{6}$.
351 ff.... — V 412.
360,$_{6}$ ... — III 164,$_{13}$.
404,$_{1}$ ... — IV 320,$_{19}$
415 ff.... — I 418.
— II 365.
417,$_{9}$ ... — II 369,$_{16}$.
417,$_{23}$... — II 381,$_{21}$.
418 ff.... — II 175.
419 ... — II 178.

Dīpavaṁsa

page 26 ..... — III 454.

Jātaka

(I 88....... .. — VI 479).
I 126....... — I 170.
I 133....... — IV 148.
I 160....... — III 64.
I 241,$_{29}$..... — III 524
I 278....... — II 206.
— III 133.
I 279,$_{24}$..... — I 31,$_{15}$.
I 308....... — II 234.
I 369....... — III 193.
I 404....... — II 181.
I 411....... — II 179.
I 480....... — III 84.
I 495....... — II 132.
— III 97.
II 23........ — II 314.
II 74........ — II 208.
II 125....... — II 206.
II 132....... — III 97.
II 158....... — III 133.
II 206....... — II 125,$_{10}$.
— III 133.
II 267....... — III 197.
II 282....... — III 78.
II 314,$_{21}$..... — II 23,$_{25}$.
II 318,$_{24}$.... Jāt. III 524.
II 404...... — IV 342
II 404,$_{8}$ .... — IV 343.
II 406,$_{5}$ .... — IV 345.
II 408,$_{14}$.... — IV 349.
II 412,$_{4}$ .... — IV 39.
II 429...... — III 193.
III 18....... — III 397.
III 51....... — V 33,$_{17}$.
III 58 ...... — III 435.
III 90....... — V 424. 428.
III 99,$_{8}$ ..... — IV 48,$_{16}$.
III 100...... — III 193.
III 154...... — IV 30.
III 208...... — III 397.
III 213...... — III 388.
III 215...... — III 390.
III 238.... . — V 247.
III 412...... — IV 422.
III 454...... — II 311.
III 463...... — V 132.
III 469...... — IV 401.
III 487,$_{30}$.... — III 490.
IV 11,$_{18}$..... — IV 435.
IV 37....... — V 247.
IV 41,$_{20}$..... — IV 48,$_{10}$.
IV 111,$_{25}$.... — IV 422.
IV 361,$_{10}$.... — VI 255.
IV 422...... — V 123.
V 359,$_{3}$ .... — V 336.
V 359,$_{4}$ .... — IV, 132,$_{15}$.
VI 99,$_{9}$ ..... — VI 202. 203.
VI 100,$_{8}$ .... — VI 198.

Dasaratha-jātaka ed. by V. Fausbøll

p. 9 .... Jāt. III 98,$_{22}$.
30 .... — III 155.
39 .... — I 126.

Five Jātakas, ed. by V. Fausbøll.
p. 1 .... Jāt. II 101.
8 .... — II 164.
12 .... — III 25.
14 .... — II 109.
16 .... — II 175.
48 .... — III 102.
51 .... — III 51.
Ten Jātakas, ed. by V. Fausbøll.
p. 1 .... Jāt. II 1.
107 .... — III 109.
111 .... — IV 332.
Khuddaka-Pāṭha, ed. by Childers.
p. 5 .... Jāt. I 446.
— III 369 (18).
11.......... — I 446.
14.......... — II 414,16.
Mahābhārata (Calc. edit.)
12,(917. 529. 6841 Jāt. VI 54,27.
Mahāvaṁsa, by Upham.
3,801 .... Jāt. I 454,14
Mahāvastu, ed. by Senart.
I p. 281...... Jāt. V 123,15.
— VI 94,20.
282...... — V 109,2.
338...... — V 412.
366...... — IV 43,16.
II p. 49...... — V 387,12.
Majjhima-Nikāya, ed. by Trenckner.
I p. 130,28 ..... Jāt. V 210.
III 4.......... — IV 482.
Milinda-pañha, ed. by Trenckner.
p. 172....... Jāt. III 24,1.
202....... — III 454.
220....... — III 32,28.
230....... — III 354,17.
p. 384...... Jāt. IV 14,1.
402...... — IV 71,24.
421...... — IV 496 (25).
422...... — IV 166,1.
Petavatthu, ed. by Minayeff.
p. 23.......... Jāt. VI 13,22
24.......... — VI 13,17.
Rāmāyaṇa, ed. by Schlegel.
vol. II 63 ...... Jāt. VI 68.
Saṁyutta-Nikāya, ed. by Feer.
Vol. I p. 1 .... Jāt. IV 476,23.
— 2.... — IV 398,6.
— 3.... IV 487,18.
— 7.... — VI 57,25.
— 17 ... — V 483,18.
— 18 ff.. — IV 64,9.
— 19,3 . — VI 571,17.
— 20-22 — III 472,10.
— 31... — III 471,20.
— 71... — V 483,15.
— 204-5 — III 305,16.
Sumaṅgala-Vilāsinī, ed. by Rhys Davids & Carpenter.
Vol. I p. 155,17 Jāt. V 140,17.
— 156,1 — V 65,24.
— 177.. — VI 316,13.
20. 320,15.
— 178... — VI 320.
Sutta-Nipāta, ed. by V. Fausbøll.
v. 44—45 .... Jāt. III 488.
50 .... — IV 313,1.
98 .... — IV 184,15.
105 .... — III 260.
124 .... — IV 184,15.
253-57 .... — III 196,10.
574....... — IV 151.
p. 45 ff....... — IV 73.
173....... — V 413.

Theragâthâ, ed. by Oldenberg.
p. 22 . . . . Jât. IV 325,8.
35 . . . . IV 54,30.
496,13.
v. 969 . . . . - V 50,27.
Therîgâthâ ed. by Pischel.
p. 126 . . . . Jât. IV 320.
Vinaya-piṭaka, ed. by Oldenberg.
Vol. I p. 36 . . Jât. VI 220,8.
-- 337 . . -- III 486.
— 349 . . — III 488,8.
IV p. 204 . — III 28-29.

Aelian 16,11 . . . Jât. I 20,34.
d'Alwis, Buddhism.
p. 11 . . . . Jât. V 246.
d'Alwis, Nirvâna.
p. 121 . . . . Jât. III 501,14.
d'Alwis, Sidath Sangarawa.
p. CVI . . . . . . Jât. IV 129, (2).
CLX . . . . . . -- III 42,11.
Bastian, Völker d. östl. Asien
vol. II p. 233 . . Jât. VI 30,20.
Beal, Catena of Buddhist Scriptures.
p. 5 . . . . Jât. VI 479.
Bibliotheca Indica
vol. II p. 3; p. 128 Jât. VI 54,27.
Bigandet, Gaudama.
p. 36 . . . . Jât. VI 479.
412 . . . . - VI 30,30.
Feer, Journal Asiatique.
1871 T. 18 p. 248 Jât. VI 14,5.
p. 269. 320 — VI 1.
1874 T. IV p. 265 — III 139.
1875 T. VI p. 260 -- II 111.
1875 T. VI p. 265 . J. II 429.
III 193.
— 282 . — I 248,11.
295 . -- II 60.
1876 T. VIII p. 520 — I 126.
Grimblot, Sept Suttas Palies.
p. 299 . . . . . . Jât. IV 26,30.
309 . . . . . — III 234 (22).
Sp. Hardy, Manual of Budhism.
p. 290-91 . . . . Jât. V 246.
Hultzsch, ZDMG.
vol. 40 p. 60 . . . . Jât. VI 95.
Indian Antiquary
1875 p. 91 . . . . . Jât. VI 68.
L'Institut.
1853. II sect.
T. 18 p. 23 . . . Jât. VI 157.
Journal of the Am. Or. Soc.
XXXI . . . . Jât. VI 1
Journal of the Royal As. Soc.
1870 V p. 8 . . . Jât. II 152.
— 170 . -- VI 479.
1870 Dec. . . . . . — I 208.
1871 p. 173 . . . . — VI 68
1892 p. 77 . . . . . -— VI 157.
1893 p. 357 . . . . — VI 1.
Minayeff, Grammaire Pâlie.
p. XXIV n 24. Jât. IV 320.
p. XXVIII . . . . — III 108,16.
Minayeff, Mél. As.
T. VI p. 591 . . . . Jât. III 126.
Monatsberichte d. k. Akad. Berlin.
1858 p. 265 . . . . . Jât. I 246.
Morris, Journal of the Pâli Text Soc.
1885 p. 62 . . . . . . Jât. VI 95.

Müller, Pâli Proper Names.
J. P. T. S. 1888 . . Jât. V 246
Ralston, Tibetan Tales.
p. 247 . . . . Jât. VI 1.
p. 267 . . . . — VI 479.
Sacred Books of the East.
Vol. I p. 300 . . Jât. VI 30,20.
Thiessen, Legende v. Kisâgotamî.
p. 41 . . . . Jât. III 164,18.
42 . . . . III 165.
45 . . . . — IV 61.
Trenckner, Pâli Miscellany.
p. 75 . . . . Jât. III 513.
Weber, Indische Studien.
Vol. III p. 128 . . Jât. III 25.
IV p. 387 . . — I 246.
V p. 412 . . V 412
V p. 415 . . — II 311.
— III 454.
Westergaard, Codices Orientales.
I 34 . . . . Jât. IV 498.
Zachariae, Die 16te Erzähl. d. Vetâlap. Beitr. z. K. d. idg. Spr.
Vol. IV p. 375 ff. . . Jât. V 209. 214.

V.

ADDITIONS AND CORRECTIONS

to Index I.

Akatti, see: Akitti.

aggasāvakā, (cfr. Sāriputta-Moggallānā).

Aggi, (cfr. Jātaveda).

Ajjuna, Paṇḍurājaputto V 424,20. 426 (10. 31. 36.) 427 (16). (— Kuṇālo sakunarājā (Bo.)).

Ajjuna, (sahassabāhu) rājā Kekarājadhāniyaṁ Mahiṁsakaraṭṭhe V 135,24*. 143*,12. 27. 145 (9). — VI 201,20*. (cfr. Kekakādhipa).

Ajjuna-vatthu V 119 (15).

Aṭṭhakathā II 299 note[24].

Aḍḍhakāsī, gaṇikā V 447 (29). (cfr. Vin. II 277).

Aṇimaṇḍavya (Āṇimaṇḍavya).

atītavatthu I 136,18. 375,2. 473,4. — II 212,14. 234,20. 333,27. 429,18. etc.

Anāthapiṇḍika, (cfr. Mahānāthapiṇḍika.)

Anūpiya, nagaraṁ (Mallaraṭṭhe). (cfr. Dhp. p. 139. Vin. II p. 180).

abhimāra-payojana, (cfr. III 97,14 (v. l.). Sumaṅgalavilāsinī I 152,6. 154,11.)

Amarādevi-pañha, v. l. B Channapatha-pañha. (cfr. VI 366,6).

Ayojjhana-nāgara, read: Ayojjha- (ɔ: Ayojjhā).

Arindama, Kāsirājā (cfr. V 352,15*).

Alāta, (cfr. Piṅgala).
Alīnasattu, (cfr. Kampilla).
Avāriya-pitā (v. l. Āvāriya-).
Avīci, (cfr. Mahā-avīci).
Assaka², (cfr. Aruṇarājā).
Ājañña-jātaka I 181 82.
Āṇimaṇḍavya, see Aṇimaṇḍavya.
Āditta-jātaka = Sucira-jāt. IV 360,24. — Sovīra-jāt. IV 401,12.
Āḷāra, add: V 175,31*. — Videhaputto V 166*,4. 16. Vedehaputto V 167 (28).
Āvāriya, see: Avāriya.
Inda, sa-Inda-devā V 223,28*. — sabbe Indakā devā V 276 (24). — sa-Indakā IV 356,17. — VI 104,6.
isigili, read: Isigili.
Isisiṅga, (tāpaso).
Utta-thera, (cfr. Datta, Mantidatta).
Uttarāpathaka (adj.), II 31,1*.
Udaya-jataka, read: -jātaka.
Upacara, v. l. B Upavara, Uparivara.
Uprimaṇḍalaka, read: Uparimaṇḍalaka.
Ubbarī, devī Cūḷani-Brahmadattassa (= Nandā) VI 473*,5. 18. 475,19*. (ubbarī = orodho VI 473 (11).)
Ussada-nirayā soḷasa III 473 (11).
Ekarāja-jātaka, cfr. Cariyā-piṭ. 351, read: III 13 v. 8.
Kakaṇṭaka-jātaka, = Kakaṇṭaka-pañho, Mahāummagga-jātake VI 347,5.
Kaccāyana² VI 327,17*, read: 323,17*.
Kammāsadamma, (cfr. Mahā-Kammāsadamma).
Kalyāṇi IV 422bis 11 (read: kalyāni (?). cfr. V 124,28*).
Kāpilānī I 289,15.
Kāmāvacara-devā N 47,24.
Kāḷudāyin, (cfr. Udāyin).
Kuṇāla V 428 (31) (cfr. Garuḷa).

Kūṭāgārasālā I 504,6. — II 392,18.
Komārabhacca, to be inserted after Komāyaputta-jātaka.
Kolita V 151,30.
Kosambakā, (cfr. III 486,21).
Kosiya-jātaka c) (cfr. Jāt. (535)).
Khaṇḍahāla-jātaka, (— Candakumāra-jāt. Ood. B).
khantivādi-tāpaso VI 257 (26).
Gaṅgeyya (adj.) II 151*,26. 27. 152,1*.
Gaṅgeyya, nāgarājā III 362 (10).
Gotama, isi (— Aṅgiraso G.) V 267,6*. (cfr. Aṅgirasa).
Gotama, brāhmaṇo (?) IV 371,11*.
Gotama Buddha, add: (Gotamo, Gotamo Buddho, Samaṇo Gotamo) II 262,11. 13. V 334,4. 7. 14—10. — Mahā-Gotama-Sammāsambuddho II 434,2 — Gotama-sāvakā II 417,13. — dele: IV 371,11*. V 144,1*. 267,6*.
Candakumāra-jātaka, see: Khaṇḍahāla-jāt.
Calākā, see: Talatā-devī.
Cittalatāvana N 52,19.
Cittasambhūta-jātaka, see: Citta-.
Cullatuṇḍila, (cfr. Tuṇḍila).
Cūḷajanaka-jātaka, (cfr. Mahā-janaka).
Cūḷani-Brahmadatta, (cfr. Pañcāla).
Cūḷabodhi-tāpasa, (cfr. Bodhi-kumāra).
Cūlasubhaddā, dhītā Anāthapiṇḍikassa.
Channapatha-pañha, (— Amarādevī-pañha I 424,21. Cod. B).
Takkāriya-jātaka II 175,19 (Mahā-Takkāri-jāt.).
Talatā-devī, (v. l. B Calākā).
Tāvatiṁsā devā VI 105,5 read: VI 104,5. add: IV 366,17.
Tidasā V 20,17*. 390,22*.
Tidiva IV 450,10*. — V 14,20*. 15 (3.
Tiracchāna-yoni I 168 (17).
Duṭṭhakumāra[1] (cfr. I 506,24*).
dussasahassapaṭilābha-, read: (cfr. sāṭakasahassap-).

Devadattassa vadhāya parisakkanaṁ, add: IV 444,7. — °assa Sugatālayo II 162,8 read: 162,18.
devorahanaṁ read: devorohanaṁ.
Dhammaddhaja, (— Bodhisatto).
Dhūmakāri, (cfr. Vāseṭṭha).
Nandavatī, (dhītā Bodhisattassa) I 475,20*. (Cod. B).
Nāgadīpa III 118,5* read: 188,5*.
paccuppanna-vatthu I 136,12. 480,13. 484,12. 487,4. 495,18. — II 64,21*. 212,18. 234,26. 359,4. 382,3. 410,1. 429,18. 440,6. 443,3. — III 8,17. 13,11. 115,11. 232,21. 238,8. 314,17. 317,5. 341,21. 351,24. — IV 1,4. 45,2*. 90,2. etc.
paccekabuddho V 245,15* read: 249,15*.
Paṇḍukambalasilāsana III 53,9*.
Pāli, add: Pāḷinayena IV 338 (16). — V 258,17*. Ekanipātapāli I 345 (15).
Purindada V 260*,5. 7.
Bahubhāṇi-jātaka, (— Kacchapa-jāt. (215)) II 176*. (cfr. Dhp. p. 419).
Belaṭṭhiputta, see: Sañjaya.
Bodhisatta, p. 105 l 7 add: Bhaggavo, paribbājako (408).
Brahman, sa-Brahmakā (devā) V 223,28*.
Mahosadha-jātaka, (— Mahā-ummagga-jāt. Cod. B).
Mahāsutasoma-jātaka, — Sutasoma-jāt. V 460,15*. (Cod. B).
Mūgapakkha-jātaka N 46,25. (— Cariyā-piṭaka III 6, v. 18.)
Vidhurapaṇḍita-jātaka, — Puṇṇaka-jātaka IV 14,24. 182,19*.
Vīmaṁsanakhaṇḍa, Mūgapakkha-jātaka VI 9,24. (Cod. B).
Sabbasaṁhāraka-pañha (cfr. VI 336 (16).)
Sammodamāna-jātaka dele: V 97,9.
Sutasoma-jātaka, see: Mahāsutasoma-jāt.
Sundarīnandā, (dhītā Bodhisattassa) I 475,20*. (Cod. B).
Hemavataka IV 374,4.

CORRECTIONS AND ADDITIONS.

Vol. V. 202,4 fr. bottom read so ali
332,22 read patiṭṭhāsi
333,13 — balavā vedanā
334,18 — Buddha-

Vol. VI. 9,24 add after sa Vīmaṁsanakhaṇḍe.
48,17 read gāmaṇiyehi
52,2 — gāma-
73,7 — mayhaṁ for mayaṁ in all three MSS.
81,17 — abhari
81,18 — bharissante
111,17 — gīvāya
145,25 — mattesaṁ
159,22 — vīmaṁsissāmi naṁ
164,23 — -putto mama dhītā
165,23 — Virūpakkha-
168,24 — Virūpakkhe
324,2 — Inde-
359,31 — Niṭṭhitā
556,16 — abhidhāviṁsu
594,24 add te after sesaṁ

Formerly published:

Dhammapadam. Ex tribus codicibus Hauniensibus Palice edidit, Latine vertit, excerptis ex commentario Palico notisque illustravit V. Fausbøll. Haunim 1855. 8 Danish crowns.

Five Jātakas, containing a Fairy Tale, a Comical Story, and Three Fables. In the Original Pāli Text, with a Translation and Notes, by V. Fausbøll. Copenhagen 1861. 3 Danish crowns.

Two Jātakas. The original Pāli Text, with an English Translation and Critical Notes. By V. Fausbøll. 1870. (From the Journal of the R. A. S.). 1 Danish crown.

The Dasaratha-Jātaka, being the Buddhist Story of King Rāma. The Original Pāli Text with a Translation and Notes by V. Fausbøll. Copenhagen 1871. 1 crown 33 øre Danish.

Ten Jātakas. The Original Pāli Text with a Translation and Notes, by V. Fausbøll. Copenhagen 1872. 4 Danish crowns.

The Sutta-Nipāta, being a collection of some of Gotama Buddha's dialogues and discourses. Edited by V. Fausbøll. Published for the Pāli Text Society. Part I. Text. London 1885. Part II. A Complete Phraseological Glossary to Suttanipāta. London 1894.

The Sutta-Nipāta translated by V. Fausbøll, Sacred Books of the East, vol. X. Oxford 1881. Sec. Edit. 1897.

Nogle Bemærkninger om enkelte vanskelige Pāli-Ord i Jātaka-Bogen. (Fra det danske Videnskabs-Selskabs Oversigter). 1888.

The Jātaka together with its Commentary. Vol. 1 7, with an Index by D. Andersen. London 1877—97.

Catalogue of the Mandalay Mss. in the India Office Library. J. P. T. S. 1897.

Smaahistorier fra Österland. Efter det Persiske ved V. Fausbøll. Kbh. 1852. 50 Ører.

Vægter-Versene i deres ældre og yngre Skikkelse, udgivne af V. Fausbøll. Med Afbildninger af Vægtere fra forskjellige Tider. Kbh. 1862. 2det Oplag. ibidem, eodem. 20 Ører. (Med Melodier). 3dje forøgede Oplag. ibidem, 1894.

Beretning om de vidtbekjendte Molboers vise Gjerninger og tapre Bedrifter. Ved V. Fausbøll. Kbh. 1862. 3dje forbedrede Udgave. Kbh. 1887. (Illustreret.)

Bidrag til en Ordbog over Gadesproget og saakaldt Daglig Tale, oplyst med over 5000 Exempler, hentede fra trykte Kilder, og med Henvisning til beslægtede Ord og Talemaader i andre Sprog. Ved V. Kristiansen. Kbh. 1866. 2 Kroner.

Om [illegible] der hidtil ikke have været [illegible] Gilvlyde. (I Universitets-Jubil[illegible]

www.ingramcontent.com/pod-product-compliance
Lightning Source LLC
Chambersburg PA
CBHW030633030726
47497CB00006B/1771
9783337384920